PRAISE FOR JAN BURKE AND
HER **IRENE** SERIES

"An entertaining series, this novel gives the reader a thought-provoking puzzle and a cast of endearing characters."
—*Dallas Morning News*

"Burke continues to invite praise for her gutsy heroine and intricate plot twists."
—*Mostly Murder*

"A satisfyingly complex plot for mystery buffs to enjoy."
—*St. Louis Post-Dispatch*

"Sue Grafton fans who get impatient between letters of the alphabet need to check out Jan Burke, a similarly gifted mystery writer with an intriguing central character and engaging plots. . . . A deliciously tense mystery that hungry whodunit fans will devour."
—*Colorado Springs Gazette Telegraph*

"Burke is in top form here."
—*Publishers Weekly*

IRENE KELLY MYSTERIES

Goodnight, Irene

Sweet Dreams, Irene

Dear Irene

Remember Me, Irene

REMEMBER ME, IRENE

IRENE

Jan Burke

HarperPaperbacks
A Division of HarperCollinsPublishers

HarperPaperbacks
A Division of HarperCollins*Publishers*
10 East 53rd Street, New York, N.Y. 10022-5299

This is a work of fiction. The characters, incidents, and
dialogues are products of the author's imagination and are not to
be construed as real. Any resemblance to actual events or
persons, living or dead, is entirely coincidental.

ISBN 0-06-104438-5

HarperCollins®, ▦®, and HarperPaperbacks™
are trademarks of HarperCollins*Publishers*, Inc.

Cover photo: by Yamamoto /Photonica

A hardcover edition of this book was published in 1996 by
Simon & Schuster.

First HarperPaperbacks printing: May 1997

Printed in the United States of America

Visit HarperPaperbacks on the World Wide Web at
http://www.harpercollins.com

❖10 9 8 7 6 5 4 3 2 1

TO THOMAS WILLIAM BURKE
who welcomed a stranger

There are three kinds of lies: lies, damned lies, and statistics.

—BENJAMIN DISRAELI

Over and over, they used to ask me
While buying the wine or the beer . . .
How I happened to lead the life,
And what was the start of it.
Well, I told them a silk dress,
And a promise of marriage from a rich man . . .
But that was not really it at all.
Suppose a boy steals an apple
From the tray at the grocery store,
And they all begin to call him a thief,
The editor, minister, judge, and all the people—
"A thief," "a thief," "a thief" wherever he goes.
And he can't get work, and he can't get bread
Without stealing it, why the boy will steal.
It's the way the people regard the theft of the apple
That makes the boy what he is.

—EDGAR LEE MASTERS,
from "Aner Clute" in Spoon River Anthology

1

His last address was his own body, and what a squalid place it was. Someone told me he cleaned up just before he died, and I now know it's true. But when I last saw him, the place was a mess.

He was sprawled on a bus bench, stinking of alcohol and urine, drooling in his sleep. He was an African American man, and while it was hard to guess his age, I judged him to be in his fifties. His skin was chapped and one of his cheeks was scraped and swollen, as if he had been in a fight. I took more than a passing interest in him: noted his matted hair, his rough beard, his rumbling snores, the small brown paper sack clutched to his chest like a prayerbook. The last prayer had been prayed out of it sometime ago, judging by the uncapped screwtop bottleneck.

I stood to one side of the bench, studying him, thinking up clever phrases to make the readers of my latest set of stories on public transportation in Las Piernas smile at my description of my predicament, smile over coffee and cereal as they turned the pages of the *Express* at their breakfast tables. I would be ruthless to the Las Piernas Rapid Transit District—perhaps call it the Rabid Transient District. My small way of repaying it for forcing me to be two hours late getting back to the paper.

I had been on buses all day. My back ached and my feet hurt, and one more ride would take me back to the *Express*. I was tired and frustrated. I felt a righteous anger on behalf

of the citizens who had to use the system every day. I had yet
to see a bus pull up at the time it was scheduled to make a
stop. I could see exactly why the regular riders were angry.
This was one day's story for me; for them it would mean being
late to work, to doctors' appointments, to classes, to job interviews. One missed connection led to another, turning what
was planned to be my four-hour, see-it-for-myself test ride
into six hours of hell on wheels.

My series of rides had taken me all over the city, and the
man before me now was not the first drunk I had encountered,
not even the first sleeping drunk.

Perhaps the guilt I've felt since that day now colors my
memory of my attitude at the time. There is, in any job that
requires a person to observe other people and publish the ob-
servations, an aspect of being . . . well, a user. I used the man
on the bench. Took notes on him.

He awoke suddenly, and I took a step back. Awake, he was
a little more fearsome. He looked bigger. Stronger. He
yawned, wiped a dirty sleeve across his face, and moved to a
slumped sitting position. When he noticed me, he cowered
away, tucking the bottle closer, eyeing me warily.

He was afraid of me. That startled me more than his abrupt
awakening. I looked at the swollen cheek again as I stopped
taking notes.

"Hello," I said, and stuffed my pen and notebook into the
back pocket of my worn jeans. (No, I wasn't wearing high
heels and a tight skirt. A day on *buses*. I do have a little sense
left, even if I am still working for the *Express*.)

He just studied me, as if trying to fit me into the scheme
of things, as if I were someone familiar and yet unfamiliar to
him. His eyes were red and he blinked slowly and nodded forward a little, not past the danger of passing out again.

After a time, I wished he would pass out. The relentless
stare began to unnerve me. I stepped a little farther away, bal-
anced my stance, looked for potential witnesses to whatever
harm he might intend. No one. This stop was along a chain-
link fence surrounding an old abandoned hotel. No cars in the
parking lot. Windows broken. Redevelopment, almost.

A few blocks down the way, Las Piernas could show off the benefits of its redevelopment plan. But at this end of the street, there were no polished glass skyscrapers, no new theaters or trendy nightspots. Just empty lots and crumbling brick buildings. Weeds pushing up through neglected asphalt, curbs and sidewalks cracked. The sporadic traffic along the street moved quickly, as if the drivers wanted to get their passage along this blighted block over and done with.

I watched longingly for the bus. No sign of it.

"I know you," he said, one careful word at a time. I looked back at him. "I know you," he repeated. Some teeth missing. Knocked out or lost to decay?

"My picture sometimes runs in the paper," I said. "I'm a reporter."

He shook his head. "No."

"Yes, really," I said, taking another step back. "I'm a reporter for the *Express.*"

Shook his head again. Kept studying me.

Where the hell was that bus?

With fumbling fingers, he started to unbutton his worn denim jacket. I was mapping out the safest place to run to when he reached down beneath several layers of T-shirts and pulled out something truly amazing: a large, gold school ring with a red stone in it, dangling from a long metal chain. He held it out toward me, swinging it back and forth like a hypnotist's watch, and beckoned to me.

"Look at it," he said.

"I see," I said, in the tone one might use in speaking to a child holding a jar full of wasps. I wasn't going to venture close enough to see which school the ring came from.

He looked up at me again and his eyes were misty. He turned away, curled his shoulders inward, as if afraid I might hit him after all.

"I'm sorry," I said, feeling as if I *had* hit him.

He shook his head, still keeping his back to me.

Where the hell was that bus?

He turned around again, and this time, the look was pleading. "You don't remember me. I'm . . . I'm . . ." He ducked his head. "Not who I used to be," he mumbled.

I didn't say anything for a moment. "I'm not who I used to be, either," I said, ashamed.

"It's okay," he said in a consoling tone. "It's okay. Okay. Okay."

I didn't say anything.

"You didn't change," he said. *"I know you."* He winked at me and pointed at my face. "Kelly."

It only took me aback for a moment. "Yes, I'm Irene Kelly."

He grinned his misshapen grin. "I told you!"

"Yes, well, that's what I was saying before. You've probably seen my picture near one of my columns in the paper."

He shook his head and batted a hand in dismissal of that notion.

"I know you. You could help me."

Uh-oh, I thought, here it comes. "I don't even have fare money," I said, holding up the transfer that would take me back to the parking lot at the paper. And my beloved Karmann Ghia. My nice, safe, *private* transportation. I looked up the street, and to my delight, one of Las Piernas's diesel-belching buses was in sight.

"No, no," he insisted, standing up. "I don't want your money."

Yeah, right, I thought, moving to put the bench between us. "That's good. Well, nice talking to you. Here's my bus."

He glanced toward the bus, which was trundling slowly up to the stop. It passed us and stopped just beyond where we stood. I moved toward the forward door.

"No, don't go! You're good at math."

I paused at the open door, staring back at him. Two passengers alighted from the rear door, ignoring us.

"You're good at math!" the man called again, as if it were a password between us, one that would cause me to embrace him as a compatriot.

"You gettin' on this bus, lady?" the driver asked.

I nodded and started to step aboard.

"No!" the man cried, stumbling toward me. I rushed up the steps, shoving my transfer at the driver, dismayed to find the bus so full that I could not retreat back into it. The man drew closer.

"Not today, Professor," the driver said, snapping the door shut in his face.

But the "Professor" wasn't giving up so easily. He pounded his fists on the glass, staring at me. "You're good at math!" he shouted. "You're good at math!"

The driver pulled away.

For a moment, my fear of the man turned into fear for him. But peering into the side mirror, I saw him stare after the bus, then turn away in defeat.

"The Prof didn't scare you, did he?" the driver asked. When I didn't reply, he said, "I haven't ever seen him like that. Usually he's real easygoing, even when he's drunk. I've never known the Professor to hurt anybody."

"Why do you call him that? Was he a professor?"

"Oh, I don't think so. But he gives little informal tours to the passengers when he gets on the bus. If he cleans up a little, people enjoy it. Don't let it out to my supervisor, but I sort of let the Prof ride around with me, you know, stay warm when it gets chilly out. Naw, he's no professor. Just a bum. But he knows all about this area. Grew up in the neighborhood, back when it was one. You ask him about any building on this street, and he'll tell you when it was built, what it was used for, how many people lived in it, all kinds of stuff like that. I think it's the only part of his brain that still works. Remembers old buildings."

Remembers old faces, I thought. By then, the Professor seemed vaguely familiar to me. Why? I couldn't have told you then.

But he was right: I'm good at math.

I just hadn't yet put two and two together.

2

"A boob job, I tell you."

"Alicia," I said, wishing for the one-millionth time that *any* other member of SOS—Save Our Shelter—would come along and distract her away from my side, "I really do not give an otter's bottom *what* Helen Ferguson has done to her breasts."

"Not just her breasts, Irene." She smiled wickedly over the brim of her glass of chardonnay. I blinked, once again blinded by a reflection off her rings. Alicia Penderson-Duggin's fingers carry jewelry on them the way the walls of a hunter's den display animal heads. "And speaking of bottoms," she went on, "I'd bet hers has been lifted."

"I don't care if it's lifted! I don't care if she's got the ceiling from the Sistine Chapel tattooed on her buns!"

"Tattooed? You think so?"

Just as I was regretting making any remark that could become part of Alicia's ongoing gossip marathon about Helen, the (possibly somewhat altered) woman who had been the subject of the discussion began to make her way toward us. A half-dozen or so other women followed in her wake. While I didn't know all of the people who were at this fund-raiser for the local battered women's shelter, I recognized every face in the group Helen brought with her—most of them had been part of SOS from its inception.

"Irene!" Helen said, embracing me but ignoring Alicia, "I'm so happy for you!"

"Thanks," I said. Before I could say more, several of the other women greeted me in much the same way, adding "Great news!" or "It's about time!"

"About time for what?" Alicia asked.

Seemingly oblivious to Alicia's extended lower lip, Helen lifted her glass toward me and said, "I'd like to propose a toast. Irene, as *most* of you know, was recently married to Las Piernas Homicide Detective Frank Harriman. And even though she was rude enough to exclude us from the wedding, we wish them long life and happiness together."

The others gave a small cheer and laughed as they touched their glasses together. Alicia was staring at me, slackjawed.

"First molar on the left," I said to her in a low voice, causing her to snap her mouth shut. "If you want me to know about any other hidden gold, please just tell me about it."

"Irene Kelly—Irene Harriman—I will never speak to you again!"

Oh, if only it were true. No chance. She didn't even last two seconds.

"I can't believe you didn't invite me to your wedding!"

I could have told her that no one other than the witnesses (Pete Baird, who is Frank's partner, and Pete's own new bride, Rachel Giocopazzi) were invited. But I've never liked Alicia, so I didn't make the clarification. We've known each other since Catholic school, and the relationship has not improved with age.

Luckily, the others stayed to talk to me, even the ones who had previously ducked away when they saw Alicia standing near. Ivy Vines, who works at the college radio station, asked, "Are you going by Harriman or Kelly?"

"Either one."

"Either?" Alicia said. "That makes no sense at all! You might as well go off and make up a name, like Ivy did."

"I didn't make it up," Ivy protested.

Alicia made a sniffing sound. "You were Ingrid Vines when we were students."

"*That* was made up," Ivy countered.

"I'm using Kelly professionally," I said, trying to turn my

back to Alicia. "I've got over a dozen years of contact with
my sources using that name. But I'll answer to either Harriman or Kelly elsewhere."

"Sensible," Ivy said.

"Ridiculous," Alicia declared behind me.

"Congrats, Irene!" a voice called. I turned to see Marcy
Selman.

"Hi, Marcy. Thanks. How's your daughter?"

"Lisa's great," the woman next to Marcy answered—
Becky Freedman, an emergency physician at Las Piernas
General. She grinned. "Lisa met me for lunch today. Does that
mean I got to see her before you did?"

"Lisa's in town?" I asked Marcy.

"Yes, in fact she'll be here later. And she'll probably hit
you up for money, just like she did Becky."

"I didn't mind at all," Becky said. "Mark my words, Lisa's
going to be California's first woman governor."

"Lisa's running for *governor?*"

"State Assembly," Marcy answered, finally getting a word
in.

"For now. She'll be governor someday," Becky main-
tained. "I've never met anyone with more determination than
Lisa Selman."

The possibility of Governor Selman didn't seem far-
fetched. Lisa was only twenty-nine, but she had always
achieved her goals faster than most of the rest of us. She had
graduated from high school at fifteen, earned a master's degree from San Diego State University before her twentieth
birthday. Currently the top aide to State Senator Barton
Sawyer, she was already experienced in the world of politics.

"So, she's making her move," I said. "Let's see. A San
Diego State Assembly candidate . . . Doug Longmore's seat?"

Marcy nodded.

Longmore, who had health problems, had recently announced that he would not seek another term. "Has Longmore
endorsed her?" I asked.

"Not yet," she said.

"Well, it's a little early yet. I suppose Bart Sawyer's helping her out?"

"Yes, he's been talking to Longmore about supporting Lisa. And Bart's being . . . very generous."

Lisa would need that generosity. A campaign for a State Assembly seat could easily cost half a million dollars—more than double that if the race was hotly contested. "She deserves Sawyer's support," I said. "She's served him loyally for what, now, ten years?"

"Longer than that, I think," Marcy answered. "She was seventeen when she worked on his first campaign. I remember that, because she was just a little too young to vote for him, even though she was working for him. That frustrated her. But he really inspired her, even then. Bart's been like a father to her."

There was a slight pause in the conversation, during which I suppose all of us probably had the same thought: Andre Selman, Lisa's father, had never been much of a parent.

"You going to fork over a few bucks for her, Irene?" Becky asked.

I held up my hands in mock surrender. "Sorry. Can't contribute to any campaign and keep my job."

"Really? Even if she's running outside of the districts you cover?"

"Really. The *Express* has a written policy on it. But with Barton Sawyer's backing, Lisa should do fine. His constituents are in love with him, he's a helluva fund-raiser, and he's got one of the cleanest reputations in state politics."

"So Lisa's headed for Sacramento!" Becky said.

Marcy laughed. "Filing hasn't even opened yet, Becky."

"Still, not bad for a Survivor of Selman," Ivy said.

Among some of the original members, the notion that SOS actually stood for Survivors of Selman was an old joke. Somehow, applied to Lisa, it didn't seem so funny. Another small silence ensued, and Ivy blushed furiously. As one who has done my share of blurting out remarks that kill conversation, I felt sympathy for her.

"I guess none of us have done too badly, have we?" I said.

"No," Becky chimed in, and began to talk about a research grant that one of the other "survivors" had received.

I glanced around the banquet room at the Cliffside Hotel, and saw the faces of a few of the others who had joined the organization not long after it began. A number of them held degrees in law, medicine, and business. There were also artists, writers, homemakers, bureaucrats, educators, entrepreneurs. Their political leanings ran the gamut. But the first women to join SOS all had one thing in common: they had survived a marriage, relationship, or affair with Dr. Andre Selman, professor of sociology at Las Piernas College.

Professionally, Dr. Selman was highly respected in his field. He had not yet come into his own when I knew him. In the mid-1970s, his studies of changes in urban populations were just under way, not yet published. These days, he was one of the college's most prized faculty members; consulted globally, not only by his fellow sociologists, but by media and moguls alike. Andre Selman was now a man of affairs.

Privately, you might say he had always been a man of affairs. About thirty of the women who were now in SOS had personal knowledge of that fact. Four of them were ex-wives; the rest of us had experienced everything from a few weeks to a few years with him, but got out without the help of lawyers.

Lisa had survived being his child. While I could now laugh at my own foolish decision to become involved with him, Lisa didn't have a choice.

"Marcy, why isn't Lisa here tonight?" Alicia asked, as soon as Becky stopped to draw a breath. "There's all kinds of money walking around in this room."

"She wanted to come along," Marcy said, "mainly to see her old friends. But I asked her to wait until after the dinner. She thought I just didn't want her hitting everyone up for campaign contributions at a fund-raiser for the battered women's shelter, but that wasn't it." She hesitated, then added, "Sometimes, when we all get together, we start talking about her father or her brother. And even though she's an adult now and even *she* certainly survived Andre, I don't think it's right for her to hear us go on about him."

"I agree," said Roberta Benson, who had just walked up. Roberta, Becky, Helen, Ivy, Marcy, and I were the founders of SOS. We had all known Marcy first, because we had all dated her ex-husband. We were also all especially close to Lisa while she was growing up.

Roberta's a therapist, and Marcy's remark allowed her an opportunity to wax on about contemporary psychological theories on why a child—even an adult child—should never hear rude remarks between exes.

Not especially interested, I looked around to see a local artist talking to a real estate broker about finding a location for a new gallery. The conversation was just part of the typical networking that goes on at an SOS meeting.

Helen had moved back to the front of the room. Alicia was still too close for comfort, but she had Ivy in a one-on-one now. "My Harold gave me this one for letting him keep his tacky old easy chair in the guest house," she said, rocking her hand back and forth to catch the light on a diamond. "The chair's gone now, of course, but . . ."

Ah, poor Ivy. Alicia had more history to her rings than a Hobbit.

Roberta drew my attention away from them by placing a hand on my arm.

"I wanted to tell you—" she began, but was interrupted by Helen's call to dinner. "I'll catch you afterward," Roberta said. "I need to get in there and try to sit next to Helen. She's on the board where I work now. But I want to talk to you, too. Can you stick around for a minute after dinner?"

"Sure."

The group made its way into the dining area, and once we had feasted, Helen stood up and gave a quick speech. Applause followed her report that we had donated a record amount to the shelter and its programs against domestic violence. Nominations for officers for the next year were called for, and I deftly avoided being drafted.

Becky sat next to me throughout the evening. Ivy sat at my other side. Alicia, unmerciful, was at our table, too.

"Andre's married to his fifth wife," she said. "That's five years now, and a record."

"Alicia, who the hell cares?" Becky said, and asked if I wanted my dessert. It was something that was supposed to be mousse, but looked closer to moose, so I told her it was all hers.

"All I'm saying," Alicia went on, "is that at the age of fifty-five, he seems to have settled down."

Becky leaned over and whispered, "Not that the women in this town are safe. Word is, Jerry is just as bad as his old man."

I had already heard rumors that Andre's son by his first marriage was a womanizer. I looked over at Sharon Selman, Jerry's mother. Becky caught my glance. "Not Sharon's fault, of course."

"No," I said, "I guess not. Maybe not even Jerry's. Andre has kept Jerry as close as he's kept Lisa distant."

"Andre's loss," Becky said.

"I agree." I found myself thinking about what Alicia had said. "Becky, Andre had a heart attack five years ago. Think that made him decide to change his ways?"

"Maybe, but Lisa told me that Andre's on hypertension medication, too."

"He has high blood pressure?" Ivy asked.

"Yes. Lisa was telling me about all of his prescriptions. The one for high blood pressure—well, my guess is that old Andre may suffer the occasional side-effect of impotency."

"Someone should have diagnosed his high blood pressure years ago," I said.

Becky laughed. "Maybe someone did. Another possible side-effect of that medication is priapism."

"What's that?" Alicia asked.

"A condition that's very hard on a man," Becky said—with a straight face.

Alicia didn't seem to get it. Or maybe she did, and that's why she went home early.

Later, after the meeting wound down to a close, I stood talking to Marcy and Roberta in the lobby of the Cliffside. Becky and Sharon and several other women were nearby, all of us reluctant to end this year's time together. At one point, I looked over my shoulder toward Claire Watterson, who was married to the president of the Bank of Las Piernas. Each year, at SOS meetings, she made a point of spending some time talking to me. I enjoyed her company, but tonight, she didn't seem to be herself. Normally vivacious, she had been quiet and withdrawn all evening. I beckoned her to join us, but she shook her head and gave me a little smile, then walked farther away from the group.

I turned my attention back to the others. Roberta was telling us about her work as the director of counseling at a privately operated community services center. Most of her work was with the homeless.

"I've heard about the center," I told her. "I remember that the business owners in the area went before the Planning Commission about it."

"They were opposed to it at first," Roberta admitted. "But we had help from some local philanthropists—including Helen—who convinced the commission that it was the best place to let us locate—right among the people we serve. Now that we've been there a while, they've accepted us."

"I'll have to come by and see it."

"Sure. I'm leaving for an out of town meeting tomorrow, which makes my schedule a little hectic this week. But call me next week and I'll give you the grand tour of the center— oh! I almost forgot to tell you! An old friend asked me to say hello to you . . ."

She stopped speaking and, looking over my shoulder, smiled broadly. When I turned around to see what had distracted her, I saw Lisa Selman strolling toward us.

Lisa was smiling, too. She had her father's blond hair and her mother's light gray eyes and dark brows. Her other features were clearly her father's and yet not masculine on her, giving her a strong but pleasant face. Even though she was ostensibly there only to give her mother a ride home, she

wore a modest but sleek black dress—one that was not at odds
with the elegant evening wear of the women coming from the
banquet. She looked poised, sure of herself. A woman, I realized. No longer the adolescent prankster I was introduced
to in the mid-1970s. An adult.

I go through this every time I see her, which is usually no
more frequently than once a year. If those were the only moments in which I received a reminder that time was advanc-
ing, I don't think it would bother me much. Unfortunately, I
get these reminders more frequently than I get membership
renewal notices from my local public television station.

"Lisa! You're looking great," I said, and gave her a hug.

"Hello, Assemblywoman Selman," Roberta said, smiling.

We chatted for a while, then Lisa said, "Give me a call,
Irene, and we'll make plans together while I'm here. I'm
staying at my brother's place." She wrote the number on the
back of a business card. Her smile changed slightly as she
handed the card to me, and I saw a hint of her old mischief in
it. "No room at my mom's place—she's renting my old bedroom to a college student."

"You could have stayed with me," Marcy said. "There's
still plenty of room. The couch folds out into a bed."

Lisa laughed. "Mom, even the attic at Dad's is better than
that old sleeper sofa."

They laughed, but I wasn't so comfortable with the memories she had evoked. Andre had a three-bedroom house.
Back when I was dating him—when Lisa was about twelve
or thirteen—Andre used one bedroom for an office and slept
in another. The third was reserved for Jerry. When Lisa visited, she stayed in an attic room that was finished, but had no
closet. "He doesn't want me here," she once told me with a
shrug, as if it were an accepted fact of life.

Marcy suddenly realized she had left her purse in the banquet room, and went back to get it. As one of the other women
began to talk to Lisa, Roberta turned to me and said, "I've got
to be going. I just wanted to let you know that seeing you has
really made a difference in Lucas Monroe."

"Lucas Monroe?" I said, puzzled. "I haven't seen him in years. Not since before I went to work in Bakersfield."

She looked troubled. "Really? He claims—well, maybe he was mistaken."

"He claims what?"

"That he saw you about a month and a half ago," she said. "While you were waiting for a bus."

3

L ucas Monroe = The Man on the Bus Bench.
     Try as I might, it was impossible for me to completely accept that equation as the truth.

Lisa, Becky, Sharon, and others overheard Roberta mention his name, and remembered him. Roberta glanced around at their expectant faces and looked uneasy.

"Roberta . . . ," I said, then shook my head. I couldn't make sense of what she had just told me.

She put an arm around my shoulders, keeping her voice low as she said, "Look, he wants to have his act together when he sees you."

I pulled back a little, looking at her face.

"Don't worry," she said, misreading my distress, "he's cleaned up, and I get the feeling that the things he wants to talk to you about are *important*. I suspect that when he makes his case this time, he wants to do it right."

"Is Lucas a lawyer now?" Becky asked, making us both aware that we were still within earshot of the others.

Roberta looked at her watch. "I've got to get going. Good-bye, everybody! It was good to see you!"

"Wait," Lisa called as Roberta reached the doors. "Will we see each other before I go back to San Diego?"

"Sure, if you can meet me for lunch tomorrow," she said.

"I'm traveling to a meeting in Sacramento tomorrow night."
Lisa nodded in agreement, and Roberta left. Lisa extracted
similar promises from several of the others as we walked out
of the hotel.

As its name suggests, the Cliffside is built above the ocean,
and outside, the salt air was damp and cold. The others has-
tened their movements. I needed the coldness, the briny smell,
and found myself walking more slowly than the others. Their
voices eddied around me, surging bits and pieces of conversations passing me as the women moved on to their cars,
leaving me standing on the steps of the Cliffside, until the only
remaining sound was the whispering of the sea below the
cliffs.

I heard it beneath a chorus of relentless self-accusation.

"Irene?"

I turned to see a tall blonde standing behind me. "Oh—hi,
Claire. I thought everyone else had left."

"They have. I was going to call a cab, then I saw you
standing out here alone. Are you all right?" she asked.

I nodded. "How about you?"

"I—I need a favor, actually. I wonder if I could get a ride.
My car is in the shop, so Ben was going to pick me up this
evening, but I guess he's fallen asleep. I've called, but I just
keep getting the answering machine."

"Maybe he's on his way over here. I'll wait with you, if
you'd like."

She shook her head. "At first I thought he might be on his
way, but it's been too long. And he doesn't answer the car
phone in his Jag."

She literally meant "his Jag," as in "his and hers." Ben and
Claire Watterson had matching Jaguars. This proved they
were frugal—they could have afforded a chauffeur-driven
limo. And she wanted a ride in my drafty old heap? Right. Cab
fare, even all the way across town to their mansion, could have
been paid for with about two minutes' worth of the interest

on Claire's pin-money account. So I figured that Claire needed a favor, but it wasn't a ride.

"Sure, I'd be happy to give you a lift," I said. "Just let me go back into the hotel and call Frank. He's turned into a real worrywart."

"Please, use mine," she said, reaching into her handbag and pulling out a cellular phone.

I started to say "A pay phone would be cheaper," but realized what a ludicrous remark that would seem to Claire. I called home. I also got an answering machine, and left a brief message saying I'd be later than expected.

"Frank must have been called out," I said, handing the phone back to her. "Come on. I'm parked in the self-parking lot—I'm too cheap for valet." I paused, wondering again why she would want to ride with me. Even though Claire was one of the women who had survived Andre Selman, I usually only saw her at the annual dinner. But in the next moment, I thought of the last time I had turned my back on someone. "I've only been to your house for a couple of fund-raisers," I said. "Seaside Estates, right?"

"Yes. I hope it's not too far?"

"Don't worry about it. I didn't get to talk to you much tonight. This will be our chance to catch up."

"Yes," she said, but didn't say more as we walked to the car.

As I started the Karmann Ghia, she asked, "What did you mean, 'called out'?"

"Pardon?"

"About your husband. You said he must have been called out."

"These are his prime business hours. He's on call tonight."

"On call? Is he a doctor?"

"He's a homicide detective."

She made a face. After a moment she said, "Doesn't it bother you that he spends his time around dead bodies?"

"Cuts down on the office sex."

"Irene!"

"Sorry. No, the dead ones don't bother me. In general,

bodies don't tend to be dangerous. It's the folks who left them that way that worry me."

Her perfect brows drew together. "Yes, I suppose the fact that he's out looking for killers is more frightening."

"Right. I begin to feel relieved if it's a suicide case."

She was silent for a time, then suddenly asked, "Who's Lucas Monroe?"

Good question, I thought. I couldn't bring myself to tell her that Lucas Monroe was a drunk on a bus bench, partly because I couldn't understand how it could be that Lucas was that man. "I'm not who I used to be," he had told me. No kidding.

"An old friend," I said. "I haven't seen him in years. I met him in college." When he was strong, good-looking, and dressed more neatly than about 98 percent of the student body. So clean-cut, he wore a suit and tie every day. "He was a graduate student, a teaching assistant in sociology. I took a statistics class from him."

"Statistics?" She was openly puzzled. "I thought you majored in journalism."

"I did. And Introduction to Statistics wasn't required for my degree. I took the class at my father's urging."

"Your father must have been a cruel man."

I laughed. "I fought the suggestion. But my father argued that government decisions were constantly being made on the basis of statistical studies, and that I would be a better reporter if I could analyze those studies on my own."

"Statistics was the most boring class I ever took," she said.

"I told my dad that I had heard that complaint from lots of stat students. He pooh-poohed that, told me to ask around the various departments until I found someone who had a reputation for teaching the subject well. Lucas Monroe had that reputation."

"You must have really loved your father to take that class."

"My father and I were close, but we weren't getting along very well at that time. Growth pains, I suppose."

"But you took the statistics class anyway."

"To prove him wrong. When I later reported that Lucas

Monroe made a convert out of me, my father was pleased. When I graduated, Dad ignored my journalism professors and sought out Lucas." I shook my head, remembering. "He made his way through the commencement crowd to shake Lucas's hand. They talked for a while, and later my father said, 'That young man is destined for great things.' "

"Was he right?"

I swallowed hard, pretended fascination with the road for a moment. "My father's prediction wasn't remarkable. Just about everyone who knew Lucas saw the same bright future. Lucas had won scholarships and awards, and he had obtained his bachelor's summa cum laude. He was doing well in his graduate studies—had a gift for both teaching and research."

"What does he do for a living? Is he a professor at Las Piernas?"

"I don't know what he's doing now," I said, thinking that was at least partly true. "Like I said, I lost track of him. Lucas was gone from the college by the time I returned to Las Piernas. Later, when I was working at the *Express,* I ran into some complex studies that were far beyond my abilities. I called and asked for him, and was told that he was no longer with the department of sociology. I wasn't surprised, really, because he had talked of going on for a doctorate at one of the big universities. He told me he wanted to try to get on the faculty at Las Piernas, but I just figured he found something elsewhere."

"You said he was a graduate assistant in sociology? Andre Selman's department?"

"Yes. Lucas was one of the researchers on one of Andre's first well-known studies. In fact, I met Andre while sitting in Lucas's office."

"You know, Andre really is a rat, but he knows some great people." She was quiet, then added softly, "I met Ben through Andre."

Claire came earlier in Andre's lineup than I did. As I recalled, she had one of the more short-lived encounters with him. I was an intern at the *Express* the year she married Ben; I remember the sensation caused by Claire's courtship with him. Ben was widowed, had no children, and was her senior by a quarter of a century. They had now been married for over fifteen years, and all but the most vicious tongues had stopped wagging.

I glanced back over at her. To my surprise, she looked like she was about to cry.

"Claire? What's wrong?"

She bit her lower lip, hesitating. Claire and I weren't close friends, partly because we moved in such different circles. I wasn't sure she would confide in me.

She took a deep breath and said, "I'm worried about Ben. He says he wants to retire."

"Why are you upset? You've been trying to get him to retire for at least five years now."

She waved a hand in dismissal. "And he hasn't wanted to. So why now?"

I made the turn on to the road that leads to Seaside Estates, one of Las Piernas's upper-crust enclaves. The Seaside Country Club golf course was on our right, huge houses on our left. "What does Ben say about it?"

"He says exactly what you said. 'You've wanted me to retire, so I'm retiring.' "

I laughed. "That's a pretty good imitation of Ben's voice."

She smiled a little. "Lots of time listening to him. I suppose I'd be happier about this retirement if *he* seemed happier about it."

"Most people have mixed feelings about retiring. Ben's been at the Bank of Las Piernas for a long time—and in a very powerful position in the community. President of a bank that has helped businesses get started, financed much of the growth and development of the city." I thought of the one person I knew who worked for the Bank of Las Piernas. "The people who work with Ben respect him. My friend Guy St. Germain speaks very highly of Ben as a boss."

"Guy is an exceptional employee." She sighed. "Maybe I'm borrowing trouble. It will be great to have Ben all to myself. I don't know why it bothers me."

I made a turn that brought me to a security gate. She

handed a keycard to me. "You'll have to guide me from here," I said, as the gate rolled open.

"Turn right, then keep heading uphill. Sorry to put you to so much trouble."

"It's nothing."

"It's not like Ben to leave me stranded somewhere," she said, looking worried again.

"You seem to think this is connected to his retirement. Could something else be troubling him?"

She opened her mouth as if to reply, then closed it.

"What?" I asked.

"Nothing." After a moment, she said, "I don't know, maybe it is something else. I worry about his health. He hasn't been sleeping well, or eating enough. I wake up in the middle of the night, and he's over at the bedroom window, just staring out into the darkness. Or I'll find him sitting up in the study at three or four in the morning."

"Does he give a reason for any of this?"

"No. He just tells me that he didn't mean to worry me. Says he's getting old, and . . ."

"And what?"

She closed her eyes, leaned her head back against the seat. "Sometimes he'll say, 'You should marry a younger fellow next time.' "

I didn't say anything.

"It hurts to hear him say that," she said. "Makes me wonder if—oh! Turn at the next corner. You can only go right."

I made the turn. After a short distance, we were in front of another gate. She reached into her bag and pressed a remote control button that caused this gate to open, pushed it again once we were through. We drove down a dark, tree-lined lane that gave way to a long, curving driveway that sloped up to the mansion. There was a Jaguar in the driveway.

"Looks like Ben is home," I said.

But she was concentrating on the house, a puzzled look on her face. "The lights are out."

It took me a moment to register what she was saying, because there were plenty of lights on—but then I realized that they were all exterior lights. The house itself was dark.

"Maybe he's gone to bed," I said, but she was shaking her head.

I barely noticed her denial, because at that moment, what I at first took to be a berserk, woolly bear came bounding toward the car. As it drew closer, it started barking, and I realized it was not ursine but canine—the biggest dog I have ever seen in my life.

"Don't jump, Finn!" she called out. Apparently he heard her, or saw the censure on her face. He scrambled to a halt and plopped his rear down just outside the passenger door—close enough to her window to steam it with his breath. Sitting, he was nearly as tall as the car. He started whining. "He's an Irish wolfhound," she said, anticipating my question. "Back up, silly," she said to him with affection. "I can't get out."

His response was to lift a paw as big as a saucer and smack it against her window. When he set it down again, Claire drew in a sharp breath.

There was blood on the window.

4

"He's hurt!" Claire cried, but even as we hurriedly opened our car doors, I wondered how he had managed to lope across the lawn if he was badly injured.

Finn wasn't waiting for sympathy. He ran away from us, barking his deep-throated bark. We were both wearing heels, so we couldn't follow very fast. He turned, came partway back, ran from us again.

"Finn, stay!" Claire called. He seemed to consider this option for a moment, gave a big "woof" of dissent, and took off once again.

I kicked off my shoes and closed some of the distance. He rounded the corner of the house and headed for the backyard.

There weren't any exterior lights here, so it was dark along that side of the house, causing me to slow a little. The ground was cold and uneven beneath my stockinged feet. I stumbled once, but didn't fall, and glanced back to see Claire taking off her shoes.

I wondered if we should change tactics. Maybe it wasn't blood on his paws. Maybe he was just making mischief, playing a game of chase. He came back into view, his tousled fur backlighted as he stood in silhouette at the far corner of the house. The bark changed to a baying sound. I ran faster.

A large patio came into view, and as I rounded the corner I saw a swimming pool; I stopped cold when I saw a series of crazy-eight patterns of red paw prints along its deck. The dog's baying put me in motion again. He stood outside what appeared to be a cabana; it was small compared to the house, but I guessed it to be about as large as my first apartment. It was white. One of a pair of French doors facing the pool was open. A light was on inside the building, spilling out through the open door. As I came closer, Finn quit baying and started watching me intently. It made me slow to a walk, then stop—about twenty feet away from him.

I heard Claire coming up behind me. I reached out and motioned for her to wait next to me.

"What's wrong?" she asked.

"Call the dog, Claire," I said. "Just let me go in while you hold him."

For a moment I thought she would protest, but her face went pale as she looked down and noticed the bloody prints on the deck.

"Come here, Finn," she said in a shaky voice.

He twisted his head to one side in canine concern, but stayed put.

She took a deep breath and said in a commanding tone, "Finn!"

He trotted over and sat prettily in front of her.

"Check to see if his feet are hurt," I said. "I'm going to take a look in the cabana."

I walked toward it before she could object.

"Ben?" I called from the open door. There was no answer.

I stepped inside and found myself in a small sitting room decorated in soft hues of rose and gray. A small white refrigerator hummed in one corner. To either side of the sitting room, there were changing rooms, two on each side; their open doors showed them to be empty. A short hallway led to another door, also open. Over the gray tiles which led to it, I saw a trail of bloody paw prints.

"Ben?" I called again.

Nothing but the hum of the refrigerator.

With wide, awkward strides, as if stepping on stones across a stream, I crept along, careful to avoid the blood on the cold tiles.

"Ben?" I said, a little louder.

Nothing.

But there was a smell, I realized, a smell that grew much stronger as I neared the door.

My palms started sweating, my heart drumming. I wanted nothing so much as to turn around and run out of that hallway, out to where there might be sweet, cold air—big gulps of air—air that didn't reek of blood.

I braced my palms on either side of the doorjamb and made myself peer around the corner, look inside the room. It was a bathroom. The shower stall door had been pushed open. On the floor, lying half out of the shower stall, was a man, fully clothed. Ben Watterson. He held a gun. The back of his head was missing. It might have been in the big mess in the shower. I didn't stick around to find out.

As I came running out of the cabana, I saw Claire, staring at me.

"Don't go in there," I said.

She immediately let go of the dog and started to do what I just told her not to do. She had a wild look on her face. I grabbed on to her. "Claire, don't—"

The dog barked at me, scared me enough to make me let

go of her. I don't know if she heard me or if she heard the dog, but she didn't move.

Finn barked at me again.

"What—?" She left it at that. I don't think she wanted to ask the question. I might answer it.

"Let's go into the house," I said.

She looked at the cabana again, didn't budge.

"It's Ben," I said. "I'm sorry, Claire."

"No."

I waited.

She just shook her head. "No. Not Ben. Not Ben. No, you're wrong. It's not Ben."

"Yes, it is."

She bit her lip, then said, "Let me see him. He might need help."

"Claire—it's too late. I'm sorry."

"You weren't in there very long. You don't know that he's—you don't know! I want to see him." She hurried toward the cabana.

"No!" I shouted. "For Godsakes, Claire, don't—"

She stopped moving, turned toward me.

"Please don't," I said. "Please, please don't go in there."

She hesitated a moment longer, then came stumbling back to me.

"We need to go into the house," I said, trying hard to keep my voice steady. "We need to call the police."

"No," she said, but let me put an arm around her shoulders.

She leaned against me, and let me guide her away from the cabana. She just stared at me when I asked for the key to the house. I finally took her purse from her, found the keys, then tried a couple until I found one that would unlock the back door, which led into the kitchen. She stood nearby, petting the dog. "Good boy, Finn," she said, at least half a dozen times.

As I opened the door and fumbled for a light switch, the air was suddenly pierced with an obnoxious whooping noise, quickly followed by horns and bells.

"You set off the alarm," she said dully, and pushed past me to enter a code on a keypad. Blessed silence returned.

She turned on the kitchen lights and went to a wall phone, pushed an auto-dial button, and said, "This is Mrs. Watterson, that was a false alarm." She gave them a code word, then hung up.

"Do you need to use the phone?" she asked, as if she hadn't just missed a perfect opportunity to contact the police.

"Yes," I said, and dialed Robbery-Homicide.

"Frank's not here," Detective Jake Matsuda said when I identified myself. "He got called out on a case."

"This is about something else, Jake." Aware that Claire was listening to every word I said, I tried to give him as much information as I could without being cruel to her. He told me he would send someone right out.

"You want me to page Frank?" he asked.

"Yes, thanks. Could you let him know that it may be a while before I'm home?"

As I hung up, I noticed that Claire had started shaking. Her face was colorless.

"Sit down," I said, afraid that she might faint. She took a seat at the kitchen table, and Finn immediately sprawled out at her feet, head between his paws. "Can I get you something?" I asked her.

She looked out toward the backyard. "It might not be Ben," she said.

"How about a glass of water?" I went to get it without waiting for an answer.

I'll confess that I thought about calling the paper—a reporter's impulse when the town's leading banker kills himself. Already, I was wondering what had led Ben to pull the trigger. But looking at Claire as she took the glass of water, I couldn't bring myself to make the call.

"Why?" she said.

"What?"

"I heard what you told the police. Why would Ben want to kill himself?"

"I don't know, Claire. I was just wondering about that myself."

"Everyone will wonder, won't they?"

"Yes."

Once again, she stared toward the backyard. She reached for the glass of water but knocked it over, breaking the glass. "Now look what I've done," she said, and started crying.

I felt a little uneasy with the detectives who had drawn this case. I didn't have any problem with David Cardenas. But Frank had once knocked Cardenas's partner, Bob Thompson, flat on his rump. Why? For making a remark about me. Not the kind of thing that will make a guy sign your dance card at the Policemen's Ball.

Things seemed to be going okay at first. Cardenas took my statement while Thompson talked to Claire in the living room. I told Cardenas about the dog, and he had me show him the car window, and from there, to retrace most of my steps as I told him what had happened. He didn't force me to go inside the cabana again; a photographer and other technicians were at work in there. When they first arrived, Claire had been forced to calm Finn, who grew upset as other strangers came near the cabana. A uniformed officer was petting and cooing to him now, as a technician took a sample of hair from the dog's paw.

"The dog stayed outside, with Mrs. Watterson, when you went in to look?" Cardenas asked me.

"Yes."

"About where was she standing then?"

I showed him. "About here."

"Was there a reason you asked her to wait?"

I shrugged.

He waited.

"I'm not sure I thought about it at the time. There was blood, the lights were out everywhere else, and Ben hadn't come to the hotel to pick her up, as planned. He hadn't answered the phone when she called. Given all of that, by the

time we were standing here, I had a bad feeling about what
might be in the cabana."

"Did you open the door to the cabana, Mrs. Harriman?"

"No, it was already open."

"There are two doors. Were they both open?"

"No, just one. The one on the right."

"As we face the cabana, the one on our right?"

"Yes."

"All the way open?"

"No, but nearly wide open."

"Did you reach out as you approached it?"

"No."

"Touch the doorknob?"

"No . . ."

The questions went on. Cardenas was good at his job. He
helped me to concentrate on remembering a sequence of
events and details that my mind was already trying to lock
away from me. As we finished at the cabana, he paused to ask
the technicians to check out the blood on the car window, then
continued to go over the details of our entry into the house.

He thanked me for my help, asked me to wait in the
kitchen, went into the living room for a few minutes. When
he came back he said, "I think Mrs. Watterson would like to
talk to you for a moment."

I nodded and went into the living room.

Somewhere along the line, Claire must have gathered her
wits; she told me that she had called her sister, Alana, and told
Thompson that she'd wait until Alana arrived before she'd answer any other questions. Then she explained that Alana was
an attorney. Thompson apparently took that in stride.

Claire asked me to wait with her until her sister arrived. I
sat next to her on the couch. It seemed to me that she was more
herself; perhaps not completely cool and self-possessed, but
getting there. Her face was swollen from crying, her eyes red
and puffy, but there was defiance there. It occurred to me that
somehow, Thompson had made her angry.

He was sitting in a chair, swinging his foot back and forth,
watching her.

"Why couldn't they send your husband?" she asked me.

"He isn't allowed to work any case that his friends or relatives are involved in," I said. "But even if I hadn't been here, Detectives Thompson and Cardenas would have been the next ones called. Frank was already on another case."

"Mrs. Watterson," Thompson said, "you *do* understand that this woman is a newspaper reporter?"

Claire lifted a brow. "Why, Detective Thompson! I had forgotten all about that."

She reached over to the end table nearest her side of the couch and picked up the phone, then handed the receiver to me. "You probably need to call the paper about what has happened here," she said. "What's the number of the newsroom at the *Express?*"

For a moment, I was too stunned to give it to her.

"Go ahead," she said, then added quietly, "It's not as if this is something I can hide from the world."

I gave her the number, and she repeated it as she punched each digit. She gave Thompson a look that said *What are you going to do about it?*

He just kept swinging his foot, but his neck turned red.

Alana arrived just before the police showed Claire the note. Alana was slightly taller than Claire, but there was no mistaking them for sisters.

The note had been found on a desk in the study, beneath a small desk lamp. Apparently, when we arrived, that was the only lamp that was on inside the house. We hadn't seen the light from outside—the drapes in the study were closed.

Cardenas showed the note to Claire. She had to read it through a plastic cover. It said:

Claire—

Forgive me for not telling you. There is no cure. This has nothing to do with you, my love. I simply choose to avoid days of pain.

Ben

Claire broke down when she read it. "I thought he might be ill," she said, "but not so ill that he . . . why didn't he tell me?" Her sister embraced her and asked the detectives if they could have a moment alone.

I reached for my purse, thinking that I should probably leave, too. It was at about that time that I looked up to see Frank walking into the room. It was an awkward moment to give an introduction, but he managed without me. He nodded to Thompson and Cardenas, then walked toward us. He's tall, but he lowered his big frame so that he was eye level with us. He took my hand, gave it a quick squeeze, then said to Claire, "Mrs. Watterson? I'm Frank Harriman. I'm Irene's husband. I'm so sorry we had to meet under these circumstances."

The words themselves weren't extraordinary, but something in his manner or his tone must have soothed her. She stopped sobbing. Tears still ran down her face, but she quieted.

"Thank you," she said. "Irene has been very good to me tonight, but I think she should probably go home now. It's been—it's been a long night. Alana will stay with me." She looked at me and said, "I won't ever forget all you've done for me, Irene."

I wished her good night, and we left.

"You okay to drive home?" Frank asked when we reached the driveway.

I nodded.

"I'll see you there, then." He gave me a hug. He looked tired.

I had a bad moment when I first got into my car and saw the blood on my car window. I looked up into the rearview mirror and saw the headlights of Frank's car, and calmed myself. I don't always appreciate his protectiveness, but there are times when it feels good to have him watching over me. This was one of those times.

When we were on the road near the golf course, I saw Mark Baker, a friend and fellow reporter, drive past me going the other way. He gave me a puzzled look and honked, but I kept on going. I spent most of the trip home praying that Claire would be all right, and that she would forget every smart-alecky remark I had made about Frank's job.

5

John Walters, my news editor, called a meeting at the *Express* the next morning. The paper had already gone to bed when I had discovered Ben Watterson's body the night before, but it was looking like tomorrow's paper was in danger of becoming the Ben Watterson Memorial Edition.

John had gathered any of us who had interviewed or covered Ben Watterson in the past. Nobody had anything scandalous to say about him; he was credited with being a major force in Las Piernas's growth and development. He had known some opposition from antigrowth groups, but even among his opponents he was highly respected. To others, he was all but a god. The Bank of Las Piernas had financed many local businesses.

Lydia Ames, who works on the city desk, was at the meeting. She had been dating Guy St. Germain, one of the bank's vice presidents, for eight or nine months. Because she socialized with people in the bank's higher echelons, she had been able to talk to a number of people that might have remained close-mouthed otherwise. John asked her to give us an update.

"Several of the executives say that during the past week Watterson seemed agitated. Some of them are pretty upset. They feel they should have seen this coming."

"Why?" John asked. "Did Watterson drop hints, talk to any of them about killing himself?"

"No, but his activities in recent days fit those of someone

who was suicidal. Watterson was settling unfinished business, tying up loose ends in his personal estate, destroying sensitive office files, talking to board members about naming his successor."

"He tell anyone he was sick?" John asked.

"No. He told several board members that he had decided to retire," Lydia said. "But now, in hindsight, they see some of the things he said and did as warning signs they didn't heed. He gave away personal items. He gave one man some archival photographs, saying BLP might want to use some of them in a history one day. The guy now feels as if Watterson was saying good-bye."

John turned to me. "You were with the widow—right, Kelly?"

"Yes."

"At some kind of party?"

"A fund-raiser for the battered women's shelter."

He paused for a moment. "So the widow is out on the town while her husband is committing suicide?"

"You're off base, John. I was there. She took it very hard. Last night, on the ride home, she was worried about him, wondered why he suddenly wanted to retire, said she had noticed that he seemed unhappy. But she didn't even hint at being concerned that he might be suicidal."

John was thoughtful for a moment, then started barking out orders. "Got lots of angles to cover. Business section will be looking at the financial picture, including real estate." He listed reporters' names, assigning an aspect of the story to each. "Baker," he concluded, calling on our crime reporter, "try to get more out of the grieving widow."

John's bad moods are so perpetual that we usually find ourselves afraid of him when he's cheerful. We've all suffered his temper, so his moods allow the often competitive reporters of the newsroom to band together in defense. But today no one complained about him. The suicide of Ben Watterson was one of those stories that made everyone want to do a little more digging. We all knew there was more to the story.

No one had any real reason to believe that, but no one had any doubt about it, either.

When I got back to my desk, a light was blinking on my new phone. The *Express* had just invested in a voice-mail system, and the light meant that I had a message. I entered the required codes and eventually got to my section of this glorified answering machine. "You have one new message," the overly pleasant voice of the system said. "Sent today at 9:37 A.M." What followed was a series of telephone tones, as if someone were dialing in my ear. I didn't mind—they played "Goodnight, Irene," a signal from one of my city hall contacts.

I called Nina Howell, a secretary who works in the Zoning Department. She calls me whenever she has one of those days when she feels like she's working for a crook. This means she calls me on a fairly regular basis.

"Zoning Department," she answered. "This is Ms. Howell. May I help you?"

"I sure hope so. You called?"

"Yes. Moffett is leaving. He resigned this morning."

"Allan Moffett, the city manager?" There weren't any other Allan Moffetts running around city hall, but the idea that the most powerful employee in the city government was resigning wasn't easy to grasp.

"Yes. Word is, he's running scared." There was noise in the background, and she hesitated for a few moments before saying, "Yes, that's right. This is the Zoning Department, and I'm afraid there's no one here by that name."

"I take it this means your boss is back in the room?"

"Yes, well," she went on, "if you spell the name for me, perhaps I can look it up in your directory."

"Okay. I've just spelled the name of someone who might be able to help me out. You're stalling?"

"Exactly."

"Can we meet for lunch?" I asked.

"I don't seem to be finding that one here, but perhaps you

should try our main switchboard. Would you like for me to transfer you to the operator?"

"Whatever you need to do."

"Please hold the line," she said.

No choice but to wait and see what happened. There was a click, and then a new voice came on the line.

"Charlotte Brady," a strained voice answered.

Allan Moffett's secretary. Trying not to sound too surprised, I said, "Hello, Charlotte. It's Irene Kelly."

"Irene Kelly?"

I waited for her to snub me or to harangue me about calling her on what she probably thought of as one of the saddest days in Las Piernas history. Charlotte Brady was fiercely protective of her boss. Nineteen years as Moffett's secretary had ingrained certain ideas about me into Charlotte's loyal mind, most of which identified me under one heading: The Enemy.

"Irene Kelly . . . ," she said slowly, as if weighing my name on a scale.

"Uh, Charlotte, are you all right?"

"Am I all right?" she shouted. "Hell, no. What would make you think I would be all right?"

I was stunned into silence. Charlotte is usually so calm and controlled, you could say "Charlotte, your clothing is on fire," and even as she did a drop and roll, she'd smile and reply that she couldn't confirm or deny anything without Mr. Moffett's say-so.

"Do you know what that son of a bitch said to me this morning?"

"No," I said, not even sure she meant Moffett.

"He said, 'Charlotte, you've been wonderful. Thanks for all you've done. I talked to Glen, and you can keep that desk set if you like.' "

"Mr. Moffett asked the mayor if you could keep the desk set?"

"Yes! I sat here for about thirty minutes, just . . . just in shock, I suppose. But I got over that stage about an hour ago. Guess which stage I'm at now?"

"Well—"

"Anger. That's where I'm at now. I'm the angriest I've ever been in my life. Wouldn't you be?"

"I imagine I would."

"Nineteen years of loyalty. Not one day out sick. Nineteen years of organizing that man's life, putting up with his moods, serving him his morning coffee in a white china cup, addressing his Christmas cards for Godsakes! A desk set! Nineteen years, and his big damned favor to me is a desk set!" She drew in a deep breath and let it out on a long sigh, then laughed. "Well, Irene Kelly, after practically hanging up in your ear several times a month for the last ten years, let me ask—*very sincerely*—what can I do for you, my dear?"

"Perhaps you could tell me why he left?"

"Oh, he claims it's because of his health."

Those words made me think of Ben Watterson, and I felt a chill. "His health?"

"Oh, it's not true. Not unless 'skeletons in the closet' can be called a bone disease."

"What skeletons?"

"I'll be honest. If I knew the details, I'd be down there dictating them to you. All I know is that all hell broke loose after that man came in to see him."

"Wait—what man?"

"I don't know, but someone ought to give the guy a medal. I should have seen this coming when I saw how Allan treated his ex-wife."

"Allan's ex-wife has something to do with the man who came in to see him?"

"No, no, sorry. I meant, I should have seen how rotten Allan could be to women. But no, this man came in here yesterday, and I almost called security. He wouldn't give his name, and he acted nervous."

"Can you describe him to me?"

"He was a black man. Hard to guess his age. Late forties? Maybe early fifties? Not well dressed. His clothes didn't fit him right—wore an inexpensive suit that was kind of loose on him. I tried to tell him that Mr. Moffett was very busy and couldn't see anyone without an appointment. But this guy was determined. If you work as a secretary long enough, you can spot the ones you can get rid of easily and the ones that are going to be persistent—like you. You have nearly driven me crazy on more than one occasion, you know."

"The admiration is mutual."

"Oh, I hope you weren't insulted by that remark?"

"Not at all. Tell me more about this man."

"Well, I gave in. I don't know, I guess it seemed to me that he wasn't asking for much. He didn't exactly ask to see Allan."

"What did he want?"

"He had a letter with him, and he asked me to take it in to Allan."

"Did you see what the letter said?"

"No. But I was very curious about it, because Allan went white as a sheet when he read it. Then he got kind of blustery and stood up and marched out into the waiting room. But the man just sat there calmly and looked Allan in the eye. Allan said, 'Come into my office.' The man nodded and went on in."

"You hear any of their conversation?"

"Not a word. He talked to Allan for a long time. He didn't seem especially happy when he left, so maybe Allan didn't give him what he wanted."

"If he left unhappy, what makes you think he had anything to do with Allan's resignation?"

"It was what happened after he left. Allan sat alone in his office for a long time. He wasn't using the phone—I would have seen a line light up on the phone. Then he buzzed me on the intercom and asked me to work late. I had to call all of his old buddies last night. He set up a dinner with them."

"They met last night?"

"No. Allan was too busy packing up his office and shredding documents last night to go have dinner. I didn't know that's what he was up to, of course. I was making dinner arrangements." She paused, then said, "Maybe that's how you can supply me with my sweet revenge, Miss Kelly. The dinner is tonight at the Terrace. I'll bet you'd like to be there."

"The Terrace is usually a little out of my price range, but

maybe I'll splurge tonight. Mind if I ask who's on the guest list?"

She gave me a list of six names, seven with Allan added on as host. I knew all of them. They were the names of men with high profiles in Las Piernas; mostly, they were involved in a mix of planning, banking, real estate, and construction. But as I typed the names into my computer notes, two of them gave me an uncomfortable feeling.

I had been hearing one of them too often lately: Andre Selman.

The other name led me to tell Charlotte to change the number in the reservation.

Ben Watterson wouldn't make it to dinner.

6

Charlotte hadn't seen or heard any of the news about Watterson's suicide. Once she got over her initial shock, I asked her about her conversations with the men who were going to the meeting.

"What were you supposed to tell them to get them to this dinner?" I asked.

"Nothing special, really. Allan said I should just mention who would be at the dinner, and then to say, 'Mr. Moffett is certain you already understand the importance of meeting as soon as possible.' Ben Watterson. My God. I can't believe it."

"What time did you talk to Mr. Watterson?"

"Let me check my phone log," she said. I heard paper rustling in the background, then she came on the line again. "At about seven o'clock."

"Allan didn't ask you to destroy your phone log?" I asked, temporarily distracted.

"No. Either he forgot about them or he figured my notes wouldn't be very important."

"Hang on to them, all right?"

"Sure. Now that I think of it, he called twice that day. The first time, it was to tell Allan that he was sending a fax."

"Do you remember the fax?"

"No, I didn't get it. Allan said it was some confidential information from the bank. He stood next to the fax and picked it up himself."

"Wasn't that unusual?"

"Well, it didn't happen too often, but Allan would do that on occasion. He had his secrets, even from me. Obviously, or I wouldn't be packing up my desk today."

"Did Mr. Watterson seem upset when you spoke to him about the dinner?"

"No, he seemed very calm. Very quiet. Just said, 'Thank you, Charlotte, I've been expecting a call.' "

"Nothing else?"

"No, not a word."

"No indication that he wasn't planning to show up?"

"None at all. I guess that's why I'm shocked . . ."

"Any of the others say anything when you called?"

"No. I figured they all knew that Allan would be contacting them. They all just took down the information and said to tell Mr. Moffett that they would be there."

"Do you know what, if anything, these men have in common?"

"No, not really. Allan had dealings with all of them from time to time." She paused, and I waited while she thought it over. "Nothing too surprising as far as their connection to this office. When I look down the list, they've all worked on city redevelopment projects in one way or another. Roland Hill, of course, as a developer; Keene Dage has done a lot of big construction; and as you know, Corbin Tyler is an architect. Ben Watterson's bank has financed some projects. The other two, Booter Hodges and Andre Selman, are from the college. Las Piernas College has supplied most of the research and

planning studies for redevelopment. So all of these men have
legitimate business with Allan."

I told John about Moffett's resignation and the connection between Ben Watterson and Moffett. Then I drove over to city
hall and spent time that did little more than confirm my initial impression that Moffett's resignation was as unexpected
as a queen's belch at a banquet. People were either trying to
pretend that nothing happened or nervously hiding glee or
horror, depending on how they felt about Moffett. Up on the
sixth floor, where the city manager's offices are housed, only
the most minor officials were available to see me, and they
had little to say. The most powerful had left for lunch appointments. Each of their secretaries quickly closed any appointment books that were open on their desks, then calmly
lied to me, saying they had no idea where their bosses were
eating lunch.

I looked at my watch. Just after one o'clock. I made a big
show of leaving and talking about being too late for my deadline (my own lie) and took an elevator down to the lobby and
left the building to call the paper. The potential of this story
had rated me the use of a cellular phone for the afternoon, but
it was cheaper to make the call from a pay phone, so I used
my own coins. I hoped John would balance the righteousness
of that sacrifice with the fact that I had bupkis to report. He
didn't.

I grabbed lunch at a noodle shop near city hall, went back
in through the lobby, and stood around acting as if I were fas-
cinated with a sculpture that I had seen at least two thousand
times before. The sculpture is big enough to hide behind if
you're not wearing red or some other color that will show
through the holes in it; I was wearing a dark gray outfit that
blended in perfectly.

I saw the secretaries from the sixth floor—those liars—
come back from their own lunches, and figured that was as
good a sign as any that their bosses would be back soon.
They chatted while waiting at the elevator, and the pieces of

conversation I strained so hard to overhear turned out to be about a baby shower for a coworker. Not wanting them to warn their bosses that I was in the building, I took the stairs. A few other hardy souls took the stairs as far as the fourth floor, but after that I was on my own.

I stopped on the landing of the sixth floor, looked through my purse for the big rubber eraser I carry for such occasions, and jammed it in the door to hold it open a crack. From this vantage point, I couldn't see the elevator or any of the office doors. That didn't matter. Years of covering this particular beat had taught me a lot about the habits of Las Piernas city executives, and I knew where to wait for my prey. I had an excellent view of the door to the men's room.

Sure enough, Ray Aiken came walking down the hall. Ray was the assistant city manager, and to my good fortune, he preferred the city hall facilities to those of whatever restaurant he was returning from. Ray was nearing sixty. He's a big man with a small bladder. I know this from watching many long city council meetings.

Ray was alone. My lucky day. I retrieved my eraser and waited in the hall.

He was still tucking the tail of his shirt into the wide waist of his pants when he shouldered his way out of the men's room door. He looked up, saw me, and said, "Oh, cripes," turned around and went back in.

I pushed the door open and followed him. "I know no one else is in here, Ray, but I'd prefer not to interview you in here so soon after you've—"

"Goddammit, Kelly, this is the men's room!"

"Really? And I thought those things were baptismal fonts."

He turned beet red and said, "Have you no shame?"

"All kinds of it, but it won't keep me from talking to you in here if I have to."

"What if someone comes in here and sees you in here with me?"

"They'll think neither one of us has any shame. Come on out into the stairwell and talk with me, Ray."

He sighed in resignation, and after a furtive look down the

hall, followed me into the stairwell. I sat on a step, but he stayed on his feet. "I don't have to talk to you," he whispered, craning to look at the landings above and below.

"I know."

He looked back to me in surprise.

"You don't have to," I went on, "but I think you will."

"Really? What makes you so sure?"

"You're the guy most likely to be the next city manager. You'll need the paper's help to keep you clear of the stink that Moffett's leaving behind. And it's especially smelly that Moffett has quit the day after Ben Watterson killed himself."

"I was sorry to hear about Ben," Ray said quietly. "I don't think the two are connected."

"Maybe not. We'll leave that for now. But as the man most likely to be the new manager—"

"Big assumption, Kelly."

"No, think about it. The new mayor has an unexpected chance to reshape the office. He likes you. A total newcomer would bring the city to a grinding halt while he or she learned the ropes—the mayor can't afford that. You're known as someone the city employees trust. You're experienced, but you're not one of the fossils."

He laughed at that, but sat down next to me. "Kelly, if I know you, you'd love to see everyone on the sixth floor replaced."

"Not necessarily. I'll admit, I'm not one of Moffett's fans. I don't think you are, either. You've worked hard for him, and he's needed your expertise, your way with people. But he hasn't always treated you with the respect you deserve. That's why I picked you instead of one of his cronies."

He sighed. "You knew his cronies would never talk to you, so you picked one of his drudges to harass. As for all that respect I supposedly deserve—if some male reporter had followed a woman into a restroom—"

"Look, I apologize. I wouldn't have followed you in there if I thought you were—"

"Never mind, never mind. I can't stay in this stairwell all afternoon. What do you want?"

"Just tell me why Moffett's resigning. The real reason."

"Resigned. Past tense. He's out. But the man put thirty years of service into this community, Irene. I can't drag him through the mud."

In spite of the actual words spoken, when Ray stops calling me Kelly, I know he's giving in. I waited.

"I need a cigarette," he said, and lit one in blatant disregard of a city ordinance banning smoking in public buildings. I kept waiting.

He took a long drag and exhaled slowly. "You don't need me to tell you that there are many opportunities offered to a man who holds the title of city manager. He's not elected, but because the council relies so heavily on him for information and to carry out their will, he's powerful. In fact, Allan has been the city manager longer than any of the current council members have been in office. If certain offers were made to him, well, even a saint would find it tempting to accept an offer now and again."

"And Moffett is no saint."

Ray shook his head.

"So just what kind of sinner are we talking about here?"

He stayed silent, watching the end of his cigarette for a moment. He took another drag, then said, "You remember what downtown was like about twenty years ago?"

"Sure. Depending on your point of view, it was a historical district full of beautiful but aging buildings in need of renovation, or it was a seedy, festering dump that needed to be demolished."

He smiled. "Liked the old buildings, did you? You were probably some damned hippie."

"Sorry, Ray, I just missed out on the hippies. The nuns wouldn't let us out of our plaid, and by the time I got to go to public school, it was all over. To use a hippie expression, I'm not too bummed out about it. The Las Piernas High School imitation of hippiedom was pretty pathetic."

"Too young to be a hippie. Dammit, Irene, you are making me feel very old."

"So this is related to downtown redevelopment?"

"I didn't say that."

"But I'm close."

He smiled, crushed out his cigarette, and carefully pocketed its remains. "You're closer than you were to being a hippie, I suppose."

He stood up, brushed his pants off, and left me sitting there. I thought about what he said. I left when a bureaucrat from the next floor up opened a door, sniffed the air, and told me in a nasty tone of voice that it was illegal to smoke *anywhere* in the building.

7

I thought Frank might resist the idea of dining at the Terrace that night, but I was wrong.

"Of course I'll go with you," he said. "You know how I feel about your being out alone late at night. And these guys might not appreciate your attention."

"I'm not asking you to come along as muscle, Frank. We just haven't seen much of each other lately."

He looked skeptical. "Sure that's it? Or do you just want to avoid attracting attention by dining alone in a fancy restaurant?"

I turned red, but said, "The last of the great romantics."

He took that as a personal challenge. He met it admirably, so even though we weren't due there for a couple of hours, we were a little late getting to the Terrace.

Driving to the restaurant, we passed through the part of town where I had seen Lucas. I started telling Frank about him.

"It's a cold night," I said, watching the empty streets as if I might see him again. "I hope he's in a shelter."

"Sounds like your friend at the center looks out after him. He's probably okay."

"Roberta's out of town," I said. "I wouldn't even know where to look for Lucas. I was such a jerk that day. Ran away from him."

"You expect too much of yourself," he said. "You didn't know who he was. He scared you. That's not your fault. And you didn't make him crawl into a bottle, either."

"No," I said, but grew silent.

"Listen, from what you've told me about him, you're probably right—some time after graduate school, something must have really gone wrong. But right now, until he contacts you, there's not much you can do about him. I could ask the guys who work that section of town—"

"No, don't. Just knowing where he is wouldn't be enough. And it might embarrass him. I don't want Lucas to think I'm putting pressure on him. He'll come to see me when he's ready."

We came to another section of the city, this one much more affluent than the one we had just left. Separated by one of the oil fields that have brought money into Las Piernas since the 1930s, the two neighborhoods might just as easily have been separated by outer space. Here in the Knolls, as the enclave was called, big, sloping lawns fronted large homes.

The Terrace isn't in one of the fancier parts of the Knolls, but it is on an actual knoll. It's at the end of a small street, bordered by the high walls of one of the housing developments. One of the smaller lots of oil pumps is across from it. Despite the noise made by the rhythmic, rolling, rocking-horse motions of the pumps outside, the restaurant itself is quiet.

Even though it's packed every night, something about the Terrace invites its diners to speak in low voices. Dark paneled wood, candlelight, and traditional fare—no menu items that belong in a lab notebook. Perhaps a little straitlaced, but reliable.

Before the maître d' could do much with his look—one that said he wished he wasn't too polite to pinch his nose shut—

I said, "We're just here for a drink," and guided Frank into the bar.

"Going to drink your dinner?" Frank asked as we sat at a small table.

"No, but you can make a meal out of the appetizers. We can't have dinner here tonight, anyway. They didn't have any tables open in the dining room by the time I called."

"Now you tell me."

I shrugged. "This will be cheaper."

He laughed. "I guess we can stop by Bernie's on the way home." He wasn't looking at me as he said this. He was looking around the room, checking out the occupants. Cop habit of his. He caught me catching him at it and asked, "Do you need to take a stroll around the restaurant to look for Moffett and his guests?"

"I could, but I think I already know where he is. We're sitting next to a private dining room," I said, pointing at a hallway off the bar.

"So that's what the note on the reservation's list meant."

"Mr. Harriman, I'm dazzled. I didn't think you had a chance to read it while the maître d' was snubbing us."

"I'm full of tricks. You've been in this private dining room?"

"Not as an invitee. Are you familiar with the Brown Act?"

"The law that gets you and all your pals at the *Express* into government meetings, right?"

"Well, yes, but there's more to it than that. Without getting into a lot of details, let's just say one of the most important things the Brown Act does is to prohibit local public agencies from meeting secretly."

"Public agencies?"

"Local legislative bodies, for the most part. School boards, city councils, and commissions are included. It's a state law. One of the best sections of the Brown Act—great for reporters, anyway—extends the requirement for open and public meetings to any committee or task force those councils and commissions appoint—even advisory groups."

I paused in my civics lecture while the waitress came to take our drink order.

"You're going to tell me what this has to do with the private dining room at the Terrace, right?" Frank asked.

"Patience. So—these commissions can't exclude reporters from meetings, right? And 'meetings' aren't just those formal gatherings in the council chambers. The law can extend to social functions. Parties, picnics, you name it."

"Wait a minute. You mean the city council members can't have a party without inviting the *Express?*"

"Maybe, maybe not. Depends on what they discuss. If the city council members all get together for a picnic, they don't have to invite the public—*unless* they start discussing public business. They can't evade the law just by going to the park and playing Frisbee while they tell each other how they plan to vote on a zoning change."

"I'm beginning to see where this is leading. Someone held a meeting here and you found out about it."

"Right. The Redevelopment Agency. People with business and construction interests used to invite the city planning commission members down to the Terrace for dinner meetings. That's in violation of the Brown Act. Someone leaked word of one of the meetings to me, and I barged in on it—it was a great story."

Frank shifted a little in his chair. The drinks arrived, and he took a long sip of scotch before asking cautiously, "You do remember that I'm employed by the city? I mean, I won't get in the way of your doing your job, but—"

"Don't worry, I'm not going to barge in on this meeting, Frank. I can't."

"Why not? You just said—"

"Moffett doesn't qualify. He was the city manager, and now he's a private citizen. The people who are in there with him have been involved in city projects, but none of them are members of a public board or advisory committee—at least, not right now. So it's a private meeting."

"So why are we here? Were you going to try to eavesdrop?"

"The *Express* may be cheap, Frank, but we haven't crawled down to tabloid level yet. No, I just want to know who showed up for this cozy little gathering. And I want them to know that I'm around—that will be enough to make a couple of them nervous. If I get a chance, I'll try to corner one of them on the way out. Even if I don't, someone may want to talk later."

"Any ideas about what's up?"

"Not exactly. But it's got to be connected to whatever caused Moffett to resign."

We ordered enough appetizers to keep the alcohol from going straight to our stomachs. We made the most of our chance to be alone, to talk, to catch up on the day's events—even though I was keeping one eye on the hallway near the private dining room.

After we had been there about an hour, Andre Selman came out of that hallway. I hadn't seen him in more than a decade. His once-blond hair had turned silver, he had gone soft in the middle, but otherwise he hadn't changed much. For some odd reason, he seemed shorter.

Most of the women in SOS would probably say that Andre's charm was more powerful than his looks, but at the moment, neither was in evidence. He looked like hell. He was dabbing a handkerchief across a perspiring forehead and he was pale. His blue eyes watched nothing but the carpet as he hurried along. I thought he might be headed for the restroom, but his destination was one of the telephone booths. Like everything else in the Terrace, the phone booths are old-fashioned—real booths with doors made of wood and glass. By the time I figured out that Andre hadn't gone into the rest-room, he was returning to the dinner party. It was on his way back that he spotted me. His eyes widened, then his face screwed up in anger. For a moment it looked as if he would storm his way over to me, but then he seemed to notice Frank.

Frank had realized some moments before that I was watching someone, and had turned in his chair and started watching, too. I couldn't see Frank's face, but Andre's seemed to go pale again. Andre hurried down the hallway to the dining room.

Frank turned back to me, a self-satisfied grin on his face. "Well, well, well," he said, and finished off his drink.

"Out with it."

"That, I take it, was the old boyfriend?"

I cringed. "Do I go around reminding you of your mistakes?"

He laughed. "No. But none of my old girlfriends have whole societies dedicated to honoring their memories."

"What are you talking about? SOS isn't about Andre."

"You sometimes call it 'Survivors of Selman,' right?"

"As a joke."

He didn't say anything, just sat there looking bemused. His smug mode. He was inviting a fight, but escalating the argument in the middle of the Terrace was an unappealing idea. I had the feeling this topic could get loud. I kept my eyes on the hallway and changed the subject.

"Tell me a Bakersfield story," I said.

After a brief moment of hesitation, during which he probably figured out that he had pissed me off, he said, "Okay. This one happened not long after I made detective."

The story was about a hardware store owner who had disappeared. His wife reported him missing, and she was convinced that the guy's business partner had done him in. They questioned the business partner at the store and didn't learn much, but Frank thought he seemed nervous. Frank's partner, a senior detective, agreed, and they kept an eye on the guy. Frank talked to a nosy neighbor. The neighbor was full of complaints about the suspect: didn't keep his lawn mowed, left his garbage cans out for a day or two after pickup, his house needed painting, his leaves needed raking, so on and so forth. Only thing the guy cared about was his car. Then the neighbor mentioned that the suspect had changed one habit lately: he had been leaving his car out in the driveway, instead of parking it in the garage.

The story was interrupted when we heard a commotion near the front door. I turned to see the maître d' blocking the way of a dark-haired man wearing jeans, refusing him entrance.

Frank pushed his chair back. The man at the door hovered over the maître d', saying angrily, "I don't want to dine in your goddamned restaurant! I'm just here to take someone home. Move out of the way!"

Although I hadn't seen the man in many years, his face was immediately familiar. "It's Jerry Selman," I said. "Andre's son."

Before the maître d' could reply to Jerry, Corbin Tyler came bursting out of the private dining room, panic-stricken. He looked blindly around the room, his gaze finally settling on me. "Help!" he shouted. "He's having a heart attack!" He ran back down the hall.

Frank was out of his chair and moving after him in no time, pausing only to shout back at me, "Call 911!"

Jerry and I rushed past one another as I made my way toward the maître d', who was already dialing the phone. I waited until I heard him asking for an ambulance, then went back to the private dining room.

I realized as I walked into the room that I had assumed that Corbin had been shouting about Andre; as it turned out, the assumption was true. In a quick glance, I took in Corbin Tyler, Booter Hodges, Allan Moffett, and Keene Dage all watching nervously from the other side of the room. Roland Hill was with them, too, but seemed merely curious, not at all upset. Frank and Jerry were on the floor with Andre. Frank straddled Andre, doing chest compressions while Jerry knelt near his father's face, giving him mouth-to-mouth.

"Stay back," Booter Hodges warned.

"I know CPR," I said, moving a chair and kneeling down on the floor.

"Pulse," Frank said between counts.

I reached toward Andre's neck, my fingers searching for his carotid artery. At first, I felt nothing, and then, a few seconds later, it was there. "He's got a pulse!" I said.

Frank stopped, felt for it, too. "She's right."

"He's breathing," Jerry said, and started weeping.

We stayed there, not speaking, waiting to make sure our luck would hold. I heard someone leaving the room, but I was too focused on keeping my fingers on Andre's pulse to see who it was. Andre's color changed from a claylike gray to a shade that still didn't look great, but wasn't half as frightening.

Paramedics arrived, and at last we stood and moved away. I turned to see that only two of Andre's friends were still there: Roland Hill and Keene Dage. Keene said, "If you need me, I'll be in the bar."

Roland lifted an eyebrow, then said, "Really? Well, I don't suppose I'll need you this evening. We can talk about our business tomorrow." He nodded toward me on his way out, cool as the shady side of an iceberg.

Frank had an arm around Jerry's shoulders, and talked to him as they followed the paramedics outside. I was left standing alone in the room. I had that wobbly knees feeling that sometimes comes after the adrenaline leaves your body, so I sat down for a moment.

I wondered how hard Lisa would take it if her father died. There had never been much affection between them, but that wouldn't mean that she still didn't hope for his approval. Jerry—well, Jerry would probably be crushed. I didn't wish that kind of suffering on him. And even though Andre was a genuine shitheel, I didn't wish pain or death on him, either. I considered the fact that I had never really known Jerry, who was away at college when I was dating Andre, and that Andre was all but a stranger to me now. They might have changed over the years. Might have. Seemed unlikely in Andre's case.

Had something upset him this evening, something besides seeing me? I didn't for a moment believe I meant enough to him—good or bad—to give him a heart attack. I looked around the table.

Most of the dinner dishes had been cleared; it appeared that the meal had been at the coffee-and-dessert stage. I got up and slowly walked around the table, but nothing of importance had been left behind. Even if I had known who was sitting where, all I would have learned was who drank his java black and who took cream and sugar. There was no point in sticking around. I left the room.

Keene Dage was at the bar, doodling on a cocktail napkin.

"What are you having, Keene?" I asked, sitting next to him.

"Just finished a club soda," he said, standing up. "Not much of a headline, is it?"

He walked off.

I waited until he was out of sight, nabbed his cocktail napkin, and left enough cash to cover our bill before hurrying out to follow my quarry. A cold wind made me hold my coat around me with both arms as I stepped outside. I didn't see Frank or Jerry, but Keene Dage was waiting for the valet parking attendant.

I called out a greeting.

He stared stonily ahead.

"Now Keene, this just isn't like you. You've never been rude to me."

Keene Dage was a big, rough-hewn man, and even at seventy he looked like he could build a skyscraper with his bare hands. He had been in the management end of construction for decades before he retired, but he had come up the hard way and hadn't forgotten it.

"Goddammit, Irene," he said, shaking his head. "Go back inside. You look like you're freezing your ass off."

"I can take it if you can, old man."

He laughed, long and hard—much longer and harder than my remark called for, but it probably afforded him the kind of release that club soda won't provide. "Still full of piss and vinegar, I see," he said, wiping his eyes.

"Tell me about your dinner meeting, Keene."

The levity was gone. "Forget all about this. Just forget it. It was a private dinner. Allan's retired. Until Selman became ill, we were just spending an evening thanking Allan for his service to the city. A sort of farewell for Allan, that's all."

"Somehow I don't imagine Allan will have to make a lot of last-minute, urgent calls when it's time for his going-away party. When that really happens, you'll have a little more time to plan a trip in from—where is it now?"

He fidgeted with his tie, loosening it. "Fallbrook."

"Right. You're growing avocados now."

"I'll send you a box of them next time we pick them. Now here's my car."

"Come on, Keene. You can do more for me than this. This isn't about Allan. You aren't really all that fond of Allan."

He had started to tip the valet, but now he paused, still holding the cash in his hand, the wind whipping the bills as the valet looked at them longingly.

I glanced at the valet, and Keene paid him. When he was out of earshot, Keene said, "Where the hell—when did you ever hear of me saying an unkind thing about Allan?"

"Never. You were doing business here, and you needed Allan, and you were too smart to go around saying you didn't like his style. But I've always sensed it. I even mentioned it to O'Connor."

"O'Connor's dead," he said, getting into the car.

"Well, yes, Keene, I certainly know that O'Connor is dead. When you work with a man for over a dozen years, you notice such things. This is not something I said into a Ouija board. I talked about it with him when he was alive. You haven't been in town for a few years now. This was before you left, before O'Connor died. He agreed with me—there was some kind of tension between you and Allan."

He hesitated. "So your old friend talked about me, eh?"

"Yes. He liked you, Keene. Said you and Corbin and Ben were the only honest men in that bunch who had worked on redevelopment in the 1970s."

Keene looked away for a moment, then turned back to me. "O'Connor was wrong," he said, and closed the car door.

I thought he would drive off, but he rolled down the window. "Sorry, Irene, guess I'm rude after all. Hope you don't take this personally. It's not about you."

I pulled out a business card.

"I sure as hell don't want to take that thing from you," he said. "I've got to get back home. Long drive. I'll be making it again in a few days."

"Why?"

"Ben's funeral. You going?"

"Yes."

He frowned. "Don't come up to me and talk to me there, okay? I'll send you a box of avocados."

He drove off.

O'Connor was wrong, Keene said. About Keene's dislike of Allan Moffett? Or about his honesty?

Frank wasn't in the restaurant, so I burrowed into my coat and walked around to the parking lot in the back. The sky was darkening, but we had parked near one of the parking lot lampposts, and I could see Frank sitting in the Volvo. As I drew closer, I saw that he had his arms folded over the top of the steering wheel, his forehead resting on them. He didn't look up when I got in the car.

"Are you all right?" I asked.

"No," he said.

It hit me, then. I reached over and placed my hand over his. "Thinking about your dad?"

I heard him let his breath out, a long sigh. He took my hand, held it tightly as he leaned back in his seat. His face gave me the answer before he said, "Yes."

Frank's father had a heart attack three or four years ago; Frank was with him shortly before he collapsed. Although Frank hurried back into the room and did CPR, his father had died.

For a long time, we just sat in that parking lot, holding hands, Frank looking out into the night. Rain began to fall. I watched the reflections of the rivulets on the windshield move across his face.

"You never finished telling me that story," I said. "The one about the man who didn't park in his garage."

"No, I didn't, did I?" he said, and then a look of mild amusement crossed his face. "We waited until the guy came out of his house, and my partner asked him, 'Could we see the garage?'

" 'Sure,' he says, 'no problem.' He opens the garage door, and the entire floor of the garage is red."

"Blood?" I asked.

Frank shook his head. "Paint. The guy has painted the entire floor of the garage. The exterior of the house is cracked and peeling, but he's painted his garage floor. When my partner comments on this, the guy says, 'Yeah, well, I'm gonna paint the whole house, I just started here.' "

"Right."

"That's what we thought," Frank said. "So while my partner is talking to him, I'm kind of snooping around. This is the cleanest garage on earth. Too clean. It's been scrubbed. I look up, and I can see that even the light fixture has been cleaned. I wander over to the sink. There's a shiny new trap under it. I start wondering if anything might be left under the rim of the drain. But then I look next to the sink, and I see a mop leaning against the wall. A good old-fashioned cotton mop. I move it around a little, and poke through the strands, and guess what I see?"

"Bloodstains."

"Well, no. But I take it over to the guy. What I was showing him was rust from the metal clamp, but he didn't know that. I made out like I was sure it was blood, and my partner kept his mouth shut. I asked the guy, 'Why'd you go to all this time and trouble, and then forget to throw the mophead away with the sink trap?' He started crying—to this day, I'm not sure if it was because we had caught him, or because he had done a lot of unnecessary cleaning. Anyway, he confessed."

"Was there any blood on the mop?" I asked.

"Oh yeah, the lab guys found traces of it all over the place, even before they wrecked the paint job on the floor." He smiled. "I got to tell the guy what we were doing to his paint job."

"I think this is one of your best Bakersfield stories."

"My dad was still working then. He loved the business with the mop—told it to the other guys so often, it's a wonder I didn't end up with a nickname out of it. I'd say, 'Dad, we would have caught him without the mop.' He wouldn't hear a word of it."

He started the car, turned on the windshield wipers.

"You okay to drive?" I asked.

"Yeah." He leaned over and gave me a quick kiss. "I'm okay now."

We were almost home when I remembered the cocktail

napkin. Frank saw me pull it out and try to read it, and flipped on the dome light. "What's that?"

"Keene Dage's cocktail napkin."

"What's on it?"

"The letter *Z*." I turned the napkin and frowned. "Or the letter *N.*"

"Or just a doodle," he said.

"Right," I said glumly, which made him laugh.

That was okay.

8

On Friday morning, my time was whittled away on the phone, to no apparent purpose other than strengthening my dialing finger. I was trying to contact people who might know more about Allan Moffett's resignation. Most of my time was spent talking to receptionists and secretaries whose bosses supposedly weren't in. Not in now, not expected back in today, probably not in as long as I was the caller.

The people who were willing to talk to me were his political enemies, and although Moffett's long tenure in a powerful position allowed him to gather quite a few adversaries, it was clear they were not knowledgeable on the subject of his sudden retirement. It was all well and good to allow a few of these frustrated souls to tell me how happy they were that Moffett was gone, but I wanted to do more than gather reactions to his departure.

I listened to their theories, hoping some useful lead might be found. There had been the disappointment around the convention center plans, they pointed out. The city and its developers had suffered a defeat at the hands of the Coastal Commission, which had recently denied approval of a waterfront convention center. But when I countered that Moffett had weathered far worse, no one disagreed.

There were budget shortfalls and an increasingly uncooperative city council. Budget shortfalls didn't fit with sudden flight, though, or account for the guest list at the dinner meeting, although I kept that to myself. And even Moffett's enemies couldn't blame him for problems caused by cutbacks from the county and state. If anything, Moffett had relentlessly urged the city to budget more realistically when cutbacks occurred.

His priorities might not have been universally embraced by the city council, but even I knew that the council had been at his mercy—not the other way around. The city manager could slow a council member's pet projects to a standstill, just by making sure that his own staff was overly meticulous in discharging their bureaucratic duties. The council also received much of its information from Moffett and his staff, and no politician who wants a second term fails to realize what a valuable commodity information can be. Council members came and went, Moffett stayed. Until now.

His friends weren't helpful to me in the least, and after the disrupted dinner at the Terrace, his closest pals were all taking the day off—if their secretaries were to be believed.

Throughout the morning, I wondered how Andre was doing, but realized my concern was not really for Andre himself. I was worried about Lisa and, to some extent, Jerry. I pulled out the card Lisa had given me and dialed her brother's home number. I got an answering machine.

"Jerry," I said, after the beep, "this is Irene Kelly. I don't know if you remembered me last night at the Terrace, but"—I stopped myself from saying "I used to date your dad"—"er, I was just wondering how things are going today. If there's anything I can do for you or Lisa, let me know." I left my number.

I was still holding on to the receiver, wondering why I had done such a lame job of leaving a simple message, when the intercom line buzzed. I punched the button. Geoff, the paper's security guard, announced that I had a visitor, a Ms. Lisa Selman. He put her on the line.

"Lisa?"

"I don't suppose you'd be free for lunch today?"

"Sure. Give me a minute, I'll be right down."

She was engrossed in reading a copy of the paper in the lobby when I came downstairs. I stood on the stairway, watching her for a moment. She was wearing jeans and a sweater, but even in the casual attire she looked sophisticated. She glanced up and saw me, and as the light struck her face from this new angle, I noticed dark circles under her eyes. "Just now reading the paper," she said, shaking her head. "I overslept this morning and haven't caught up since."

"Lisa—"

"Don't get that sympathetic look on your face, Irene, you'll make me cry. My father's in stable condition now, thanks to you and your husband, I hear." She held up the paper, pointing to my article on Allan's resignation. "Jerry told me that you and your husband happened to be at the restaurant last night." She paused, drawing her lips together as if suppressing a smile. "Poor Jerry. He really does think you *happened* to be there."

I shrugged. "I didn't actually talk to Jerry last night."

"Well, whatever your reasons for being there, he was very grateful for your help."

"I think it was pretty rough on Jerry."

"It was," she said, her eyes welling up.

I put an arm around her shoulders. "Not easy for you, either, I suppose."

She shrugged, then glanced at Geoff.

I understood the signal. "There's a burger joint not far from here. Feel up to a short walk?"

"Sure. I—I hope you're not too busy. I mean, I saw the article and I know you must have your hands full with this story—"

"That was yesterday. Today I'm busy but not very productive."

When we stepped outside, I reconsidered our plans. In the

sunlight, she looked pale and drawn. "Would you rather drive somewhere? You look tired."

"Oh, I'm all right. I'm concerned about Jerry, that's all. He's up at Las Piernas General with Cinco, glued to Andre's side. He's exhausted, physically and emotionally."

Lisa had long referred to her father by his first name, and I should have been used to it, but I guess some old-fashioned notions of mine are more ingrained than I like to admit. I could let that slide, but I found myself unable to keep the censure out of my voice when I asked, *"Cinco?* As in five? Is that how you talk about your stepmother?"

"Oh, I'm sorry, I've offended you. And you're right, it's unkind of me. Nothing personal against Maureen—I hardly know her. I started calling my mom 'Tres' as a joke some years ago—she's my father's third wife. Just a joke, not an insult. I suppose it was an attempt to cope with my 'stepmother' situation. Maureen is my father's fifth wife, but I've lost count of all the other women my father asked me to form some sort of mother-daughter relationship with—you were one of them."

I felt my cheeks growing warm.

"I'm not criticizing you, Irene. It's my father's problem, not yours. You and some of the others were good to me, but most—Maureen included—have no interest in me whatsoever. For the most part, it's mutual." With an impish grin, she added, "I do have some marvelous dirt on some of them from the attic days!"

"I had forgotten about that feature of the attic room," I said. "You mean your dad never found out how well sound carried up through those heating ducts?"

"Never! Isn't that rich?"

I couldn't help but return her grin. As we walked a little farther, though, we both grew silent and serious. "Are you doing okay?" I asked.

"You mean because of my father's illness?"

"Yes."

She stopped walking and said, "Are you talking to me as a reporter or as my friend?"

"Your friend, of course."

"Then I'll tell you the truth. Of course I'm worried about Andre. But for Jerry's sake. That's all. I know you think I'm a terrible daughter, but I can't lie to you about that. You've watched me struggle with all of this over the years, Irene. Before you judge me, think about what it would be like to have Andre for a father."

"Not exactly a typical childhood, I suppose."

She sighed. "I don't know. I don't know about other people. I just know I can't change Andre, can't make him a different father. Sick or well, he will never love me. It's a simple fact. I could wallow in self-pity over that, but I prefer not to. I've got my mom, I've got Jerry, I've got friends like you. Andre ceased to matter to me long ago, but not before I ceased to matter to him."

I thought about my father. I had been a rebellious daughter, but I had never questioned his love for me. Lisa was right; my childhood was nothing like her own.

"You were in my father's house when I was growing up," she continued. "Are you surprised by my feelings?"

"No," I admitted. "Andre's just reaping what he has sown."

The burger joint, currently being called the Lucky Golden Palace, didn't appear to be any of these things. Lisa ordered a burger and fries, I ordered a salad.

"Jerry know anything about the meeting your dad was at last night?" I asked, my curiosity getting the better of me.

She laughed. "I wondered when you'd ask about that. I suppose I smell the same rat you do. Some redevelopment connection, obviously. Roland Hill buys old run-down properties, Corbin Tyler designs new buildings for them, Keene Dage builds what Corbin draws and Roland pays for."

"With money Ben Watterson's bank has loaned."

"Right. The head of the Redevelopment Agency reports to—or reported to—Allan Moffett. My father has supplied a lot of statistical studies for redevelopment projects over the years. Booter Hodges arranges for the college to get grant money from the city for the studies."

It was good to be talking to someone who understood all of the political and economic connections. "That's the dinner party. So what's your guess? Why would Allan resign?"

"You don't have any leads?"

I considered telling her what I had heard from Charlotte Brady about Allan Moffett's visitor, but decided against it. Charlotte hadn't insisted on confidentiality, but if she got another job in city hall, I wanted her to think of me as someone who could be trusted.

"Nothing very substantial," I said.

"Maybe I can help you, Irene."

I looked up from my salad.

"Roland Hill has expressed concern about my father. Maybe I could ask him about the meeting, ask if anything upset Andre."

"I don't know—"

"Why not? I'm staying in town a little longer than I had planned. I don't want to leave Jerry here to cope with all of this alone. The next time I see Roland, I'll ask."

"Just ask him to return my phone calls." I wasn't too excited about the idea of getting a story second- or thirdhand. "Tell me what you've been doing for Barton Sawyer lately."

The change of subject didn't seem to bother her. In fact, she became quite animated. As she talked about her job, it was apparent that she respected her boss.

"He's been so good to me," she said. "Once I had my master's, I was afraid I'd be pigeonholed, that he'd have me working on demographics forever. But he's allowed me to branch out from there, to pursue my own goals."

"Still, your background in statistics has been helpful to him, I'm sure," I said.

"Of course, it's very useful. And it will help me plan my own campaign. I guess I do owe that to Andre—I was never afraid of numbers."

"So you aren't completely without admiration for him?"

" 'Admiration' might be a little too strong," she admitted. "But I'm not ungrateful. Barton pointed a few things out to me. He said that Andre taught me to be thorough, not to be afraid to take on challenges, to follow through on what I started. He was right."

"You turned out just fine, Andre or no Andre."

"Jerry did, too."

"I don't know your brother very well. Is he still teaching at Las Piernas College?"

"Yes. I don't know if he's happy there or not." She bit her lower lip. "Let's quit talking about sociologists. Tell me about your husband. He's a cop, right?"

"Yes, a homicide detective."

"Homicide!" Her eyes widened. "How did you meet him?"

"Meet him? Hmm. We met a long time ago—remember when I moved to Bakersfield?"

"Of course. I was just a kid, and I thought I'd never see you again. You mean you've dated this guy for a dozen years and never told me about him?"

"No—we didn't date then. But we met there, and became friends. I moved back here, and as it turned out, he moved here, too. There were a number of years in between the two moves, and all kinds of complications once we were both here. We finally got together last summer."

"Last summer? And now you're married? Las Piernas must have been a little more conducive to romance than Bakersfield."

"It wasn't that," I said. "It was the timing as much as anything. Besides, I was a green reporter, he was a rookie cop, and even among the more experienced ranks, members of the two professions are discouraged from mixing socially—for good reasons."

"I can see why. He might leak information to you, you might not be as critical of the police as you need to be."

"Among other problems. But Frank's worth the hassles I get at work, and so far, he seems to think I'm worth the ones he gets where he works."

"Any chance of my meeting him before I go back to San Diego?"

"Sure. His schedule is pretty erratic, but we can try. Why

don't you come over for dinner on Monday? I'll check with Frank and let you know if there are any problems."

I came back to my desk to find a voice-mail message waiting for me. Jerry Selman had returned my call.

"Hello, Irene," the message said, "I'm glad you called. I'm here at the college now. I'll be in my office until three." He left his work number.

I started to dial the number, hung up, and walked over to the city desk to tell Lydia where I'd be.

"You mean you'll be at Las Piernas College if you can find a parking space," she said. "Want me to call ahead and try to get one for you?"

"No, thanks. Some of the members of the administration get a little antsy when they know the local press is around. I'd rather not have anyone announce my arrival."

"Oh, forgive me," Jerry Selman said, finally stepping back to allow me to walk into his office. "I guess I wasn't expecting you to go to so much trouble. The campus isn't very accessible to the public, I'm afraid."

Only a moat full of piranhas would make it less accessible, I thought, having hiked up a steep hill from a distant parking lot.

"I should have called," I said, "but I was going to come up to the campus anyway, so I thought I might be able to catch you in your office." As I said it, I told myself that wasn't a lie. I didn't have any appointments, but I did plan on trying to corner Booter Hodges after I saw Jerry.

"Let me take your coat," he said. "Have a seat—the chair by the windows is the best of the three. And let me get you a cup of coffee. How do you drink it?"

"Just black is fine, thanks. Oh—this isn't from—"

"The vending machines? Never." His smile was contagious. "But you've just proven that you truly were a student on this campus. The coffee out of those machines is noxious."

"We used to say that if you saw someone buying a cup of it, he just wanted something to pour on the cockroaches under the sandwich machines."

He laughed and went down the hallway to another room and soon emerged with two cups of office-brewed coffee. He carefully set mine on a corner of his desk and seated himself, holding but not drinking from his own cup. This opening round of hospitality completed, he seemed at a loss, his expression solemn.

Serious, he was hardly less attractive than he was when he had smiled. Andre had been pleasant-looking but no knockout. Even as a younger man, Andre wouldn't have received a second glance if you could have placed him next to his adult son. Jerry's hair and eyes were dark brown, like his mother's, but his other features were Andre's—Andre's, but somehow improved upon. Long fingers, thick eyelashes, a mouth a woman might want to coax into a smile or a kiss. It would be easy for this Selman male to surround himself with women. If he was half the manipulator his father was, he probably had a list of ex-lovers that would take longer to read off than roll call in a sultan's seraglio.

"I cannot tell you how grateful I am to you and your husband," he said in a broken voice, snapping me out of my sins-of-the-father attitude.

"It was truly nothing on my part," I said. "You and my husband did all the work. Lisa tells me that your father is in stable condition?"

He nodded, setting his coffee down. "He's still in intensive care. There's talk of surgery. I don't know. He doesn't take care of himself. Out last night without his medication! With a heart condition! And I kept telling him that he can't let things get to him. The past few days—I think it was all too much. Ben Watterson's suicide, Allan's resignation, problems here at the campus, that old photograph—he let himself get too worked up."

"Photograph?"

He waved a hand in dismissal. "Someone sent a photograph of Dad and an old girlfriend to Dad's house. Actually, it wasn't a photograph, but a color photocopy of a photograph—as if to say 'There are plenty more where this came from.' Maureen saw it and was understandably upset. She asked him to explain it to her, and he lost his temper. You know how he can be."

"Yes."

He turned red. "Well, yes. So . . . he said some hurtful things to Maureen. They patched things up, but it was just one more episode of stress. I can't help but think that whoever sent that photocopy to him had to know he had a heart condition. It was a despicable thing to do. Not that he takes care of himself anyway. He had no business being out alone last night without his medication."

"The dinner meeting—do you know what that was about?"

He looked away. "No, I'm sorry, I don't. I didn't even know where he was until I came home and got his message on my machine. It's lucky I came home when I did—and that I know enough to carry a few of his pills with me. Not that there was time for that last night."

"You weren't home when he called?"

He shook his head. "Neither of us were home. Lisa was out with one of her friends and I was here, grading papers. I had a fierce headache, so I went home."

"I saw him go to the phones. He didn't look well."

"He was such a fool! He should have called an ambulance, or had one of those men take him to the hospital. Didn't he learn anything the last time?"

"You were able to save him. That's what matters."

He took a deep breath and exhaled on a sigh. "I hope so. I wish I could be more certain of his recovery. When I saw him last night, hooked up to all those tubes and machines . . ."

"Not easy on you, I know. You look like you could use a few hours' sleep."

"Impossible. I thought I might be able to work, but I can't concentrate."

"Your sister's worried about you, you know."

"Yes," he said, smiling faintly. "She's not likely to worry about Dad. Not that I blame her. He made her so miserable as a kid."

"She hasn't done bad as an adult. And she seems happy with her life in San Diego."

"Probably because she got away from Dad. She was smart there." His cheeks colored. "I suppose I'm destined to remain under his thumb."

"Destined?"

"Perhaps that's not a good way of speaking about it. But I'm trapped, in any case."

"You're not trapped. Just leave. Do what Lisa did. Live somewhere else."

"No, no, I can't. There aren't many teaching positions available these days. Even if I were willing to throw away all my years of study and look for some other kind of work, there's Dad's health. He needs someone to take care of him. I'm the only one who'll do that now."

"What about his wife?"

"Maureen? She's good to him. But then, all of Dad's wives were good to him, right? And taking his . . ." He paused, turning slightly red again. "Well, let's call it his romantic history. Taking his romantic history into account, I can't expect Dad to be cared for by any woman. It's his own fault. He's failed at marriage four times and seldom stays with anyone more than a few months. He's a hopeless cad, I'm afraid."

A strange analysis from someone who—if the rumors had any foundation—was supposedly something of a cad himself.

He glanced over at me. "I'm not being entirely honest."

"Oh?"

"Let's face it. I'm afraid. My worst fear is that he'll have another heart attack and I won't be there with him. I was with him when he had his first heart attack. He complained of chest pains, and over his protests, I drove him to the hospital. By the time we got there, the pains were much worse. That one wasn't so bad, but still, it scared the hell out of me.

"All the way to the hospital, and for days afterward, I found myself saying three words over and over: *Please don't die, please don't die, please don't die.*"

He paused, shaking his head, then went on. "This from someone who has wished him dead countless times. As much as I've hated how he treated my mother, Lisa, all the women in his life—as angry as I've been with him for trying to control my life—knowing he's a real bastard, I still wanted him to live." He let out a long sigh.

"I don't know why I'm telling you all of this," he said suddenly. "I guess it's because none of the other women from SOS—yes, I know the inside joke—has ever tried to talk to me. Maybe I'm jealous of Lisa, because the members of SOS are so taken with her, while they all seem to assume I'm my father's clone."

"I don't know if I've ever thought—"

"It's okay. How could you know anything about me? Naturally, his former girlfriends would assume that—what's the old saying?—'The apple never falls too far from the tree,' right? And what a tree! When I was younger, I used to fantasize that he'd get back together with my mother. By the time I was in high school, I was grateful he left her alone."

"Even though you were away at college when I was dating him, my impression was that Andre adored you."

He shrugged. "He did. Still does, I suppose. But that isn't all it's cracked up to be. It meant that the only sibling I'll ever have—Lisa—grew up hating me. And no one thinks of me as Jerry Selman, an individual in his own right. I'm always Andre Selman's son." He laughed. *"His* reputation precedes me."

"Academically, that can't be bad."

"Unless you are expected to exceed your sire's abilities. I never will. I'm a better teacher, frankly. But I'm no good as a researcher. Sometimes I think his frustration over my lack of scholarly ability must have given Dad that first heart attack."

"You don't seriously believe that?"

He hesitated only slightly before saying, "No, of course not."

I felt off-balance. I had expected Jerry Selman to be a smug, spoiled little bastard, not this vulnerable creature. Trying to regain my footing, I asked, "Do you know why I wanted to talk to you today?"

This time he turned a furious red. "Not to hear my tale of woe, I'm sure."

"Listen, don't misunderstand me. I'm glad you've talked to me about all of this. You're right—I've never tried to get to know you before now. My former relationship with your father isn't a source of great pride for me, and for obvious reasons you are someone I associate with him. But I'm sure I'll think of you differently after today."

"Thanks," he said. He finished off his coffee and tossed the paper cup into the trash. "But then, I don't suppose you came here for my thanks. All the same, I do wish there was some way I could show my appreciation." He frowned, then said, "While I was waiting at the hospital this morning, I read your article in today's paper—the one about Allan Moffett's resignation—and then I realized that you weren't at the Terrace by coincidence. I take it you're here in connection with that dinner for Allan."

So, Lisa's brother wasn't nearly as thick-headed as she imagined him to be. I began to wonder if he wasn't often underestimated. "Yes," I said, "I thought your father might have talked to you about it."

"I'm not going to be of much help to you, I'm afraid. I wasn't invited to it. Dad had mentioned that he was going to be there, but just said that Allan was going to get some of his friends together. I didn't think anything of it."

Outside the building that housed his office, I stopped at a concrete bench and took a moment to collect my thoughts. Chill air frosted my breath. I was near a big tree full of noisy blackbirds, but otherwise the campus was quiet. It was that time of day when morning classes were over and evening classes had not yet begun. A few students drifted by on their way to the library. I looked around me. Thomas Wolfe was right, except that home isn't the only place you can't go back to.

I pulled my coat collar up around my ears and headed down the sloping walkways toward what a friend of mine used to call "the lower kingdom"—the administration building, nestled into the bottom of the hill. It was my fervent wish that Booter Hodges would find my visit there an unpleasant surprise.

9

"Hello, Irene! How nice to see you!" Booter wore a big grin as he welcomed me from his office door. "Pammy," he called to his secretary, who was standing a few feet away, posed in the ready mode, "take this girl's coat from her, would you?"

Grateful that I had taken it off and draped it over my arm *before* Booter could help me out of it, I handed it to Pamela and thanked her.

"Would you like a cappuccino or an espresso?" Booter asked.

"This won't be from one of the vending machines, I take it?"

He laughed as hard as if it had been one of his boss's jokes. I looked at the long-suffering Pamela, who stood waiting for the next command. "No need to bring me anything," I said. "I'm fine."

"Come on in, come on in," Booter said.

The enthusiasm didn't fool me. Booter is paid to be enthusiastic. He was once an economics professor. He received lousy student evaluations, but he got along well with his colleagues—a gift in an academic setting—and was made department chair. What he lacked in teaching ability he made up for in administrative skill. He continued to rise quickly through the ranks, from department chair to dean and on to his current vice presidency. His ability to raise money from alumni and other sources had kept him there for many years.

His real name was Lynn. He hated it. He was fond of telling male companions that he earned the nickname "Booter" by kicking ass in his college days. I knew better. An old chum of his gave me quite a history of the alias. Said Booter used to get drunk at frat parties, and then suffer a side effect of drinking, the one dry cleaners and cabbies hate. At his college, this charming act was referred to as "booting."

He motioned me to a plush white leather seat. Booter was slender and tanning-salon brown. His gray hair was styled perfectly, his hands were manicured. He was wearing an expensive dark blue suit and a dark red tie. As he sat at his big cherrywood desk, he moved a wide gold band with a diamond in it up and down his left ring finger like the bead on an abacus. I hoped his wife was saving for a rainy day, because it didn't look like Booter was sure he wanted to keep that ring on.

"Didn't get a chance to talk to you at the Terrace last night, Booter," I said. "You disappeared not long after you saw me come into the dining room."

"Oh, now, Irene, no need to take offense. I was just shaken up by Andre's collapse. I'll tell you a little secret."

I waited.

"Promise not to tell anyone?"

"Depends on the secret."

He laughed, a little bass chortle this time. "Spoken like a true journalist! Well, all right. Here it is: I can't stand the sight of blood. I'm a decorated Korean War veteran, but I am an utter yellow-belly when it comes to anything having to do with doctors or medicine. I can't even date nurses!"

"Imagine that," I said.

"Say, was that your husband I saw you with last night?"

"Yes, that's Frank."

More movement with the ring. "Now, that man's a hero. In fact, I'm going to recommend that the president send him a letter of thanks."

"The president," in this case, would be the college president.

"Entirely unnecessary, I assure you, Booter."

"No, no! I'm going to do it. He saved one of our most important faculty members."

"Jerry Selman did just as much," I said. "And I don't think Frank would be comfortable with the attention."

"Frank? Is that his name?"

I nodded, wishing he would listen to someone else besides himself.

"Good-looking man."

I was trying to figure out if saying "thanks" was the appropriate response when he irritated me by adding, "But then, you're a good-looking gal, right?"

Trying not to do a little booting of my own, I forged ahead. "What brought the six of you together for dinner last night?"

"You were there, you saw us. Nothing to hide. Allan retired and wanted to thank those of us who stood by him over the years."

"In what way does the college foundation stand by the city manager?"

"Oh, in my case, it's the other way around. Allan's an alumnus, of course. He's done a great deal over the years to keep community leaders in touch with the college."

"Just how much money has he brought in, Booter?"

"Well, hard to say. Hard to say. Helped immeasurably. Let's just put it like that."

"And the college has helped Allan, of course."

"We've helped him stay in touch with experts here at the college, helped the city as well. Is that what you're driving at?"

"Experts like Andre Selman?"

"Certainly. Andre has done a number of studies for the city."

"And that brings in city grant money to the college?"

"We apply for them, compete for them like everybody else. It's cost-effective to use local experts whenever possible. Allan knows that."

"I'm sure Allan has done the college a world of good."

Booter leaned back, making the chair creak. He began stroking his tie. It was a nervous habit of his, pulling on his

tie like that. Wouldn't take a Freudian psychiatrist to figure
out why Booter didn't wear bow ties.

"Is there something wrong with that?" he asked.

"You tell me."

"Why no, of course there isn't. That's the trouble with the
media these days. That's why a lot of Americans are just plain
fed up with the press. You're all so negative—"

I tuned out while he went on and on about what a heart-
less bunch we were. I've heard it all before. Every clown who
ever read the funny papers is a media expert these days.

It was especially irritating to hear someone like Booter
rant about the media's supposed failings. People like Booter
believe that newspapers (and almost everything else in the
world) exist for their convenience. Their idea of cooperating
with the press is to try to use it. They want to be interviewed,
but only if the interview flatters them. We exist to supply
them with public favor, whether they deserve it or not. Their
motto seems to be "Don't buy advertising, get the newsroom
to hand it out for free." But begin to tell the whole story,
and suddenly, we're the negative press. This gets damned
tiresome.

Booter ground to a halt, suddenly realizing his mistake.
"Oh, Irene, I'm just an old windbag."

Although I was tempted to tell him that I knew exactly
where he had found the wind to fill up that bag, and that he
had his head stuck up in the very same place, I kept my temper in check and asked, "Did the six of you get together
often?"

"Not too often. We're all busy."

"I've been saying six, but I guess it should be seven. Ben
Watterson would have been there."

His smile disappeared, his eyes grew moist. Booter is such
an oily fake, it was hard to trust what I saw on his face.

"Ben was a good man," he said. "The best. He was always
kind to me. I wish he would have talked to me, confided in
me. Maybe I could have cheered him up. I wish he would have
just let me *try* to cheer him up. I wish he had called."

His wishes were wasted, of course, as are all our wishes for what we could have done for the dead. But it seemed his sadness was genuine.

"Did you know Ben was ill?" I asked.

He shook his head.

"I'm sorry, Booter, I didn't know you and Ben were close."

"We weren't, really. But Ben—well, he was a good man," he repeated, half to himself. "Better than most."

I decided to change the subject, finding myself uneasy with a Booter that didn't bluster.

"Last night, did Allan Moffett ever get around to explaining why he resigned so quickly?"

"No call for that, either," he said absently. "A man shouldn't panic."

"No," I said, keeping my voice low and coaxing. "And Allan doesn't scare easily. So he must have had good reason to panic, right?"

"Huh?" he said, sitting up in his chair. I watched one other true emotion cross his face—his horror at speaking to me in an unguarded manner. He recovered quickly. "I'm sorry, I was talking about Ben. Allan had no need to panic. No, no. Allan simply decided to enjoy life, get away from all the hassles. That's all."

He was about as forthcoming as a clam with a bad case of tetanus after that. Except for delivering another meaningless and infuriating lecture—on how unduly suspicious the members of the press were—he had nothing to say.

My own jaw started to lock. I managed to mutter a good-bye. His secretary had my coat waiting for me.

I had met with two men who—each using his own style— might have been trying to feed me a load of crap.

A typical day; maybe even better than average.

10

Keene Dage might not have wanted to see me at Ben Watterson's funeral services, but Roberta Benson made sure she got a seat next to me in the church. The place was fairly packed, and people were still filing in by the dozens. Keene and his friends were already in the crowded front pews, as were my friends Lydia and Guy. But I hadn't known Ben very well, so I settled for a place near the back.

The high number of "mourners" should have been a tribute to Ben's power and contributions to the community. But in the course of a few short days, the community's regard for Ben Watterson had changed. The man whose remains lay in the closed casket at the front of the church had become an enigma, and at least part of the throng was there because his suicide had become the focus of public curiosity. According to the coroner, Ben had no disease.

Why would a man lie in a suicide note? The question had been asked at every lunch table and watercooler in town. Rumors ran rampant. One was that his widow—his *young* widow—had somehow managed to kill him for his money. Quiet, withdrawn, and now very, very rich, Claire was a favorite target. Supposedly, she had either done some fancy sneaking in and out of the SOS meeting or hired someone else to kill Ben. The coroner continued to say it was suicide.

Another rumor claimed that the Bank of Las Piernas was on the verge of failing. So far, the bank examiners were declaring it healthy and sound. No financial cancer, either.

It was also speculated that Ben had led a double life, but no one could figure out where he had found the time to lead the second one. And the rumor that some doctor was going to be sued for a mistaken diagnosis was also false—Ben's doctor hadn't seen him in over a year. The last visit had been a checkup. Ben had been told he was in fine condition.

The metal casket stood mute before us, as impervious to rumor as it would be to the earth that would soon cover it— while Claire was left to brave more than the elements. Still, it seemed to me that she, too, was encompassed—in a numbing, bewildered grief that allowed her to be absent from all that went on around her.

I moved down the pew to make room for Roberta, thinking her worried look was for the widow. Roberta's sense of vocation is seldom confined to her office, and I figured she wanted to talk to me about how we could help Claire through this crisis. But Roberta had another friend in mind.

"Have you seen Lucas?" she asked in a whisper.

"No," I whispered back, leaning to catch a glimpse of Claire from my new position on the pew. "He hasn't contacted me yet. How's he doing?"

"I don't know."

I turned to her in surprise. "What do you mean, you don't know?"

She leaned a little closer and whispered, "He's missed two appointments with me. I'm worried. I'm afraid he may be drinking again."

I thought back to Lucas on the bench, my own hurried judgment of him. "Maybe he has some other reason for missing the appointments."

"No, you don't understand," she said. "I haven't seen him since I got back into town. He hasn't reported to his rehab program during the last three days—not once. He's missed his AA meetings. The shelter told me he hasn't slept there since Wednesday night."

"Are they sure? It's been so cold the last few days. Haven't they been overcrowded?"

"Yes. They're sure. They've held his place for him as long

as they could each night. But he hasn't checked in. I even looked at the log for the locker room. He hasn't been to his locker since Wednesday night."

"Wednesday night? The night of the SOS meeting?"

"Yes. I guess I was too optimistic about him."

I felt myself bristle. "You said he was doing well, was on the mend."

She sat back a little, then said in a low voice—each word enunciated as if English were not my native language—"He was. But when you've been in my line of work long enough, you learn that nothing is very certain when it comes to substance abuse recovery."

"This isn't about your line of work," I hissed. "This is about Lucas Monroe. A human being. You said—"

"Keep your voice down!" She looked toward Claire, then went on. "I said seeing you really made a difference, and I never should have said a word to you about him." I knew the look on her face. Every reporter has seen it a million times. It was the whoops-I've-told-you-too-much look. The look that always follows it is one you can see on a mule. "If he hadn't asked me to say hello to you," she went on peevishly, "I wouldn't have mentioned him to you. It came very close to breaking a professionally privileged confidence—"

"Cram your professional confidence!" I snapped, only to realize that I had spoken loudly enough to cause heads to turn. A lady in front of me scowled so hard I was afraid she'd never get her face straightened out again.

I was ashamed to notice that even Claire had been disturbed by my voice; she was looking toward us. In the next moment her heretofore blank gaze seemed to focus on me, and her brows drew together. I mouthed an apology, but she leaned over to the woman who sat next to her, an older person who sat between Claire and her sister. From the back, I could only see gray hair and a broad back stretching a dark dress. The lady glanced over her shoulder at me, holding the corner of her glasses as she peered over the rims. She nodded, rose, and moved slowly toward us. She was an apple-shaped woman, a wonder of balance as she trod carefully in her sensible shoes.

Oh hell, I thought, this old biddy is going to scold me and ask me to leave.

In the next moment, I decided that would be a blessing. The growing crowd made the air in the church steadily more stuffy, and my desire to escape the room had grown proportionately. I was angry with Roberta, probably unreasonably, which only made me more anxious to evade the "closure" she would undoubtedly seek. And, as will happen at funerals, I selfishly remembered those friends and family members I had lost over the years, and fought hard to prevent each shard of old grief from piercing whatever get-on-with-life barrier I had built around it.

Roberta seemed to think the lady was approaching her, but the woman bent over and laid a cool, paper-dry hand on my wrist. Roberta leaned back to avoid smothering in the woman's pillowy, ample bosom. I heard a lovely drawl when the lady said, "I'm Claire's Aunt Emeline. Forgive me for disturbing you, sugar, but Claire wondered if you might be willing to please come up and sit beside her. You will, won't you?"

"Certainly," I said, and stood up to move out of the pew.

Roberta also stood. "I should be with Claire, too."

"Oh, don't trouble yourself," Aunt Emeline said to her, with a cool look that made Roberta sit back down.

Claire nodded a greeting, but didn't say anything to me or to her aunt. Alana moved over, so that Claire sat between her aunt and me. Claire remained silent, staring at the coffin throughout the service. I tried very hard not to think of Ben Watterson as I had last seen him. When it was time to leave for the cemetery, Aunt Emeline leaned over a little and said, "Ride with us, won't you?"

I stayed with Claire and her aunt and sister throughout the rest of the ceremonies, even through the brief and subdued gathering at the Watterson home. During that time, her aunt would simply suggest something and add "won't you?" and I'd follow along.

I had balked at one point. Claire had been seated at the graveside. Out of Claire's earshot, Aunt Emeline encouraged me to sit next to her niece. This seemed to me a place for family or very good friends of the deceased.

"Please," I protested, "there must be someone who was closer to Ben, or who is closer to Claire."

She eyed me for a moment, then said, "Sugar, sometimes after a man dies, he just pulls the ladder right down with him."

"The ladder?"

"All those people who were climbing up after him are brought low. You know, like the Bible says, 'Whosoever exalteth himself shall be abased; and he that humbleth himself shall be exalted.' "

"Still—some of these people truly were his friends."

She nodded. "Yes, sugar, they were. But she's the one that's living now, not Ben. And of all those friends of his, wasn't a one of them happened to be there with her on the night he died. You were. Come sit by her now, won't you?"

In the Watterson house, Claire said little more than "thank you" or, "yes, a shock" to her guests, who generally took the hint fairly quickly. Even Alana left early on. When I mentioned leaving, I was "won't you"-ed into staying by Aunt Emeline.

When only the three of us remained in the house, Aunt Emeline brought a silver tray into the room where I sat with Claire, the study where Ben had left his note. The tray held strong black coffee in two fragile white cups. Emeline set it down and left, closing the door behind her.

Obviously, plans had been laid between the two of them to keep me there after the others had left. I waited.

Claire took her cup and stood, idly touching the spines of the books with her long, graceful fingers. "I'm glad it didn't rain," she said.

"Me, too. It was even a little warmer today."

"Not much." She stopped touching the books. "Not much." She looked over at me. "I've imposed upon you all day."

"Not at all. If it helped you in any way, I'm glad."

"It did. I—I still need your help."

"Like I said, glad to offer any help I can."

"You can say no. I would understand. You may even feel angry with me . . ."

"Claire, ask."

She nodded, and sipped her coffee.

I waited.

"I need—I need to understand why this happened. As much as I will ever understand it."

"Of course. But I'm not sure I'm the best person to—"

"Forgive me. I'm not making myself clear." She sat down, drew a steadying breath, and said, "I want you to contact your old friend."

"My old friend?"

"Lucas Monroe."

I was dumbstruck.

"That night . . ." she went on haltingly. "The night of the meeting—the night when Ben—when Ben died. You were talking about him. About Lucas Monroe. That's why I asked you about him when we were in the car. On the way out, I overheard people saying that Roberta had seen him—and you had seen him, too. I could go to Roberta, perhaps, but—" She shrugged. "Roberta means well, but—I always feel as if She's trying to make a project out of me."

"I know what you mean," I said. "I'm sure there's some psychological diagnostic term for people who have her problem. *Theraputis Interminus.*"

That earned a small smile, the first I'd seen from her in some time.

"So why do you need to talk to Lucas?" I asked. "What does he have to do with Ben?"

She walked over to the desk and opened a drawer. She pulled out two envelopes.

She handed one to me. "This arrived in Ben's office about two weeks before he died. He brought it home the day he told me he wanted to retire."

It was a plain envelope postmarked from Riverside, with a typewritten address to Mr. Ben Watterson, President, Bank of Las Piernas. Although it had been sent to Ben at the bank, it was marked "personal and confidential."

It contained a single black-and-white photograph. I saw the back side of the photo first. "Be in touch soon" was inscribed in a delicate handwriting. I turned the photo over.

A young African American man was smiling proudly, holding an oversized check—the type that are mocked-up for publicity shots. Ben Watterson was also smiling, his arm around the young man's shoulders. "Bank of Las Piernas Scholarship Fund" was printed at the top of the check, which was signed by Ben. The date was June 1, 1969. The amount was $2,500. The payee was the young man—Lucas Monroe.

11

"The envelope was addressed to Ben's office," I said. "How did you get this?"

"Ben was in here one night, staring at it. He seemed unsettled. I asked him about it, and he said, 'Oh, this is just a young man who won a scholarship from the bank a long time ago. Probably wants to see me about a job.' There was a fire in the fireplace that night, and he reached over as if he were going to burn the photograph. That time, I was able to stop him."

She looked over to the fireplace, as if she could still see Ben reaching toward it. That blessed numbness of hers seemed to give way a little. She closed her eyes and covered her mouth with a trembling hand, as if her emotions were right there, right at her lips, being held in by the pressure of her fingers. But after a moment or two, she drew in a deep breath, straightened her shoulders, and dropped her hand. Although her voice was a little less steady than before, she went on.

"I took it from Ben, and told him that it looked like someone had saved that photograph for a long time, and that he ought to return it. After all, there was the note, 'Be in touch soon.' "

"You said, 'that time.' What did you mean?"

"There were at least two pictures sent to Ben by this Lucas Monroe." She handed me the second envelope, postmarked the day after the first one.

It was empty.

"Do you know what was in it?" I asked, turning it over in my hand.

"Yes. A color photocopy."

A color photocopy. Andre Selman, who had certainly known Lucas, had recently received one, too. "A photocopy of what?"

"Some people on a boat. I only saw part of the page, and only for a few seconds. Ben succeeded in burning that one."

"Did he say why?"

"No. Just that it was something someone had sent him to remind him of old times. He said it was a picture of our old boat. But I didn't actually get a good look at it, so maybe that wasn't true."

"Was he in the habit of burning papers he didn't need?"

She shook her head. "No, in fact, I think he was embarrassed when I caught him burning that one. He shoved the envelope into his desk drawer and tried to change the subject. I was mildly curious, but knowing how much Ben hated boats, it didn't surprise me that he burned a picture of one."

"Hated boats? I thought you just said you owned one."

"For a time. Ben became completely disenchanted with it—in fact, he never went out in any kind of boat after we sold that one to Andre. That was years ago."

"Andre Selman?"

"Yes. Anyway, knowing how he felt about being out on the water, you can understand why I didn't question him when he burned the photocopy. It didn't seem important at the time." She closed her eyes, then added in a shaky voice, "Famous last words, right?"

I decided to keep the discussion on neutral ground. "Nothing else in the envelope?"

She shrugged. "I don't think so. But maybe there was—maybe something was in it before he showed it to me, before he came home with it. All I know is, when Ben received these letters, something started eating at him. He started talking about retiring, about getting away from Las Piernas all together."

"Ben talked about leaving Las Piernas?"

"Yes. Unbelievable, isn't it? Things only got worse from there. I should have tried to get him to talk to me more. I should have seen this coming. Looking back—"

"Looking back is useless. I remember what you said to me on the ride home, Claire. You had been trying to get him to talk to you. He wouldn't."

She bit her lower lip, hard. "I think Ben was being blackmailed," she said. "I think he was being blackmailed by your friend Lucas Monroe."

"Hold on, Claire. I admit there are some suspicious circumstances here—"

"Suspicious! I would say so!"

"Please hear me out."

"Ben . . ." She was shaking now. The tears started flowing. I stood up and reached out to her. She could have turned from me, but perhaps because I had been in this house with her the last time this happened, she let me hold her while she cried.

"I'm sorry," she said after a moment.

"It's okay."

She pulled some tissues out of a pocket and tried to dry her face, the tears continuing to thwart the effort. "I'm sorry," she said again, "it wasn't fair to call him your friend. You told me you haven't seen him in years."

"Uh . . . that's not exactly true."

That stopped the tears. She looked at me over the tissue.

"I saw Lucas. I just didn't know it was Lucas when I saw him. And I want to believe that I am still his friend."

"You aren't making any sense."

"No," I agreed. I briefly told her the story of my encounter with Lucas, and of Roberta's conversations with me at the

Cliffside and in the church. "I want to hear Lucas's side of all of this before I jump to any conclusions. There's a logical explanation for his contact with Ben." And Andre, I added silently. "Lucas is trying to straighten out his life. He's probably looking for a job. Ben is obviously someone who knew him in better days."

"I understand you want to feel compassion for him," Claire said slowly. "You're a compassionate person. But—"

"Claire, please don't go into a lecture about alcoholics and what a hopeless sap I'm being. I got that one from Roberta. But think about it as calmly as you can. Please just try to do that. There are so many unanswered questions about Ben— and about Lucas Monroe. You said you wanted to try to understand what happened to Ben. Did you mean it?"

She nodded, fighting tears again.

Her struggle got to me. "As I said earlier, Claire—perhaps I'm not the person you need to talk to about this. You may not want to trust my judgment on something like this."

"No, you're wrong. I trust you," she said. "That's why I came to you for help. But I'm trusting you to be fair, Irene. If you discover that Lucas Monroe is guilty of blackmailing my husband . . ."

"I can't be his judge and jury. But if I find proof that he was blackmailing Ben, then I'll admit I was wrong about him. It will be a matter for the police at that point. Are we agreed?"

"Yes." She looked away for a moment, then said, "I have to do something anyway, don't you see? Ben's reputation meant everything to him. The things that are being said about him now . . ." Her voice trailed off.

"Look, nothing can stop that entirely. I'll be blunt. Here in Las Piernas, Ben was too rich and too powerful to be ignored when he was alive—and he won't be ignored in death."

"Of course not," she said, the numbness coming back. "So what should we do next?"

"Let's go over what we have so far. Let's start with the photocopy. You said there was a group of people on the boat. Did you recognize any of them?"

She shook her head. "I didn't get to look at it, really. I might have recognized them if I had been able to catch more than a glimpse of it. I have an impression of a group of men, but that's all. There could have been a woman in the picture. I'm not sure."

"Did Ben take other people out in the boat very often?"

"It was a long time ago . . ."

"Try to remember."

"Well, yes, lots of people."

"Anyone who went out on it often?"

"Andre Selman, of course. Andre loved fishing, so Ben took him along. Sometimes it was just the two of us. Sometimes he took business associates."

"Roland Hill?"

"Yes."

"Booter Hodges?"

She smiled a little. "Yes. I remember that, because the first time Booter went out with them, the sea was a little rough. Booter became violently ill and they had to turn back. They made fun of him, because he ruined Corbin Tyler's brand-new deck shoes. The others all said that Booter couldn't come along after that, but Ben wouldn't let them pick on him. He just made sure Booter took a pill for motion sickness before he came aboard."

"Somehow the story about Booter's seasickness doesn't surprise me."

"Actually, Booter was braver than Ben about that. At least Booter took the medication and had the courage to try it again. The last time Ben went out on the boat, *he* got a bad case of seasickness. Came back from a fishing trip with Andre, looking awful. Ben said he didn't want to set foot on it again, that he was going to sell the boat to Andre. He sold it, but he was in a blue mood about it for weeks. I remember that much."

"How long ago was this?"

"Hmm. Ten, fifteen years ago? I don't know."

"Let's work on that for a moment. We'll assume that Ben told you the truth, that the color photocopy really was a picture of people on your boat, and not some other boating party. Did Ben already own the boat when you married him?"

She shook her head. "We bought the boat after we were married." Her brows drew together. "Not long after we married, so about seventeen years ago? And we didn't own it for very long."

"Would you still have records on it?"

"Yes, somewhere around here. Why?"

"If we figure out which years you owned the boat, that may help us learn when the photograph was taken. So that's your first assignment."

"Okay. But about this Lucas Monroe—" she began.

"I know he's in the other one, but that doesn't mean he sent the photograph. Lucas is homeless. He's unlikely to be walking around with photo albums."

"But who else would send them?"

I started studying the envelopes. The postmarks caught my eye. "Riverside! Why didn't I think of that before? There is no easy way to get to Riverside from Las Piernas on public transportation," I said. "Greyhound might take you there. Not much else without lots and lots of transfers."

"You've lost me," Claire replied.

"These are postmarked Riverside. Lucas wouldn't go all the way to Riverside just to mail a couple of letters, would he? Why? To hide an address? He doesn't *have* an address."

"Oh." She seemed disappointed, then said, "Well, he might go to Riverside—or anywhere else, for that matter—if he could make a lot of money by doing it." Seeing my look of obstinacy, she added, "You don't know who he has become over the years, or how desperate he may be now."

"No. I need to talk to him. But for now, let's not jump to conclusions."

She was silent as I kept looking at the envelopes and the photo. Finally she said, "That's not a man's handwriting on the back of the photo."

"Probably not." Something else occurred to me. "It's certainly not Lucas's."

"Certainly?"

"He was one of my favorite teachers, remember? I took

one of his classes. His handwriting was terrible. We used to tease him unmercifully every time he put something up on the blackboard. No one could read anything but his numbers and stat symbols. He usually used an overhead projector with typed transparencies for anything else that had to be written. Sometimes he taught the whole class period using transparencies. No way is this his handwriting."

"I suppose a person would remember something like that." She sighed. "It's sounding less and less like Lucas Monroe sent the photos. But if he didn't, who did?"

"I don't know. And we don't know that he isn't in some kind of partnership with whoever sent these. Give me a few days to try to find him."

"You're going to go looking through the skid row area alone?"

"Oh no, not alone. I've got an excellent partner in mind."

12

"You've got a really great ass."

"So you've told me," he said.

I sighed. "Ah, the bloom is already off the newlywed rose. I tell him he has a great ass—"

"A *really* great ass," he corrected.

"A really great ass, and he just acts bored."

"Hmm. A little more to the left."

I moved my hands to the right.

He peered over his shoulder, smiled at me. "Okay, okay. I apologize." He didn't mean it.

I was giving Frank a back massage, trying to get him to relax a little before I told him my plans. Running my hands over his muscles, I was having trouble concentrating on what those plans were. I moved to the left, gently working out the tension.

"Hmm. Yeah, right there," he said. "Oh God, yes! Yes, yes!"

"No need to overdo it, Frank."

I felt him shaking beneath me. There was a little snort into his pillow. I slapped that ass I was so fond of and climbed out of bed.

"Ouch. Hey, where are you going?" he asked. For all his size, he can move like lightning; before I was out of reach, he had pulled me back into bed.

"To find Cody. He *purrs* when I rub him."

"Hmm. But Cody doesn't know that you're hatching some scheme."

Busted. Well, hell.

"You're turning red. Does that mean I'm right?"

"Yes, Frank. Feel free to gloat a little more."

He didn't, just rested his chin on top of my head, rubbed his hand along my neck. "Nothing to gloat over," he said after a moment. "I just did something really stupid. Only a fool would have interrupted a backrub like that. I should have at least collected my bribe."

"How did you know?"

"Well, let's see. The glass of my favorite scotch? The one you handed me as I walked in the door? That raised suspicions. The dinner you cooked when it was my night to cook? Made me a little more suspicious, but you were smart, you didn't push it too far—no candlelight, no music playing in the background. Just a nice dinner together. Spaghetti. Not even one of my favorite pasta dishes."

"Didn't have time to run to the store," I admitted.

"Hmm." He kept rubbing my back and neck.

"So the massage must have been a real tip-off."

"I knew before then."

"How?" I said, looking up at him in disbelief.

"You're upset about something. At first, I thought it was the funeral. Funerals upset you. I understand that; they upset me, too. But you're not acting like you've been to a funeral.

You're hyper—tense. That doesn't make any sense. You're distracted."

"What do you mean?"

"The pasta? Overcooked. The queen of al dente made soft spaghetti tonight. Cody chases Deke and Dunk around the house, you don't even come to the dogs' rescue."

"Oh."

"Shall I go on?"

"No thanks."

"What's on your mind, Irene?"

When I didn't answer, he said softly, "Why don't you tell me about your day?"

So I did, only I think the day changed as I talked to him. Feelings I had set aside to concentrate on one problem or another throughout the day took their place in the order of things. The remembered horror of seeing Ben Watterson in that shower; my concern for Claire; my fears for Lucas; my guilt over my nastiness with Roberta.

So by the time I got around to the part about my plan to ask Rachel to help me search for Lucas, I should have felt drained, I suppose. But oddly, I just felt better.

"It's a good idea," he said.

"What? Forgive me for saying this, Frank, but I expected a lot of objections."

"You would go looking for Lucas anyway, right?"

"Yes."

"See, I'm learning. But maybe you are, too. Taking Rachel with you is a good idea. She'll provide good protection," he said, and absently rubbed at his shoulder. I knew he was thinking of a recent hard throw to the mat she had given him in a martial arts workout, but he didn't say anything. "She's a hell of a shot," he added.

He was being generous. She didn't stand a chance against him on a firing range. She had told me as much herself. They had gone to the firing range the day after the throw to the mat. His idea, I believe.

"She didn't get to where she was in Phoenix by being careless," he added. I think he had convinced himself. He paused, then laughed. "Pete is going to have a fit. Let's get dressed and have them over for a drink."

"No way," Pete said, pacing our living room, then stopping to point a finger at me. "No effing way are the two of you going to do this."

I looked over to Frank, who sat quietly in my grandfather's old armchair, drinking a glass of merlot, acting as if his partner hadn't said a word. The dogs lay on the floor in front of the fireplace, watching Pete intently, ready to come to my defense if need be. Cody, my cat, was curled up next to Frank's dog, Dunk, getting the benefit of fur on one side and fire on the other, and faking sleep—his ears pivoted once in a while, giving him away.

Not long after Pete and Rachel arrived, I told Rachel my plan to enlist her help in finding Lucas. As predicted, Pete had gone nuts.

"Rachel, tell her no," he pleaded.

"I already told her yes," Rachel said. "Since people who live in cardboard boxes seldom have private attorneys, I'm down in the skid row district all the time now."

This was part of my reason for asking Rachel if I could hire her help. She had retired from the Phoenix Police Department after twenty years' service; at forty-two, she was still young enough to work elsewhere. Elsewhere had turned out to be Las Piernas, where she moved when she married Pete. She got a private investigator's license, and part of her income now came from doing contract work as an investigator for the public defender's office. This irritated Pete on two counts: first, because she was "working for the other side," as he saw it, and second, because Frank had helped her find the job.

"Skid row is no place for a woman to be," he moaned.

"You've got a real problem, you know that?" Rachel said. "What'd you think I was going to do? I told you I was going to keep working."

"I know! I know! But did you have to go from being a cop to being a—a—Christ! I hate to say it!"

"An investigator for the public defender. Oh, how awful. Better I should be home making raviolis for you, *caro?*"

Apparently, she would have stuffed them with sarcasm.

"There's no shame in being a homemaker," he snapped.

"No. And there's no shame in what I'm doing, either."

I noticed Frank's glass of wine was empty. I reached over to refill it. He smiled his thanks and stroked a finger along my forearm. Newlywed gesture. I had been wrong about that earlier.

"Pete," Frank said in that quiet way of his, the tone that Pete seems to hear better than a shout.

"What?" Pete said, lowering his own voice.

"You can't win this one."

Pete made a face and wrung his hands together, but sat down. The dogs relaxed. We managed to get along peaceably through the rest of the evening.

"See you early tomorrow morning," Rachel said as they left. "If Lucas is a wino, he's probably hanging out with other winos. Early in the day, his old friends may be hungover, but probably at least half-sober. We'll try to get to them before they've panhandled enough cash to get too far along in the day's drinking."

"We start the next round here."

I stared out of Rachel's car window. Five faces stared back. The faces were weathered and unwashed; most were bearded. Three of them were so bleary-eyed they hardly seemed able to focus. All male. *What are you doing here?* the faces wanted to know. I was beginning to ask myself the same question.

We had started at the shelter and at the detox program. The most we had learned there was that Lucas wasn't able to get into the shelter on Thursday night—the night of Allan Moffett's dinner party. He had tried to get a bed, but had come by too late.

Like all shelters, this one had its rules. He had to show up by a certain time or risk being turned away. It had been especially cold that night, and although his bed was held until the deadline of nine o'clock, it was given away when he failed to show by then. He had arrived at about ten o'clock, when the shelter was already overcrowded for the night, even the floor space gone.

Five degrees colder, and city regulations would have opened up other public buildings for the night. The doors stayed shut.

We had spent the rest of the morning talking to people under railroad bridges, beneath freeway overpasses, on the beach. Some of them were loners, but many huddled together in small groups, some around trash-can fires. "They watch over each other's stuff," Rachel explained, "and sometimes each other's backs." The groups had different turfs; even spots for panhandling were claimed and defended.

"It's not so different from Phoenix," she said. "They're not all panhandlers. Some of these people work. They have temporary or part-time or low-paying jobs, but they don't make enough to pay for shelter. Sometimes they spend their money on booze or drugs instead of a place to sleep, but other times, they just fall in a hole and have a hell of a time getting back out. Some are what we used to call hobos—wanderers, don't want responsibilities. Some are crazy." She paused, then added, "It makes me angry to see the crazy ones out here, because basically, they're out here because nobody gives a damn. So they become a problem for the cops. As usual, cops are supposed to solve anything no one else wants to deal with."

"You've only been here a couple of months," I said, "and yet a lot of these people know you by name."

"Partly because I come down here trying to help the public defender. But any cop—or investigator—who has any brains gets to know the street people. If I can get them to trust me, then I can learn things from them. People living on the streets watch what goes on. They have to, just to try to stay safe. And if you're in their territory, you're walking around in their living room. They can spot an out-of-towner or a newcomer, a young runaway—they'll know who's doing what and where."

"So why hasn't anyone seen Lucas?"

"He cleaned up, you said. They all agree that he has. If he's smart, he's avoiding bad company. You'd be lucky not to find him among these people. It sounds like his favorite old drinking buddy is hanging out with Blue now. If Lucas isn't with them, then maybe he's still sober."

Now, looking at this group of men huddled together outside of a restroom in a small park, I wondered if we had any hope of ever learning where Lucas had gone after being turned away from the shelter.

Rachel got out of the car, the men watching her all the while.

"How's it going?" she said, pulling out a pack of cigarettes. "Anybody need a smoke?"

"Ah, you're an angel, Rachel," one of the men called. He was dressed in several lumpy layers of clothing, the outer layer all blue—sweatshirt, sweatpants, running shoes, and ragged knit cap—and seemed a little more attuned to his surroundings than some of the others. He had the build of a wrestler. He began walking toward her, and the others followed, all glancing nervously in my direction. Rachel was obviously someone familiar to them.

Watching her, I felt a sense of relief. She knew exactly what she was doing. Once again, I was struck by her ability to appear in command of any situation. Part of it was her height, her athletic build. Most of it was something in her attitude. I stepped out of the warm car into weather cold enough to chill my breath. As I closed the car door, the men watched me with open curiosity.

"It's okay," Rachel said easily. "She's a friend of mine."

The man dressed in blue stepped forward again. "Squeaky send you down here, Rachel?"

"Not today, Blue. And you know Ms. Wentworth doesn't like to be called Squeaky."

I had to stifle laughter. Given her high-pitched voice, "Squeaky" was the perfect nickname for Wentworth, one of the public defenders Rachel worked for.

He shrugged. "She ain't here, so she can't take no offense.

Ain't here and never will be. She wouldn't want to soil her little self, right, boys?"

The others nodded.

"Give her a break," Rachel said. "County isn't exactly heaven on earth. She's too busy keeping you guys out of jail to come down here and socialize."

"This cold, she mightn't be doin' anybody a favor," Blue said. He looked over at me. "Who's this lady with the great peepers?"

"This is Irene. Irene, meet Blue. No need to tell you why he likes the color of your eyes."

I extended a hand. He nodded, stayed where he was, but said, "Pleased to make your 'quaintance."

The others hooted at him.

"You boys got no manners," he said stiffly. He gestured to the other men. "This here's Decker," he said, pointing to a man with fists like hams. Then, as he pointed to a skinny fellow, a short, gray-haired man in a fatigue jacket and a heavyset man, "Beans, Corky, and Rooster. Not their right names, of course, but they earned them. You want to know how?"

"Sure," I said, causing Rachel to mutter something under her breath in Italian.

Blue grinned. "Decker 'cause he can flatten anybody, Beans 'cause he smells like that's all he eats, Corky 'cause— I dunno, he's always been called Corky, and—" He paused and grinned, waiting.

Before I could ask, Rachel said, "And Rooster, because he can't keep his pants up. No need to demonstrate, Rooster, I don't like to laugh too much before noon."

The men hooted again, Rooster included. "You come up into my coop sometime, Rachel," he said, hitching up his belt. "I'll show you that I got something to crow about."

"That's all right, Chicken Little."

"Oooh, she got you good," Blue said, laughing.

"Give it up, Rooster," a man in a fatigue jacket said. "The Amazon just might send you on a ride."

"Amazon, huh?" Rachel said. "Well, you aren't the first one to think that one up. No, I'm not in the mood to put anyone in an ambulance today. I'm really much daintier than I look."

This brought another round of laughter.

"You're Corky?" she asked the man in fatigues.

He nodded.

"Irene is trying to find one of her friends," Rachel said. "We thought you might know him."

No laughter. They all looked away from me then.

"Come on, now," Rachel said. "Nobody is trying to get anybody into trouble. She really is just looking for someone she knows."

"You know how it is, Rachel," Blue said. "Somebody don't want to be found, we ain't gonna find 'im. It's the way of things."

The others all murmured their agreement. Following Rachel's lead, I let the silence stretch. Corky nudged Blue and whispered something to him.

"Well, Corky, that's a good point. Corky was saying there was no harm in listening to you say who you was lookin' for, but—well, first off, you wouldn't happen to have another one of them cigarettes, would you, Rachel?"

"Sure I do," Rachel said, but didn't reach inside her jacket for the pack.

Blue narrowed his eyes. "You don't smoke, do you?"

"No, I carry them just in case I meet somebody who might like one."

"Tradin' on our bad habits, you mean," Beans said.

"Tell her what she wants to know," Corky said crankily. "You all knew she was a snoop before she drove up."

"I'm looking for a man named Lucas Monroe," I said.

They looked at one another blankly, all except Corky. He was studying us.

"You might know him as the Professor," I added.

"The Prof," Corky said.

"The Prof?" Blue said. "You looking for a black dude?"

I nodded. The cigarettes came out of Rachel's pocket, but she didn't extend the pack.

"Corky knows the Prof real well," Blue added.

The pack made the rounds again.

"Now Rachel, don't get mad at me," Corky said. "This is the God's truth. The Prof isn't around much anymore. He got religion or something. He's living at that new shelter, going to AA and the whole bit."

"Hell, Corky, you haven't told me a thing I didn't already know," she said.

"How could I know what you do and don't know already? What am I, woman, a mind reader?"

She gave him a look that made him bundle up tighter in his worn fatigue jacket.

"He hasn't been to the shelter for a few days," I said. "He missed his curfew on Thursday night, and hasn't been back since. Have you seen him in the last three or four days?"

Corky shook his head. "Any of you seen him?" he asked the others.

Solemn head shaking.

"Before he cleaned up," I asked, "where did he sleep?"

"Buses, mostly," Corky said. "Sometimes he stayed in one of the old hotels."

"Which hotels?" Rachel asked.

"The Hyatt and the Hilton." It brought out a round of laughter from the others.

When Rachel and I didn't join in on the joke, he scowled. "How do you know the Prof?" he asked me.

"I was his student once."

"The Prof was a real prof?" Blue asked.

"He taught at Las Piernas College," I said. "I ran into him at a bus stop one day. A friend at the shelter told me he might be looking for me."

"Wait a minute," Corky said. "You the reporter?"

"Yes."

The others stepped back again.

"Aw, relax," Corky told them. He turned back to me. "You're not here to do a story on any of us, right?"

"Right. Just want to find Lucas—the Prof. Did he mention me to you?"

He nodded. "Yeah. Saw you when he was sleeping one off

on a bus bench. That was before he went on the wagon." He paused, a distant look coming over his face for a moment. "Twenty."

"Give me a break," Rachel said. "I could start an auction right here among your pals and do better than that."

After some arguing with the others, Corky said, "If you fellows don't learn to stand your ground, others will continue to take advantage of your misfortune."

"Cork it, Corky," Blue said, then turned to Rachel. "The minute he starts talking like that, he knows he's beat. He'll tell you for fifteen."

Rachel looked to Corky, who scowled, then reached out a filthy hand.

"Oh no, let's hear it first."

"Prof said he knew some reporter on the *Express*. Said one day he was going to go see her, tell her his story. Said it would be big news."

"That's worth zero to me," Rachel said, "unless you know what this big story was."

Corky got a speculative look in his eye.

"Don't even bother making something up," Rachel said.

Corky looked resigned. "Nah, he didn't give away a lot, even when he'd been drinking. Christ, Rachel, give a man a break."

"We've been talking to people all day. They tell us you're his buddy, the one he hangs out with."

"Used to. Until he sobered up," Corky said.

"Tell me where he stayed when he wasn't sober."

"Prof likes the Coronet, the Sunset Arms, the Angelus, the Piccadilly," Corky said. "He likes the tall ones, the upper floors. Used to make me climb all those damned stairs with him."

"Those hotels are all condemned," I said.

Corky laughed. "Right. Never have to worry about them having a vacancy."

"It's a start," Rachel said, and gave over the fifteen bucks. Corky quickly stashed it inside his fatigue jacket.

"Have any of you seen him at one of these places in the last few days?" I asked.

Another round of head shaking.

I was noting the names of the hotels when I heard Rachel ask, "Who else has been looking for him?"

Complete silence. I looked up to see them shifting uneasily.

"Ten bucks," Rachel said.

No takers.

"Five bucks each," I said. Rachel rolled her eyes.

The others looked at Corky. "All right, all right," Corky grumbled. "But I better not find myself standing up against him alone."

"Ain't we stood by you so far, Corky?" Blue said. "I'm not scared of tellin' her." He turned to Rachel. "There's this one guy—name of Two Toes. Used to call him Holler. You know him?"

"Haven't had the pleasure," she said.

"Won't be no pleasure. Guy's a 5150. Nuttier than a damned fruitcake. Makes up weird poetry, talks all kinds of religious stuff. And he's a real knucklehead to boot. Used to call him Holler 'cause that's all he does, day-in and day-out—hollers at people. He was always hassling Corky, but the Prof made him lay off."

"Long as he could, anyway," Corky muttered.

"That's right," Blue said. "Two Toes punched the Prof a good one a little while back." He pretended to wallop himself on the cheek, complete with sound effects. "Pow! Old Prof swelled up like a damned chipmunk." He laughed a little, then slanted a glance my way and grew quiet.

"When was that?" I asked.

"Not too long before he sobered up, I'd guess," Corky said. "Few weeks ago."

"Where'd Two Toes get the new nickname?" Rachel asked.

"Cut off two of his own toes," Corky said.

"And ate them!" Blue said.

"I don't believe that," Corky said, looking as if he did.

"He's been looking for Lucas? For the Prof?" I asked.

"Always. Thinks the Prof's ring is magic," Beans said.

"His college ring?"

"Yeah," Corky said with a wheezy laugh. "I told him if it

was magic, it would have been from my alma mater, not some lousy place like Las Piernas College."

"Your alma mater?" Rachel asked.

"Yeah, UCLA. And if you're a Trojan, I'll just thank you to keep your mouth shut."

The others stared at him. He looked down at his pair of stained Adidas, as if suddenly embarrassed. I began to despair of getting any further information from him.

"Where's that five bucks?" Blue asked.

No one paid any attention to him. We were watching Corky.

When at last he looked up at me, his eyes were hard. "Keep your lousy five bucks."

"He don't mean it," Blue said, but I was watching Corky walk away.

"Corky and Prof were good friends," Rooster said. "Prof only hung around with the rest of us because he liked to talk to Corky."

There was a lot of nodding on this point.

"Where can I find Two Toes?" Rachel asked, as I reached into my jeans pocket and pulled out a handful of fives.

"It's Sunday," Blue said, not taking his eyes off the cash. "He'll be out in front of St. A's."

"St. Anthony's?" I asked.

He nodded. "He stays on his knees in front of that statue out front. Can't miss him. He's a big guy with a crazy kind of hat on, and a big beard. He's been Catholic the last few Sundays. Better catch him before he turns Baptist or something. And watch out for them fists of his."

St. Anthony's is a beautiful old Catholic church. I like it better than my old parish church, which—after redecorating— went so ultramodern that I feel like I'm on the set of a cheap science-fiction film every time I set foot in it. (Which is admittedly so rare, it could have changed back to something more traditional since the last time I was there.)

But St. Anthony's has stained-glass windows, mosaics

covering the walls and parts of the ceiling, marble on the altar, and all sorts of alcoves and nooks and crannies with statuary and candles and holy water. If you're the kind of Catholic who knows what it is to own a calendar with red fish printed on the Fridays, then St. Anthony's is your kind of place.

I wasn't going to see the inside that day, though, because the man we were looking for was right where Blue had told us he would be—outside, kneeling before a statue of St. Anthony of Padua. Patron saint of the poor.

The "crazy kind of hat" turned out to be a long stocking cap of rainbow colors—it vaguely resembled one an aunt gave me in the 1960s, the Christmas after she got a knitting machine. His beard, which was dark brown, was almost as long and pointy as the cap. There was a sort of symmetry in it, I suppose.

Inside the church, a mass was being said. I could hear the congregation singing the Gloria. "Glory to God in the highest, and peace to his people on earth," they sang, a group of guitars strumming in the background.

Two Toes was a big man. I could see that, even while he was on his knees. He heard us approaching and suddenly stood. He turned toward us, his feet planted wide apart. He pointed at us, his eyes narrowed, and he sniffed the air, as if catching a scent.

Rachel immediately put me behind her, her own stance one of calm readiness. "Hello," she said, watching him.

"Who are you?" he thundered.

"I'm Rachel," she said in a quiet, but firm voice. "This is Irene. We just wondered if we could talk to you for a minute."

He tilted his head to one side, tried to peer around to see me. "Tell her not to hide behind you," he said to Rachel, not shouting now. "This is the Sabbath. A day of rest. Peace be with you."

I stepped over to one side, but Rachel said in a low voice, "Whatever you do, don't get between me and him."

"Have you lost something?" he asked.

Rachel looked puzzled, but I said, "Yes, that's why we've come to St. Anthony."

"Good, good," he said. "St. Anthony prays for those who have lost something. Then the Lord helps them find what they have lost. A saintly service, free of cost."

"Of course," Rachel said, her own Catholic days coming back to her.

"What have you lost, my dear? I have St. Anthony's ear."

"I've lost a friend," I said.

He closed his eyes and swayed a little on his feet, began humming to himself. "Tell me more," he said after a moment.

Any minute now, I thought, Toto will pull back the curtain. But if this was the way he was going to play it, there wasn't much I could do about it.

"My friend is named Lucas. Some call him the Prof."

His eyes flew open. He raised a fist over his head.

"Step back," Rachel said to me in a low voice. "Slowly."

"No!" he roared. "You are not worthy!"

Inside the church, the congregation began singing the Alleluia. It distracted him. He tilted his head again, listened. He lowered his fist.

"Our Lord loves sinners. He takes sinners and makes them winners. He wants me to tell you." He lowered his head, then raised his eyes up to us again. "An angel watches over the Prof—watches over him all the time. Seen it with my own eyes at the Great Wall of China." He smiled and started singing in a loud voice—to the tune of "Chattanooga Choo-choo"—"Nothing could be finer, sittin' in the diner, than eat your ham and eggs in good ol' China." He stopped singing and frowned. "Wall of China. An angel led me to him. Got to say it three times, when the bells ring. The ring, the ring, the ring."

"What?" Rachel asked, though I doubt she had high hopes for an explanation.

"Amen, amen, I say to you." He turned back to the statue and dropped back down to his knees. He began humming "Chattanooga Choo-choo" again.

"What angel?" I asked.

"Many angels," he replied. "I follow the angels. Go in peace. Go while you can."

We stood there for a while, but he only hummed. We gave up trying to get his attention. As we walked back to the car, I could hear the parishioners of St. Anthony's singing again. The Lord's Prayer.

Give us this day . . .

But in an association of ideas perhaps only slightly less random than those of Two Toes, the singing of that prayer gave me an idea about where we might find Lucas.

13

"**S**top the car," I said.

Rachel complied, pulling over. "Do you see it?"

"Over there. Look at the building across the street."

"The one they're working on?" she asked, indicating a scaffolded tower, where on a weekday, workers with jack-hammers and cement mixers and other equipment would create the cacophony of construction work. Today, it was silent.

"No, the one to the right of it," I said.

On the next lot, a tall, gray building stood, its dignity sagging like the chain-link fence which surrounded it. Like a lonely old woman whose dress and makeup are passé, it was both ornate and abandoned. At the top of the building, at each corner, a pair of angels stood, wings long and tucked close, hands folded in prayer, long robes draped heavily to their feet. Faces solemn and watchful.

If they were guardian angels, there was little left to guard, but perhaps it was through their protection that one or two of the large street-level windows miraculously remained unbroken. The owners and patrons of what I would guess were once opulent shops and elegant restaurants were long gone, no wares displayed in the windows dull with dirt and brick dust from the project next door. Still, the bright red Chinese characters painted on one of them were plainly visible, as were the words which had caught my attention: Great Wall of China Restaurant.

My gaze moved to the building's front entry. At the top of a set of stairs, a banner held by two smaller stone angels spelled out a name: The Angelus Hotel.

An angel watches over the Prof—watches over him all the time. Seen it with my own eyes at the Great Wall of China . . . Got to say it three times, when the bells ring.

"Looks like you were right," she said. "Two Toes was talking about the Angelus."

"It was the only hotel on Corky's list that fit with anything Two Toes was saying. I'm not sure they ever served ham and eggs in there, but maybe he was just saying that it was a restaurant, not the actual Wall of China."

"Saying?" she chided. "I think it was as much a secret code to him as to us."

We got out of the car and started walking toward the old hotel. It looked like it had been built in the 1920s, one of Las Piernas's boom periods.

"Domini angelus . . ." Rachel intoned, reciting the Latin opening which gave the prayer its name. "Should have known. Used to say the Angelus three times a day. You, too?"

"Sure. I went to Catholic school, remember? Should I sing a few bars of *O Salutarus Hostia* for you?"

"Some other time. Wonder if a Catholic built the hotel?"

"That or someone who was trying to connect this town up with Los Angeles. But L.A. might not have been such a big place itself when this was built, and given all those angels on the corners, I'm betting this was put together by one of our more devout brethren."

"One of our more affluent brethren," Rachel said.

The fence along the front of the hotel was intact, if not exactly forbidding. We walked outside it to our right, away from the construction site and toward an alley on the other side of the Angelus. The alley was deserted, cut off from a one-way street by three large metal posts with bent reflector signs on them. I burrowed my hands into my coat pockets and followed

Rachel as she walked down the alley, studying the building.

Ahead of us, in a section that would have been out of sight from the construction workers, the fence had been cut. Rachel pulled back on the mesh of chain link and made an "after you" bow.

Squatting low, I made my way through, then waited for Rachel. We now stood on a long strip of ground that might have once been a lawn or garden. A pair of tall palm trees and a few clumps of weeds were all that remained of it.

A long paved drive ran between the strip and the hotel. Beyond the drive was what must have been a parking lot—what I could see of it was cracked asphalt studded with weeds.

Rachel stood still, looking at the hotel, and then at the ground. "Good thing it rained the other night," she said. "That will help us find the preferred entrance."

"Footprints."

"Right. The ground is dry now, but some folks definitely took shelter here when it rained. These ought to point the way."

The trail of bent grass and depressions in the dried mud angled to and from the back of the building. We followed them.

"Don't slip on this palm crud," Rachel said as we crunched our way across the messy drive. The "palm crud" was actually hundreds of unfertilized dates, dropped onto the concrete over God knows how many seasons without a gardener.

We made our way closer to the building. At one end of the hotel, we went past a metal door at street level—it was welded shut. Two floors above it, a series of small windows began, going to the top of the building. The lowest windows were broken out.

"So much for the stairwell," Rachel said, looking up as we continued toward the back of the building. "Look—even the fire escape has been welded in place. Bad news."

"Because of the danger to the unofficial tenants?"

She nodded. "These guys light fires to stay warm; if they fall asleep, or if they're drunk or high or careless, there goes the building—and maybe everybody in it. Or they suffocate—the fire stays under control, but they don't have proper ventilation in the room, and the fire burns up all the oxygen."

We climbed some concrete steps at the back of the building. A little less picturesque than the front, the back was comprised mainly of a series of doors that had been boarded up.

"Wood's fairly new," I said. "Doesn't look like this was done so long ago."

"No, but look—here's one that's already been jimmied back open. Let me go in first, just in case any of the unofficial residents are in."

She pulled the big flashlight out of her belt and turned it on. As she cautiously opened the door, we were greeted with the sharp, overpowering smell of excrement.

"Yeeech," I said, backing away.

She laughed. "You weren't expecting the maid service to have the place all clean and tidy, were you?"

"No, but I wasn't expecting to walk into the bottom of an outhouse, either."

She turned her back to me, flashing the light around the large room, which was lined with rusting pipes and sets of valves. A shaft of some sort rose from one end of the room.

"Laundry room, I think," she said.

"Maybe so. But nothing's been cleaned here for a while."

"This isn't so bad. Think how awful it would be if it were a warm day—just watch your step in this one place near the door," she said, spotlighting it with the flashlight. It was about two feet away from where I stood.

"Let's move on, okay?"

"Prop that door open," she said. "I want to be able to get out of here in a hurry if we have to."

The door still had a stop attached to it, so I kicked it down. It held.

We made our way to an interior door. We stepped into a long, dark hallway. Several doors led off it. The floor was sticky, and the odor of urine permeated the cold air. I tried not to think about it, and swore I'd throw my shoes away when I got home.

"Prop that one open, too," Rachel said. "Make it easier to find our way out."

As we walked away from the door, the hall grew darker, and it was the darkness and sense of confinement, not the stench, that began to stir a growing panic within me.

I once spent a few days locked in a small, dark room as the guest of a couple of creeps who got their kicks out of hearing people scream. One result of the experience is that I sometimes have to sleep with the light on. Other times, it's better not to go to sleep at all. Darkness is not my old friend.

I tried to keep my mind away from memories as we went on. Rachel kept moving forward. I followed more closely. She looked back at me, holding the flashlight so that it didn't blind me.

"You okay? You want to wait outside?"

I wanted it more than just about anything, but I shook my head. "Lucas knows me, he doesn't know you."

"He's not likely to be hanging out here during the day."

"I'm going with you."

She shrugged and moved on. She stopped often to listen as we approached doors. The only noises to be heard were the now-distant sounds of occasional traffic on the street, our sticky footsteps, and the hammering of my heart. My claustrophobia was kicking in.

"We're making our way to a stairwell," she said, her tone gentle, coaxing. "There should be more light there."

I couldn't answer.

She looked back at me again, then put the light on the doors around us. Some were marked, most weren't. She paused, as if debating something. I started shaking. I tried to force insistent images from my mind. This is different, I told myself. You're safe, you're safe. I heard my own breathing—quick, short breaths.

"Slow down," she said. "You want to carry the light?"

"No." I made myself take slower breaths.

She reached back and took my hand, then started walking again. My own hand felt cold in hers. I wanted to protest, to

say she was making me feel like a child, but I was grateful
for her warm, firm grip.

"Hope that *stronzo* we found back there didn't bother you
too much."

I shook my head. Useless in the dark. *Get me out of here!*
I wanted to scream.

"Look at it like a hunter would," she said. "Think of it as
fresh spoor. Maybe your friend left it."

"No, he didn't," I said, my voice tight. "Somebody else,
maybe. Not Lucas."

"Oh, so your friend the bum is such a saint he doesn't ever
take a shit, eh?"

I pulled my hand away.

"Oh," she said, in the darkness, "so he's a saint, just like
St. Anthony?" She kept moving forward; I was forced to follow at a faster pace. "The saint who never took a dump," she
went on. "What a fantastic miracle to have to one's credit!"

I felt my fists clench. "Stop it."

"Maybe the pope will make him patron saint of the asshole. St. Bum of the bum."

"Goddamn it, Rachel," I shouted, "shut the fuck up!"

The words echoed in the hallway. She stopped, and flashed
the light on the door just ahead of us. EXIT was painted on it.
She turned back to look at me, bouncing the light off a nearby
wall, illuminating both of our faces. She was smiling. "Much
better."

I realized what she had done, why she had done it. I
dropped my gaze. "Forgive me if I don't say 'thank you' right
away."

She laughed and opened the door.

There was light in the stairwell, and more air, a combination which helped me to calm down. I raced past her, up
the stairs to the first broken window. I put my face up to the
opening, took deep, gulping breaths of cold, fresh air. The
knots went out of my stomach, I stopped shaking. Then, on
that wave of relief, for the next few moments, I felt as if I
might start crying.

At one time, an emotional reaction like that would have

made me ashamed of myself. Now, I was growing used to it, and perhaps because I knew it would pass, it passed more quickly. I looked over at Rachel, who was waiting behind me on the landing, pretending to be studying her cellular phone. Her long hair cloaked her face, hiding her expression.

"Are my nose and cheeks as red as yours?" I asked.

She looked up. "Yes, and your *orecchi*—your ears, too."

I reached up and rubbed a hand through my hair. "I can't wait for this to grow out again."

"It will, it will. That stubbornness of yours will push it right out of your head. Your hair will be longer than mine by summer."

I laughed.

She smiled. "A good sound, that laugh of yours," she said, putting the phone away. She began to lead the way upstairs again. "I figure we should start at the top. That okay with you?"

"We're thinking the same thing. Corky said Lucas liked to go to the upper floors in a building."

"Right."

There was little conversation after that. The task of climbing fourteen flights of stairs kept us both warm and quiet. Rachel was in terrific shape; Frank, Mr. Really Great You-Know-What, once told me that Rachel had shamed *him* into a more rigorous workout. I was still making a comeback from having been laid up for a while; for the last few floors, I had to put real effort into it.

At the top floor, we stepped out into a dark area near a set of elevators. We rounded a corner into a dimly lit hallway. The light was coming from two large glass doors, long plates of frosted green glass. Deco-style woodwork of mahogany and chrome framed the doors. Twin angels, as solemn as their counterparts on the exterior of the building, faced us. Draped in heavy robes, each held a sword.

"The angels on this building are the saddest heavenly creatures I've ever seen in my life," Rachel said, pushing one of the doors open. "Maybe I won't feel too bad if I go the other way."

The doors opened on to one large room. Light streamed in

from three directions, from long windows that must have once offered a fantastic view of the city and the water. Now, taller buildings blocked much of that view. Behind us, a long bar carved with smiling cherubs stood before a big mirror that had lost a lot of its silvering.

"The happier angels are here at the bar," I said, my voice echoing in the empty room.

"I guess those serious types at the door are the bouncers," she said.

"Guardian angels. Must be—if my guess about the age of the building is right, that glass and the rest of this place survived the big quake of 1933."

Rachel shivered and made an Italian gesture to ward off evil. "Don't say the word 'earthquake,'" she said. A hardwood floor, scarred and buckling, remained in place, although I doubted that anything other than dust motes had danced in this room in the last few decades. I squatted down closer to the floor to look at it from another angle.

"Doesn't look like anyone has been staying up here," Rachel was saying.

"No, but look at the floor. Someone sat up here and admired the view."

There were places here and there that might have been old footprints, but a set that was clearly newer led across the floor to a place along the south-facing windows, and back again to the doors. Whatever tables and chairs had been in the room had long ago been removed, but an overturned crate was propped up near the windows where the footprints ended.

"Let's take a look," she said.

"These windows face south, toward the ocean."

"Do you think he was trying to look at the water?"

"Couldn't see much of it from here."

Near the crate, the view from the windows took in a narrow glimpse of the sea. The buildings directly across the street didn't block the view, but several blocks away, especially along Broadway, a long cluster of skyscrapers stood between the Angelus and the Pacific Ocean. One in particular caught my attention—a black glass monolith, one of the tallest buildings downtown. Three letters crowned the giant: BLP. The Bank of Las Piernas. Ben Watterson's bank.

"Let's try the next floor down," I said.

There was no light in the hallway on the fourteenth floor of the Angelus Hotel, but there was still plenty of cold air. It didn't stink like the first-floor hallway, making me wonder if that was one reason Lucas took the trouble to climb all of those stairs in the buildings he slept in.

Rachel grew cautious again, listening carefully before opening the first door we came to. As it creaked open, she waited a moment in the hallway before stepping into the room. I crept in after her.

Only when a hotel room is absolutely empty do you realize how small it is. No carpet, no drapes, no bed. A radiator against the wall beneath the window. Only the window trim and wainscoting kept the room from being utterly plain. I could see our breath as we looked around.

No sound.

Rachel glanced in the small bathroom and closet.

"Nobody has been in here for ages. Let's keep looking."

As we left the room, I started to pull the door shut.

"No, leave it open," she said. "More light in the hallway." She paused, then added, "Would you like me to open one of those windows?"

I shook my head. "I'm okay now. Thanks—for offering, and for what you did earlier."

"You know I didn't mean it, right? It's just that you were looking like you might pass out down there, and that was the first thing I could think of to distract you."

"You were successful. And yes, I know you didn't mean it. But next time, let's just argue politics or religion."

"Wouldn't have worked as fast," she said, then leaned an ear to the next door. We opened six doors on six small rooms on the fourteenth floor of the Angelus, and found nothing.

On the seventh try, we found Lucas.

14

He looked different from when I had met him on the bus bench. Cleaner, for the most part. He had cut his hair and shaved since then. He wore the same jacket, but it had been washed. Beneath it, he was casually dressed—in worn jeans, a flannel shirt, running shoes.

Near him, in an open duffel bag, was a neatly folded suit. A pair of dress shoes next to the bag looked as if they had just been polished. If he had been wearing those clothes, he would have looked even more like the man I knew in college.

It's strange, the things that will haunt you. In many later moments, I would think about the care he took with the suit and the shoes, and I would waste wishes.

He lay face-up on a sleeping bag. His breath wasn't chilled like Rachel's or mine—he wasn't breathing at all. There was a small amount of dried blood on his face, as there was on the floor and the radiator. A thermos bottle lay on its side near his feet; on the floor beneath its gaping mirror mouth, a pool of liquid had congealed into a pancake-sized stain.

And someone had placed dull pennies on his eyes.

That much I saw.

Rachel had seen him first, and quickly turned and tried to block my way, but I looked over her shoulder. She held on to me, pushing against me as I tried hard to push past her. I learned that I'm no match for her—but I put up a decent struggle before I stumbled backward out into the hall. She followed, somehow keeping me from falling. When I had regained my balance, she quickly reached back and closed the door behind her.

"No—stay back," she said, seeing I was willing to go at it again.

"It's Lucas," I said.

"Not anymore."

"Yes—"

"No, it's not," she said. "Come on, you don't want to march your big feet all over the evidence now, do you?"

Evidence.

There's something of a blank in my recollections from the point that she asked that question until a little later, when we were sitting on the floor of the room next to Lucas's. I was too numb, I suppose, to register most of it. I heard and didn't hear Rachel talking to me. Felt and didn't feel her arm around my shoulder.

I suddenly realized she was swearing like crazy in Italian. It startled me out of my detachment. She was holding her cellular phone in her free hand.

"What's wrong?" I asked, sitting up straighter.

"Can't get a signal in here. Wait right here, okay?"

"Where are you going?"

"I'm not going anywhere," she said firmly, "just over to the window."

I watched as she struggled to get the window open. "Dammit. Fricking thingamajiggy won't work. Probably hasn't been opened in fifty years." To my amazement, she pulled out her flashlight and used the grip end to bust out the window. "Destroying private property," she muttered, clearing the last fragments from the frame. "Pete will really be thrilled."

With phone in hand, she leaned out the window, then pushed some buttons. "This will only take a minute," she said to me.

"*Caro?*" she said into the phone. "Listen, we've got a situation here . . . No, just a . . . no, will you listen? *Si calmi!* Christ. *Stà zitto!* Put Frank on . . . No, I'm not going to say another word to you . . . oh, really? Well, *va f'an culo,* Mr.

Big Shit Detective. I'm hanging up. And if this phone rings, it had better be your partner calling!"

She pressed a button. "Excuse me," she said to me—very calmly, as if she hadn't just been insulting her husband bilingually and with enough gestures to make a mime envious.

I just looked at her. I felt as if I were watching an experimental theater production from a front row seat. Up close, and it still didn't make sense. I put my head down on my knees.

"Irene," she started to say, but the phone chirped. She pushed a button and leaned out the window again.

"Frank? What do you know—he's catching on. Listen, we found Irene's friend. Possible 187 . . . Yeah. Well, exactly. I'll tell you in a minute—we're in an old hotel, and it's a little hard to describe how to get here. You out of earshot of your boss? Good. Now, what I want to say is, I think the situation could use a little TLC, you know what I mean? Yeah, I'll let you talk to her. She's right here. But about the, er, business aspects of all of this . . . exactly. Good . . . And can you talk Carlos Hernandez into handling this one himself?" There was a long pause, then she said, "No. Not from the looks of things." She glanced over at me. "Coins on the eyes, for one thing. Also some sort of head injury, although—no, of course not. Stepped right back out of there . . . Yeah. We're at the Angelus Hotel. Fourteenth floor." She gave him the address, and when she started to describe the entry, I interrupted her.

"Tell them about the footprints near the drive."

She passed the message along, gave him a few more details, then gestured for me to come near the window. I took the phone, and leaned out as she had done.

"Irene?" I heard him say.

"Tell Pete not to blame Rachel."

"They'll be all right. How are you doing?"

I didn't know how to answer that.

"Irene?"

"I know it won't be your case," I said. "But do you think you could come over here, maybe take me home afterward?"

"Of course. We'll be there soon."

"Thanks. Here's Rachel." I handed the phone back to her

and sat against a wall, the one facing the wall which adjoined Lucas's room.

Questions and guilt and disbelief took turns somersaulting through my mind. Rachel talked for a while to Frank and somebody else in the homicide division, then hung up the phone and sat down next to me.

She didn't try to force any conversation out of me. I was grateful.

A few minutes passed before I said, "Nothing went the way it should have gone for Lucas."

She just listened.

"I don't know how he ended up on the bus bench that day I saw him there," I went on. "It doesn't matter. What matters is that he was trying to make something of his life. He was trying to come back from that. I believe that with all my heart."

"Sure he was," she said gently. "Everybody who knew him said so."

"I want to look around in there."

"You hired the wrong PI, then. I spent too many years as a cop to go in there and fuck with a crime scene. We'll end up pissing off a bunch of people whose cooperation we're going to need."

I sighed. "I suppose you won't let me go back in by myself."

"No. Frank's going to do what he can to make sure we don't get locked out of this. My guess is they're going to want to talk to us, because otherwise, they probably won't have jack."

"Don't try to convince me that this is going to be investigated with much enthusiasm. Lucas wasn't exactly the biggest mover and shaker in Las Piernas."

"You're wrong, Irene. All kinds of people end up as homicide victims. The *press* may treat them differently, but that doesn't mean the cops will."

"Forgive me if I'm a little slow to buy that."

She shrugged. "Believe what you want to. Me, when I was working homicide, I didn't care if the victim was a prince or a pauper. I wanted to nail the killer. I didn't want that son of a bitch walking around thinking he was too smart to get caught, thinking he beat me.

"Besides, if you don't think the police are doing the job they should be doing on this case, you've got a powerful way to put pressure on them."

"Which reminds me of something, Rachel. Can I borrow your phone?"

I dialed John Walters' home phone number.

John listened patiently as I told him about finding Lucas.

"Well," he said, "sorry about your friend. Sounds like you've had a tough day. Tell you what. Tomorrow, come in a couple of hours late if you like. But before the end of the day, I want you to do some serious work on Moffett's resignation."

"What?"

"Yeah, take a couple of hours off. I *do* have a heart—no matter what you tell the interns."

"Serious work on Moffett? Is that what I heard you say?"

"Exactly. You tell me some cock-and-bull story about some bum causing everything from Watterson's suicide to Moffett's resignation. You've pulled this kind of shit on me before, so I know to let you have a little time to spend the morning trying to find out what happened to your friend, or you're not going to have your mind on your work."

"This wasn't some ruse, John," I said, trying to hold on to my temper. "I'll admit, there have been times when I wasn't exactly working on a story in the way you asked me to—"

"—Oh, yes, Ms. Kelly. It *has* been known to happen. Like the time you spent the day sailing when you were supposedly doing an investigative piece on the harbor?"

"That harbor piece won a CNPA!"

"And the *Express* is proud of that award. But the California Newspaper Publishers Association didn't give it to you for anything that skipper taught you on the way to Catalina."

Not for the first time, I cursed the storm that came up that day, trapping me in Avalon with a guy who turned out to be a bigger drip than anything that fell from the sky.

"Look, John, I don't have time to dredge up old history.

This is different. Lucas Monroe is the key to all of this. You should have Mark down here on this."

"Mr. Baker is busy with other assignments."

"If not Mark, then—"

"Then nobody."

"Nobody!"

"Nobody. Irene, think like a reporter, will you? The death of your friend is not newsworthy."

"Why? Because he's black? Because he's homeless? Because he died in a part of town that everyone wishes would just sink into the core of the earth?"

"You know what Wrigley's going to say if I start printing stories about druggies OD-ing and bums croaking in abandoned hotels?"

"This is not about—"

"You've heard his speech. Right after he tells me that our subscribers do not want to open the morning paper and read about dirtbags dying—good riddance, etc.—he'll ask me if I'd like to try another line of work."

"It's a bullshit policy and you know it. If we aren't going to print anything about 'dirtbags,' then pull Wrigley's name off the masthead."

"I'll tell him you suggested it. I'm certain it will cause him to reconsider his position."

"I hate this crap," I said, my anger not lessened by defeat. "I absolutely hate it. The policy's wrong. And you're wrong, too, John. You're wrong about Lucas. He wasn't—" Something caught in my throat, and I couldn't speak. I was thinking of the man who had patiently taught me one of the most difficult subjects I'd ever studied. A man who had given me a great gift, the ability to tell at least a few of the lies from a few of the truths—a man I respected, no matter what had become of him since those student days. That man, reduced to this.

"Kelly, listen to me," John said. "I'm not trying to insult the memory of this friend of yours. I've got nothing against him. I'm just trying to get you to see it from the paper's point of view. I know you're upset—hell, if I could, I'd give you the whole day off tomorrow. But I've got a nasty feeling that if we don't get a handle on this Moffett thing, the *Times* is going to beat us in our own backyard."

"What, they're going to put out an extra supplement this week? They care less about Las Piernas than Wrigley cares about the homeless."

"Maybe. But I wouldn't like to see it happen, would you?"

"No. That's exactly what I've been trying to tell you. This *is* about Moffett and Watterson. Too many coincidences. I've got to follow up on this, John."

"On your own time, Kelly. Like sailing."

I handed the phone back to Rachel. I knew she could tell that I hadn't gotten very far with the paper, but she didn't rub it in.

A little later, we answered questions from a group of people who weren't too happy about climbing up over a dozen flights of stairs. Reed Collins and Vince Adams had drawn the assignment; I had met them once or twice before, but didn't know them well. Frank had spoken highly of them, though, and I wondered if this was part of what Rachel meant when she talked to Frank about TLC. Reed explained that Frank would be up in a minute, but procedure required them to talk to me alone first. We showed them where the body was; my second look wasn't much longer than the first. Reed and Vince had us wait in the hall for a few minutes while they talked to a pair of technicians.

When they came out of the room, they wanted to question us separately. Vince talked to Rachel, Reed talked to me—vacancy rates being what they were at the Angelus, we didn't have a problem finding separate rooms.

It took a while to explain to Reed why we had been looking for a homeless man, and why we had looked in this hotel. I could see that I was doing just as terrific a sales job on him as I had on John Walters—no one was buying that Lucas had influenced Las Piernas's rich and powerful. Reed never said that he doubted my theories—which I admit were only half-formed at the time—but his questions all led away from any talk of Ben Watterson or Allan Moffett.

"Can you describe this man Corky?" he asked.

The other questions were in a similar vein—always returning to the other homeless men.

"This Toes," Reed said. "Are you sure this is what he said? It seems a little jumbled."

"Two Toes. *He's* a little jumbled."

"So how can you be certain you're remembering it correctly?"

"I'm not. I didn't take notes or record him, so it may not be absolutely accurate. But I'm pretty good at recalling conversations."

"Well, yes, I guess you need to be able to do that in your line of work."

We talked a little longer, then he walked out into the hall, leaving me alone. While the door was open, I saw Carlos Hernandez, the county coroner, go by. Hernandez was followed by two men wrestling with a stretcher.

A few seconds later, Frank came in. He didn't say anything, just walked up to me and put his arms around me. It was the best thing that happened to me all day.

"Postmortem lividity," Carlos said. He was standing in the hall outside the room. I could hear the photographer at work, the quiet conversation of the men who were gathering physical evidence. "The patterns prove that someone moved his body after he died."

"The pennies on his eyes ought to be proof that someone else was in there," I said.

"The pennies tell you someone was here after he lost consciousness," he corrected. "But the discoloration of postmortem lividity—the places where blood and other fluids settle after death—are on the front of the body. The body was moved after death."

"When was he killed?" I asked.

"I'm not so sure he was killed."

"Not killed! But I saw blood—"

"Yes, on the forehead and the radiator as well. I doubt that blow to the head killed him. I'll know more after the autopsy, but my guess is that he fell against the radiator, perhaps after a . . ." He glanced at Frank. "Well, perhaps after a dizzy spell."

"What were you going to say?" I asked.

"Dizzy spell will do for now," Carlos said, then seeing I wasn't satisfied, added, "I understand he had a history of alcoholism?"

"Past history. He's been clean for at least six weeks."

"You're absolutely certain?"

I hesitated. "No."

"Even if he was clean, as you say, there are no signs of a struggle, and the blow to the head was not too severe. There is bruising on his knees and the palms—the palms, not the knuckles or fingers—as if he fell." He paused, glancing back toward the room. "It's very early to say, of course. I'll know more after the autopsy."

"What about the time of death—can you estimate that?"

"Time of death isn't easy to judge under the circumstances. The room is very cold and dry. That has retarded the rate of decomposition. The weather has stayed cold, but there is no way to be certain the room has stayed cold—as I said, judging from postmortem lividity, we know someone was here several hours after the time of death, moved the body, and— well, before I say more, I have a favor to ask. Would you mind coming into the room, taking another look at the body?"

"Of course not," I said, not sure I really meant it.

I was glad when Frank came with me.

Carlos asked the technicians to step outside for a moment, making the room a little less crowded. The body had been bagged and moved up onto the stretcher. I felt Frank's hand on my shoulder; Carlos moved over to the bag and unzipped it. The sound made me long for the days of sheets and shrouds.

He beckoned gently. Frank stayed with me as I moved a step closer.

"Now that you have a little more time to look," Carlos said, "would you please make sure this man is . . ."

"Lucas Monroe," I said, my mouth dry. "Yes, it's Lucas."

Carlos nodded, then began unbuttoning Lucas's flannel shirt. I found myself concentrating on Carlos's fingers and the buttons, the pattern of the flannel. Carlos pulled the shirt open.

Lucas's brown skin was darkly discolored in places, those on which a face-down body would have rested.

"You see this?" Carlos said, tracing the outline of an odd-colored blotch on Lucas's chest. He reached into the body bag and pulled out Lucas's hand. A matching spot was indented into the lifeless palm. "Here and here?"

I nodded.

"Did Mr. Monroe wear jewelry?" Carlos asked.

"His ring."

"No, not on his fingers, but—"

"He didn't wear it on his finger. He wore it around his neck, on a metal chain. Didn't you find it on him?"

"No. Can you describe it?"

"It's a gold Las Piernas College ring. Ruby or some other red stone in it."

"This man was a college graduate?" Carlos asked.

"Yes. Probably bought the ring when he earned his bachelor's degree. Sometime in the 1970s. The school could tell you." I looked back to Frank. "I told you about it, remember?"

Frank nodded. He called to Reed, who was out in the hallway talking to Vince. "You may be interested in this," Frank said, and asked me to repeat the description of the ring.

"It was removed several hours after he died," Carlos added, as Reed took notes.

"By the way, Irene," Reed said, "any ideas on how we could contact his family?"

I shook my head. "No, but you might try Roberta Benson down at the homeless shelter. She could probably tell you a lot more about him. He's one of her clients."

At the word "client," Frank and Reed exchanged a look, but Reed said, "Thanks, I'll give it a try."

Rachel came in to see how I was doing. The room was fairly crowded then. There was nothing more that I could add to their reports, so I managed one last look at Lucas, said a silent good-bye, and asked Frank to take me home.

"I'll call you later," Rachel said, and reached to give me a hug. As her arms came around me, I heard the body bag being zipped shut.

15

The phone was ringing when we came into the house. Cody was yowling and rubbing along my ankles as I tried to make my way to answer it. The dogs were barking greetings, and Frank went to let them in. Cody sniffed at my shoes with utter fascination. I slipped them off quickly as I lifted the receiver.

"Irene? This is Claire." There was a pause, then she added, "Have I called at a bad time?"

The dogs had stopped barking, but Frank was saying "Down, get down," in the background as they let us know how happy they were to have us return.

"That's only our welcoming committee," I said, forcing a lightness I didn't feel into my voice. "We just walked in the door."

"You have pets?"

"At the moment, about three too many. What can I do for you?"

"I found the information on the boat. We bought it in 1974 and sold it in 1977. Does that help?"

"And Ben never went out on the boat with Andre after he sold it to him?"

"No, but why does that matter?"

"You said he burned a photocopy of a picture of your old boat. It helps me to determine when the picture was taken. If Ben never went out on the boat after it was sold, the photo was taken sometime between 1974 and 1977."

"But couldn't Lucas Monroe tell you more about the photo, anyway?"

"Claire—I should tell you . . ." But I couldn't. I couldn't speak. Or swallow. Or breathe. Claire said nothing. Frank stopped petting the dogs.

"Irene?" he said. The dogs, Cody, and Frank all looked at me expectantly. I closed my eyes.

"I should tell you," I began again, "that Lucas is dead. We found his body a few hours ago."

For several long moments, neither of us said anything. I listened to Frank building a fire in the fireplace.

"I'm sorry," Claire said. "He was your friend."

"It's strange," I said. "You were right. I don't know who he had become. Haven't really known him for years now—I lost track of him a long time ago. Our lives obviously went in very different directions, but at one time we were friends. And I know he wanted to talk to me. The last time I saw him, he said 'You could help me—' "

"Now you've lost the chance," she said, filling in the silence. "Yes, I know."

I figured she did know. "I respected Lucas," I said after a moment. "That hasn't changed."

"He was young, wasn't he?" she said.

I answered the real question. "The cause of death hasn't been determined. The coroner hasn't given an opinion yet."

"Coroner? Was Lucas killed?"

"Hard to say. It will take some time. We found the body in an abandoned hotel. The coroner doesn't even know how long Lucas has been dead."

"This must all be very difficult for you."

"Look, I'm still going to try to learn about the photographs."

"If you want to drop it, I won't be angry with you."

"No. Tell me you won't give up on this, Claire."

"Oh, I can't, Irene. And now, I suspect, neither can you."

We talked a little longer, moving to safer subjects as she asked me about our dogs and Cody. Just before we said good-bye, she said, "Oh, I just thought of something. Ben kept calendars. Should I look for the ones from those years?"

"Calendars—you mean, something like appointment books?"

"Yes, only more detailed."

"Well, yes," I said, trying not to let my hopes soar. "I think they would be very helpful."

As I hung up, I turned to see that Frank had dragged all of our pillows and blankets out of the bedroom—and apparently from the linen closet as well—and arranged them in front of the fireplace. He had changed into a pair of jeans and a sweater, and was mixing drinks.

"Are you building a fort?" I asked, studying the pile of bedding.

"Yes," he said, "and here's the ammo." He handed me a Myers's with a spot of orange juice in it, took up a scotch and water, then led me to the pillows and blankets. The dogs and Cody gathered around as I downed the drink. It was a stiff one, and I felt it burn its way from my throat to my chest.

Frank watched me, took the empty glass, and set it aside.

He pulled the blankets and pillows around us, dogs and cat protesting but resettling. He held my head on his shoulder and stroked my hair. I didn't start crying until he said, "Whatever you do, don't cry on my fort."

I awoke in the middle of the night, vaguely aware of troubling dreams. It was a relief to hear Frank's soft snoring. My thoughts soon turned to Lucas, and the fact that his family might not even know he was dead. Where was his family? I thought of the envelopes Claire had shown me.

Frank murmured something unintelligible as I got out of

bed, but he fell right back to sleep. Cody followed me into
the living room. I picked up the phone and dialed long-
distance information for area code 909.

"City and listing?" a voice said.

"Riverside. Last name Monroe."

"First name or initial?"

"I'm not sure."

"I'm sorry, ma'am, there are a large number of listings
under the last name Monroe. I'll have to have a first name."

"Try Lucas."

I heard the clacking of computer keys, then, "Sorry, no
listing."

The next morning, Frank escaped the house only after I bad-
gered him into promising me that he'd find out if the family
had been contacted. He called me at work to say that it would
take a little time, since Lucas hadn't given the shelter any information on his relatives.

That's why, throughout the rest of the morning, whenever
John wasn't cruising by my desk in the newsroom, I was
pulling a Riverside phone directory out of my desk drawer and
hiding it on my lap.

After Frank's call, I had skulked over and snatched the directory from the bookcase near Stuart Angert's desk. It wasn't
Stuart's bookcase; the items in it were for the use of the entire newsroom. But given John's warnings and a lack of broth-
erly love among some of my coworkers, I didn't especially
want anyone keeping track of what I was doing. Bad enough
that Stuart had returned to his desk, seen the gap in the di-
rectories, and glanced around the newsroom. His glance settled on me, picking me out the way Sister Mary Joseph used
to be able to pick me out of a crowd of identically dressed
Catholic girls whenever someone had pulled a prank on a nun.
I smiled, he smiled back, and I knew that if he had indeed
guessed what I was up to, he was one of the few people who
wouldn't rat on me.

On my twenty-third call to a Riverside Monroe, a woman

answered the phone, and there was just enough of a pause before she said "Nobody here by that name," to make me call back after she hung up in my ear. I got an answering machine this time.

"This is Irene Kelly of the *Las Piernas News-Express*. I knew Lucas in college. I need to talk to you about him. Please. It's very important. Call me at the paper, or later at home. Call collect. But please call me." I left the 800 number for the paper and my home number.

I hung up, then stared at the phone for a few moments, willing it to ring. Nothing.

In between absolutely fruitless calls to my city hall contacts about the resignation of Allan Moffett, I also made twenty-six additional calls to other Monroes in Riverside. Either they weren't home or they didn't know a Lucas. I chatted with a couple of the more lonely Monroes, left messages for others.

Still, the only one I made a note of was number twenty-three: J. Monroe, no address.

The day had turned the corner past noon, the hours were galloping toward deadline, and I didn't have a thing written up. I could have blamed all the Monroes in Riverside or the people in city hall for my frustration, but I knew what was really irritating me. I wasn't working on the story I wanted to work on—at least, not from the right angle.

I reached into one of my desk drawers and pulled out a pile of loose scraps of paper bound with a couple of rubber bands. It was a treasure I inherited when the contents of the desk were returned to the *Express* by the police, who had held them while trying to solve the murder of the desk's previous owner, my friend O'Connor. In the bundle I found a scrap with a 619 area code number on it, and written beneath the number, in O'Connor's personal shorthand, symbols that meant "Dage's Little Rancho." I dialed the number.

"Keene? It's Irene."

"Oh, for Chrissakes—"

"Hold on, Keene. Just slow down and think for a minute. You have a chance to distance yourself from all of this, so you might as well take it. The pressure is on. You think all of your dinner companions are going to keep their mouths shut forever?"

"Assuming there *was* anything to talk about, you'd have to admit they've kept them shut this long. I'm not going to be the first to blab anything."

I stayed silent.

"You don't know what you're after, do you?" Keene said at last.

"You're forgetting that Lucas Monroe and I go way back."

"You give Lucas Monroe the same advice I'm giving you: just forget it. Go on with your lives. No good is served by this."

So Keene didn't know Lucas was dead. Or was pretending he didn't know. I postponed what had started to be a sense of relief.

"Have you seen Lucas lately?" I asked.

"No, apparently Mr. Monroe doesn't know how to get in touch with me. So I guess he can't threaten me the way he did some of the others."

"How did he threaten them?"

"Shit. I should have known you were on a fishing expedition. You don't know squat, do you?"

"Fishing expedition? Like the kind you used to take on Ben's boat?"

Silence.

"You received a photocopy, didn't you?" I asked.

"Shit," he said again. There was a long pause before he said, "Leave me in peace, Irene."

"Are you at peace, Keene?"

There was a sigh. "I'm an old man."

"O'Connor used to say there was no accomplishment in being young."

He laughed. "Seems I've heard that somewhere before."

"Entirely likely. He never claimed to have made up all of that stuff."

"Look," he said. "I don't think your friend Lucas Monroe knows how to get in touch with me and I don't want him to learn. Don't give him this number."

"He mailed the photocopy to your office?" I said.

"Yeah. And I'm not in there much anymore. My kids run the business now. They bundle my personal mail together and send it off to me every few days. We do everything else by phone and fax."

I thought for a moment. "You have a fax at home, then?"

"Sure."

"Fax the photocopy to me, Keene."

"Christ! You haven't even seen it, have you?"

"Fax the photocopy to me, Keene."

"No. I am sure as hell not faxing something to a god-damned newspaper."

"I'll stand by the machine."

"You'll stand there a long time. Wait a minute—what's going on here? Why doesn't your friend just give you a copy of it? He had enough of them made."

Decision time. Could I trust him? After a moment, I said, "There's a good reason why he hasn't given me the photo-copy. I'll tell you that reason, if you swear to me that you will not discuss this with your cronies or anyone else."

"They are *not* my cronies. Not all of them, anyway."

"Swear it, Keene. And swear it on something that means something to you."

"I swear it on my wife's memory," he said, and there was nothing casual in the offering.

"Lucas Monroe is dead."

"What?! Oh God, tell me you're shitting me again."

"You know I'm not."

"You see how dangerous this is? You see?"

"You're talking as if you don't believe my friend died of natural causes, Keene."

"Did he?" There was a plea for hope in the question.

"No, I don't think he did. Coroner is still working on it, but nothing he comes up with will make me believe that Lucas just happened to die at such a convenient time. And I can promise you this: I won't let this one rest."

He groaned. I waited.

"I don't really know anything," he said again, but without much heat.

"Keene, if you don't know anything, you have nothing to worry about. And if you don't, why are you afraid to send me that photocopy?"

There was another long silence.

"Too dangerous. Find somebody else. Maybe Tyler will give you his copy," he said. "Talk to Tyler. Call him at his office."

"I haven't been able to get past his first line of defense."

He paused, then said, "I'll give you his direct line. But you better swear an oath of your own to me—you swear on O'Connor's memory—that you won't tell Tyler who gave you the number."

Oaths and numbers exchanged, I promised him I'd keep in touch.

"I wish you wouldn't," he said, and hung up.

"Hello," the low voice said on the other end of the line.

"Corbin Tyler?"

"No one who has permission to call this number needs to ask," the voice calmly replied. "Who is this?"

"Irene Kelly of the *Las Piernas News-Express*. Before you hang up—"

"Forgive me for interrupting, but I have no intention of hanging up, Ms. Kelly. That would be rude. Not as rude as divulging a private number to a newspaper reporter, but I imagine my chances of learning who did so are very slim."

"Nonexistent, Mr. Tyler."

"I understand. Perhaps this is for the best. My secretary has felt quite annoyed for the past few days."

"So have I. Why didn't you just tell her to put the call through?"

"If you called again on that line, Ms. Kelly, I would refuse your call. But for the moment, you have my attention."

"I'm calling about a color photocopy. Do you need me to spend time telling you which one?"

"No."

"I'd like to see it, to talk to you about it—and about a few other things."

I heard him sigh. "We will compromise, Ms. Kelly. Give me one hour. At the end of that hour, come to my office." He gave me directions. "Park in the underground lot, near the north elevators. Use the one marked 'private' and enter this code on the keypad." He read off a short list of numbers. "I'll be waiting for you. Good-bye until then."

He hung up.

At the top floor of the building that houses Tyler Associates, the elevator doors open directly onto the reception area of Corbin Tyler's offices. There was no one sitting at the big marble-topped desk that stood facing me as I stepped out. I heard the faintest kiss of rubber as the elevator doors closed behind me. I listened, but heard no other sounds. In fact, the place seemed deserted.

Highly polished marble, glass, and brass surfaces were made less forbidding by soft, wintry light from skylights overhead and plush carpet below. A model of some new project stood off to one side in a glass case. Several doors led off the large room; all but one was closed. I walked toward the desk, my footsteps nearly soundless on the carpet. I stood there for a moment, then called a tentative "Hello?"

No one answered. On the large phone on the desk, none of the buttons for the multiple phone lines was lit. I studied the room for a moment and spotted two security cameras. I murmured a little prayer of gratitude—I hadn't done any scratching or adjusting.

The open door led to a long hallway; along the passage, as in the reception area, all but one of the doors appeared to be closed. I couldn't be certain, though; the hallway itself was almost completely dark. In contrast, the light filling the one open doorway was bright; so bright, I couldn't see who or what was in the room.

I stepped into the hallway. The bright light beckoned at the end of the corridor, but once I was within the passage, I could barely make out anything right in front of me. I reached out and found a wall, and kept walking with my hand gliding along the cool surface.

Each step away from the elevators made me more uneasy. I didn't know this place, or who Corbin Tyler might have contacted in the hour that had passed since we had spoken. In my eagerness to avoid John Walters, I had left the office without telling anyone where I was going. Only Keene would even know that I might have made contact with Tyler. "Hello?" I called again. "Mr. Tyler?"

There was no answer. I kept walking. My own heartbeat, my breathing, sounded loud to me. I kept my eyes on what I now thought of as the light at the end of the tunnel.

A voice behind me said, "Ms. Kelly."

I shrieked.

I whirled around to face him, clutching my hand to my chest, embarrassed but too startled to say so. The afterimage of the bright light floated between me and a person who said, "I frightened you."

"Yes."

"My apologies. Continue down the hallway, please."

I didn't like the way things were starting out. Rachel had taught me a few self-defense moves. I was going over them in my head, considering my options as I walked to the open door. Hoping to quickly evaluate the situation before committing myself any further, I slowed down and listened. I could hear Corbin Tyler slowing as I slowed. *Think!* I told myself. I could turn and run now. One man, I might be able to get past. If there were more . . . I peered into the room.

The sight which greeted me took my breath away.

There are probably better views in downtown Las Piernas, perhaps from some of the taller buildings, but I haven't seen them yet. Directly ahead of me, a wall of windows faced the water, where I could see ships, the bridges over the harbor, the breakwater and marinas. The windows curved with the room, so that to my left, they faced slightly inland, overlooking a section of downtown Las Piernas. I finally noticed Corbin Tyler.

He had entered the room while I stood gawking. He was standing at the farthest curve of the windows, silhouetted by the afternoon light. He seemed to be staring at a building. I quickly realized that his attention was on the Haimler Building, a tall, graceful structure crowned by a complex glass design. The Haimler was one of Tyler's award-winning creations.

"This isn't the best time of day to see it," he said without turning around. "A little later, it captures the light in an entirely different way." His voice, as before, was calm, low, even. It unnerved me in a way that Booter Hodges' self-involved rambling never would.

"Where is everybody?" I asked, looking back over my shoulder to make sure the door remained open.

"I sent them home. Right after you called. I don't want anyone to know you were here today."

"But the cameras—"

"Are off," he said, finally turning around.

"Oh." I felt a chill go down my back as he silently assessed me.

Corbin Tyler's eyes and hair were raven black, which was all the drama on the playbill of his features. He was a slender man of average height. His face was pale and thin, his mouth soft and unsmiling. There was a look of cool determination in his eyes. Everything about him said he was serious.

"There is an envelope for you on the desk, Ms. Kelly. Take it and go."

"I appreciate this more than I can say, Mr. Tyler. But I also have a few questions—"

"I will not discuss it further with you."

"Why not? It's not as if—"

He held up his hand like a traffic cop. I fell silent.

"Don't push your luck," he said. He folded his arms. Something in his manner told me that I should be grateful for the photocopy and go, but as Popeye might say, I am what I am.

"Do you know why Allan Moffett resigned?" I asked.

"Yes."

I waited.

"Thank you for asking. Now, if anyone has seen you arrive and asks why I met with a reporter from the *Express,* I will tell him that you came up here to ask about Mr. Moffett. Take the envelope and go, Ms. Kelly."

I walked over to his desk, picked up the 9 x 12 clasp envelope on it, and paused, my eyes drawn to the only other objects on its surface—two framed portraits. One was a wedding photo, of a bride with a round, merry face; the other a graduation photo, of a young woman who had inherited the best of her parents' features.

"My wife and daughter," he said from behind me, then added, "My late wife."

I turned to look at him. He hadn't moved from the windows, but his face had changed. I thought it had changed, anyway, at least for a moment. He still looked serious.

"Your daughter is beautiful," I said.

He turned his back to me. "She's all I have now, of course. Over the years, I've learned that I will do almost anything to protect her. Now, *please go.*"

I reached the door and looked back at him. He hadn't moved.

"Why are you letting me have this?"

"You speak as if I have given you a gift, Ms. Kelly. You're wrong."

I didn't actually run to the elevator, but I thought about it. About halfway down the dark hall, I began to ask myself if this all hadn't been too easy. As I passed the receptionist's desk, I glanced at the phone and saw that one of the lines was lit. I paused and listened. I heard the low murmur of Tyler's voice but couldn't make out anything he was saying. The light on the phone went off. He had called someone. Who?

My instincts told me to get the hell out of there. I hurried to the elevator and pressed the call button several times, as if the elevator would somehow recognize my sense of urgency if I kept signaling it. Tucking the envelope under one arm, I searched through my purse, looking for something that could be used as a weapon. My keys were all that was handy.

I heard noises from the hallway, someone moving about, closing a door. The elevator car arrived. I stepped in, pushed the button for the garage, and watched Tyler emerge from the hallway just as the shiny brass doors closed in front of me, leaving me with nothing but a funhouse reflection of a tense woman's face. Mine.

I clutched the unopened envelope as the car began its rapid descent, seeming to pick up speed at each floor. My mind raced with it. Corbin Tyler had easily handed over something which might damn him, and then made a phone call. Did he hand it over because he knew it wouldn't leave the building? Would someone be waiting for me when the doors to the elevator opened?

The car suddenly slowed, a roller coaster dropping motion that was echoed in the lurching of my stomach. This wasn't the garage. The elevator was stopping at the second floor. I moved away from the doors, leaned my back against the bank of buttons, my hand ready to press the alarm bell. I held my breath.

The doors slid open. I waited. Heard the stairwell door close just before the elevator doors slid shut.

The descent began again, and again the car lurched to a stop. The doors opened, this time in the cavernous underground parking lot. I held my hand on the "open doors" button as I peered out.

The stark overhead fluorescent lighting cast shadows everywhere. I saw no one. The elevator buzzed at me in annoyance. I stepped out into the garage; the doors closed softly behind me.

I heard every single footstep I made on the concrete floor, all the while wondering who else might be listening for them. I had my keys out, but still I fumbled to get the car door open. I got in, locked the door, and started the car. I heard the squeal of tires somewhere in the garage, hurriedly backed out, and roared toward the exit, my own wheels screeching. The startled attendant at the gate pressed a button and raised the gate arm just before the Karmann Ghia would have smashed into it, a contest I'm not sure my car would have won. The car jolted hard onto the pavement as it burst from the garage onto a blessedly empty street. I slowed, glanced in the mirror, and saw no one leaving the garage behind me.

I took a series of unnecessary turns just to make sure no one was tailing me, finally ending up at the *Express*. I sat in my car for long moments, staring at the clasp envelope on the seat next to me. Finally, I reached for it, opened it carefully.

There was a plain white envelope inside it. This one was postmarked Las Piernas. Except for that and Tyler's office address, the white envelope looked identical to the ones Claire had shown me. Typewritten, marked "Personal and confidential." Inside the envelope, the slick paper of a color copy was folded in thirds. There was no writing on it. I unfolded it.

In what appeared to be an enlarged copy of a color photograph, I saw a group of people on a boat. It was a good-sized boat, a boat set up for serious fishing. I couldn't tell its exact size or model from the photo, but it had the look of an expensive craft. There were seven men visible in the photo: Booter Hodges, Allan Moffett, Roland Hill, Corbin Tyler, Keene Dage, Andre Selman, and Ben Watterson. Hill was at the helm. Ben and Andre had their arms around a young woman. The other men were standing behind the woman, lifting cans of beer, as if in a toast. She was perhaps in her mid-twenties; the men spanned a range of ages, but all older than she by at least a decade. She had straight red hair, worn in a bowl cut. She held out a small sole; she was keeping the fish at arm's length, but smiled proudly at the camera, in triumph.

I had no idea who she was.

I had the uneasy feeling that I was no better off than the fish.

16

$\mathbf{B}$ack at my desk, I decided to face up to the worst possibility—that Lucas wanted to use me in some way, to help him blackmail seven of Las Piernas's leading citizens.

Setting aside all the objections I had to that theory, thinking of Lucas as a blackmailer raised other questions. The worst thing portrayed in the photograph was "refusing to toss back an undersized fish," not exactly an offense that would drive someone to commit suicide or tender a resignation. So what did the photograph represent? What did Lucas want? Had someone killed him in order to be relieved of his threats? If so, who?

Keene Dage and Corbin Tyler had just confirmed a link I had only guessed at. Ben Watterson was not the only one who had been contacted by Lucas. According to Charlotte Brady's description of the visitor who upset her former boss, Allan Moffett's visitor could have been Lucas. I was willing to bet that Allan's response to that visit was to call the other potential blackmail victims.

The dinner party, with Ben added.

"A man shouldn't panic," Booter had said. Allan had done just that. But what the hell could a homeless man hold over their heads that would induce that sort of panic? Something that could be hinted at in a photograph of a fishing trip.

From Keene, I gathered that everyone had received this same color copy, but perhaps that wasn't the case. Jerry Selman had mentioned a picture of his father with a former girlfriend. Ben had received a picture of a group of men on a boat now owned by Andre Selman. Was this woman in the photo the old girlfriend?

Maureen Selman (I had to fight the impulse to think of her as Cinco) might have been upset at a photo of Andre with an old girlfriend, but she had been with Andre long enough to know that she hadn't married a virgin. A photo—taken a dozen or so years ago—of Andre with a woman couldn't really be very threatening. And the photo was hardly one of Andre and the woman in flagrante delicto. I looked at the rest of the list. Keene was a widower, as was Corbin. Allan and Roland were both divorced. I didn't think this was about old girlfriends.

Old girlfriends. I smiled to myself as I realized that SOS would provide me with a resource not everyone would have in this situation: old girlfriends who knew one another. Maybe one of the other members of the group would know the woman in the photo.

What did Lucas want? Money was the easiest answer, but was it the right answer? It didn't fit with the Lucas I had known, but that man hadn't been living on the streets, either.

The coroner might not believe that Lucas was killed, but I was nearly certain of it. Beyond a strong hunch, beyond bodies being moved and pennies and missing rings, there was the simple fact that he had been some sort of catalyst. Allan had felt threatened. So did half a dozen other men.

Those men were linked before Lucas threatened them, and I became convinced that the more I discovered about their connections to one another, the more likely I was to learn not only why Allan Moffett had resigned, but why Ben Watterson and Lucas Monroe had died.

I decided I needed to have a long talk with Murray Plummer, the real estate expert for the *Express*. I called his extension, but he wasn't in, so I left a message on his voice mail. I wondered if he was in but not taking calls.

I looked over the list of attendees at Allan's dinner party. They came from three areas. From the college, from the city, and from local business. The businessmen were Keene Dage, Corbin Tyler, Roland Hill. Ben had belonged to this latter group.

Roland Hill. Moffett may have called the dinner meeting, but years ago, Hill would have been the one who originally brought this group of people together. Whatever significance the picture of the boat had, it was apparently regarding something that was going on in the late 1970s.

Like most newspapers, the *Express* had only recently started indexing stories on the computer, so I wouldn't be able to look up stories from that decade at my desk. I was going to need to go to the morgue, or library, as we were now supposed to refer to it. With men as publicly prominent as Ben Watterson and Allan Moffett, the noncomputerized files would be huge, going back over several decades. Of the remaining men, Hill was a much more controversial figure than most of the others. His development projects had not been universally welcomed or successful. I decided he would be my best bet for a starting point in a search through the clipping files.

It would help to have guidance from Murray. I tried calling him again. Voice mail. I hung up without leaving a message.

My thoughts went back to Lucas. As far as I could remember, Lucas was working on his thesis when I left Las Piernas in 1976. He couldn't have been far from finishing his master's degree.

John Walters' shadow across my desk startled me out of my reverie.

"Where in the hell have you been all day?" he growled.

"I was only out of this office for an hour," I said. I thought of telling him what I had done during that hour, but didn't think he'd approve of the meager results.

"Going to have anything for me by deadline, Kelly?"

"Uh, probably not today, John," I said, closing the drawer with the phone book in it.

"Goddammit, why not?"

"I need to talk to Murray, for one thing."

He scowled, but then apparently decided that working with Murray meant I wasn't chasing after stories on Lucas. "Okay, Kelly. But one of two things is going to happen after a while. Some other newspaper is going to get the story first, or the story's going to grow so cold that no one in this town will remember who Allan Moffett is, let alone care about why he resigned. Go look for Murray."

"Sure, John."

"And Kelly? Don't forget to put that phone book back."

I scowled at Stuart, who was shaking his head.

"I can still observe things on my own," John said, and walked off.

The *Express* is laid out like a rabbit warren. Hallways appear where you don't expect them, and a doorway that would seem to lead to a small office often turns out to be the entrance to a large room. Murray and I probably passed one another a couple of times without knowing it, but I finally caught up with him in the composing room. It's called the composing room even though no one composes pages in it, and the machines in it are called typesetters even though they don't really set type. Nothing wrong with tradition.

Black and turquoise cubes, about four square feet each, the typesetters sit along one wall of the composing room. The typesetters are really gigantic film processors that turn out "film," slick black-and-white prints which are a little larger than a newspaper page.

Murray was standing at a dump, one of the counter-height metal tables in the room. I saw him reach into a pocket and pull out a thick packet of folded proofs.

"Were you just downstairs?" I asked.

He turned around and smiled. "Hello, Irene. No, I was scheduling something with a photographer until a few minutes ago. Now I'm waiting to sign off my pages for the real estate section."

As he spoke, he smoothed out the proofs, which had corrections and changes circled with red china marker here and there.

"Here you go, Plummer," the compositor said, handing Murray the film that had just dropped into the typesetter's tray. I stayed quiet while Murray double-checked the folio—the upper corner information which includes the date and page number—and then found the corresponding proof.

"So, you've been looking for me?" he asked, uncapping a pen. It was the kind that marked in a special light blue ink known as "nonreproducing blue."

"I'll give you a chance to check your page over," I said.

"Thanks." I watched him check the headlines first. As they say, if you're going to make a mistake, don't do it in 42 point type. Next he went over the cut lines under photos, the jump lines and jumps, and then checked to see that all the corrections on his proofs had been carried out.

"Turin is spelled wrong," I said, looking over his shoulder. "Your reporter has this Italian architect coming from a soup bowl."

He sighed as he made the correction. "Do they teach geography in schools these days? Thanks for catching that—one of those words that makes it past the computer spelling-checker." He noted the change from Tureen to Turin, sent the page back, then turned his attention to me.

"What's up?"

"You've covered real estate since the early 1970s, right?"

"Right."

"I saw a group of men having dinner together the other night—the night after Ben Watterson killed himself. Allan Moffett called the meeting."

Murray lifted a brow over the rim of his glasses. "Who were they?"

I named them. "I know they were also meeting in the mid-to-late 1970s. Back in the seventies, Ben Watterson was meeting with them, too, and would have been invited for the dinner party, except—"

"Except now he is permanently unavailable for dinner parties. How do you know about all of this?"

"Another time, Murray."

He grinned. "Okay, okay. But before you turn in your story, help me to be ready with a tie-in for my section, will you?"

"If it's at all possible, I will. I'll need your help on this anyway."

"Hmm. Yes. Let's take a look at this group. Name them again for me."

I did. He noted the initials on a scrap of paper.

"You want to know what projects they were involved in from, say, 1970 to 1980?"

"Yes. Especially 1974 to 1978."

This time both brows went up, but then he studied the initials again. "Andre Selman has done many studies for the Redevelopment Agency, of course," he said. "He's one of their regular paid consultants."

"Yes, I know," I said. "It all goes hand in hand."

He nodded.

"I need a quick way to figure out which projects they worked on together. I can't just go through four years of microfilm—not and keep my sanity or my eyesight, let alone make John happy. As you say, the college and city have worked together many times. So, for the moment, if we just stick with the private sector, we're left with Tyler, Hill, Dage, and Watterson. Can you tell me about any projects they were working on back then?"

"Off the top of my head? Lord. Dozens of them."

"Oh."

"Hill was putting deals together like crazy then. But you're looking for redevelopment, right?"

"Yes." On a hunch I said, "Maybe something in the area near the Angelus Hotel."

Murray frowned. "The Angelus?"

The compositor came over with another page. Murray took it absently, still studying me.

"Look," I said, "I'd just as soon we kept this between the two of us, okay?"

He chuckled. Hell's bells. What could I offer Murray in exchange for keeping his yap shut?

"Did I ever tell you that Jack Fremont is a good friend of mine?" I asked.

He stopped chuckling. "Jack Fremont? The man who owns over half the beach property in Las Piernas?"

"The very one. The one who's been so media shy."

"You're bribing me with an interview possibility?"

"Emphasis on possibility."

"I would never betray you, Irene."

My turn to laugh.

"Let me sign these pages off, then I'll go back to my office and do a little research for you. I'll have a list for you by tomorrow morning at the latest. Would that seal the deal?"

"I'm only promising to *talk* to Jack about letting you interview him, right? He makes the decision on his own."

"Right."

"Murray, you've got yourself a bargain."

17

I got back to my desk, ignored the message light, and called Jack. He agreed to do the interview with Murray.

"I'm not going to tell him this right away," I said. "I've got to make sure he comes through on his part of the bargain."

"Okay," Jack said. "If he calls, I'll just say I'm thinking about it."

"Thanks, Jack."

"By the way, did Frank get in touch with you?" he asked.

"No, but I haven't picked up all of my messages. Why?"

"Well, if you don't have a message from him, give him a call, okay?"

"What's this about?"

"Oh, no. I'm not getting in the middle of this one."

I checked my messages. A few answering-machine Monroes saying they were sorry, but I had reached a wrong number when I had called. Nothing from J. Monroe. Two other calls, one from Frank and one from Rachel. I called Frank first.

"Harriman," he answered.

"Me, too," I said. "What's up?"

"I'm glad you called back. I've been a little worried about you."

"Stop the presses."

"I'm serious. There have been a couple of developments in this Lucas Monroe situation—"

"Situation? It's a little beyond a situation, isn't it? The man is dead."

"Okay, have it your way. Something has come up in connection with the death of—"

"Has Carlos finished the autopsy?"

I heard a sigh of utter exasperation.

"Okay, I'll be quiet. Say what you have to say."

There was no reply.

"Are you pinching the bridge of your nose?" I asked.

"How the hell could you know that?"

"You sometimes do that when you're about to lose your temper."

"Call Rachel. She'll fill you in on what's happening."

"Whoa, whoa, wait!"

He didn't say anything, but he didn't hang up, either.

"Don't be angry," I said.

I heard a little snort. We were getting somewhere. "Please," I added.

"This evening," he said, in that quiet, measured tone he uses when most people would be shouting, "I would sincerely appreciate it if you went straight home."

I started to say that I already planned to, then remembered that I wasn't going to interrupt.

"Jack has promised to go with you when you walk the dogs, so just call him whenever you're ready. Otherwise, please stay home. Humor me, if you will, and lock the doors. I'm working late, but Rachel will be coming over."

"Frank, dearest," I said, "there's just one teensy-weensy problem with all of these plans you've laid out for my evening."

"Namely?"

"I've got others."

"Cancel them."

"Do you want to tell me what the hell is going on, Frank?"

"Two Toes is looking for you."

That surprised me, but I was too mad to let it register. "Oh, so what? He's not exactly fully functioning. How would he ever figure out where I am? The guy spends his time on his knees in front of religious statues."

"So what?" That cool tone was going all to hell—he *was* starting to shout. "I'll tell you so what. While he's out looking for you, we've been looking for him. And guess where he was last seen?"

"Where?" I said softly. He was scaring me a little, not with his shouts but with what I guessed the answer might be.

He didn't speak right away. He calmed himself, then said, "On Broadway, standing around outside the Wrigley Building. Maybe waiting for you to come downstairs, go out to lunch. Turns out a patrolman told him to move along before he learned we were looking for the guy."

"Let's start this conversation over. The Las Piernas Police Department is looking for Two Toes."

"Right. Reed wants to question him. Based on what Two Toes told you, we think he might have been the last person to see Lucas alive. Then we picked up word on the street that the guy has Lucas's ring and—"

"His ring? Wait—Carlos said the ring was taken after Lucas died. So you think Two Toes was there when Lucas died?"

"Maybe. If nothing else, Two Toes robbed a dead man. He also seems to hold you responsible for bringing the police into the Angelus. A couple of people heard him ranting that you had desecrated Lucas's tomb."

I wasn't paying strict attention to what Frank was saying. I was still wondering if Two Toes killed Lucas for a lousy college ring. "Has Carlos come up with a cause of death?" I asked.

"He says Lucas had a heart attack, but—"

"Heart attack!"

"Hang on, let me finish. Carlos and Reed worked this out from the patterns of bruising. Carlos said Lucas might have grown dizzy, stumbled, grazed his forehead on the radiator, then collapsed to his knees, probably clutching his chest as he died. He said it would have been quick. There's only one thing that's bothering him."

"What?"

"Lucas's liver wasn't in great shape. But his heart—Carlos can't figure out why the heart gave out on him."

"What are you saying?"

"I'm saying," he said, "that you might not have won Reed over, but Carlos was impressed by your concerns. With or without your concerns, he's a very thorough man. He wants to make sure the heart attack wasn't induced."

"Induced . . . you mean by some chemical means? A poison? Maybe a drug?"

"Maybe."

"Did Carlos check for injection marks?"

"Yes. There were no injection marks. Not even old ones, so your friend wasn't a junkie."

"The others said that. He hit the bottle, stayed away from drugs. He had real problems with booze, I guess, but even his street friends said he had been staying sober." I thought for a moment. "He had a thermos with him in the hotel—"

"Carlos has ordered toxicological reports on the body. I'm sure they'll check any food or drink that was in the room as well."

"When did Lucas die?"

"Carlos isn't positive, but he thinks it was probably about three days before you found the body."

"The day Allan Moffett resigned."

"Yes."

I mulled this over. "Did Roberta have any information about Lucas?"

"No, not that's she's sharing with us. She said he didn't give any family information when he signed up with the center—claims confidentiality about anything else."

"Even though he's dead?"

"It's still privileged. We may get a warrant."

I wondered if Roberta would tell me more about what was going on with Lucas, then I remembered my last conversation with her. Roberta probably wasn't willing to speak to me about anything. Maybe I could try mending fences. That brought my thoughts back to my husband.

"Frank, about tonight——"

"Look, before you make up your mind, let me apologize about coming on so strong. I guess I sort of panicked. This Two Toes has a reputation for using his fists. I didn't want him using them on you. I couldn't reach you, and I started making arrangements. I wanted you to be safe."

Safety. There's no such thing, I wanted to say. Instead I said, "I understand, Frank. But Lisa Selman is coming over for dinner, remember? She's coming over to the house at seven. I was going to cook dinner for the three of us."

"Hmm. I forgot about that. Look," he said, "could you reschedule the dinner?"

"I don't know. Her dad's in the hospital and——"

"You're right. So she meets Rachel instead of your domineering, overprotective husband."

"Somehow it won't be the same. I'll call Lisa and see if she's willing to let Rachel sub for you."

"Thanks, Irene." There was relief in his voice.

Neither Lisa nor Rachel objected to the change in dinner plans. That settled, I took out the photographs that Claire and Tyler gave me and studied them for the one hundredth time. I dialed Booter Hodges.

"Hello, Irene! How nice to hear from you! What can I do for you?"

"I was thinking about Allan Moffett. You're old friends, right?"

"Well, yes, although I hardly move in Allan's circles."

"Oh, c'mon, Booter. You're even fishing buddies, aren't you?"

There was the slightest pause before he said, "Oh, I may have gone fishing once or twice with him."

"When?"

"Nothing lately. Five or six years ago we went once or twice, that's all." He forced a laugh. "Who has time to go fishing now?"

"Andre Selman has a boat."

"No kidding? Well, what do you know about that?"

"You didn't know?"

"Oh, maybe I heard something about it. Why do you mention it? Did you want me to ask Andre Selman to take you fishing?"

I laughed at that. "No, no thanks, Booter. I just thought you might have been out on his boat."

"No, sorry. Never. I'll have to ask him to show it to me— if I ever find a free moment. Now, I'm sure you're busy, too. Don't let's waste time talking about fishing. Is there some way in which I may be of assistance to you?"

"Yes, I think you may. Tell me if the Alumni Foundation has heard from a graduate named Lucas Monroe."

There was another pause, then Booter said, "I couldn't give that information out, as I'm sure you know—privacy laws, of course. I know they're a bother to you reporters—they can be pretty darn tough on an alumni foundation, too."

"You remember him?"

"Who?"

"Lucas Monroe."

"I don't believe I've ever heard of him."

"Worked with Andre. Used to share an office with him."

"How long ago?"

"Oh, back when you were fishing with Allan and the other boys."

"Well, then, no wonder. We have thousands of students here, and I can't be expected to recall a man who went to school here back in the 1970s."

You blew it, I thought. Once or twice five or six years ago. Sure. "You haven't heard from Lucas Monroe since the 1970s?"

"No—I mean, I've never heard from him."

"But you mentioned the 1970s, not me, Booter."

There was a pause, then he said, "I guess I assumed you were asking about one of your old friends, someone who went to school here when you did."

I tapped my pencil. "That's strange, Booter. I mean, strange that you don't know him."

He laughed nervously. "Why? Why do you keep mentioning this fellow?"

"Oh, this brings us back to the dinner party, I believe. And a few other matters. If I were to ask Mr. Monroe if he's seen you lately, I suppose I'd get a different story. He might be able to name a date and place and time."

I heard the chair creak. I could picture him, leaning back, stroking his tie.

"If someone named—what did you say his name was?"

"Monroe. Lucas Monroe," I said.

"Well, if he claims he knows me, or has been to see me, he's lying, pure and simple."

"Lying."

"Yes, the man's a liar."

"A liar," I repeated. "Well, you should know. By the way, Booter, did I ever tell you that I know how you got your nickname?"

"Oh, I suppose you've heard I was something of a pugilist in my day," he said with a laugh.

"Pugilist? You mean boxing? I thought your sport was hurling."

"Hurling? Why, no! You mean pitching, a baseball player?"

"Not exactly."

"Oh, maybe you said 'hurdling.' I never went out for track and field. I'm slow as molasses."

"Whatever you say, Booter. Well, if you remember anything about Lucas Monroe, let me know."

Poor Booter. A man builds a certain kind of reputation, thinks no one will learn his secrets, then one day some stupid little story catches up to him. Suddenly his name is mud—or something worse.

Booter was a strange man. Not as dumb as he acted, but not as smart as he thought he was, either. I didn't think he knew Lucas was dead, but I couldn't be sure.

I needed to step back a little. I had been sort of mean to Booter, partly because I didn't like hearing him call Lucas a liar.

Perhaps I had taken it all wrong. Coming from Booter, calling someone a liar could have been a statement of admiration.

18

Deke and Dunk were snoozing after a hard run on the beach. I had showered and changed, a chicken was roasting in the oven, and Rachel had set the table. Now she sat at the counter, drinking a glass of white wine, scratching Cody's ears, as I worked on a batch of biscuits.

"So, tell me about this group you're in," Rachel said, obliging Cody when he lifted his chin to be scratched where *he* wanted to be scratched. "This SOS—Pete thought Frank was crazy to let you go to that meeting the other night. I told him it was none of his business, but you know Pete. If he thinks something is bothering his partner—"

"What? Bothering his partner? Frank told Pete that my going to SOS *bothered* him?"

Her hand stilled. "Uh-oh. Listen, I don't know that for a fact. Pete borrows trouble, you know?"

I went back to kneading biscuit dough, she went back to spoiling the cat. I decided to set aside my worries about Frank, since there was nothing I could do about them until I had a chance to talk to him.

"SOS is Save Our Shelter, a group that supports the battered women's shelter," I said, "but I'm guessing that you're not asking about that group."

"No, Pete called it something else."

" 'Survivors of Selman'?"

"Yeah, that was it."

"That's a joke that I regret letting Frank in on. It's just what brought a few of us together years ago. Even then, calling it that was intended to be a joke. Women who had gone on with their lives after being with Lisa's dad."

"You make it sound like a crowd. How many old girl-friends does this guy have?"

"How many? Let's see. Every now and then, Andre lasted a year with someone. He's been with his current wife for about five years now. But before that, the man averaged two or three girlfriends and a dozen quick affairs each year for twenty or twenty-five years . . ."

"Merda, well over a hundred women! What derailed this freight train of love? Fear of AIDS?"

"No, I don't think so. Maybe. There are several theories floating around. I don't care, really."

I knew she was studying me, but I kept my eyes on the bis-cuit dough, as if its white sameness inspired fascination. I was hoping she would let this line of questions drop. That went the way of a lot of hopes.

"So you still haven't told me how the ex-girlfriends man-aged to meet each other the first time."

"Lisa—the woman you'll meet tonight?"

She nodded.

"She asked about five of Andre's ex-girlfriends to attend her high school graduation. I was one of them. Later, Lisa's mom invited us back to her house for coffee, while Lisa and her friends went on to a party."

"You knew these other women were Andre's ex-girlfriends?"

"No. It was the first time I had met most of them. I knew Marcy, Lisa's mom, of course. And Sharon, Jerry's mom—Jerry is Andre's son. But the others were women I'd never met before. I turned to one of the others and asked, 'So how do you know Lisa?' and that was that."

"Must have been weird."

"Not really. In fact, it was a relief. Here were some other women who—" I stopped, felt the heat rise in my cheeks.

"What's wrong?"

I shook my head. "Rachel, of all the stupid relationship moves I've ever made, getting involved with Andre was the stupidest. In the end, I felt—I don't know, *conned,* I suppose. So here I was—meeting smart, strong women—and every one of them had been conned in exactly the same way."

"He took money from you?"

"No. I was a student. I didn't have money."

"Your virginity?"

I laughed. "No, the precious prize of my virginity was long gone."

"I didn't mean—"

"I know you didn't. Andre took my pride. That's all. Just my pride."

Rachel didn't say anything for a while, just kept scratching Cody. I realized that I was kneading the dough a little too vigorously, and decided to roll it out while it would still make something resembling biscuits.

"Andre always courted and broke up with women in the same way. In fact, he always arranged—with the help of his best friend, Jeff—that you'd walk in on him having sex with another woman. It had happened exactly the same way for all of us."

"Good God!" Rachel said. "I'm surprised he hasn't been killed by one of those women—Andre and his friend!"

"As far as I know, I'm the only one who didn't leave it at shouting obscenities or running away in tears. Some even tried to get back together with him."

"What did you do?"

I smiled. "I grabbed one of his prized fishing poles and started flailing his naked behind with it."

She laughed. "Literally whipped his ass, eh? So then what happened to you?"

"I moved to Bakersfield. I worked the police beat for a local paper for a couple of years before the *Express* offered me a job down here. My father's health was starting to fail, so I moved back home." I started cutting out biscuits, putting them on a baking sheet, allowing the memories of my father's illness to get lost in a more pleasant recollection, that of standing next to my mother when I was little, watching her make biscuits. Mom made the biscuits from scratch. I was using a mix, telling myself that was one step closer to homemade than popping open a tube of refrigerated dough.

"Maybe it was just time to come home, anyway," Rachel said quietly, bringing me back to the memories of my father's illness.

"Maybe." Think of something else.

"Isn't Frank from Bakersfield?" she asked.

"Yes. We were just friends in those days. It took us another dozen years to meet up again, but that's where I first met him."

"So—I guess I still don't understand why you formed this SOS."

"We all said things like, 'I wish I had talked to you back then. It would have helped to know I wasn't the only one.' Becky—one of the women there that night—suggested we go around picking up survivors after Andre broke up with them. You know, let them know that they weren't the first person to go through this routine. Someone said that the only thing Andre didn't do was batter us."

"Hmm." She shook her head.

"Well, the comment made us think. 'There but for the grace of God,' and all that. As it happened, around the time we were having this conversation, the battered women's shelter had lost some grant funding. We decided to make something positive out of what had been a negative experience for us. Sort of mushroomed after that."

Cody protested as Rachel stopped scratching him. I looked up to find her staring at me. "Tell me the truth. This Andre didn't hit you, did he?"

"No, Rachel. As far as I know, he never physically abused anyone. Psychologically—that's another story."

She looked as if she wanted to comment on that, but the dogs started barking. The doorbell rang.

"I'll answer it," she said. "Your hands are covered with dough."

If I had any worries about Lisa and Rachel feeling comfortable with one another, those fears were proven groundless within the first few moments after Lisa's arrival. Throughout dinner, they talked as much to one another as with me, discussing Rachel's move to Las Piernas and Lisa's upcoming candidacy. If Rachel thought it strange that Andre's name didn't come up until the meal was nearly finished, she didn't show it.

"By the way, Andre's condition hasn't changed much," Lisa said. She turned to Rachel. "I don't know if Irene has told you about the person who is nominally my father. He suffered a heart attack the other night."

"Yes, I know about his illness," Rachel said. I knew her well enough to see that she was displeased by Lisa's flippancy. At first, I doubted Lisa saw it. I was wrong.

"I'm sorry. I've offended you. I did the same thing with Irene the other day at lunch. The problem is, I don't think very highly of my father. Among friends, I tend to let my guard down. My father's illness hasn't changed my relationship with him. No miraculous healing of old wounds or finishing of unfinished business. To Jerry, his son, he has been a very affectionate father. To me, worthless."

"That seems a little harsh," I said.

She lifted a brow. "Does it? Think back to when you were dating him. When it was my father's weekend to have custody, what happened?"

"We all shared—"

"Not *we*, Irene. You and I. I'll grant you, there was always the 'doting father' show. It drove me crazy for years. He put this big act on whenever he first dated a woman. I was baffled—going from being adored to ignored, unable to comprehend what was triggering the change. What was I doing that made him suddenly turn cold? Until I grasped the fact that his affection was connected to the impression he wanted to make on his date, and not on my behavior, I never knew what to expect."

"You seemed to have that figured out by the time I met you," I said.

She laughed. "Rachel, when Irene first met me, I was an absolute monster."

"You were not," I protested. "You just tested me. Kids do that to adults."

"Oh, sure. But most women in their twenties didn't catch on. Trust me. I *tested* lots of them."

"Tested how?" Rachel asked.

"At first, just by whining a lot and generally being obnoxious. Irene would pretend to be bored by it—she'd just yawn and say things like, 'Most people quit that baloney by the time they're three years old.' So then I moved into phase two. Let's see . . . there was the time I put cod liver oil in your shampoo bottle—"

"It washed out. Eventually."

"The time I put shoe polish on the rims of the eyepieces of your binoculars, so that when Andre took you to a hockey game, you—"

"—looked like a raccoon until Andre finally broke down and told me why people were laughing at me. Yes. An old trick, but Andre was deeply amused."

"Actually, I think most of them were old tricks. The plastic wrap beneath the toilet seat, salt in your cola—"

"Makes it foam up, right?" Rachel asked.

"Yes," she said. "Oh, there was also the time I put laxative in your coffee."

I made a face. "That was one of the worst."

"If Irene was reading an article in a magazine and got interrupted," she told Rachel, "I'd tear out the last page of the story."

"That one was irritating, but at least it didn't ruin my day."

"You see, a brat."

I shrugged. "You were just trying to get my attention. I wasn't an angel when I was twelve, and I didn't expect you to be one. Besides, you were treating me the way I treated my older sister. I figured I was doing penance."

"I don't know about the penance, but you're absolutely right about the attention." She turned to Rachel. "I was devastated when Irene moved to Bakersfield. She was one of my favorites. I really hated Alicia."

"Alicia?" Rachel asked.

"Alicia Penderson," I said. "A girl I had known since grade school, was the one who—"

I caught myself, but Lisa just laughed. "She was the one who was in bed with my father when Irene whipped his butt with a fishing pole!"

She saw our mutual discomfort and said, "Oh, please! I've been an adult for years now, Irene. You don't need to act embarrassed about the fact that I knew about my father's sexual activities. Lots of sounds carry up along that heating vent to the attic."

"Maybe I'm still a little old-fashioned about some things," I said. "I know you didn't get it all from eavesdropping through the furnace. Your father thought it was oh-so-progressive to tell you things most parents keep from their children. I think you had to grow up a little too fast as a result."

"Nothing can be done about it now," she said. "I survived. I didn't turn out so badly, did I?"

"No," I said, smiling. "Not at all. I'm very proud of you."

She looked down at the table, turning a deep shade of red.

"Nothing to blush about," I said. I turned to Rachel. "Lisa graduated from high school when she was fifteen—"

"You told me *you* graduated early," Lisa said.

"Only a semester early. And I wasted it completely. If I hadn't taken college classes during a couple of summer sessions, I might still be an undergrad. You, on the other hand, finished your master's degree when you were nineteen—and graduated with honors."

"You're a sociologist, like your father?" Rachel asked.

"Oh no. My life is in politics. But I did get a degree in sociology."

"There seems to be a family love of the subject," I said. "Her brother is also a sociologist."

"Are you close to your brother?" Rachel asked.

She hesitated for a moment before saying, "Close? No. He's six years older than I am—"

Rachel glanced over at me. "You dated a guy who had a son your age?"

"Thank you, Rachel," I said dryly. "Jerry's three years younger than I. He was just starting college when I was about to graduate."

"Oh, I see. You were *much* older then."

"Don't give Irene a hard time," Lisa said. "My father's conquests are legion—and most of the women were in their twenties when he met them."

"I'm not sure I've been defended," I said. "To go back to Rachel's question—I think age differences didn't matter so much as the fact that he grew up in a different household."

"You're right. Jerry's my half-brother, Rachel. For the most part, he lived with his mother, and I lived with mine. But he sometimes spent months at my father's house, and he lived with Andre all summer, every summer. When I was young, I was very jealous of him, of course. Eaten up with envy. I would have loved to have had one-thousandth of the attention he received from Andre. For a while, when I was in school, we grew further apart. But in the last few years, we've started to get to know one another again."

We shifted to less volatile subjects, eventually leaving the table to make ourselves more comfortable near the fireplace.

"I should be getting home," Lisa said at about eleven o'clock. "Oh, by the way, Roland Hill said that he would talk to you if you called tomorrow."

"How did you ever get him to agree to do that?" I asked.

She smiled. "I wouldn't be very good at my job if I couldn't get a little cooperation from people like Roland Hill."

The phone rang as I was about to thank her. The machine picked it up before I could get to it.

"This the Irene Kelly that called here earlier?" a voice asked over the speaker.

I quickly picked up the phone and said, "Yes, it is," to the twenty-third Monroe.

19

"This is June Monroe. Are you the reporter who's going to help my son?"

Her son. Oh hell, I thought, my mouth suddenly dry. I glanced over my shoulder to see Rachel and Lisa watching me intently. I hunched closer to the phone, took a deep breath. "I need to talk to you, Mrs. Monroe, but I'd rather speak to you in person."

"Hmm. This sounds like trouble to me. Have Lucas call me, then maybe I'll talk to you. But I need to talk to him first."

"I'm afraid—I'm afraid that's not possible."

"Why not?" She paused, then added, "Don't tell me he's fallen off the—" She caught herself, but I knew what she had started to ask.

"No," I said. "He hasn't been drinking."

"Oh? Then what's making you sound so nervous?"

"Could you hold on, please? I need to switch phones."

I excused myself from my guests for a moment; Cody followed me back into the bedroom, where I picked up the extension. I waited while Rachel hung up the kitchen extension.

"Mrs. Monroe?"

"I'm still here."

"I need to talk to you about Lucas, but I don't want to do it over the phone. It's late now, but—"

"Late to you, maybe. I work nights. This is the middle of the day."

Cody jumped up onto my lap. I stroked his fur, trying to

steady my nerves, while my mind frantically sought a way to gently handle this situation. "You'll be up for a while, Mrs. Monroe?"

"Yes. Why?"

"I'd like to drive out to see you."

"Now? A white woman planning on coming all the way to Riverside from Las Piernas at eleven o'clock at night, just to talk to some old black woman?" She paused, but before I could reply, she said, "What has happened to Lucas?"

I opened my mouth, but I couldn't make my voice work.

"I asked you, *what has happened to him?"*

"Please, Mrs. Monroe—"

"Don't you 'please Mrs. Monroe' me. You've got me worried past all reason now. I don't like it. You drive out here, it will take you at least an hour to get to my place. What am I going to do all that time except worry?"

"I'm sorry," I said. "I'm sorry."

There was silence on the other end of the line. Cody batted at the phone cord.

"Just tell me," she said, but her voice was softer now.

"I'm a stranger to you, Mrs. Monroe. I knew Lucas many years ago—"

"He's told me all about you. You were one of his students. You don't know me, but he's been telling me a lot about you. Lucas trusts you. He leads a lonesome life now; he doesn't trust many people. But he trusts you. That's good enough for me."

"I don't deserve it," I whispered, and never meant anything so sincerely in all my life.

"God will be the judge of that, as He will be of all of us. My son may have a few problems, but he's smart. I've never seen a child so smart as he was. He's straightening out now, getting himself on the right path. Just like I knew he would," she said. "I have always known it. Charles—his older brother—thinks I'm crazy, but he just doesn't know Lucas like I do."

"I didn't even know he had a brother," I said. Oh, yes, I thought. Let's talk about his brother, his uncles, his cousins— about anything but what has happened to your hopes.

"Well, now, never mind that. Let's just talk about Lucas," she said, taking up the reins as if she had heard my thoughts and feared I would bolt.

"I wanted to find Lucas," I began, voice unsteady. "I don't think he was ready to talk to me yet, but I needed to ask him about a photograph."

I paused, but she didn't offer any comment on the photo, so I went on.

"I was also worried about him. He hadn't been to the shelter for a few days. I called a friend of mine who—well, let's just say she works with the homeless every now and then. We asked around; talked to a lot of people who knew him, men who live on the streets. No one had seen him since Thursday."

Silence. Cody's purring not enough of a comfort.

"Eventually someone gave us some information that led us to an abandoned hotel. We found Lucas there."

"Was he hurt?" she asked, and I knew she wanted that to be the problem, knew that she had already somehow heard the truth before I spoke it.

"No. He was—he was in one of the rooms. Up high, one of the highest floors. He was lying there, very peacefully."

She made a short, high-pitched keening sound.

"His heart," I managed to choke out.

"No . . . not Lucas. Not Lucas!" she said, again and again and again.

When I thought June Monroe might hear me, I said, "You shouldn't be alone. Is there anyone who can be with you tonight?"

"You're going to be with me. I'm coming down there right now, you understand?"

I did. Perfectly. I wasn't going to be able to sleep, anyway.

"I'll call Charles. He'll take me down there. You're going to take us to see my boy. I'll call you right back."

She hung up. I sat there numbly until the phone rang in my hand.

As I held up the receiver, an angry voice came from it. "What the hell is wrong with you, calling my mother up and telling her something like that on the phone?"

"Your mother called me. And I didn't want to tell her—"

"All I got to say to you is, this damn well better be my brother. If it's anyone else, you're gonna find yourself in so much mess, you're gonna wish you were in a refrigerated drawer right next to Mr. John Doe."

"Listen, I'm sorry about your brother—"

"Save your 'sorry,' bitch."

I was on the verge of hanging up in his ear when I thought of his mother. I owed it to Lucas and to her to keep my mouth shut. I only half-listened as he spouted off a mixture of anger and abuse; it occurred to me that a lot of it was predicated on the assumption that I must have misidentified the body. If my sister, Barbara, had been lying in a faraway morgue, I probably would have held on to a similar thought—as fiercely, if not in quite the same way.

When it looked as if he would not wind down any time soon, I said, "I can give you directions, or I can let you figure it out on your own. But while you sit here giving me a hard time, your mother is alone. Either way, I'm off this phone in about another thirty seconds."

He used about five of those seconds to brood, then said, "Give me the damned directions."

When I emerged from the bedroom, Lisa was at the door, just waiting to wish me a final good night before going home. I apologized for being tied up on the phone so long.

"Was that Lucas Monroe's mother?" she asked.

"Yes," I said, surprised.

"I saw Roberta today. She told me Lucas had died of a heart attack, and that she didn't even know how to contact his family. That seemed so awful; I'm so glad you were able to help. Hard on you, though, isn't it?"

Her face was full of sympathetic concern. "I didn't know you knew Lucas," I said.

"He worked with my father. He was an unforgettable person. Very bright, always concerned with others. He was always very kind of me—used to stick up for me with Andre.

No matter what has happened since, that's how I'll choose to remember him."

If only the rest of the world would be so kind to his memory, I thought. She secured a promise to get together again soon and left.

"How will you recognize them?" Rachel asked as we waited outside of the county morgue.

"I don't think I'll have much trouble figuring out who they are," I replied, twisting a tissue to shreds. "Won't be too many people coming down here this late."

Rachel had insisted on keeping her promise to Frank to keep an eye on me, and wouldn't let me meander through town on my own. She asked me to page Frank to let him know where we would be. This set off an electronic chain reaction: Frank called back, called the morgue, and then paged Reed Collins, who then asked the coroner's office to page him when the Monroes arrived.

As it turned out, we needed Frank's help anyway. Even though the morgue is open twenty-four hours a day for receiving bodies, the normal "viewing" hours were 8:00 A.M. to 5:00 P.M. If Frank hadn't pulled some strings, I would have been the one to tell the Monroes they'd made the drive for nothing. I'm sure that would have gone over big with Lucas's brother.

We were almost twenty minutes early. I decided to wait outside; a vain attempt to not think about what went on inside of the building.

I looked up to see a woman quietly and resolutely making her way toward us on a younger man's arm. She was a fine-looking woman, a woman who took care with her appearance without becoming a lacquered mannequin. Not afraid of a few wrinkles or the gray in her short-cropped salt-and-pepper hair. Something both old-fashioned and yet lively about her.

When the man walked into the light as they drew nearer, I felt a moment of unsettling recognition. Had Lucas Monroe never lived on the streets, I thought, he would look very much like the man standing before me. I quickly amended the thought—had he stayed off the streets and grown to hate me, he would look like this man.

The woman looked at me, then glanced at Rachel, but quickly let her gaze come back to me. "You're more upset than this other one," she said. "I think you must be Irene."

Charles lost the very brief argument that would have allowed me to wait with Rachel while they went in to see the body. I wish he had won.

I do not ever again want to be in the county morgue, not unless I am dead. I do not want to stand at the side of a mother who must say of a video image of a body pulled out of a drawer, "Yes, that's my son." June Monroe did not carry on loudly, did not sob or wail. She swayed a little, and so ferociously bit the hand that flew to her mouth in a balled fist, that she drew blood from it. Charles folded her to him, setting aside the glare to make a silent request. I acknowledged it and excused myself. Reed followed me out of the room, and asked me to wait for the Monroes in a small conference room across the hall. He kept the door open, and watched for June and Charles Monroe. I spent some time dodging his questions about how I had located Lucas's mother. He wasn't very happy with me.

After a while the Monroes came out into the hallway. Reed asked her a few questions about when she had last seen Lucas. She told him that he had come to Riverside a little over two weeks ago for a brief visit. It was the first time she had seen Lucas in several years.

Reed carefully worked his way toward asking, "What did he talk about on that visit?"

She caught him at it anyway. "Nothing that would concern the police," she said, then seemed to change her mind. "He asked my forgiveness," she said, looking at Charles, not Reed. "He asked my forgiveness and he got it. He had it before he arrived."

"Just working his twelve steps, that's all," Charles said.

"My son Charles thinks that the fact that his brother went to AA somehow made that apology less sincere. I don't. Lucas wanted and received my forgiveness." She folded her arms across her chest in a gesture that said that would be that.

"When was the last time you saw your brother?" Reed asked Charles.

Charles didn't answer.

"He hasn't seen his brother since Christmas," June said, ignoring Charles's glare. "Charles came down to Las Piernas every year, as a favor to me." She paused, then added, "Not to speak to Lucas, just to let me know if he was still alive."

"Guess I ought to be grateful," Charles said. "Lucas has gone and saved me from making that trip again."

I saw June Monroe stiffen in her chair. She pursed her lips together, as though to hold back a retort. She pointedly turned her back to Charles and began to ask questions of Reed Collins. Her son was a young man, too young to have a heart attack. What did the police know about his death?

Reed was straightforward in his answers, if not detailed. He told her that although Lucas's college ring was missing, so far there was no evidence that he had died anything other than a natural death. He told her again that tests were being done just to make sure. I wondered if all of this was going right past her; she seemed numb. But she merely thanked Reed and then drew a breath and asked for time alone with me. After protests from Charles, they left us alone in the small conference room.

"Mrs. Monroe," I began, but she waved my sympathy aside before I could offer it.

"Nothing can hurt him now. I have faith, Irene Kelly. Faith. My faith sustains me. I know my son was a good man, a good, good man. I know the Lord will take care of him. Charles, he doesn't believe. He tells me he lost his faith in Vietnam, but I don't know if that's so. This will be much harder for him, I'm afraid." She closed her eyes for a moment, drawing another deep breath. When she opened her eyes again, she gave me a look that was so no-nonsense, she could have X-rayed me with it.

"Are we going to work together, Irene Kelly?"

20

"You can help my son," she said when I hesitated. "He wanted your help before he died, and you can still give it to him."

"You know what he wanted to talk to me about?"

"Yes. His reputation."

"Oh," I said.

Her mouth set into a thin, tight line. "Don't tell me I was mistaken. I told you I would trust you. Don't tell me that you're no better than that detective—Collings? Was that his name?"

"Collins. Reed Collins."

"Well, Lucas was just a bum as far as that man is concerned. I could see that from the moment he met us. Mr. Collins has other work to attend to, I'm sure. And Lucas wouldn't count for much around here, would he? So this Mr. Collins, he's just ready to just wash his hands of this whole mess."

"It's hard to tell," I said. "Reed has been following up on some things he might ignore if he just wanted to take the easy way out of this."

"Be that as it may, I'm asking you if you think Lucas was just a—a nothing, a nobody."

"Of course not. Look, Mrs. Monroe. I don't know what happened to Lucas, or how he ended up on the street—"

"That's easy. He drank. He drank and drank and drank. His father drank—drank himself to death. They say alcoholism sometimes might be genetic. I don't know if Lucas got it from his father or what. It's an illness, that's all. Some folks,

well, to them, it's a name you call somebody. Alcoholic. Like
that settles something."

She shook her head. "Well, none of that matters to me now.
All I know is that my son spent the end of his life sober. And
I know he had this idea, this dream of his. It was a quest, you
might say." She paused, then added, "I think you had something to do with that. He saw you, and he saw a way to get
back something he had lost."

"I'm sorry, I don't know what it was he—"

She didn't wait for me to finish. "Do you like the name
Lucas?"

"Well, yes, it's a fine name."

"Lucas Monroe *used* to be a good name. That's what he
lost, and that's what he wanted back. His good name. He told
me he would come home, you see, but first he—"

She was interrupted when the door opened. Charles started
to enter, caught her look of disapproval, and stayed in the doorway. He frowned back at her. "How long you gonna be?"

"You need eyeglasses?" she said.

He didn't answer.

"Did you see me walk out of that door?"

"I have to get back home."

"Go on, then," she said. "Go."

"I'm not leaving you here."

"Oh yes you are. Just get my bag out of your car. I can get
a taxicab to a hotel. You go on back to Riverside."

"I'll wait," he said in martyred tone.

She cleared her throat. "Excuse us for a moment, Ms.
Kelly."

I stood and moved toward the door. Charles was blocking
it.

"Charles Monroe," I heard her say behind me.

He put on a false smile and stepped back, bowing with ex-
aggerated politeness. "Oh, pardon me."

I went out into the hall and looked for Rachel. She was in
a waiting room at the front of the building, reading an old copy
of a tabloid magazine. She looked up over the top of it and
smiled. "Aliens will arrive any day now," she said. "This is

reported by a woman who just came back from the future."

"Does this mean I won't get a chance to collect my retirement?"

"Sorry, you're out of luck. You look tired. Ready to go home?"

"No, sorry, Rachel."

"Why not?" another voice asked. I turned to see Pete coming down the hall, Frank behind him.

"What are you guys doing here?" I asked.

"Good to see you, too," Pete said. "We come here all the time, remember?"

"Just decided to let Rachel go home," Frank said. "Reed said you were in the conference room with Monroe's mother. Has she already left?"

"No, not yet. In fact, I wanted to ask you if we could put her up for the night."

"She's staying here in town?"

"There's a lot that needs to be settled. I just can't imagine her staying in a hotel. Not after all that's happened tonight."

"You going to put both of them up?" Rachel asked.

"Both?" Pete asked.

"Her son's with her," Rachel said. "A real asshole."

"Come on, Rachel, his brother just died," I said.

She shrugged, nothing apologetic in it.

"You know these people?" Pete said. "I thought—"

"It will be fine," I said, feeling my patience slipping from me.

"I'm sure it will be," Frank said quickly, giving Pete a quelling glance. "Rachel, thanks for everything."

She laughed and put an arm around her husband. "Let's take a hint, Pete." She steered him toward the door, then called back to us over her shoulder. "Good night, Frank. *Piano, piano,* Irene."

Softly, softly. Sort of an Italian version of "take it easy." Pete was muttering complaints as the door closed behind them.

"You okay?" Frank asked.

"Honest to God, I don't know."

Charles Monroe picked that moment to come walking down the hall. "She wants to see you," he said, as if the words were full of lemon juice. He kept walking, going outside before I had a chance to introduce Frank.

"The asshole?" Frank asked.

I scowled at him. He held up his hands in mock surrender and took a seat. "I'll be right here if you need me," he said, picking up the tabloid. "Reading about this boy who can see with his ears."

When I got back to the conference room, it was clear to me that June Monroe had been crying, but her voice was steady as she said, "I want to talk to you, Irene, but I believe I'm all talked out for now. Can you recommend a good place to stay? I haven't been in Las Piernas in years, but I figure a newspaper reporter knows her way around."

"I'd like it very much if you and Charles would stay at our house."

"Oh, no. I couldn't impose. And Charles won't be staying here at all; he owns his own business in Riverside, so he has to be there early in the morning."

"It wouldn't be an imposition. We have a guest room. Please—unless you'd really be more comfortable in a hotel? I should mention that we have pets—two dogs and a cat—"

"Oh, that wouldn't be a problem. I love animals."

"You'll stay with us, then?"

She considered the offer for a moment, then said, "Thank you, yes, I will."

Charles was just about as pleased with the plan as he was with anything else connected with me that night. June merely crossed her arms and asked him to please open the trunk. He angrily obeyed, yanking the small suitcase out and setting it on the ground with a thump, then drove off without saying so much as good-bye to her.

Frank pretended not to notice what had happened, helped

her with her overnight bag, and struck up a conversation with her about the night classes she was teaching in Riverside—algebra and geometry for the adult education program.

It was two in the morning when we got home. After a raucous greeting from our pets, everyone settled in for the night. Cody decided that June needed a big cat on her bed, which seemed to please her. I was grateful for that; he might have yowled all night if denied his preferences.

Frank was in bed, drowsy, but waiting for me. He snuggled up against me, behind me, wrapped an arm around me. We talked for a while about the evening's events.

"Why did you let her son give you a hard time?" he asked.

"He's having a hard time, too. He just learned that his brother died."

"Didn't appear to be grief-stricken."

"In his own way, I think he was. Even if I had felt like arguing with him, I wouldn't have done it. It would have upset Lucas's mother."

"I guess that makes sense. Still, the guy was an—"

"Don't say it." I turned to my other side, so that I could look at him. "I don't know why you're upset with him. You've seen all kinds of reactions to death in a family—some people cry, some people get real quiet, some get angry."

He sighed. "Yeah, you're right. If I had met him under other circumstances, I might have seen it that way. But I just haven't ever watched anyone act that way toward *you*. Not and get away with it."

I smiled. "I'm okay, Tarzan."

He laughed, then reached up and stroked my hair. "If I wasn't so damned tired, I'd make you regret that remark."

I kissed him. "I'll take a rain check."

I turned back into spoon position. He nuzzled my neck, then yawned. I listened as his breathing became deep and regular.

That rhythmic breathing acted as a counterpoint to my troubled thoughts. It calmed me, kept me from dwelling on questions that could not be answered that night, kept me from worrying about June Monroe, Claire Watterson, and all the other wounded souls I could not heal. Holding me in bed that night, Frank was warm and solid, his simple act of affection as important to me as the beating of my own heart against his hand. "I like being married," I whispered, thinking he was asleep.

"Me, too," he murmured against my ear.

I woke up almost as tired as I was when I fell asleep, and twice as cold. In the soft gray light of the approaching dawn, I saw that Frank had rolled to the other side of the bed, taking the covers with him. I lay there for a time, asking myself if it was worth waking him to reclaim the blankets; I decided that the possibility of my going back to sleep was so low, I would let him get away with the theft.

I eased out of bed, wrapped myself in a robe, and stood there for a moment, watching him sleep. His big body was wrapped up in the blankets almost mummy-style, although the toes of his left foot peeked out. One arm held a pillow over the top of his head—something he does when he's especially tired. Only the lower half of his face showed beneath the pillow. To anyone else, right at that moment, he probably would have looked kind of silly. To me, well, he was going to have to make good on that rain check.

I slipped on a pair of jeans and a big sweater, put on a pair of running shoes; I thought I might take the dogs for an early morning romp on the beach. But as I approached the sliding glass door that leads to the backyard, I saw that June Monroe was sitting out on the patio, the dogs basking in her attention.

I almost stepped away, but the mutts had heard me, and came running over to the door. I went outside.

"Good morning," she said. "This surely is a beautiful yard. Did you plant this garden?"

"No," I admitted, sitting down next to her. "Frank's got the green thumb."

She looked out over the riot of crocuses, jonquils, daffodils, and other bulbs that were just coming into bloom and smiled. Deke nudged her hand and Dunk moved back and forth between us, vying for ear-scratching. "I'm surprised you can keep this garden with these two dogs back here."

"When we first got them, they nearly destroyed it more than once. Fortunately, we have a neighbor next door who thinks of these dogs as shared pets—he even helped us pick them out at the pound. He has a remarkable ability with them. I would swear to you that he just talked them out of ruining the garden."

"I believe it."

She looked weary; her weariness, I suspected, was caused by more than a lack of sleep.

"Last night you said that Lucas lost his good reputation," I said.

"Yes."

"Because he was drinking?"

She looked surprised. "Drinking? No, no. That came later." She leaned forward, lowered her voice. "You don't know about the scandal?"

"No. What scandal?"

"At the college. Lucas was accused of cheating."

"What? I don't believe it!"

"Well, that's a good start then," she said with satisfaction. "A very good start. I never believed he cheated on anything. He was too smart to need to cheat. But they kicked him out of that college anyway."

"This doesn't make any sense." The morning suddenly seemed colder. "Come inside, I'll make some coffee and you can give me this story from the beginning."

She took a seat at the kitchen table. "When was the last time you saw Lucas?"

"In about 1975 or '76."

"Hmm. Yes, that was just before the whole mess happened. Things started getting bad in about 1977. Lucas almost had his master's degree. He had just turned in his thesis. He was so proud of that thesis . . ."

Her voice trailed off, and she looked away from me. I busied myself with the coffeemaker. When it looked as if she had regained her composure, I asked, "What was the thesis about?"

"It was a study of one of the old neighborhoods in Las Piernas, how it was changing, what might be done to help make life better for the people that lived there. It was one of the neighborhoods included in the redevelopment plans."

"I suppose it makes sense that Lucas would choose something like that for his thesis topic. He was doing work with Andre Selman."

"Hmph. Andre Selman," she said. "Someday the Lord just might teach me how to forgive that man."

"Why?"

"I'm not saying he's responsible for everything that happened to Lucas. Far from it. Some of that started in our own family, and before our family. But Andre Selman caused a whole lot of trouble."

"What kind of trouble?"

"At first, he looked like a hero. Helped Lucas get a job on campus, teaching that statistics class. Took Lucas under his wing for the redevelopment study for Las Piernas. Told Lucas all this high and mighty stuff about how he was going to help Lucas go to a big university, get a scholarship—all on account of the work Lucas was doing for him with the redevelopment study. Even shared his office with Lucas; let him keep all his books and his work there. Lucas thought the world of him."

I poured two cups of coffee, gave one to her. "That must have been what was going on when I knew Lucas. If he wasn't out in the field doing research, or teaching a class, he was in that office. He seemed happy with his work and with the project. Although now that I think about it, he did warn me not to become involved with Andre."

"That doesn't surprise me. Lucas said that professor was always making a fool out of one woman or another."

I tried not to flinch. Failed.

She didn't notice. "Of course he was happy with Dr. Selman," she went on. "Try to understand what that kind of attention meant to him. Lucas was the first person in the Monroe family to get a college education. His father, his father's father, his uncles and great-uncles—none of them ever went to college. I was the first college graduate in my family, and there were days when I would have sworn to you that Lucas's father married me because he wanted his children to go to college and thought I could get them there. Charles never did too well in school, not because he wasn't bright, but because— oh, he just let things distract him. But Lucas, he was driven. He loved school, loved sociology. He thought he could make a difference in the world."

"I saw that when I was his student. You must have taught him something about teaching—he was very good at it."

"Thank you," she said softly, "but I think he was just naturally gifted." She looked away from me then, looked back out toward the garden. "Yes, he loved school . . ." Her voice trailed off. But when she looked back, her expression was one of indignation, not sadness. "You can imagine," she said, "how shocked we were when he called up to say he was being kicked out of the college."

"What happened?"

She shook her head. "You know, Irene, the biggest problem was that it took so long to figure out what really did happen. The trouble started when Lucas turned in his thesis, and this other professor, a Dr. Warren, convinced everyone on the committee that they should reject it."

"Wait a minute— Warren? Andre never got along very well with Dr. Warren. What's the connection? And what was the reason for rejecting the thesis?"

"He claimed that Lucas had cheated to make the data come out just the way he wanted it to—said Lucas had faked the numbers."

"I don't believe for a minute that Lucas would have resorted to something like phony data," I said.

"Andre Selman said the same thing. Said there must be some mistake. Made a big show out of taking out the thesis and going over it and acting real surprised. In fact, when Lucas got called before the committee, *he* was real surprised, too."

"Why?"

"It wasn't his thesis."

"You've lost me."

"Oh, there was a thesis with 'by Lucas Monroe' on the front of it all right, even lots of pages in there that were from his original thesis—most of it, really. But mixed in with the pages Lucas wrote were ones that weren't his."

"How could that be?"

"Well, that was the question, of course. Andre Selman stood up for Lucas in front of the committee, went on and on about how he knew that Lucas did fine work and was honest and so on. Then he said, 'Lucas, you must have your own copy of this thesis. Can you bring it in?'

"And of course, Lucas says he doesn't even have to go home to get it. Everything is in his office."

"Which is also Dr. Selman's office," I said.

"Exactly right. Now what do you suppose he found there?"

"It was missing."

She shook her head.

"It was there," I said slowly, "but Lucas's own copy matched the committee's."

"Yes."

"But he must have had notes, or some other way to prove—"

"This is where they really did him dirty. This is how someone knew they could get away with this. Did you ever see Lucas's handwriting?"

"Yes. It wasn't the best."

She laughed. "It wasn't legible, you mean. He used to have trouble reading it himself. Couldn't always make out his own handwriting if a week or two went by. So he had been typing up his notes since high school. And the same thing was true of his college work; he used to type almost everything. He'd take his notes and forms from the field and type them up. The good part was, it made him go over everything, organize it."

"I was talking to someone about this the other day. I remembered that he hated to write on the blackboard," I said.

"He even typed up overhead transparencies to teach his stat class."

She nodded. "So going back to that day—he's in this office, frantic. It's like something from the *Twilight Zone*. He's searching and searching for something to prove his innocence, and everything he looks at seems to prove his guilt. Things are missing, or they've been changed."

"Who had access to the office?"

"Only a few people. The chair of the department, Lucas, Dr. Selman, another research assistant, and the custodians— who weren't likely to be typing up fake pages to a thesis. Lucas said the chair of the department was in the clear as far as he was concerned. At first he was just plain puzzled. Figured somebody must have broken into the office. But of course there was no sign of that, and so the committee was growing openly skeptical about Lucas's innocence.

"So Lucas asked if he could talk to the other student who had access to the room. Nadine Preston was her name. Lucas was about to graduate—at least, that's what everyone thought—and so, at Dr. Selman's request, Lucas had been training this Nadine to take his place on the project. Did you know her?"

"No," I said.

"Pretty little red-haired gal."

"Red-haired?"

"Yes."

"She wear it in a bowl-cut?"

"Yes! I thought you said you didn't know her?"

"I didn't. But I've seen a photograph of her. Quite recently."

21

"Did you mail a set of photographs to Ben Watterson?"

"Who?"

"The president of the Bank of Las Piernas."

Before she could answer, Frank came into the kitchen. He was dressed for work, which reminded me that I needed to get myself into gear.

"Good morning," she greeted him.

"Good morning," he answered, and gave my shoulder a squeeze as he walked over to the coffeemaker.

He looked between us as he poured a cup of coffee, then asked, "Are you going into work today, Irene?"

"Yes, although I might go in a little late. June, what are your plans for the day?"

"I guess the first thing I'll need to do is rent a car."

"If you only need to get around town—"

"No, I have things to do here, but I need to get back to Riverside to . . . to make arrangements for the funeral and so on."

No one said anything.

"Charles offered to drive back down here and pick me up," she said. "But he works so hard and was up so late last night, I just hate to make him come all the way back out here. And the bus takes twice as long as driving. Besides, what it would cost to take cabs around town and then take the Greyhound home, I'd just as soon rent a car."

"There's a rental place downtown," I said. "I can drop you off on the way to work."

"Thank you."

"Do you have any other friends in Las Piernas?" Frank asked.

"Other friends?" She laughed softly and shook her head. "No, not now. I moved away from here just after Lucas started college. Our old neighborhood doesn't even exist anymore. I might be able to find some of the people I knew from the church. Some of those people might still be around here somewhere. I could find out where the church moved to, see if any of my old friends are still in the congregation. But I haven't seen any of them in so long, I wouldn't even know who to ask for."

"What do you mean, your old neighborhood doesn't exist?" I asked.

"I mean, you go to look for it, you won't find it. It's gone. You might find a lot of empty buildings and some vacant lots. That's all. We used to live in a big old hotel that had been turned into apartments. The landlord let it get so run-down, I hated that place. It wasn't the worst by any means, but it wasn't where I wanted my children to live. Lord, how I wanted to move out of that old place."

"You worked as a teacher then?"

"Yes, but that was before I had a permanent position. We moved a lot when the children were small. My late husband was a good man, but he had trouble holding down a job. And he wasn't the money-saving kind, if you know what I mean. We never had the ends to pay the rent, nothing. By the time we were living here in Las Piernas—must have been when Lucas was six or seven years old—my husband's health began to fail. A man can't drink like that and not have some kind of problem. Soon as I'd get money saved, he'd go into the hospital. Even after he died, it took me a long time to pay off all the hospital bills." She shrugged. "About the time I got free of that, I wanted to save for Lucas's college education. As it turned out, I was able to move sooner than I planned. Lucas got those scholarships and Charles made up the rest of it."

"Charles?"

"Yes. I told you he was in Vietnam. Charles sent his soldier's pay to us. Lucas used some of it, and I bought a house in Charles's and my name. I was able to move, and Lucas was able to live on campus. When Charles came back home, he lived with me in Riverside while he started his business. Later, he got his own place. Charles even helped Lucas with his graduate school expenses."

I began to understand Charles a little better. Investing his combat pay in a brother who was kicked out of school must have caused some bitterness between them. And I began to see Lucas differently as well. The committee had denied him more than a degree. Lucas had been the bearer of dreams, the one who was supposed to make it.

"Where was your old neighborhood?" Frank asked.

She named a set of cross-streets. I looked up at her.

"Do you know where that is?" she asked me.

"Yes," I said. "I was just there a few weeks ago."

I didn't tell her that her son was there as well, sleeping on a bench.

I was running late by then, so I called the city desk. But before I could tell her what was going on, Lydia said, "John wants to talk to you."

"Uh-oh."

"I'm not sure you're in trouble. He seemed cheerful when he told me that I should transfer any calls from you to his office."

"Cheerful. Lydia, cats are cheerful when they have feathers sticking out of their mouths."

"Hmm," was her only answer to that, and she transferred me.

Figuring I'd go for the "best defense is a good offense" strategy, I explained to John what had happened the night before and said that I'd be in late.

"You're not punching a clock, are you, Kelly?" he said easily.

"Not until deadline."

"Exactly," he said. "See me when you get in."

That didn't sound too promising.

"I remember one photograph, and a letter, now that you mention it," June said as we drove downtown. I had asked her again about the letters to Ben Watterson. "The letter was addressed to someone at a bank, I believe. Lucas asked me to mail it for him. He called one day, said he had left it behind when he was visiting me. Left it in his bedroom." She looked out the car window, then added, "I always had a room ready for him, whenever he wanted to stay with me. When he was in college, he'd come out there to see me all the time. Not so much—not so much later on."

When I asked her about his last visit to Riverside, she told me he had made the two-hour bus trip to Riverside one weekend; that was a few days before the first envelope arrived in Las Piernas.

"He only asked me to mail one, but he had been sending out a lot of résumés that weekend."

"Did he tell you they were résumés?"

She frowned. "Well, no, but he was down to the copy shop one day, and I guess I just assumed that was what he was doing. He had some copies made, then typed up letters and took them with him. But he forgot the one envelope. That was the only one I really saw for more than a minute or two."

"Do you know what was in it?" I asked.

"Well, I think so," she said. "He asked me to write something on the back of a photograph for him—that photo of him and the man from the bank, where Lucas was receiving a scholarship from them. His own handwriting was so terrible, and I don't think he wanted to type on the photograph. He had a letter all typed up and ready to go with it."

"Letter? Are you sure you saw a letter?"

"Of course I'm sure. I saw him put the photo in that envelope with a letter. I figured he might be looking for a job there."

So there was more than the scholarship photo in the first

envelope, which Lucas must have mailed himself, sometime before he left Riverside. June, not knowing that first letter had been mailed, would think the second envelope—the one with the photocopy—contained the photo she wrote on.

"Did Lucas show you any other photos while he was visiting?"

"No, just the one. Why do you ask?"

"I'm just trying to figure out who he was in contact with, what kinds of things he was doing during the past six weeks. Did he make any phone calls while he was in Riverside?"

"Yes, now that you mention it, he called and talked to someone named . . . let's see, what was it?" She murmured to herself for a moment. "Ed? No, Edison!"

"His last name was Edison?"

"No, his first name. I don't know what his last name was. But Lucas called him when he was at my place. I remember because Lucas insisted on leaving some money for the call. He had spent twenty dollars to ride out to see me, didn't hardly have a nickel to his name, but he left money for that call."

"Was he working?"

"Nothing too steady. But he told me he took on odd jobs from the shelter—mostly handyman work—painting, carpentry, things like that. I think he was a little embarrassed to tell me that was what he was doing, but I told him, if carpentry was good enough work for the Lord, it was good enough for him."

I wondered about the suit I had seen in the hotel room. I doubted even Jesus wore a suit to a carpentry job. I needed to talk to someone who had seen Lucas more recently.

"Do me a favor," I said. "Go over your phone bill. Try to find the number he called, the one for this Edison."

She smiled. "You *are* going to help, aren't you?"

"I would have anyway."

I figured she already knew that, but she seemed relieved all the same.

She didn't say much after that, just kept looking out the car window. Soon I realized she was studying the street people.

She was watching a man huddled in the entryway of a jeweler's shop; a bone-thin woman picking at her matted hair as she sat at a bus stop, talking to herself. At one stoplight, June stared at a sleeping figure—a man in a knit cap, curled up in a ragged sleeping bag on a wooden pallet. A man about Lucas's size. She turned to me and asked, "Where did he live?"

She meant Lucas, of course. There were so many answers to that question. I picked what I supposed was the best answer of the not-so-great alternatives. "Would you like me to take you by the shelter?"

She nodded.

I hadn't especially wanted to run into Roberta, but as it happened, she was one of the first people we saw. She had her arm around a teenager. The teenager held a pale, sleepy toddler, one child seeming not much larger than the other. Roberta was walking to the door with them when we opened it from the other side, in time to hear her say, "The clinic is just three blocks away. They'll take good care of your son—" When Roberta saw me, her arm tightened on the young mother's shoulder, causing the woman to eye me warily.

"Irene," Roberta said, then surprised the hell out of me by bursting into tears.

"What's wrong?" the young woman said with sharp concern, but Roberta only moved to embrace me. I held her a little woodenly, my own exhaustion and emotional state making it hard for me not to start crying myself. The toddler beat me to it—June and the teenager were left staring at us as the boy began to wail in sympathy.

That, fortunately, brought out Roberta's caretaker instincts. "Oh, I'm sorry!" she said, straightening and pulling tissues out of a pocket. With reassuring words she sent mother and child on their way, and I finally got a chance to introduce June Monroe.

"Lucas's mother?" Roberta asked in a strained voice.

June nodded.

Tears welled up in Roberta's eyes, but she kept them in check this time. Roberta swallowed hard and motioned us to follow her, her face a mask of misery. We walked past a roomful of people who stood in small groups, people who were chatting amiably until the kid had started howling. We were watched with curious eyes, but no one approached us as we made our way to a staircase.

That common room was the warmest-looking of the ones we passed through. The shelter had been converted from an abandoned military warehouse and office building. The living quarters had been divided into roughly two sections, one for women and children, the other for men. A food bank, job training, and other services were carried out in common areas. There were Alcoholics Anonymous and groups for dealing with other addictions and problems meeting several times a day—you couldn't stay at the shelter unless you were clean and sober.

The shelter had the look of most institutional buildings: cinder block painted over with thick coats of bargain colors, concrete floors occasionally covered with gray carpet that was not much softer, harsh lighting sporadically relieved by skylights and high windows, metal doors with shiny round doorknobs and scuffed kickplates.

And yet, here and there, someone had tried to make this fortress yield a little. Painted a mural on a wall. Put an artificial ficus tree in a corner. Taped up posters, some of which bore images of faraway vistas, though most were commercial reproductions of inspirational messages in pastel scrawls.

We turned down a hallway. Two men at the far end of it nodded and smiled at Roberta. "Tree planting tomorrow, Robbie," one called out. "Guy from the nursery came through."

"Great," Roberta said. "We have some people working on improving the playground for the family center," she explained to us.

As we passed a couple of open offices, I noticed the carpeting in them was thicker and less worn, but the furniture had the mix-and-match look of donated goods. A secretary looked up from a computer that sat on a battered wooden desk, saw Roberta, said "No messages," and went back to her keyboard.

Roberta unlocked one of the metal doors and let us into her office. Neat but crowded, it had won the struggle against starkness. Fresh-cut flowers, four big chairs, a bright blue file cabinet, and a bookcase—all helped to draw my attention from the orange sherbet walls. But not much of the walls showed anyway; they were covered with drawings by children.

A range of ages and skills were represented, in colors dark and bright—as were the subjects depicted. I was first struck by the drawings of houses. Roberta saw me studying one and said, "Yes, children without homes draw houses." Some of the houses were drawn with bars on the windows—safety or a prison? I wondered. There was a picture of a boy being stretched between a woman and a man, another of a tiny girl surrounded by four huge adults; there were pictures of Godzilla, of sharks with teeth, of boats on the water, of gravestones, of trees with big holes in them. Some depicted small figures crying big tears. Others were of hearts, flowers, smiling faces. More than one said "I love Robbie," *R*'s and *b*'s facing whichever way they pleased.

In one corner, an easel and paints stood next to a set of shelves full of toys.

"Sit down, please," Roberta said. She seemed to have regained her composure. "Mrs. Monroe, we were all very sad to hear of Lucas's death. Is there any way in which I can be of help?"

"I just wanted to see where he lived."

"Of course. I'd be happy to show you around the shelter. It's come a long way from what we started with, but there's still a lot of work to be done." She looked down at her hands folded in her lap, then said, "I will miss Lucas. I admired him."

You've changed your tune, I thought, then became angry at myself for being so critical of her. She had actually helped Lucas, while I had only run from him.

"Admired him? Why?" June asked.

Roberta looked taken aback.

"I mean," June said, "what made him any different from any other drunk that came walking in here looking for a handout? He was just another man that couldn't make it out there, right?"

While I sat wondering why June Monroe had decided to lower the temperature in the room, Roberta said, "He was not a failure. He spent six weeks sober before he died. Maybe that doesn't mean much to anybody who can pass up a drink, but to people like your son, Mrs. Monroe, that was a life—" Roberta stopped, color rising to her cheeks.

"A lifetime," June finished for her.

"Yes."

"Roberta," I said, "Lucas told you he was working on something, right?"

"I'm sorry, Irene, everything he told me remains confidential."

"But now that he's dead—" I said.

"It doesn't matter," she insisted.

"My son talked to you?" June asked.

"Yes. But I'm afraid whatever Lucas said to me in counseling sessions is privileged."

"Whose privilege?" June asked. "Yours?"

"No, Lucas's. He never told me anything intending that others would know of it. Except in cases where I believe someone may be in physical danger from a client, I have to respect confidentiality. Lucas's death doesn't change the fact that he trusted me. It's not up to me to judge what he would want others to know now that he's no longer living."

The silence which followed stretched out until I could hear the marching click of the second hand on Roberta's quartz wall clock.

"When Roberta told me that Lucas had been missing," I said, "I went looking for him. If not for her concern, I don't know how long it would have been before anyone thought of searching for him."

June Monroe nodded. "Thank you for taking care of my son," she said to Roberta. "I would like to see where he stayed."

We made a brief tour of the shelter. It offered spartan but clean accommodations. A simple bed or cot—perhaps nothing more than a floor space on a cold night. But to someone living on the street, I suppose its hot showers and flush toilets made it look like the Ritz. It seemed it would almost be like living at one's high school gym. There was no real privacy, and yet I could not help feeling that we were intruding in someone's home, and was glad when we walked on to the dining area.

One of the men in the kitchen had been a friend of Lucas, and as he told June Monroe how much he would miss her son, Roberta pulled me aside.

"Thank you for sticking up for me, but I didn't really search for him or even take very good care of him," she said. "And I wasn't very encouraging when you talked to me at Ben's funeral. Of all the people who asked me about Lucas after that SOS meeting, I think you were the only one who really cared about him."

"Who asked about him?"

"Oh, let's see. Ivy, Marcy, Becky, and even Jerry and Andre."

"Jerry and Andre? They weren't at the meeting. How—?"

"The morning before Andre's heart attack, Andre called and asked if Lucas was living here. I guess Lisa must have mentioned it," she said. "She's staying with Jerry, you know."

"Shit. I didn't realize that many people overheard us that night. And if word spread beyond— What did they want to know about Lucas?"

"How he was doing, why he was at the shelter, what had become of him, and so on."

"What did you tell them?"

"Nothing. No one seems to understand my position—"

"No, you're wrong," I said. "I understand it. There's a version of that in my business, too."

"Of course. Your sources."

"Right. It just makes it a little irritating when I want to know something and somebody *else* wants to invoke confidentiality. Think of Lucas, for example. I know he was involved in something important—something that was important not only to him personally, but also to the city, to the people who live here. But now he's dead. So what happens to that important information he had?"

"It dies with him," she said. "At least as far as I'm concerned."

I crossed my arms to keep myself from reaching out and shaking her. "For your sake, Roberta, I hope everyone believes that's true."

"What do you mean?"

"I mean, maybe someone realized that Lucas had to be sober to stay here. They overhear you say that he wants to get in touch with me—a newspaper reporter. You said . . ." I thought back. "You said, 'The things he wants to talk to you about are *important,*' then you added something about 'When he makes his case this time, he wants to do it right.' Doesn't that sound like Lucas was on some kind of quest?"

"Well, perhaps."

"Think, Roberta! Suppose someone didn't want Lucas's quest to succeed."

"But that can't matter now. He's dead."

"Don't you get it? No one is certain that Lucas died a natural death."

"The police said it was a heart attack!"

June Monroe turned toward us when she heard Roberta say this. Her eyes narrowed, and she began to walk back to where we stood.

"Be careful, Roberta. I mean it. Please."

I suddenly realized that I sounded just like Frank. I hoped Roberta wasn't as stubborn as I am sometimes.

"You should be careful, too," she said. "I heard about, well, his street name is Two Toes."

"You know him?"

"Yes, he's much brighter than he may seem, and that's partly why he's dangerous—he's delusional, not dumb. Most schizophrenics are intelligent, a few are violent. He's both. Without discussing particulars, let's just say a person may not be violent because he's schizophrenic. Perhaps he's like other violent people: he grew up with it, worked with it, or lived with it. Often it's in his history long before the onset of his schizophrenia. Even when he's not on medication, Two Toes can be very lucid and rational. In those times he controls his anger. At other times he's childlike or just withdrawn. Most of the time he's harmless, but he has had episodes of becoming extremely brutal. Don't underestimate him."

"Thanks, I won't," I said, just as June reached us. "Ready to go?" I asked her.

"Yes," she replied, studying us.

"Wait!" Roberta said. "It just dawned on me. Lucas's things."

"His things?" June asked.

"From his locker. We—we cleaned it out yesterday. But I didn't know where to send his things. I suppose you should have them, Mrs. Monroe."

She took us back to her office, and opened one of the file drawers. She pulled out a brown paper grocery sack, gave it to June.

June didn't open the sack until we were back in the car. As we sat in the parking lot near the shelter, I watched her examine Lucas's meager legacy.

At first, it appeared to contain nothing more than a few articles of clothing. She pulled each carefully folded item out of the bag and placed it on her lap.

A gray T-shirt.

Two pairs of white socks, one dark pair.

Three pairs of briefs. Perhaps someone else would have been embarrassed, or even thought it comical to see underwear pulled out of a bag. I only felt sad when I saw them. A T-shirt could have been worn by anyone. Not these most intimate items. Death with dignity. What a laugh. This kind of accounting of personal belongings is due to all of us some day, I suppose. Perhaps it's best if it comes to us only after death.

June kept reaching into the bag. Next came a handful of AA tracts. I was looking through them when I heard her moan softly. In her hand was a little Bible.

"I gave this to him," she said, and pressed it to her lips. She was crying as she handed it to me.

There was a piece of paper in the Bible, marking the Twenty-third Psalm. I was trying to make out something scrawled on the paper when June Monroe pulled out the last item in the bag.

22

"His thermos," she said.

"His thermos? Why would a man with so few possessions need two thermos bottles?" I asked.

"No, there's only one in here," she said.

"There was also one in the hotel room. At the Angelus."

"I don't understand . . ."

"There was an open thermos bottle in the room where he died. But this thermos was here, at the shelter. So someone else must own this one . . . or someone else owned . . ."

"Why are you looking like that all of a sudden?" she asked. "Is there something I'm not understanding? You're saying this Two Toes fellow who took Lucas's ring left this thermos behind?"

"No. The homicide detective you talked to last night—now that I think about how he put it, he wasn't very clear with you about this. Even though Lucas died of a heart attack, the coroner was puzzled, because Lucas seemed to have a healthy heart. That's why the coroner is doing the toxicology studies."

"Poison?"

"He thought it was a possibility. But the studies take weeks to complete."

"You're saying someone brought Lucas some kind of something in that other thermos?"

"I'm saying it's very possible. A lot of things in the hotel room didn't make sense—the missing ring, the pennies, the scrapes and bruises. But now we know that the thermos wasn't Lucas's. It explains how someone could have poisoned him."

"Someone poisoned my boy . . ." She was looking at me in total disbelief.

"Maybe."

"Who? Who would want to kill him?"

"I'm not sure. Maybe someone felt threatened by him."

"Threatened? By a man who lived like this?" she asked, motioning toward the shelter. She leaned her head back and closed her eyes. Big tears rolled down her face. "Why wouldn't he come home to me?" she whispered. "Why live in these places? On the streets of this city? I could have offered him a roof and meals. I would have taken care of him."

I didn't say anything.

She shook her head. "Pride. That devil's pride in him. So hard in him, like a rock. Nothing could break it."

I looked out across the parking lot, watching a group of men walking slowly toward the shelter door. "I'm not sure the people out here always know why they stay on the streets," I said. "Maybe there aren't any good reasons. But as for Lucas—how old was he when his father died?"

"About twelve, I guess. Why?"

"Old enough to be aware of his father's drinking, and maybe what it cost you?"

She sighed. "Yes, I'm afraid so."

"So maybe he just wanted you to be proud of him, and he wasn't quite there yet. Like that money for the phone call."

"What do you mean?"

"He probably knew you could afford the call he made to Las Piernas. Maybe he just needed to show you that he wanted to pay his own way."

"But I would have cared for him better than these people did. He'd rather be here all alone, not a friend in the world."

"He had friends here."

"Who? That man in the kitchen? You?"

"I wasn't much of a friend. I've admitted that to you. But Lucas made friends here. Even on the street. His friends helped me find him. They respected him. He protected some of the weak ones from the bullies."

"That was his way," she said. "Even as a kid."

She pulled herself together, then began carefully replacing the contents of the grocery bag. She looked over at me, and I realized that I still had the Bible on my lap. I started to close it, saw the note again.

"Can you read this?" I asked, handing it to her.

"The Lord is my shepherd," she began.

"Er, no, I meant the scrap of paper."

"Oh." She frowned over it, then said, "This doesn't make any sense."

"I couldn't make it out either," I sighed.

"Oh, I think I can make it out. It just doesn't make any sense. It says, 'She rubs.'"

She passed it back to me. I studied it again, now that I had a hint of how to proceed. "How did he get such good grades with such lousy handwriting?" I asked.

"Teachers are as good as pharmacists at reading bad hand-writing. His teachers knew he was bright—and you wouldn't believe how hard some of them worked with him on it. He printed lots of things—his printing wasn't as bad as his handwriting. But mostly it was just that they knew he was trying. Might have had some kind of learning disability, I don't know. In those days, they didn't test for things the way they do now."

"This is an *s?*" I asked, looking at the first mark on the paper.

She looked at it again. "I think so. Or maybe a *c.*"

"A *c?* Then it would make sense. Cherubs."

She smiled a little. "Well, that's a more sensible note to leave in a Bible."

I drove her over to the rental car place, wondering if she was right. Maybe the Good Book wasn't the inspiration for the note. After all, Lucas Monroe had died surrounded by angels.

Geoff's greeting didn't do anything to soothe my nerves as I entered the Wrigley Building. The old security guard shook his head slowly and said in funereal tones, "Mr. Walters is very happy."

"Any idea what's caused this monumental change in affect?"

"You mean, why is he so happy?"

I nodded.

"You."

"Oh. Well, I'm sure it can't be as bad as all that," I said, heading for the stairs.

"And I thought *I* was an optimist," I heard him mumble behind me.

I ignored the stares of coworkers, the drop-off in both conversation and keyboard clatter as I made my way across the newsroom. I had thought to stop by Lydia's desk, but decided not to prolong my misery. I glanced over to see her catching the tip of her nose between two fingers, scissors-style—as if snipping it off. It was an old signal between us from our school days, one I hadn't seen since the last time I got sent to the principal's office. *Better no nose than a brown nose,* it meant, invented long ago as a response to Alicia Penderson's shameless kissing up to the nuns. Alicia had been in serious danger of putting a new crease in the backside of Sister Vincent's habit.

I smiled, returned the gesture, and knocked on the frame of John's open office door. "Hello, John. You wanted to see me?"

My smile must have taken him aback, because he scowled briefly before saying, "Come in, Irene. And close the door." Once the door was shut, he smiled again and said, "Have a seat."

He then went back to looking at a computer monitor, where he was scrolling the wire—browsing through the long directory, looking over the lead paragraphs of stories filed on the wire service. I took a quick peek over his beefy shoulder to see what he was reading and noticed there was nothing urgent or local on the monitor. The faker.

Unfortunately for John, I recognized the trick as one that Sister Vincent herself had often used: stall and make them squirm. My immunity to this tactic built by experts, I leaned back in my chair and studied my fingernails as if they had the winning lotto numbers painted on them.

"How's the story on Moffett coming?" he asked, not looking at me.

"Oh, just swimmingly."

He turned to look at me, his scrutiny real this time.

"So tell me about it."

"I've met with Corbin Tyler and it looks like I'll finally be able to interview Roland Hill. So I'm meeting with some people who worked very closely with him. I expect to have more by the end of the week . . ."

"Dammit, Kelly, you work for a *newspaper,* not a goddamned history journal! The man resigned on Thursday. Monday, I practically had to chain you to your chair. It's now Tuesday and you're strolling in here late. Maybe I should put someone else on to this. Someone who has time to be a reporter. Maybe Dorothy Bliss should be handling this one."

That brought me to my feet. "You want a load of half-assed, meaningless bullshit on your front page, go right ahead. You'll have a column full of conjecture and nothing to back it up. She puts more filler in her stories than a flat-chested girl could stuff into a bra on prom night!"

"At least this newspaper would appear to be looking into the matter of Moffett's sudden resignation!"

"That's *all* it would be, John. Appearance! Quotes from ten people who don't know diddly, filled in with could-it-be crap. 'Could it be that Mr. Moffett really needed more time to care for his ailing poodle?' 'Could it be that younger higher-ups were demanding more than the old commissioner could deliver?' "

"Kelly . . ."

"Maybe she'll make it dramatic." I put my hand over my heart and went into a Betty Boop voice, the closest I can come to imitating Dorothy. " 'There's an empty office in city hall. Very, very empty. Outside, on the door of the office, an equally empty slot, a place where a narrow brass plaque bearing a very important name should be. Everyone here knows the missing name on the missing plaque. Could it be that these uneasy, silent coworkers know why it's missing?' "

He started stabbing his blotter with a ballpoint pen. I went for broke.

" 'As this reporter looked at the sun-faded carpet, the little bitty indentations where the big oak desk used to sit, the really, really big oak desk that once had a really, really big leather chair behind it . . .' "

"That's enough!"

"Oh, sure it is," I said, dropping the act. "Give the story to Dorothy and you'll get ten inches on the office decor alone, no sweat. Smoke and mirrors. But what the hell? You're in a hurry. Go ahead and give it to her. Call me if you start to be curious about what really happened." I started for the door.

"Sit down!"

I hesitated, decided to turn and face him. One look at his mottled red face convinced me I should sit down.

His eyes narrowed. "You are the most insolent, insubordinate—"

"This is so much better than what I expected."

That stopped him for a moment. "What the hell are you talking about?"

"You were in a good mood this morning. Scared the hell out of everyone in the building."

He rubbed a hand over his face and sighed. "Haven't seen enough of you around here lately, Kelly."

"What's that supposed to mean?"

"I was irritated with you, that's all. A suggestion was made, and I thought it might solve some of our current difficulties."

"What suggestion?"

He shook his head. "I've changed my mind."

We sat there in silence for a moment. John started tapping the pen again.

"Can we start over?" I asked.

He looked up at me.

"I mean, about the Moffett story," I went on. "I need you to forget two things."

"Namely?"

"First, forget that I ever knew Lucas Monroe."

His scowl returned. "And?"

"And forget that Lucas was homeless."

"That's quite an attack of amnesia you're asking for."

"Stay with me for a minute. Ben Watterson, Allan Moffett, and a handful of other civic leaders were very heavily involved in redevelopment in the 1970s, right?"

"*Lots* of people got involved."

"This group more than others. Think of how easy it would be for a group of investors to make money with the kind of inside information Allan Moffett could supply."

"Give me your version."

"A group of investors learns—very early on—that a certain area is going to be declared a redevelopment zone. They buy run-down buildings for a very low price. They pick up one seedy property after another. Just to stick with round numbers, let's suppose we have two general partners who put in five thousand dollars each. They pick up a hotel for ten thousand."

I saw him jot the numbers down on the back of a memo from Wrigley, more in the way of absent doodling than any serious preparation to do math. "Okay," he said. "Go on."

"Studies are done, and lo and behold, the city decides the hotel is within a redevelopment zone. The city might have reasonably decided this old hotel should be rehabilitated into low-cost housing, but the investors believe more money is to be made from office buildings. Another study is done, one that influences the Land Use Element, and somehow it reflects a need for office buildings."

"And the tenants are evicted."

"Maybe even beforehand. That might help to convince the city that this isn't residential property. Now the investors get other benefits—low-cost loans, courtesy of the taxpayer; expedited permits and special construction variances; and so on. But for now, let's just go back to our ten thousand. Their next move is to present a fancy brochure and prospectus to sell limited partnerships. Let's say they sell one hundred shares at ten thousand dollars a share."

"They've raised a million dollars," he said. "Probably from people looking for tax shelters, maybe a group of doctors who don't have any real estate experience."

"Right about the real estate know-how, but these things attract teachers, firefighters, retirees—anyone with a nest egg. The general partners get 'highest and best use' studies and market surveys and all sorts of statistics together and dazzle the hell out of the investors. California real estate was booming then. Our general partners would work to convince everyone that the boom is permanent, that the downtown area will revive and that every lousy square foot of land in Las Piernas will be worth a fortune."

"The downtown area *has* revived."

"Some of it. Certainly not all. You know what the office vacancy rate is. And not all of the construction was first-rate. But let's go back to our general partners. They pay themselves administrative fees. Let's say they charge each limited partner a five percent fee."

"That's five hundred each. Fifty thousand all together."

I shook my head. "Fifty thousand *per year.* And since the limited partners can't make decisions about the construction or leasing, if the hotel project goes to hell, they have no recourse—they pay those annual fees anyway."

"Or sell their shares."

"Which may be worthless," I said. "The limited partners are at the mercy of the general partners."

"Which is what the greedy little limited partners get for trying to avoid taxes."

"I disagree, but we'll argue that another time. Besides, what I just presented is probably a worst-case scenario. Let's suppose the general partners just sell their own shares in the hotel building for a big profit and get out. Or maybe they don't even bother with the limited partnerships—they sell the building for a more modest profit. No matter what happens, they've probably made money—and made it because they had inside information."

"Your point being?" he said, but he was leaning forward in his chair now.

"Redevelopment was one of three things that Allan Moffett and Ben Watterson had in common. They were part of a group of men who often worked together on these projects, even if some of them—like Allan—supposedly weren't personally profiting from it."

"And?"

"Second, they were longtime, active civic leaders who seemed unwilling—until very recently—to step aside from their roles. No one would have predicted that Ben would commit suicide or that Allan Moffett would resign. And yet they did so within a day of each other. What are the odds of that happening, John?"

"Go on."

"The third thing they have in common is Lucas Monroe. At least twice in each of their lives."

"Twice?"

"Remember those studies? The earliest statistics Allan needed to set the wheels in motion—to declare an area of the city a redevelopment zone—came from a study Lucas Monroe worked on in the 1970s."

"And Monroe saw each of them recently."

"Contacted them anyway." I told him about the photocopy.

"Hmm. Too bad he's dead." It was said in an offhand manner, a newsman's regret for the loss of a source. But seeing my face he added, "Aw, Kelly, for Godsakes—"

"Forget it. I've given up getting so much as an obit for him. I just want you to realize that trying to find out what he was up to is not just a personal project." Thou doth protest too much, a little voice said. I ignored it. "I'll know more about Moffett's resignation if I can learn why Lucas went to see these people."

"You think he was blackmailing them?"

I quelled an impulse to immediately deny it. "Maybe."

After a long silence, he said, "Suppose you're wrong. What if your friend wasn't doing anything more than trying to find a job?"

"Then I'm still talking to Allan's nearest and dearest pals."

I shrugged. "I'm still trying to pry things out of Allan's former coworkers. It would take a vast conspiracy or blackmail scheme of his own to keep that many people silent. I don't think he could manage it, frankly. I suspect they really don't know why he left. Even his former secretary—who would love to have her revenge on him—couldn't offer me anything more than word of Lucas's visit, tales of a night Allan spent shredding papers, and the story of his hastily arranged dinner party. I'm planning to try to talk to her again."

"Anyone else?"

"The other people who were at the meeting. I may even try to track down Allan's first wife."

"If I allow you to keep following this angle, you suppose you could devote more of your time to this story?"

"John, as far as I'm concerned, I worked on this story over the weekend—on my days off."

"Admit it, Kelly, that was a personal matter that happened to dovetail with this story."

"Okay, fine. Have it your way."

"Just like that?"

"Just like that. Maybe I'm not the most insolent, insubordinate—What else did you call me, John?"

"That's as far as I got. And no one else around here comes close to being as much trouble as you are."

"Thanks. Do I get to find out what you had planned for me this morning?"

"And like I said, follow up with the Lucas Monroe angle, too."

"I intend to. Now what was going on?"

Finally realizing I didn't intend to be sidetracked, he said, "A pager."

"A pager?" I shook my head. "I hate those things."

"I know, I know."

"Electronic leashes. You start out thinking it will help people get in touch with you, but nine times out of ten it's some nuisance message."

"I know how you feel about them, Kelly."

"It's just that once I was talking to this city hall source—took me three days of phone calls to finally get this secretary to meet with me, and four or five hours of hanging out together before she started to drop her guard a little. Just as I think she's about to confirm a rumor for me, on the verge of coming across with everything I need to know, the damn beeper goes off. Air raid sirens wouldn't have caused the woman less alarm. She was out of there. And I go looking for a pay phone, finally find one that works, and now I'm madder than hell. I answer the page and it's—" I stopped cold. Uh-oh.

"It's me, wondering if you knew where we were supposed to meet O'Connor for drinks after work."

"Well, that's not the point. But knowing how I feel about them, John, why make me carry one?"

"It's nothing personal. Well . . . at least, not between you and me. Wrigley wants everyone who works news to wear one. Half the others wear them now. Get used to the idea."

"If it's not personal, why wasn't the new policy announced in a meeting?"

"There will be one later today. But I was supposed to deliver yours to you this morning. Wrigley's request. He's impatient for your story."

"You said you changed your mind—does that mean you've figured out how to get me out of this?"

"No. But I'll wait until the meeting to give you yours."

Comprehension dawned. "I see. Wrigley arranged a show. I'd be singled out, everyone in the newsroom would know it, and they'd assume I caused the change in policy."

"Something like that."

"And you were happy to go along with it, John?"

"Don't try to blame me. You know you've made your own contribution to this mess with Wrigley," he said.

I couldn't argue with him about that. John was often caught in the middle of my ongoing war with Wrigley. "Well, screw it, then. Go ahead and give me the beeper now."

"Look, Kelly—"

"Give me the beeper. And if Wrigley wonders why I'm not at the staff meeting, tell him maybe he should try to page me."

If the people in the newsroom wondered how I had managed to return John to his crabby self, they didn't ask me to my face. I was too busy to worry about their reactions.

I checked my phone messages. Murray was waiting to see me, and Claire had called. I had been planning to call her anyway, but I wanted to follow up on a couple of other things first.

Through his secretary, I made an appointment to see Roland Hill that afternoon. You would think the woman hadn't been hanging up in my ear for nearly a week.

Next, I called Ivy Vines.

"I need your help with a couple of things," I said.

"Sure. What can I do for you?"

"I'm trying to figure something out. You dated one of Andre's friends before you got involved with Andre, right?"

"Yes. That's how I met you, remember? I was still dating Jeff when you were with Andre."

"Jeff, the setup man," I said. "Whenever Andre wanted to break up with someone, Jeff made sure she walked in on Andre and his new flame."

"I didn't know Jeff did that for Andre until much later," she said meekly. "Sorry."

"C'mon, Ivy. No need to apologize. Until we all started talking to one another, none of us knew Andre's M.O.—ancient history by then."

"I should have guessed what Jeff was up to. I've thought about it a lot since then. Anyway, what do you need to know?"

"I'm trying to fill in a blank or two, Ivy. I was with Andre after Helen. Alicia was after me. Were you after Alicia?"

"No, I was a couple of women later."

"Who was with Andre after Alicia?"

"Hmm. Alicia didn't last too long, as I recall. I think she was just trying to take him away from you."

"Yeah, well, it wasn't the first time she went after one of my boyfriends, but it was the first time she got what she deserved."

"Nobody deserves Andre. Not even Alicia."

"True," I admitted.

"I don't remember who Andre was with after Alicia. I could try to find out—wait—I know, we could ask Lisa."

I thought back to my conversations with Lisa. Lisa had sounded so embittered. "I'd rather avoid that if at all possible, Ivy. Lisa has enough reminders of what a jerk he is without having to recite a litany of his old girlfriends."

"Good point," she said.

"Actually, I don't really need a list of people. I'm just trying to find out about one woman," I said. "Someone named Nadine Preston."

"Nadine! Oh, God," she groaned. "I remember her!"

"You do?"

"Yes, because of what happened with Jeff." She paused, then said, "Nadine really fell hard for old Andre. Wonder why we've never thought of her for SOS? She holds a record."

"I'm confused. A record?"

"Burned by the same fire twice."

"What are you talking about?"

"Andre never got back together with anyone, even if she was masochistic enough to beg him to take her back—right?"

"Right."

"Except Nadine. Technically, anyway. A very brief reunion."

I was astonished. "Are you saying she went *back* to him?"

"Yes. Jeff made a big deal out of it. He was really angry with Andre about it. It was ridiculous. I don't think Nadine and Andre were back together for more than a couple of weeks. Jeff spent more time being upset about it than Nadine and Andre spent being back together."

"Why should Jeff care if Andre was reunited with an ex, especially if it was only for a few days?"

"I tried to find out, but he never told me. He just said that it could only mean trouble. Nadine ended the friendship between Andre and Jeff."

"You lost me somewhere in there, Ivy. I would think Jeff's friendship with Andre ended because Andre lured *you* from his side."

"No, their friendship was already over. It almost ended when Nadine got together with Andre the first time. Jeff told him he was taking a big chance, because Nadine worked for Andre as a graduate assistant."

"She was an exception there, too, wasn't she?"

"Right. Andre used to have a rule: none of his own students, no one who worked for him."

"And Nadine was working for Andre when they got together?" I asked.

"Yes. Jeff thought that was a mistake, but Andre told him to mind his own business. I think it must have hurt Jeff. Until Andre broke up with Nadine, Jeff stopped hanging out with him. I don't think things were ever really the same between them after that. So when Andre got back together with Nadine, Jeff really felt betrayed. Not that I have any room to talk about betraying Jeff—"

"I don't get it. Jeff wasn't attracted to her himself?"

"Not at all. That much, I'm sure of."

"Then it was a pretty severe reaction, wasn't it? Jeff must have seen Andre with dozens of women. Why would it bother him to see Andre get back together with someone?"

"Jeff just didn't like her. He said that Andre was nuts to date Nadine in the first place. He would never elaborate on it. I tried to smooth things out between them, but Jeff wasn't interested. By then, things weren't going so well with Jeff and me—he had other problems that got in the way of our relationship. But I guess Andre took advantage of that—got back at him by stealing me away from him."

"Whew."

"Yes. Not a time I'm very proud of."

"Ivy, none of us left Andre with our pride intact."

She didn't say anything.

"So why do you think Andre broke his own rules with this woman?" I asked.

"I don't know. They didn't last too long the second time—like I said, a couple of weeks or maybe even less. That's why I thought Jeff was being ridiculous. Andre used to ask me about it. Andre and I didn't last long together. I was just looking for a way out of my relationship with Jeff. And I think Andre was more interested in trying to find out what Jeff had told me about Nadine than he was in dating me. I always had to tell him what I'm telling you—Jeff thought Andre had crossed some kind of boundary by dating someone he worked with, and he didn't think Nadine was trustworthy. But maybe Jeff would have ended that friendship anyway. I don't know."

"So who arranged for Nadine to walk in on you and Andre?"

"No one. *She* left *him.*"

"What?"

"Yes. I think they must have had a fight out on the boat. Went fishing one day, and that was that."

That's three records for Nadine, I thought, becoming all the more curious about her. Andre dated his own graduate assistant, reconciled with her, and she left him before he could leave her. "Ivy—do you still have that friend in the college records office?"

"Sure. You want me to have her track down Nadine?"

"Yes. If the records office doesn't have a current address, maybe your friend could find out if Nadine Preston has asked for transcripts to be sent somewhere."

"I'll do what I can."

"Even if I could get her student ID number—it's the same as her Social Security number, right?"

"Right," she said. "You think you might be able to locate her with that?"

"Maybe. By the way, you wouldn't happen to know where Jeff is these days?"

There was a long silence. "You honestly don't know?"

"No."

"I guess you weren't around then."

"Around when?"

"Jeff killed himself not long after I left him."

"Jeff? I can't believe—" I quickly realized that it was the wrong thing to say. The trouble was, there was no right thing to say. "I—I'm sorry, Ivy. I didn't know."

"It was a long time ago," she said, sounding as if it wasn't.

"It happened when you were living in Bakersfield, I guess."

"No one told me—"

"Don't worry about it. Now, where should I call you with the information? Are you going to be in your office?"

I looked at the little black object on my desk. "Let me give you my pager number."

23

I traveled the twists and turns of the building's corridors, my thoughts so absorbed with Ivy's revelations that I passed up the room occupied by the business section and had to double back.

I worried about Ivy, thought of how carelessly I had referred to Jeff throughout the conversation. I had undoubtedly opened old wounds. Ivy had always been kind to me, and inadvertently, I had been unkind to her.

Nadine Preston occupied my thoughts as well. Andre—who was so unwavering in his relationship patterns that a hundred women could recite them chapter and verse—had been remarkably unpredictable in his dealings with her.

I caught up with Murray at his desk. He was hard at work on the Sunday real estate section, which would go to press on Thursday morning. Watching him work on predated pages, I remembered how disillusioned I was when—early on in my study of journalism—I learned that the whole paper wasn't always printed up the night before it was delivered.

Murray looked up when I cast a shadow across his desk, glanced around, and saw that we were alone. Probably in a world of his own until I stood in his light.

"What have you got for me?" I asked.

He smiled and opened a desk drawer. "I don't know how you found out about this before I did," he said. "Swear you'll keep me posted on your progress?"

"Girl Scout's honor? Or may I simply cross my heart?"

He tugged at a manila clasp envelope, pulling it out of the drawer but keeping it in his hand. "Here are the records on the area near the Angelus. You wanted the redevelopment projects for 1974–78 with Tyler, Hill, Dage, and Watterson, right? I did that, but I also looked up a couple of other items, including the current status of ownership in the area. This has turned out to be very interesting," he said, opening the clasp. "Right now, the building next to the Angelus is owned by Hill and Associates."

"Roland Hill's company. I remember seeing construction work being done on it."

"Hill owns several of the buildings surrounding it. If there's construction being done on any of them, Keene Dage's company is doing the work. He owns one or two of the properties himself, as does Corbin Tyler."

He pulled out a sheet of paper and handed it to me. It was the current list. The name at the top of the list surprised me.

"Keene Dage owns the Angelus?"

"You sound shocked. He hasn't owned it for very long; officially, just for a couple of weeks. That's not the most important thing you can learn from that list, anyway."

I studied it. "Most of these were purchased within the last month," I said.

"Keep that in mind. Now look at the list of owners for these same properties a year ago."

He handed another sheet of paper to me. There was only one owner listed for all of the properties. Pacific View Associates.

"Pacific View Associates? Didn't you write about them recently? They're on the verge of bankruptcy, right?"

He smiled. "Yes. Most of PVA's properties are going cheap, although that may change soon. But we'll come back to that in a moment. There's the list of owners for the years you asked for. Take a look."

I studied this list for a moment, then said, "Hill owned almost all of the properties that PVA owns now."

"Exactly."

"I don't get it. Why would Hill sell it to PVA, then buy it back again?"

"Hill, Dage, and Tyler—the businessmen on your list. Sometimes Hill brings in other investors, but very few others are involved. Let's just say Hill for now. He has an uncanny ability, wouldn't you say? Buys very cheap, sells higher, buys cheap again. He has an eye for choice properties."

"You said 'choice properties.' Forgive me if I don't see this section of town as 'choice.'"

"Irene, you disappoint me! You're never going to make the kind of money these people do if you don't learn to use your imagination. Where did Las Piernas plan to build a convention center?"

"I'll never make that kind of money anyway. But to answer your question—until recently, down on the waterfront."

"And?"

I frowned, thinking over what I knew about the project. "The plans for the convention center have become a big disappointment to a lot of folks; those waterfront properties belong to a mixture of owners, including the city itself. But the California Coastal Commission put the kibosh on the plans last week, and it's not clear if the city will spend the time and money fighting it because—Oh, hell."

"My faith in you is about to be restored," Murray said.

"I should have thought about the area less than a block away from the Angelus. Las Piernas may not fight the Coastal Commission, because there are alternative sites. One of the alternative sites for the convention center is near the Angelus, isn't it?" I closed my eyes for a moment, picturing the area. "It's not on the shore, so it's out of Coastal Commission jurisdiction. But it's on a slight rise, so anything built there still could be ocean view, especially if you made it tall enough. And unlike most of the other proposed sites, there is a high rate of vacancy in the area—which is partly what's killing PVA. With fewer tenants to move, if you put the convention center there, you wouldn't get many complaints."

"Bingo!" Murray said.

"So Hill and his friends buy the property for low prices in the 1970s, sell it to PVA for a profit, and then buy it back when they get some indication that things might not go well with the Coastal Commission. A commission that's looking at plans that Allan Moffett could influence."

"Easily," Murray agreed. "Even if he didn't draw up the plans himself, his lackeys wouldn't ignore his suggestions. Knowing that certain elements of any waterfront plans might cause the Coastal Commission to balk, he could use his influence to ensure those elements were included."

"Or purposely exclude elements the Coastal Commission would want. And he probably oversees the cost projections on fighting the Coastal Commission's decision as well."

Murray nodded. "Determining that it would be better to move the project away from the shore."

"But Hill and his friends couldn't have planned this from the late 1970s, could they?"

Murray shook his head. "While it's not impossible—there has been talk of a convention center for many years—my guess would be that they steered toward opportunities wherever they saw them. They got out of the Angelus area when it didn't look like it would go anywhere, put their capital to better uses. They got back in when new opportunities were on the horizon."

"Or they decided to head back to these properties when inside information was given to them."

"Yes, well, that is always a possibility," he said, then smiled and added, "Not that I would ever imagine such a thing happening in our fair city."

"Not in a billion nanoseconds. Thanks for the information, Murray. Now, I believe I owe you a favor."

He didn't deny it, and his look of anticipation caused me to laugh. "Yes, Jack Fremont will talk to you. Want me to have him call you?"

"You need to ask?"

I went back to the newsroom and pulled out the Riverside phone book again. Stuart Angert was openly curious about my meeting with John; I told him that he'd have the whole story by that afternoon and repressed the urge to tell him to page me if he had any questions after the staff meeting.

At my desk, I covertly copied my pager number down, a series of digits that seemed to defy mnemonics. I opened the phone book to the M's, looked up June Monroe's number again, wrote it down, and put the phone book back, still refusing to give in to Stuart's pestering.

I called the Riverside number, knowing she would not be back home yet. When her answering machine picked up the call, I said, "June, I need to ask you a couple of questions," and left my pager number.

I leaned back in my chair for a moment, thinking about the list of things I wanted to follow up on. I hoped the records office at the college came through. If I could talk to Nadine Preston, I might get closer to understanding what had gone on with Lucas Monroe's thesis.

I called Claire.

"I've got a lot to talk to you about," I said.

"Are you free for lunch?" she asked.

"Sure."

"Would you mind coming out to the house? I know it's a long way from work for you, but it's so hard for me to be out in public right now . . ."

"I understand. It won't be a problem for me to be away from the office," I said, wondering if maybe I could get used to the pager idea.

Naw. I knew I couldn't. Especially not after I met Wrigley on my way out of the building.

"Irene!" he called out, with more bonhomie than Santa. He was acting like we were old pals. I knew what had inspired this. I once quit the paper, and every time Wrigley worries that he's insulted me enough to get me to jump ship again, he gets avuncular at best and downright kissy at worst.

He crossed the building lobby to come closer, but kept a respectful distance. He's an ass-pincher, but he's never tried that with me. Maybe it's because I once circulated a tall tale around the building about breaking someone's nose for doing that. By the time Wrigley heard the story, I think I had supposedly put someone in the hospital.

"I hope you aren't too upset about the pager," he said. "It's really the mark of a professional journalist these days."

"Really? I thought I had to make that mark in ink."

"You know what I mean! Look, I carry one of them myself." He pulled back his suit coat to reveal the pager on his belt. "See?"

"I'm thrilled for you," I said, but already, evil thoughts were forming.

"Where are you going?" he asked.

"That's the neato-fab thing about these gadgets, isn't it? You don't need to know where I am, because you can always page me!"

"Well, I don't know about that . . ."

I almost left without telling him, but realized he would be jealous, so I said, "I'm having lunch with Claire Watterson."

"The widow?"

"We probably have more than one in town."

"I'd love to meet her."

I'll just bet you would, you slimeball, I thought. "I'll tell her," I said, and pushed the door open, but then paused on the threshold. "No, wait. Maybe she'd be willing to have you join us a little later. Shall I have her page you?"

"Oh, sure." He fumbled in his coat pocket and pulled out a business card and a six-hundred-dollar fountain pen. He flipped the card over and jotted his pager number on it.

I even kept a straight face when he handed the card to me.

* * *

Aunt Emeline opened the front door when I arrived at the Watterson house. I was glad to see her; it seemed to me that she was one of those sturdy people who would be good to have at your side in a crisis, and I was relieved to know Claire wasn't staying in this big house alone. Finn came from the back of the house to remind me that Claire still had his company as well, dancing around me in great circles and barking. Aunt Emeline said, "Hush now, Finn," and he obeyed immediately.

It was then that I heard a rumbling noise that seemed to be coming from the back of the house. "Construction workers," Emeline said. "Claire is out there with them. She must have left the back door open for it to be so loud."

I followed Emeline to the back of the house. Claire was standing outside, watching something going on in the backyard. When I reached her, I was puzzled to see a bulldozer at work behind the house—until I realized that it was leveling the ground where the cabana had stood.

Claire saw me, came back inside with me, and closed the door before attempting conversation. She was wearing a navy blue silk dress that seemed a little big on her—then I realized that she looked thinner to me. There were dark circles under her eyes. But her voice was firm when she said, "I didn't want to look out there and see that building every day."

"Of course not," I said, doubting it would be so easy to level the memories of what had happened there. I thought again of Ivy, still uneasy over Jeff's death a decade or more ago.

We sat down to lunch together—Aunt Emeline's chicken salad. "It's the best in the world," Claire had said, and as far as I'm concerned, that was the truth. Claire didn't seem to have much of an appetite, but no one fussed at her over it. Aunt Emeline led the conversation, which meant that it was centered on recipes, books we had recently read, people she had known back home, and gardening. I didn't doubt that this woman could have held a conversation on almost any subject.

I suspect she chose her topics with more care than was apparent in her easy manner. We didn't talk about Ben or Lucas during lunch, which is probably why Claire managed to eat at all.

At the end of lunch, Claire asked Aunt Emeline to excuse us, but before we left she said, "We're going to talk in the library, but don't you do those dishes, now. It's my turn."

"What happened to your help?" I asked when we were alone.

Her mouth drew into a tight line. "Gossip became a problem. When certain people wanted to buy information, my housekeeper and cook each invented something to sell. None of it true in the least, mind you."

"Did they live in?"

"No. That's why they weren't here when . . . they weren't here that night, although the police questioned them anyway. And what they told the police was quite different from what they told the media. What they told the police was just what everyone else said. Ben talked of retiring. Never mentioned illness or suicide."

She sighed. "I suppose I shouldn't have been surprised. I never mistreated anyone who worked here, never even spoke sharply to them. But they actually hinted that I . . . that I could have . . ." She drew a shaky breath. "I'm so glad the police put an end to that, anyway. I know there will still be gossip. But I don't have to have people like that in this house." She looked up at me. "To be honest, I'd just as soon do the work myself. Aunt Emeline and I take turns fussing over each other. She's been wonderful. She likes you."

"Probably because she doesn't really know me."

"Nonsense. You said you had something to tell me?"

I brought her up to date on what I had learned from Lucas's mother about the photographs, and what I had learned of Nadine from my conversation with Ivy. I didn't mention Jeff, but Claire must have known the story.

"How could I have forgotten about Ivy? Her friend—what was his name?"

"Jeff."

"Jeff," she repeated absently, gazing out a window. "That's right, Jeff."

"I just learned the story today. I wasn't living here when he died."

"All these years. My God, how has she managed?"

"Maybe you should ask her someday. When you're ready," I added quickly. I was going to say more, but it was obvious that Claire didn't want to dwell on it.

"I have something for you," she said, going over to the desk.

24

"These are Ben's desk calendars," she said, lifting a set of three leather binders, each binder in its own slipcase. "Every night, he would come home, talk to me for a while, and then spend a little time in here, making notes about the day."

She carried them over to me. The spines were labeled 1975, 1976, 1977. "They weren't as difficult to find as I thought they might be." She drew in a deep breath. "Ben apparently became nostalgic during those last few weeks. He must have gone through some of these. He was tying up loose ends, I suppose—he gave some historical photos of the bank to one of the men who worked there, did things like that." She paused. "I guess I'm feeling nostalgic, too. Forgive me for keeping the one for 1974 aside. It's the year we were married. If you need it, let me know."

"Don't worry about it for now," I said, feeling the weight of the three I held.

"He was fairly religious about making entries," she said. "When he was ill, or a little down, he might miss a day or two."

"A little down?"

"He'd get depressed now and then. Not often," she added quickly. "Not severely. I had no reason to believe . . ."

"Of course not," I said, tracing my fingers along the spine of 1975.

"Before you open them, I have another request."

I looked up at her.

"Promise me that you'll just use these to help me find out why Lucas Monroe was contacting Ben. If you want to write a story about that, I won't object. But there's a lot of confidential information about customers of the bank in these calendars and some personal information as well. Can I trust you—as my friend—not to report on any of the rest of it?"

Her trust was all that had brought me this far, and she clearly wasn't going to part with the calendars without my promise. I gave it to her.

"I think the 1977 calendar will be the most helpful," I said.

"The one for the year Ben sold the boat?"

"Yes."

"That reminds me," she said, and went back to the desk. She opened the top drawer, searched through a thin sheaf of papers, and took an unsealed envelope from them. As she handed it to me, I saw that she had written my name on it. "This is the information on the boat."

I removed the handwritten note from the envelope as Claire sat on the couch next to me. It read:

52' Bertram sold to Andre Selman for $1000.00 on 8/15/77

"A thousand dollars! For a fifty-two-foot Bertram? Hell, was the bottom missing out of it?"

She didn't answer.

"When Andre took me fishing," I said, "it was on a little Boston Whaler. A fine craft for its purpose, but I don't think it was fifteen feet long. A Bertram—what was the thousand for? Refueling it after a test ride?"

"It's bad enough without your exaggeration, Irene."

"I was wondering how someone making an assistant professor's pay could afford a boat that size. It would strain his budget just to afford maintenance and taxes and slip fees. But the boat—Andre got himself a helluva deal, wouldn't you say?"

"Andre got himself a helluva gift," she muttered.

I watched her. Her eyes were lowered, her hands folded carefully in her lap.

"Why do you think Ben gave Andre such a bargain?"

She bit her lower lip, shrugged. "As I told you, the last time he went out on the boat, Ben got a bad case of seasickness. Came back late one day from a fishing trip with Andre looking awful. Ben said he didn't want to set foot on it again, that he was going to sell the boat to Andre. I remember that much."

"Come on, Claire. A man who is nobody's financial sucker practically donates an expensive item to a college professor? Over a bout of seasickness? I know people who'd *make* themselves throw up for the kind of money he lost on this deal. There's more to this." I watched her carefully. "No guesses?"

"I didn't know he had sold it for so little! I know it looks bad," she said, then added, "Maybe that's why Lucas Monroe sent those photos—maybe *he* knew why Ben sold the boat for next to nothing! He worked for Andre, right?"

"Not by then. A lot of things had happened by August of 1977, Claire. I'll tell you what I know so far. Around 1975, Roland Hill and a few of his friends had acquired some real estate in a seedy part of town. I haven't checked into it yet, but I wouldn't be surprised if the Bank of Las Piernas financed some of the purchases. Andre Selman was hired to do a study for the city, probably at Allan Moffett's urging. The study was supposed to help the city target areas for redevelopment money, and to help the city plan for the future. Lucas Monroe was one of Andre's assistants."

"So he worked on this study?"

"Yes. He was going to include some of the work he did on the study in his master's thesis. He had some disagreements with Andre about the way the study was being done, but they weren't severe enough to damage his standing with Andre—

or so he thought. Then Lucas turned the thesis in, and it was rejected."

"Why?"

I told her the story Lucas's mother had told me, and what I had learned from Murray of the new plans for the area.

"You're saying Ben was dishonest."

"If Ben knowingly went along with what I suspect happened, yes, I suppose that makes him dishonest. It's also possible that he unwittingly dealt with some people who were bribing the city manager."

She gazed out the window again. "If he was involved at all, he would have known. He wouldn't have been 'unwitting,' " she said. "Ben wasn't stupid."

"No, he wasn't."

"That's what that photograph—the second one—is supposed to prove, isn't it? That Ben was meeting with these people before the redevelopment study was in, right?"

"That photo shows some people on a fishing trip. It doesn't prove anything, really. The people in the photo are allowed to be friends, to go fishing together. But maybe it represents something else, or was just supposed to hint to Ben and the others that Lucas knew more."

"You talk as if all Mr. Monroe would be after is a master's degree. But Ben wouldn't be the person to approach in that case, would he? If Lucas Monroe had some proof of this collusion, don't you think it's more likely that he saw a perfect opportunity to blackmail my husband?"

"Maybe. And if he was blackmailing other people as well, maybe he died because someone didn't want to pay up. From your point of view, I suppose, it would be comforting to think of Lucas as a villain who got what he deserved. If you just want to accept that as an explanation, with no proof one way or another, then go ahead and take these calendars back."

She hesitated just long enough for me to begin to regret making rash offers. "No, I want to know the truth," she said, then added, "I don't know that you'll find it in there."

I let my breath out again and asked, "Did you read them?"

She shook her head. "Not recently."

"You read them when he wrote them?"

"No, not really. He didn't hide them from me. Sometimes I would be in here with him as he wrote in them; once in a while he would call from the office, ask me to look something up for him. But they were his notes, and I didn't feel a need to study them. I preferred to have him talk to me about his day."

"So they're business notes?"

"Yes, but not just business notes. Not quite a diary, either. Part business, part diary. I'll want them back, but take them home with you for now."

I figured that was a dismissal. I knew I had upset her, and felt bad about that. She had been through enough. I picked up the heavy binders and started to stand up.

"Wait," she said softly. She wasn't looking at me, but I could see tears welling up in her eyes. Her hand came up to her lips again, pressing hard, in what I was learning was her gesture of distress.

I sat down, feeling like something that would be happier sunning itself on a rock. "Claire, I'm sorry—"

She waved me to silence. I waited, setting the binders down again.

"Ben would have wanted what was best for the city," she said slowly, then drew a shaky breath. "He loved Las Piernas. He just wanted it to be a good place to live. Whatever choices he made, he wouldn't have done anything that would harm Las Piernas."

I didn't say anything.

"You don't believe that, do you?"

"Are you asking me if I believe that Ben loved Las Piernas? Or are you asking me if I believe he was a saint?"

"I know he wasn't a saint," she said. "He was a complex man. I'm not certain of much about Ben anymore, but I'm certain of that."

"You're right about how he felt about Las Piernas."

She lifted a shoulder, as if suddenly she wasn't so sure.

"Claire, I'm worried about you. Maybe you should get away for a while."

"I'll be okay, Irene. This was just a hard day. Tearing down the cabana, thinking that Ben might have been involved in some scam. But this won't last forever." She stood up, walked over to a box of tissues, and took about ten of them out in rapid succession. "It's much harder for someone like me to run away," she said, tears starting to roll. "Not understanding why Ben did what he did is eating me alive. I knew he hit rough patches, would feel overwhelmed sometimes, even a little blue. But he would always let me comfort him, let me help him. This time, he just shut me out. Left me behind, to face whatever it was he couldn't face. To be honest, I'm really pissed off at him for that."

I listened to the ticking of the clock on the fireplace mantel while she cried quietly. When she got to the tenth tissue, she blew her nose in an indelicate trumpeting style, looked up at me, and said, "Thanks, I'm much better now."

I was about to ask her what she was thanking me for when my beeper went off.

"Damn it all to hell, I thought I had this thing set so it wouldn't do that," I said, fumbling through my purse until I found it. After watching me spend another fifteen seconds trying to figure out how to get the sucker to stop making that annoying sound, Claire reached over, took it from me, pressed a button which silenced it immediately, and handed it back. She was smiling.

"I *hate* these things!" I said, not a little irked to notice that the number on the display was Wrigley's direct line at the paper. "Show me how to fix it so it won't beep."

She took it back from me, saying, "This type won't shut off, but I'll set it so it will vibrate instead of beep. Go ahead and use the phone if you need to make a call."

"I don't. It's that toad, Wrigley, wondering why I didn't have you page him to join us for lunch."

"Oh, God, I used to see him at all the charity fund-raisers. What a creep. No wonder you want to shut this thing off. But isn't he your boss?"

"My boss's boss. Don't worry, I didn't plan to set you up

for a lunch date with him." I paused, then said, "You could help me with a little scheme, though."

When I explained my plan, she laughed. "I love it. Can I get Aunt Emeline and Alana to help out?"

"Please do," I said.

I was on my way out of the house when I remembered something else I had been meaning to ask her about. "Claire, are you sure there wasn't anything else in that first envelope, the one that held the photo of Ben giving Lucas the scholarship check?"

"No, there was nothing else. Why?"

"Lucas's mother saw him put a typewritten letter into the envelope. Have you come across anything like that?"

"No, I haven't." She appeared to be lost in her own thoughts for a moment, then said, "I'll look more carefully."

"What were you just thinking?"

"That perhaps Ben burned it that night."

I wasn't happy to realize how likely that was. Claire had stopped Ben when he tried to burn the photograph. Lucas's letter may have already gone up in flames.

I looked at my watch and realized I'd have to hurry to get to Roland Hill's offices in time for my appointment. I tried to clear my mind of concerns about June Monroe and Claire Watterson, to think of the best approach to use with Hill if he was as cool and remote as Corbin Tyler. I glanced at the stack of binders on the seat next to me. I would be parking in another parking garage, but still, I didn't want to leave them out. I didn't want to take them in with me, either. Risking being late, I pulled over and put them in the trunk. Acting a little paranoid, perhaps, not to do that in the parking garage, but I decided I just didn't want anyone to see me locking something away.

I was a little more at ease; this was unlike my secret meeting with Tyler. I had told Lydia where I would be, and Hill's secretary wasn't being sent home. A state senator's aide had been instrumental in setting up this appointment. The two meetings would be nothing alike, except that in each case, I might be visiting a killer.

Maybe it was that thought that led me to call Frank from the building's lobby and leave a voice-mail message. "I've got a pager now, Harriman, in case you ever want to literally give me a buzz." I left the number. "I'm meeting with Roland Hill. See you tonight."

Like Tyler Associates, the offices of Hill and Associates were also on the top floor of a tall building, but the similarities ended there. Hill's company also occupied several other floors. Hill's were much busier than Corbin Tyler's; no fewer than two dozen people were working in open cubicles as I walked in. Most of them were on the phone. The first receptionist sent me on to a second receptionist.

The second receptionist worked in a much quieter area. The business attire was more expensive and the offices more private. This receptionist smiled and led me through a maze to a secretary, politely introduced me, and left.

This was the secretary who had made the appointment. She greeted me warmly, took my coat, and asked me if I would care for a cup of coffee. When I declined, she took me in to see Mr. Hill himself.

His office was more spacious than Corbin Tyler's, but didn't have much of a view. At one end of the room, the top of a credenza was loaded up with golfing trophies.

Roland Hill looked like an upgraded version of Booter Hodges. It struck me that Booter probably tried to emulate Hill's look. He fell short of the mark. Hill was a big man, and he didn't seem to be carrying an ounce of fat on him. His face was wrinkled in a way that made people say "has character" instead of "old." His skin was light brown, his hair white and full. His eyes were pale blue. He was a handsome old devil, with a smile that promised you had just met the person who would become your new best friend.

"Hello, Ms. Kelly," he said. "How are you doing?"

He had a firm handshake. He seemed perfectly at ease.

"I'm fine, Mr. Hill. Thank you for agreeing to meet with me."

"First, please call me Roland. May I call you Irene?"

Not to be ungenerous, I nodded.

"I apologize for delaying this interview, Irene. I know it has presented a hardship for you in your work, but I had conflicting concerns. I didn't wish to disappoint you, but I have loyalties to consider. Allan Moffett has been a terrific city manager. You understand?"

"Yes, of course, but—"

"I love Las Piernas," he said. "Do you?"

"I've lived here almost all my life, Mr. Hill."

"Roland, please. Well, yes, but do you love it? Do you want it to thrive as a community, or whither and die?"

"Mr. Hill—"

"—Roland—I want to see it thrive. I want it to grow—in all the best ways. It takes a certain amount of vision on the part of the citizens of this community to ensure that happens. Allan had vision. That's why we were at the restaurant that night. To pay homage to a man of vision."

"Has Mr. Moffett mentioned to you his reasons for abandoning that vision so abruptly?"

"Is that what you'd call it?"

"You must admit that Allan Moffett's resignation was unexpected."

"Only by those who don't know him well. Those of us who do are aware that Allan has grown weary of the tremendous burden of that office."

"You're saying you were expecting this announcement?"

"Absolutely. Oh, perhaps not right down to the hour and the day, but I knew it was coming, Irene."

"Roland, let's be honest with one another. If you weren't surprised by Allan Moffett's resignation, you knew more about the city manager's office than the mayor himself."

He smiled. "Entirely possible."

"Which brings me to another set of questions," I said quickly. "Have you received a photocopy—"

"—of myself and a group of other individuals going out on Ben Watterson's boat for a pleasant day of fishing? Yes, ma'am, I have."

I couldn't quite hide my surprise, and he grinned.

"I'm hoping you can explain that to me, Irene," he added.

"Me?"

"Yes, word is, you've discovered who sent the photo and why he sent it. He came by here one day, but my receptionist turned him away. From what she told me about him, I gather he was some crazy bum."

"No. A man who worked on studies that you profited from."

"Really?" he said, unperturbed.

"Really."

"Well, Irene, if that's the case, I should thank him for that, and for reminding me of happier days with Ben."

I thought of asking him what he knew of Ben's suicide, but decided I couldn't bear to hear the sunshine version. I was already annoyed with his salesman's tricks—using my first name constantly and asking more questions than he answered.

"You certainly accentuate the positive, Roland."

"I'm not one of those people who will tell you that a positive attitude is all that's required, Irene. Hard work and remaining aware of your customer's needs are also important, don't you think?"

"Would you happen to know where I can find Nadine Preston these days?"

"I'm sorry, Irene, I can't. I really had no reason to think about her until that photograph arrived. I only met her a few times, many years ago, when she was dating Andre Selman."

"And you remember the name of one of Andre's dates? That's remarkable."

He smiled. "I understand your point. I do have a good memory; it has allowed me certain advantages in business. But Nadine also worked with Andre Selman. That's why I remember her."

"Her, and not the man who became—what did you call him? 'A crazy bum,' I believe?"

He shrugged. "I vaguely remember Andre's first assistant. He joined us on one or two of the fishing trips. But of course, his appearance was quite different then."

"I thought you said you didn't see him. That your receptionist turned him away."

"I didn't. I should have said that his appearance, as it was described to me, would not have led me to make the connection."

I stayed there for another half hour, mainly just to irritate him. I had already figured out that he was not going to give me a straight answer on anything. I think he started to realize what I was up to, and I saw the first little crack in the happy armor. Nothing verbal, just his eyes. Not anger, not frustration. Emptiness.

I asked for my coat and left.

In the parking garage, I opened the trunk of the Karmann Ghia, half afraid I'd find it empty. The binders were still there, along with the usual items I stored there. I moved the binders into the front seat, and headed back to the paper.

By the time I got back to the parking lot of the *Express,* it was clear the staff meeting had already started: every parking space was taken. I pulled into the alley next to the building and tried to hug the wall as I parked there. I didn't plan to be in the office long, so with luck, the car wouldn't get towed. I thought of leaving the calendars in the car, but in this alley, they might invite a break-in. Maybe in the trunk again? No, I decided against that, too. If the car *was* towed and I somehow lost track of them, I'd never forgive myself. Claire would never forgive me, either.

From the corner of my eye, as I fumbled with the binders in one hand and the car keys in the other, I caught a splash of color moving nearby. I glanced back and dropped my keys. Two Toes was standing not six feet away from me.

25

"You can see me!" he said, seeming as surprised as I was. I nodded. Alone in an alley with the man Frank had warned me about, who had bruised—if not killed—Lucas. Not good.

"That's because I chose to appear!" He stabbed a finger in my direction. "Why'd you call the cops on me?"

"I didn't call the cops on you!" I realized I was squeaking. I thought again of some of the self-defense moves Rachel had taught me, but none of my extremely rudimentary training covered what to do when your arms were full of binders and your keys were on the ground in front of you. But acting panicked could not improve the situation, so I took a deep breath, backed up a step from him, and said in a much lower voice, "You told me where Lucas's—the Prof's—body was, and the police decided they'd like to know what happened to him."

"I told you what happened!" he shouted. "You should have told them. I was there! I'll tell you one more time. Are you listening?"

I nodded again. If I scream, will you kill me? I wondered.

When he spoke again, his voice was much softer, as if he were telling a story to a child. "It was a cold, cold night. Wind and rain. All the children went to Jerusalem, and there was no room at the inn. The Prof couldn't stay, they turned him away." He smiled at the rhyme, then went on. "I watched him go to the Chinese Wall. He was seeking shelter where the angels are. The angels and I, we watched over him. I wanted his magic. I needed it to stop the voices in my head. The guardian angel came to him, but then the angel left."

"Guardian angel?" Should I go for the keys? Drop the calendars and run? Throw the calendars at him, pick up the keys and run? I was so preoccupied with evaluating these meager options, I didn't bother correcting him about what he had said to me the last time I saw him.

"The one that watched over him wherever he would go. He talked to the angel, and the angel went away. I followed the angel down the stairs. The angel went outside. It scared me to watch that angel. Made me have to go to the bathroom." He paused, then said, "I went back up to wait for the ring. I waited all night, then I heard him fall. I found him." He motioned toward his forehead. "His head bled. His head bled," he repeated, as if enjoying this rhyme as well, then grew solemn again. "He was ready for the angels. He needed to be prepared. I was the willing servant of the Lord. God said the Prof didn't need the ring. God said I could take it. He made me an angel."

He reached into his jacket and pulled out the ring, dangling it before me on the chain.

"Was God in the room, too?"

"No, God is in my mind. You are my assignment." He glared at me. "You were the first one I helped, and you called the cops on me!" he shouted. "They defiled the Prof's grave!"

I tried to think of a way to get him to forget about that. "No, they didn't, and being an angel, you know that. You're just testing me, aren't you? You know they just took him to his mother, so that she could bury him."

It must have worked. He grinned. "I like being your guardian angel."

"My guardian angel?" I repeated, my mouth going dry.

"Yes, I'll watch over you. I'll even give you the magic ring. Here, you take it," he said, stepping toward me.

I backed up again.

He suddenly cocked his head, as if hearing something. He tossed the ring at me, and it landed near my keys. He turned and ran.

Shaking, I bent to retrieve the keys and ring. I held them tightly as I leaned against the car, waiting for the fear to leave me. I heard footsteps and whirled around, but it must have been someone walking past the alley at the other end. I looked back in the direction where Two Toes had gone, but didn't see him. After a moment, I started walking toward the newspaper offices, but Two Toes' voice came from above me.

"This is your guardian angel speaking!"

I yelped and looked up. He was on a metal ladder, one which led to the roof of a neighboring building, an old two-story brick place.

"Don't park there, you'll get towed!" he shouted, and scrambled up to the roof and out of sight.

Receiving such sensible advice from my self-appointed guardian angel, I felt a sudden urge to laugh aloud. I fought it, not out of fear, but because I didn't want to belittle him.

I was still scared of him and knew he was capable of hurting me. But so far, he hadn't done anything but try to help me, and I wasn't going to repay that by laughing at him. I opened my palm and looked at Lucas's ring.

I walked into the building, went into a restroom, and splashed cold water on my face. I gathered the binders and ring and went to my desk. The newsroom was relatively empty; most people were still in the meeting. I stared up at a wall clock, waited for a slow fifteen minutes to go by, and called the police.

"He's long gone," Reed Collins said. He gave me a hard look as we stood in the alley next to my car, but it didn't win him any confessions. He frowned and pulled out his notebook. "Tell me again what Mr. Jones said to you."

Mr. John Jones, I had just learned, was Two Toes' rather unremarkable legal name. It would take some getting used to. I repeated my guardian angel's explanation of the events at the Angelus.

Reed kept frowning. "Can you make anything out of that?"

"It's hard to say what he means. Reality is just one ingredient in whatever he recalls. God knows what else he tosses into the batter before he bakes a memory."

"But you understood him when he told you where to find the body."

"Guesswork."

"So guess again," he said, looking at the rooftops—and probably silently cussing me out.

"He was telling me about the night Lucas died. I think he followed him from the shelter. That's probably what he meant by 'no room at the inn,' because there was plenty of room at the Angelus."

"So this would have been Thursday night," Reed said.

"Yes." Thursday. The night of Allan Moffett's dinner meeting. I remembered how cold and rainy it was that night.

"Go on," he said.

"The story gets a little weirder from here," I said. "He mentioned the angels at the Angelus, but then he also said there was a guardian angel. He spoke of this guardian angel a little differently. I think he meant someone else was following Lucas."

"So his story is that this guardian angel left Monroe alive."

"Right. But he heard Lucas fall, and if you believe him, Lucas was dead by the time he reached him. Two—er, Mr. Jones—hears voices, and believes that God told him to help himself to the ring."

"Aside from that, I wonder how much of it is true."

"Most of it fits, doesn't it? No one else saw Lucas any later—even his street friends hadn't seen him since the night he was turned away from the shelter. And from what Carlos Hernandez has said, Lucas was dead when the ring was taken."

"Any idea who this guardian angel might be?"

I shook my head.

"Well, I guess that's it, then." He put his notebook away, then said, "Oh, one more thing . . ."

"Move my car?"

He grimaced. "Do I look like a meter maid? No. What I was going to say is, next time you hear we're looking for someone? And you see that someone? Don't *hesitate* to call."

I kept my mouth shut. I knew he had doubted my vague excuses about taking a while to calm down and losing track of time.

"Come on," he said, "I owe it to your husband to make sure you get back inside the building safely."

When I got back to the newsroom, there were enough grim faces to let me know that the staff meeting was over and done with. I walked up to Lydia's desk and said, "I think I know how to break Wrigley's beeper habit."

"I know a dozen people who'd love you if you did."

"Anyone who wants to help should meet me at Banyon's for a pint after work."

I checked my messages again. I had a call from Steven Kincaid, a friend who was renting my old house. It had been a relief to find such a good tenant, since I am inexperienced as a landlady. I returned the call, afraid that this meant the plumbing had failed or the roof had leaked. Turned out he just wanted to invite Frank and me to his housewarming, to be held in a couple of weeks.

I was thanking him for the invitation when my purse started to rattle and hum, sounding as if I had somewhere received a hive of live bumblebees in lieu of change.

I told Steven I'd talk to Frank and call him back with an answer, said good-bye, and turned off the pager. This time the number was June Monroe's.

"I'm glad you called me," she said when I returned her call. "I almost came by that newspaper to talk to you, but decided I had probably made enough trouble for you for one day."

"Not at all."

"Well, I am just about as tired as a body can be right now, and you probably aren't much better off. So I'll make this quick. First, after I talked to you, I got to thinking about some things, and decided that I will bury Lucas in Las Piernas. You were right. He loved Las Piernas. His daddy is buried there, so Lucas will rest next to him."

"I know that must have been a hard decision to make," I said.

"Oh, not after I thought about it and prayed on it for a time. Lucas's friends may be having hard times, but they were his friends. If I hold this funeral way out here in Riverside, nobody but Charles and me would be likely to attend."

"I'm glad it will be here, but I would have come out there. Roberta, too, I think."

"Well, it doesn't matter, it will be right there in Las Piernas on Friday morning at eleven. That doesn't give you much time to let his friends know about it, but I would appreciate anything you can do to spread the word."

I told her I would do my best. She gave me the name of the funeral home and cemetery.

"After making all the arrangements," she went on, "I came straight home and looked for that phone bill. I've got the number that Lucas called."

"Edison, right?"

"Right."

I wrote the number down. "Thanks for doing that, June. I know the last twenty-four hours have been exhausting for you."

"You said you had a couple of questions?"

"Yes, but first, I wanted to let you know that the police have Lucas's ring now." I explained Two Toes as far as he could be explained.

"You don't think he's the one who killed Lucas?"

"No. I'm not sure I can tell you why, but I guess it's just that I think he'd admit it if he did. He'd be saying God told him to do it."

"Maybe so," she said, sounding unconvinced.

"I think whoever killed Lucas wanted more than a school ring. That brings me to a question I had for you. I wondered if you knew what became of Lucas's thesis—I mean, his copies of it? His raw data, his drafts, the final copy—any of it?"

"Well, it was here until recently. Had it in a box, one of those filing boxes. But he took it with him after his last visit.

I asked him, did that mean he was going to try to get his degree? He just said that it was probably too late to worry about that, and besides, it wasn't so important to him now."

I couldn't tell her how disappointed those words made me feel. If he wasn't interested in getting his degree, was he more interested in blackmail? "I wonder what he did with them. The papers weren't among Lucas's things at the shelter."

"No," she said. "Maybe he just threw them out."

"When he left, did he walk to the bus station from your house?"

"No, I gave him a ride. Even waited with him at the station."

"Did he have the box with him when he got on the bus?"

"Yes. Yes, he did. Hmmhmm. That was the last time I saw him alive, waving to him as that bus pulled out. He was smiling." She paused, then said, "Well, what else did you need to know?"

"I just wondered if you could tell me a little more about what happened to Lucas after he was denied his master's degree. Did he just give up after that?"

"No, not then. I never did finish telling you that story, did I? Sorry, I've been a little rattled. I meant to tell you about this Nadine. She was dating that professor, right? Old Andre Selman kept that real quiet, only his closest friends knew, and I guess they just sort of turned a blind eye to it. Lucas told me about this, and I said, 'Lucas, you always tell me that this man can't hang on to a woman. He just loves them and leaves them. So you just wait until he leaves this one, 'cause a woman scorned is something to behold.' Sure enough, not long after this study is finished, so is Nadine—Selman drops her."

"And Lucas talked with her?"

"Yes. He was smart, he gave her a little time, then he went and talked to her. And she admitted to him how she had done him dirty. She told Lucas that Selman had her substitute the pages of the thesis, that Selman was afraid Lucas would ruin the project, would cause the school to lose all that grant money. But by the time Lucas talked to her, I think she realized what harm she had done to him. She was sorry all over."

"He must have wanted to kill her."

"No, no. He knew she was the only chance he had of ever getting that mess straightened out. So he gets her to agree to testify on his behalf at a hearing at the college."

"A hearing?"

"Yes. Lucas went to the department chair. That man liked Lucas, and he'd been suspicious of Selman, so he set up a hearing. First time, it was just going to be the department chair, that Dr. Warren that had stirred things up in the first place, and someone from the foundation that gets the grant—strange name, I can't remember it though. Just remember thinking it was a funny kind of name."

"Booter? Booter Hodges?"

"That's it! You know him?"

"I've talked to him a few times."

"Lucas didn't like him at all. Anyway, two days before the hearing, this Nadine is acting like she's got cold feet. Says she doesn't want any hard feelings with Selman, doesn't want to sneak around behind his back. She's going to talk to him. Lucas begs her to just wait until after the hearing, but she won't have any of it. The night before the hearing, Lucas gets a call from Selman's best friend, saying that Nadine is back together with Selman. So Lucas went to talk to her, find out if it's true. She's all smiles. Tells him Selman admits he's wrong, and he's going to come with her to the hearing. He's going to face the music. Lucas didn't believe it for a minute, but what can he do?"

"And she never showed up?"

"No Nadine, no Selman, just one more round of humiliation with this Warren turkey. And that Booter says something like, 'We should have expected this.' Lucas couldn't even find Nadine after that."

"What happened to Lucas after the hearing?"

"Well, he couldn't get into other colleges, and he couldn't find a job anything like what he wanted. He was able to find work, but he wasn't happy. He started drinking then, but not real bad. But pretty soon it started to be a problem. He'd get a job somewhere, be doing fine, and somehow the story from the school would catch up to him."

"You think someone was making sure it caught up to him?"

"I don't know, I guess maybe I do. Even if the employer didn't pay any attention to the story, it embarrassed Lucas. That pride of his would suffer. He was all the time bitter and angry. He'd go drinking. Next thing you know, he's missing work and so on. It all just went from bad to worse. After a time, it was easier for him to sit around drinking than to try to keep a job, I guess. I'm not trying to excuse it. The drinking was his problem. Wasn't anybody who made him sit down and become an alcoholic. I told you before, it's an illness, that's all. Who knows?—maybe he would have ended up drinking even if he got a degree and teaching job at some university."

"It doesn't matter. If someone cheated him out of his degree, he was cheated."

"Not just his degree," June said. "Like I keep telling you. They labeled *him* the cheater. They made *him* the liar. All along, he was none of those things, but he was called those names. Being called a drunk, being poor, that's not the same. He was a good man. He deserves to go to his grave being known as one."

26

I called the number June had given me. A man answered on the second ring.

"Hello, is Edison in?"

"This is Edison. What can I do for you?"

"This is Irene Kelly. I'm a reporter with the *Las Piernas News-Express*. I'm calling you regarding—"

"Lucas Monroe!" he interrupted. "Lucas told me you might be calling me."

"He did?"

"Sure. I'm retired now, but I can give you references if you need them."

"References?"

"As a document examiner. Would you need to see my references before I go over his case with you? I won't be insulted in the least. He said you would be cautious."

"I'm afraid I don't understand."

There was a long silence. "Lucas told you about me?"

"No, not really. Mr.—Sorry, I don't even know your last name."

"Burrows."

"Mr. Burrows, I'm afraid I have some sad news. Lucas died a few days ago."

"Died? But—but how is that possible?"

"Apparently, he had a heart attack."

I didn't give him any other details. He was clearly shocked to learn of Lucas's death, and the next few moments were largely spent convincing him that I was sure Lucas was dead.

"I really liked him," he said. "And I suppose I kept hoping my son would follow his example."

"Your son?"

There was a slight hesitation before he said, "Lucas met my son on the streets. Unfortunately, my son is still drinking heavily. But I guess my son told Lucas what I used to do for a living, because Lucas sought my help not long after he began fighting his own addiction."

"If you don't mind my asking, what does document examination have to do with alcohol addiction?"

"Oh, not with addiction. I'm sorry, I forgot—he didn't have a chance to tell you. Oh, wait—there was the note—but you said it was a heart attack?"

"It's being investigated. There are some questions about his death. What note?"

"Oh, well, I wonder if . . ." He paused. "Perhaps we could meet. I know he wanted me to show you the work I've done for him. And then there is another matter, although I'm not sure . . . well, this should be taken care of as soon as possi-

ble. Could we meet this afternoon? It would be easier than trying to explain over the phone."

He completed this argument with himself by inviting me
to his home, and not wanting him to argue himself out of it,
I agreed to meet him there in an hour.

I thought about my previous plans, which would now have to
be canceled. I wasn't going to spoil everybody's fun, though,
so I took out a sheet of paper and wrote Wrigley's pager number on it about thirty times. Then I went over to the copier and
made ten copies of that page, and finally made use of a paper
cutter in the design department. I glanced at a clock and saw
I only had about ten minutes to spare, so I hurried over to
Lydia. "Can someone else cover the city desk for about two
minutes?"

Stuart Angert agreed to catch the phones, and I could tell
from his grin that Lydia had already mentioned Banyon's to
him. Lydia followed me into the women's room. I checked
the stalls to make sure we were alone and then said, "I have
a huge favor to ask of you."

"Uh-oh."

"Lydia, this is not that bad, I promise."

"Famous last words. Whenever you say 'huge favor' and
'not that bad,' trouble is coming at me downhill on roller
skates."

"Listen, I don't have time to twist your arm, so if you
don't want to do this, just say so. I can't make it to Banyon's."

"What! I just told everyone—"

"Something's come up." I told her about Edison Burrows.
"I've got to meet him, but I can't do that and be at Banyon's.
So I need you to explain my plan for the beepers."

"I knew I wasn't going to like this."

I ignored that. I've been tempting Lydia to misbehave for
about three decades, so by now I know what to expect in the
way of protest.

"Just give out these slips of paper. See? My handwriting.

It's the number for Wrigley's personal pager. I think it should be dialed. A lot."

She took the slips, her look of trepidation now replaced with a mischievous smile. That's my pal.

"How did you ever get this number?"

"The old boy thought I was going to set him up with Claire Watterson."

"He must be out of his mind."

"He will be, when we get done with him. Now, I've got to get out of here." I started to walk out, then stopped and turned back to her. "Lydia? Tell them to be creative about the call-back numbers. The pound and the sanitation department are already spoken for."

I hurried back to my desk and checked my voice-mail messages. One from Frank, one from Roberta. Frank had called me before I left my "beeper" message for him; he was letting me know he'd actually be home for dinner, so I didn't have to call him back. Roberta just left her number. I debated for a second or two, but there had been an anxiousness in her voice, so I decided to go ahead and call her now. I could always call Burrows and tell him I'd be late. But when I called, I reached her secretary.

"She's with a client," the secretary said, "and she has a meeting across town this afternoon. I'm about to leave for the day, but can I leave a message for her? I know she's anxious to talk to you."

I gave her my pager number and my home number. I gathered up Ben's calendars and left the office.

My curiosity was raging. Edison Burrows mentioned a note. Did Lucas leave a note about his activities? I was so preoccupied with trying to untangle my conversation with Burrows, I stood bewildered in the parking lot for a second before I remembered that I was still parked in the alley—or hoped I was. I rounded the corner of the building, greatly cheered to see the Karmann Ghia—until I saw the broken glass on the driver's side. A brick lay on the ground near the door.

"Shit!" I slowed my steps, trying to brace myself for finding the ignition popped or the interior vandalized. This thief might have been frustrated to find the radio gone—long gone, thanks to the work of one of his predecessors, a knife-wielding asshole who had ripped his way through the ragtop. At least the glass wouldn't be so expensive to replace. It would come out of my own pocket; the Karmann Ghia was too old to make comprehensive insurance worthwhile.

As I crunched my way closer to the car door, I noticed the hood of the trunk wasn't fully latched. I peered into the car. No other apparent damage. I brushed beads of glass off the seat, hit the release for the trunk, and went to the front of the car to see if anything had been taken from there. But my earthquake kit, flares, beach blanket, and flashlight were still there. Even my gym bag, which had a set of running clothes and shoes in it, hadn't been taken. On second thought, maybe my running shoes weren't such a prize.

I shut the trunk and got into the car, shaking loose another spray of glass beads. I started the car, relieved that nothing seemed amiss with the engine, and drove toward Edison Burrows' home.

At the first stoplight, I found myself inventing punishments for the vandal. I had a brief moment of mentally asking "What did I ever do to you?" to the unknown, would-be thief. Useless. As the wind came in through the shattered window, I clenched my teeth and told myself that I should be grateful the car was still there.

Should be.

Beyond contributing my input to local crime statistics, I knew there was no point in calling the police. Auto theft and vandalism in southern California is so rampant, those cities which don't just take reports over the phone send officers out mostly as a public relations effort, not because there is any likelihood of finding the car—let alone the thief.

I haven't owned many things as long as I've owned my Karmann Ghia, and have a sentimental attachment to even fewer. I'm not a car-worshipper by any means, but I've spent a lot of time in this one, and the broken window seemed like an injury to an old friend. But with the exception of allowing myself to engage in some rather unrealistic vigilante fantasies during the drive to Burrows' house, I knew it was best to try to shrug it off.

Edison Burrows lived in a quiet neighborhood where the branches of big oak trees were beginning to fill in their canopy above the streets with soft, bright green leaves. His house was typical of those built in the mid-1920s in Las Piernas, a small Spanish-style home with white stucco walls, a red tile roof, and arching windows. I parked on the street, got out with the calendars in hand, and caught myself just before I locked the car door.

Burrows opened the heavy wood panel door without bothering to peek at me through the small grilled window in it. The hour since we had talked on the phone seemed to have given him time to collect himself.

"Come in, come in," he said, then spying the calendars, "What have you brought with you?"

"Oh, just some things I don't want to leave in my car." I explained about the window and received just the right amount of sympathy before he seated me in a sunny kitchen and offered coffee.

He was a slightly built man, a little under six feet tall, I would guess. He bustled about the kitchen and talked energetically. His skin was pale but his cheeks were pink, and his thick brows rose and fell as he spoke. He had the look of someone who has spent most of his life indoors. He reminded me of someone, but I couldn't figure out who. The son on the streets? But which of many homeless men I had met in the last few days was Burrows' son?

"I'm so sorry to hear about Lucas," he said again, quiet for a moment. "He couldn't have been more than forty-something, right? About my son's age. I'm seventy-five—almost twice his age."

"You don't look seventy-five," I said.

"I don't act it, either," he said with a wink. "And I've got at least another twenty-five to act ornery."

He picked up a thick folder and a magnifying glass, then

sat at the table with me. He set the glass and folder to one side and began to tell me of his years as a documents examiner. He was clearly going to go about this in his own way, and I decided that it would be better to let him do so, if the alternative was something like that phone call.

"I worked for the county for years," he said.

"Las Piernas County?"

"Yes. About thirty years with them before I retired. Over that time, I had a few courses and studied with some interesting folks, and along the way I got to be pretty good at detecting forgeries and altered documents. I can tell you all about inks and papers. But my real specialty was typewriters." He laughed. "Boy, has that end of the business changed. Technology went leaps and bounds just about the time I retired."

"Computers and laser printers?"

He nodded. "That's just part of it. Anyway, it was much easier in the old days, when all the office work was done on the kind of machine Lucas used. A manual typewriter."

I thought back. "Yes, I remember now—what was it, a Remington?"

He shook his head. "Underwood. Lots of folks had moved to electric typewriters—IBM Selectrics, or Lanier word processors, if they could afford them. But to our good fortune, Lucas was used to this old Underwood. I guess he'd been using it since high school." He paused. "I'm getting a little ahead of myself here."

He patted the folder. "Lucas came to me with a challenge. He said he had some pages he had typed, and some pages someone else had typed. He said that Joshua—my son—had told him that I ought to be able to tell the difference."

"Your son is here in town?"

He was suddenly less animated. His shoulders drooped a little, and he ran a hand over his short white hair. "Yes. It breaks my heart, but I've given up trying to get him to come home. I know people have lots of reasons for being on the street, but with him it's the booze. I don't know what other reason he would have for living out there when he could be

with me. You know how many of those people living out
there with him wish they could have a warm place to stay?
He's had all kinds of advantages most of them haven't had,
and it makes not one bit of difference. Why? The booze. I
stopped giving him money. It just goes into the bottle with
him. But every time it rains or gets cold, I'm sick with
worry."

"He told Lucas to go to you for help, though. So he still
thinks of you."

Edison smiled. "Do you know how great I felt the day
Lucas Monroe called me and asked for my help—because my
son had recommended me to him? I would have helped Lucas
for free for the rest of his life . . ." His voice faltered. "Well,
I guess I did help him for the rest of his life. But not for free.
He did work around here for me. Painting, things like that. I
told him it wasn't necessary, but he wouldn't take no for an
answer."

"What was it he asked you to do?"

"He said he had a document that someone had inserted
some forged pages into. He had typed the original, someone
else had typed the forgeries. They had used the same paper,
and probably the same machine. Could I tell them apart?" He
smiled broadly. "Of course I could!"

He picked up the magnifying glass. "He told me that he
would want me to show the differences to you, that you
worked for the newspaper and might be willing to help him."
He opened the folder and tapped on the top page. "These are
photocopies—excellent copies, but copies all the same. I
worked from his originals for purposes of the examination,
of course. But I didn't want to mark those, so I copied them
and circled the places where the differences really stand out."

"Do you have the originals?" I asked.

"Oh . . . oh no. No, I don't. He didn't bring them to you?"

"No."

"I did have them for a time, but he took them with him the
last time I saw him."

"When was that?"

"Let's see. He stopped by . . . not last Saturday, but the previous Saturday."

"Ten days ago?"

"Yes. I had completed my work by then. It didn't take very long. Here—I'll show you."

27

He turned one of the pages toward me. It seemed to be a page of data gathered from a survey of an apartment building. It began with an address with cross-streets included, followed by a detailed description of the building, including number of units, parking spaces, laundry facilities, and so on. The page ended with the start of descriptions of the households in each apartment.

"This is a page that Lucas typed. What do you notice about the typing itself?"

I glanced at it. "It looks fairly neat to me. Is this from his thesis?"

Edison nodded. "Look closer." He handed me the magnifying glass, then reached over and pointed at several places on the page. "Wherever the letters *th* appear together."

As he pointed, I studied words like *the, tenth, mother,* and *father.* "The two letters are close together," I said. "Closer than some of the others."

"Very good! That's a habit of his. All typists have habits, patterns they develop over time. That's how I was able to do my job. There were the easy giveaways, of course—if someone used a different machine or ribbon. Each machine has its own characteristics—type wear and so on. But if the ribbon isn't available or the same machine was used, it helps to look at the habits of the typist.

"I asked Lucas to type something here for me," he went

on. "Had him use an old Remington I have in my den, told him just to type a note so I might have a sample of material that I had actually *seen* him type." He handed over another sheet of paper. "He was fast and quite accurate."

The paper read:

```
Thanks for the help, Edison. At least I
can now prove this part of it all. Don't
worry if it takes some time to come out
in the news. The last time Irene saw me,
I wasn't in such good shape. But I believe
she's the kind of person who tries hard
to be fair to others & when she sees what
you have discovered, I know she'll listen
to me.
    I may be able to hurry things along from
the other side, too. I've let sleeping
dogs lie for too many years.
    Take it easy,
```

Here he had scrawled his barely legible signature, then added this below it:

```
P.S. Don't worry about your son. I think
he's on his way home. I really do. I'll
call you in a week or 2. If you don't hear
from me in 2 weeks, please ask Joshua to
read PS23 to Irene.
```

I stared at this for a long time, not because I was studying his typing, but because some things will put your hands right into those of a ghost, and this was one of those things.

"Do you understand it?" Edison asked.

"Most of it, I think." Except his faith in my fairness.

When I didn't say more, Edison began talking about another page. Gradually, I tuned into what he was saying. "Could you repeat that?"

"The numerals. That's the first giveaway. You could see that even if you didn't notice the *th* pattern."

I looked at the page he was discussing. Another apartment-house survey.

"See how Lucas almost always types numerals instead of spelled-out numbers?" Edison asked, pointing to the first page we had studied, and then at the numerals in the note. "He was experienced with typing numerals, used them a lot in his work. Except in those places in the body of the thesis itself, where the style book would say numbers should be spelled out, he used numerals. I could show you many examples. But look at this other typist's work."

Sure enough, the new page showed numbers spelled out as words. "Three children: two males, aged eight and four; one female, aged six," one line read. On Lucas's survey, a similar line read: "3 children: 1 female, aged 12; 2 males, aged 10 & 9."

"He used an ampersand here, the forger didn't. Is that true throughout?"

He grinned. "Excellent. What else do you notice?"

I used the magnifying glass. "The *th* pattern is different, and . . ."

He laughed, seeing me point at certain letters. "Yes. Excellent."

"The letters *a, q,* and *z*. They're faint. And there's something weird about some of the capital letters."

"Yes, yes! When she uses the left-hand shift key, she doesn't always depress it properly, or she releases it too soon. Very good, very good!"

I looked up at him. You'd think I'd just asked him to dance. "What can you tell from this, besides that it's typed by a different typist?"

"That's quite a big discovery, wouldn't you say? But to answer your question, based on information Lucas gave me, I would suspect our culprit is Nadine Preston, not Andre Selman."

"He told you a lot, then."

"Only after I showed him I could prove two different typists were involved."

"How do you know it's Nadine?"

"I'm guessing there, but almost any sample of her typing would probably confirm my suspicions. Lucas said that the little finger of her left hand was crooked—broken in high school and never properly set. Perhaps that finger was a little weaker than the others, or so crooked her typing was impaired. That would explain what we see on the page."

"So this is what it was all about. Lucas's mother will be so relieved. If I can find the original documents, we can prove that someone tampered with his thesis. That would clear his name."

"Clear his name? Oh, that wasn't really what he was after."

"Then what?"

He picked up the pages, placed them neatly in the folder, but kept it open, staring down at the stack of copies. "Well, I don't claim to know all of his plans, of course. But we talked about a few of them. The ones concerning these." He fingered the edges of the pages, then looked up at me. "These weren't just numbers on a page, you know. Not to Lucas. They were people. Whole families. He felt a great injustice was done to them, and that he was partly to blame."

"What do you mean?"

"His statistics. He wanted the statistics to represent what was really going on in these neighborhoods. Low-income families, seniors, were living in these places."

"People who couldn't afford to move," I said, understanding where he was headed. "But redevelopment forced them to."

"Yes."

"But an argument might be made that the neighborhoods were decaying. That they needed to be brought to life again."

"Lucas said that some of the places they studied would benefit from office buildings and new retail districts. He said that was what excited him about the study in the first place. But then he saw that it wasn't enough for Andre Selman and his cronies. They saw money to be made from redevelopment."

"Andre Selman's study was used to decide where the boundary lines were to be drawn for redevelopment," I said. "I've already seen how the money-making end of this can work. But Lucas must have had some firsthand knowledge of what Andre's part in the scam was."

He nodded. "Lucas said that once he was off the project, Selman tampered with the statistics. Selman made sure that Lucas was discredited. Then he phonied up the numbers so that it looked as if fewer people were living in these places. Instead of an apartment hotel that had fifty families living in it, it suddenly had five. Fewer people to move, so the city doesn't look so bad forcing them out."

"And so Lucas decided to confront these people with his proof of their tampering with the numbers."

"Right. I think that's what he meant about awakening those sleeping dogs. All this time, they've been able to get away with it. Lucas always acted like there was more to it than disproving this study, but this was going to be the start of it."

It would have been easy to say to him, "This was all so long ago. It's too late to make amends." I wasn't even sure there was a way to make amends. The people who had lived in those buildings had either moved to other places or they were on the street. The "male aged ten" would be in his twenties now.

But I didn't say any of those things to Edison Burrows. For the most part, I didn't say them because I was certain there was more to this story, that Lucas had not told him everything. I had made up my mind after reading Lucas's note—he had wanted my help, and I would not refuse it this time.

"I need to see your son," I said. "Do you know where he is?"

"I can usually find him. If I haven't see him for a while, it will take days. But I saw Joshua last week, after that night it rained. I wanted to make sure he was all right. He was hanging out with some guy they call Blue."

"Blue? Wait—is your son called Corky?"

"Yes, that's Joshua's nickname. Have you met him?"

"I've met him." Once again, I decided against details. "He helped me out one day."

"Good, good. This will go easier if he's met you."

I wasn't so certain that was true, but didn't argue. We made arrangements to look for him the next morning.

Ensconced on the couch in a big warm blanket, the cat at my feet, dogs on the floor at my side, I started going through Ben Watterson's calendar for 1977. It was, I soon discovered, a diary after all. While he hadn't made long, journal-like entries in the seven-ring binder, these pages were obviously used to note events that had passed, not for reminders of his future engagements, although sometimes he did note that an item required follow-up, usually with an asterisk. The pages, two for each day, were preprinted from a company that specialized in appointment books. Each day was divided into twelve hours on each page, morning to the left, evening to the right. Ben put in some very long days.

His handwriting was neat and easy to read. The first time he entered a person's name, he wrote it in full. After that, he used initials or a shortened version of the name. I supposed the ones who were referred to with initials from the beginning of January were people first noted in other years. Those weren't necessarily harder to figure out. Context usually provided hints. "C." clearly stood for Claire, "R.H." for Roland Hill. Others remained beyond my ability to decipher.

The calendar was a gold mine, and I knew Claire was right—Ben never would have handed it over to a reporter.

Ben Watterson was a man who spent much of his life in meetings or on the phone. Reading it might have become utterly boring were it not for his occasional commentaries, brief but remarkably straightforward.

"Dull fund-raiser except for question re M.H.'s evening gown," one read. *"If placed on a cow, would effect reverse and make bovine look human?"*

The majority of his notations were about events and conversations I either didn't care about or couldn't make use of, owing to my promise to Claire. He was handling only the biggest decisions by 1977, but he noted the work of underlings as well. Business and social life mixed. *"Opera with C. and Chaffees,"* one January entry read. *"Horrid evening, but C. charmed them. He agreed to move accts to BLP."*

I called Claire at one point, giving her a list of some names and initials I wanted to verify—especially those in Moffett's dinner party. By that time I had reached the February entries. I had noticed a pattern that had great possibilities, so I asked for and received her permission to pull one other story out of the calendar: the one that would ensure that Allan Moffett would not return to city hall.

I was writing notes for that story when the dogs suddenly came to attention and moved toward the front door. They knew the sound of Frank's Volvo and could hear it before it was halfway down the street.

I heard him open the front door and stood up. Four things happened at once.

A scrap of paper fell out of the calendar and onto the floor.

The phone rang.

Frank asked, "What happened to your window?"

My beeper started dancing across the kitchen counter, humming as it went along.

28

Cody gleefully pounced on the note, and knowing his abilities as a hunter and shredder of paper, I made its retrieval my first priority.

"Could you get the phone?" I asked Frank, bending to snatch Cody's prize from him.

Cody was ready for me, transforming himself into a gyrating gray razorball. I managed to snatch the note from the floor while he was distracted with attacking my hand and arm with teeth and claws. I swore at him, managed to shake the little dervish loose from my arm, and looked up to see Frank motioning me to silence. He was listening intently, saying, "Just a moment."

I glanced at the paper, saw that it had been torn from something typewritten, but not much more, because Frank was calling me to the phone, I was bleeding from the cat attack, and the pager had moved up against a glass bowl and was ringing it like the closing bell at the New York Stock Exchange. That made the dogs bark.

"Could she call you right back?" I heard Frank say as I picked up the glass bowl and set the note beneath it—out of Cody's reach—then shut off the pager. As the dogs settled down, I heard him say, "Oh." I looked up to see him holding a hand over the mouthpiece, extending the receiver toward me, a kind of concerned apprehension in his eyes that made me forget everything else that had just happened, even the stinging on my arm. "It's your friend the doctor," he said.

"Becky?"

He nodded, and I moved around the counter, somehow seeing on his face that I didn't want the counter between us when I took this call.

"This is Irene."

"Irene, Becky Freedman. They brought Roberta into our emergency department a couple of hours ago."

"Roberta? Why?"

"Head trauma. Someone attacked her in her office. She's been in and out of consciousness. I did all I could, but I'm not sure she'll make it," Becky said, her voice breaking.

"You mean you were on duty when they brought her in?"

"Yes. The neurosurgeon's working on her now. No neck or spine injury, but the head trauma . . ." She paused. "I'm off duty now, but . . . I guess it's just now sinking in."

"Oh, Becky—"

"Ivy's here. Can you come down here, too?"

Frank insisted we delay only long enough to wash off my arm. As he tenderly put an antibiotic ointment on it, he frowned.

"Nothing too deep, thank God. That damn cat is a menace."
He looked up into my face, read my look of alarm, and said,
"Oh, come on, you know I'm too attached to him for that."

Jack came over just as we were leaving, offering to pet-sit
while we were at the hospital. "No rush," Jack said. "I've got
no plans this evening."

Frank lifted my arm, covered with bright red marks.
"Watch out for Cody."

We went in the Volvo. He drove. Becky was an emergency
physician at Las Piernas General Hospital, which was on the
other side of town. I spent most of the ride thinking about
Roberta.

In spite of the minor incidents of irritation between us, I
admired her. She was tireless, someone who gave of herself
in a time when that sort of generosity was treated with suspicion. She had put up with being called a do-gooder, a
chump. More than once, she had been forced to listen to the
same people who referred derisively to "psychobabble" tell
her in the next breath that she must be working off guilt. As
if the alternative—being as greedy as possible—was a supe-
rior way to live.

"You never told me what happened to your car window,"
Frank said, drawing me out of my thoughts. I told him about
the Karmann Ghia.

"Do you think it was Two Toes?" he asked.

"No. Did Reed Collins tell you about that?"

"What do *you* think?"

"That fink. I should have known."

"You should have known better than to park in an isolated
place—let alone an alley—especially when you knew this guy
was looking for you."

"Not now, Frank. You want to yell at me later, fine. You
want to talk to me like I'm five years old *after* we get back
home, great. But right now, I've got other things on my mind."

He was angry, but he didn't say anything more. I looked
down at my arm. Didn't smart as much as Frank's absolute
silence.

When we pulled into the hospital parking lot, I said, "I'm

sorry. Didn't mean to snap. I know you just want me to be safe."

He just held on to the steering wheel, not looking at me, but he sighed, which could be construed as encouragement. My eyes went to his hands on the wheel, the place where his starched white dress shirt cuffs contrasted with his tanned hands. There was something about that place where his wrists met his cuffs that made me wish my eyes were a camera, that I could somehow hold the image forever in my mind, and for a very brief moment there were no injured friends, no wrongs to be made right, no unanswered pagers or notes left unread on kitchen counters. It was a purely selfish moment.

When I looked back at his face, he was watching me, and I knew he had caught me, knew he knew exactly where I had been looking. The angry expression was gone. He smiled a little and reached up to stroke my hair. "I'm sorry, too," he said, and sighed again, just as softly, but this was a completely different sigh.

I understood it, glanced anxiously at the hospital buildings, and quickly said, "We'd better not."

He laughed and opened the car door. "Let's go, Catholic girl."

Becky was sitting on a bench in a hallway, head in hands. She was dressed in street clothes. Ivy Vines was sitting next to her, talking in a low voice. When Becky looked up at us, I saw her eyes were red-rimmed. I introduced Frank, and we moved to a set of chairs where we could all sit down together.

"They're getting her set up in intensive care," Becky said. "I decided to wait out here with Ivy." She looked at me more closely. "What happened to your arm?"

"Cat. It's fine. Tell me about Roberta."

"She was attacked in her office at the shelter. I don't know any details—I just saw the aftermath. The cops were here, tried to talk to her, but she never came around for long. Maybe I just asked you to be here for my own sake, but I also thought it would be good for her . . . familiar people around her, you know."

"I'm glad you called me," I said.

"Do you know the name of the detective who has the case?" Frank asked.

Becky searched through her pockets and handed him a business card with an LPPD detective's shield embossed on it.

He glanced at the card and handed it back to her. He excused himself and went off to a pay phone.

"She had your numbers—your's and Ivy's on a slip of paper in her skirt pocket," Becky said. "I called Ivy, and when I got another minute free, I called your home number. Ivy called your pager, too, but I guess you didn't have it with you."

"It went off at the same time the phone rang," I said. "Once I talked to you, I forgot all about the pager."

"Oh, God, I've got to call Lisa!" Ivy said, looking at her watch. "I guess she'd still be at Jerry's house. Lisa, Roberta, and I were going to try to catch a movie tonight. Lisa won't know what to think when I'm not home." She headed for the pay phones as well.

"Tell me about Roberta's injuries," I said to Becky.

"It looks like she took one strong blow to the back of her head and suffered some minor injuries from a fall—as if someone hit her from behind and she struck some furniture or some object as she fell forward. But her head injury—it's severe."

Frank came back and said, "I've talked to the detective who's handling the case. They don't know much at this stage, but apparently she walked in on an intruder. Matsuda—the detective I talked to—suspects the intruder was looking for money. Desk drawers were open, file cabinet was jimmied. Went through the secretary's office, too. Could be one of Roberta's clients, or someone from the shelter, since they seemed to know her schedule. That part of the shelter is pretty empty by late afternoon. The secretary was gone. The people at the shelter are pretty upset about it. Matsuda thinks Roberta came back early from a meeting, walked in on the burglar."

"No idea who it was, I suppose?" Becky said.

"Not really. But they've had some luck—turns out the offices were vacuumed while Roberta was out. Matsuda said that helped them to figure out there was one intruder. All kinds of people had stepped in Roberta's office—paramedics, people from the shelter. But in the secretary's office, there were only the intruder's footprints. They found some of the same prints in the places in Roberta's office where not so many other people had been walking. He's small, and he left some kind of pulp or seeds—something from some kind of plant in his footprints. The evidence technician thought it was something that had been stuck on the bottom of the intruder's shoes. The lab guys will work on it."

Ivy came back. "Lisa's really upset," she said. "She wanted to come down here, but I think I've convinced her to stay home. I told her we would call her if anything changed."

"Andre's in this hospital, isn't he?" I asked.

"Yes," Becky said. "Over in the CCU—Coronary Care Unit."

There was an uneasy silence, then Frank said, "Tell me about this group you're in. This SOS."

I let Becky and Ivy give him the explanations. They talked about the shelter, the fund-raisers, the amount of support the group provided.

"I understand all of that," he said. "About the women's shelter, and so on. Irene has told me that much. But what about Selman himself? How did he manage to inspire all of you to get together?" He studiously avoided eye contact with me when he asked this.

So it's been bothering you after all, I thought.

"Old history," Becky was saying.

"Okay, so it's old history," he persisted. "Fill me in."

Again I let the other women do the talking. Frank would look my way every now and then, but I could see that he was beginning to understand something about Andre's patterns, about the humiliation each of us had felt. "You have to remember," Becky said, "none of us had reputations as doormats."

Frank smiled. "I don't imagine you did."

"At first," Ivy said, "a relationship with Andre was mad

love. He was head over heels for you. He was passionate and generous. It was impressive, especially to a twenty-year-old—maybe women that age are more sophisticated now. I don't know. In any case, he chose younger women. You didn't have to be naive, except perhaps in one area—you had to be a romantic at heart."

"As if that leaves a lot of women out of the running," Becky said. "Besides, let's face it, we were all students, he was a *professor.* Talk about feeling sophisticated in your twenties!"

"Yes," Ivy said, then went on in the tones of a radio ad. "Young woman of today, *you* don't have to settle for those immature boys who are your peers! *You're* woman enough to have a *man!"*

"Exactly!" Becky said. "And Andre would want you all to himself during that time. What you wouldn't realize was that he was isolating you from your friends and family. You lost touch with anyone who would have been able to help you keep your balance."

Frank looked over at me.

"My father hated him," I said. "We all but stopped speaking to one another when I was dating Andre."

"It was the same with everyone. Stage two, he started the criticism bit," Ivy said. "Small things at first. How you made the toast that morning? A little too dark. The brand of spaghetti sauce you bought? Not really his favorite. What you chose to wear to a party? He hoped you'd never wear it again."

There were nods of agreement from Becky and me.

"I take it the criticisms increased?" Frank asked.

"Until that's all you were hearing," Becky said.

"Not all," Ivy said. "You'd have about six bad days with him, and one really incredibly good one. Then you'd have eight bad days, and one really incredibly good one."

"Right," Becky said, "but the bad days would be getting worse. Now it wasn't the way you wore your hair, but what went on in your head. Your opinions were groundless, just about every decision you made was a poor one. He had this saying—"

She looked at Ivy and me, and together we chorused, "Surely you don't mean . . ."

Frank laughed. "That bad, huh?"

"And worse. You liked the way an actor performed a part? 'Surely you don't mean you admire that mugging imbecile who ruined the second act?' he'd say."

"You'd like to see some of your old friends?" Ivy said. " 'Surely you don't mean those people who made that awful gaffe at the Beesoms' party? Surely not the ones who'd never read Nietzsche?' "

"By the time Andre broke up with you, at best you doubted your ability to choose men, and at worst you were severely depressed," Becky said. "He does the same thing every time."

Becky went on to tell him of Andre's breaking-up ritual, which made Frank wince, and repeated the fishing pole story, which made him grin.

"Andre never varied from that breaking-up pattern," Becky said.

Ivy and I exchanged a glance. "Yes, he did," I said. "With Nadine Preston."

"August of 1977," Ivy said.

Frank caught my look of surprise, but Becky spoke up before he could say anything.

"Wait!" she protested. "I don't know about this!"

Ivy gave a brief account of Andre's one known deviation from his script.

"How do you know it was August of 1977?" I asked.

"Jeff died that year," Ivy said. "Andre and I got together in early August, just after Andre and Nadine had their brief second fling."

"Jeff?" Becky asked.

"Jeff McCutchen, Andre's best friend. I dated him for a while before I got together with Andre. Up until the end, Jeff thought the world of Andre."

"I remember Jeff," Becky said. "But it must have been before you were dating him. Sort of a loner. I think Andre was his only—no, wait—Lucas Monroe knew him, too, didn't he?"

Ivy nodded. "After I started dating Andre, Lucas and Jeff used to go drinking together. Jeff did a lot of drugs, too, but Lucas was never into that scene."

The news that Jeff McCutchen and Lucas Monroe were friends shouldn't have surprised me—at one time, Lucas had thought the world of Andre, too.

Frank was watching me, and I could see 100 percent unadulterated curiosity on his face. I wanted to talk this over with him, but it would have to wait.

"Lucas was the one who brought Jeff to the hospital the night he died," Ivy said. "I wasn't with Andre or Jeff by then. It was about a month after Andre and I split up. Jeff came by to see me one night; he looked like hell, as if he hadn't shaved or showered or slept in days. He asked me if I was ever going to get back together with Andre."

She looked away from us, talked as if she saw some other listener.

"I said no, but then I added that I wasn't going to get back together with him, either. He said he didn't blame me for that, he just wanted to make sure I wasn't going back to Andre. He made me promise it was true. It wasn't a difficult promise to give. He smiled, gave me a hug, and said that was all he asked of me. He went home and killed himself."

"Oh God," Becky said, "I'm sorry. I didn't know that Jeff had died. I must have been at med school when this happened. I'm sorry, Ivy."

Ivy looked at her, as if surprised to hear another voice, then said, "Don't feel badly about what you said. As I told Irene, it was a long time ago. I wonder now if Jeff really knew what was going on when he acted as Andre's messenger. It's hard for me to believe he did. I don't know . . . He left a note for me and one for Lucas. I never saw Lucas's. Mine just said, 'If you ever loved me, keep your promise.' I felt incredibly guilty. Andre felt left out, I guess. In fact, the cruelest thing Andre ever said to me was that I caused Jeff to kill himself."

"That son of a bitch," Becky said. "Pure projection on his part. Ask Roberta."

The minute she said it, she clasped her hand over her

mouth and closed her eyes. When she opened them again, she said, "I'll check on her," and left.

Frank stood up and stretched. "Thanks for telling me about Selman," he said to Ivy. "I know it wasn't easy for you and Becky to dredge up the past."

"No problem," Ivy said. "If I hadn't moved on with my life, I suppose it would all be very painful. But if you look at the women in SOS, you'll see that we all kept going. We survived, we learned, we went on to better things." She smiled. "And in Irene's case, definitely on to a better man."

He actually blushed. "Well, I think I'll get a drink of water," he mumbled.

Ivy watched him as he walked off, and I could tell that she was eyeing his really great ass.

Well, I didn't care if she looked at the menu, as long as she didn't ask to be served.

"I have that information on Nadine for you," Ivy said, jolting me out of my own appreciation of his physique.

"Here?"

"No. At home. My friend just made a printout of her computer records. Should I fax it to you at work?"

I thought about this. "Sure, but call first so that I can pick it up as soon as it comes over. God knows what obscure corner of the *Express* it will end up in otherwise."

"Okay."

I thought about Roberta. "Ivy, did you know that Lucas died?"

She nodded. "Roberta told me."

I told her about the plans for Lucas's funeral, then added, "I'm going to say something that will sound a little strange, but it's really important. I think Lucas was murdered."

She drew in a breath, but didn't interrupt.

"I think he was murdered and I don't think Roberta was attacked by a burglar. Not a run-of-the-mill thief, anyway. Today my car window was bashed in, and the more I think about it, the more I'm sure it was by someone who hoped I'd left information in my car. There are other things I'm starting to wonder about, too, but—listen, what I'm saying is, be careful, okay? And don't tell *anyone*—and I do mean *any-one*—that you're helping me out with this, okay?"

She nodded, her eyes wide and fearful.

Frank came back and saw that look, and was about to ask something when Becky called to us. "She's in a room. Sorry, but the neurosurgeon will only give us a few minutes with her."

Frank took my hand as we walked to the intensive care unit, but said, "I'll wait here for you," when we reached the door.

29

A t first, the being on the bed—if it was a being—didn't seem to be Roberta. Her face was ash gray, relieved only by the black stitches on her lower lip and left eyebrow. The left side of her face was swollen. Her head was swathed in a white bandage. Tubes led in and out of her. An ICU nurse—calm, busy, the one to whom that burden of "intensive care" would fall—was making an adjustment to an IV. A man whom Becky was introducing as the neurosurgeon stood nearby, watching monitors. In the midst of all of this, Roberta seemed little and far too still.

I felt sick to my stomach.

"Only a few minutes, please," the neurosurgeon was saying.

A few minutes. How were we to take this in—to begin to believe what we were seeing—in a few minutes? What could I give her in that amount of time? I looked at her misshapen face.

Roberta?

I heard Becky saying it aloud. Becky the emergency physician. She was better at this than we were. She saw people who might be mistaken for dead all the time, right?

"Roberta, it's Becky. Ivy and Irene are here with me."

Nothing.

"Well, I guess I'll call Lisa and tell her we'll have to rent that movie on videotape, since you insist on lying around here," Ivy said. "Wonder if they'll let me bring popcorn into the ICU?"

Roberta's hand twitched. Becky looked over at the neurosurgeon, who seemed interested, but said nothing.

"I'm going to stay nearby, Roberta," Ivy said, her voice shaking as she added, "Here's Irene."

Here's Irene. Irene's tongue is cleaving to the roof of her mouth.

Find some way to encourage her, I told myself. Shouldn't be tough. What would *she* say? I suddenly remembered her office.

"Hello, Robbie," I said, and the hand twitched again. "There are all of these little strays that are going to be worried about you. Who else can they confide in? Just Robbie. There isn't any room in here to hang their artwork. Shall I tell them you'll be back soon?"

Her eyes flickered open, just for the briefest moment. I hoped she didn't really see me in that moment, hated to think my terrified face would follow her into unconsciousness. But the neurosurgeon made some kind of sound that I took to mean "good."

I told her that she was missing a chance to meet Frank, and that Ivy had already been caught staring at his buns when he went to get a drink of water, but outside of a laugh from Becky and Ivy, there was no response. I stepped back, and Becky took over. She was calling her Robbie, too.

The neurosurgeon smiled at Ivy and me, then made a shooing sign at us. We stepped out into the hallway, leaving Becky behind.

"I'm going to stick around here as long as possible," Ivy said, tears welling up. "God, she looks awful!"

No argument from me. Ivy walked with us as far as the front doors of the hospital. It was dark outside.

"Anything we can do for you?" Frank asked.

She shook her head. "I'll fax that stuff on Nadine to you tomorrow, Irene."

"Thanks. Have you read it?"

She shook her head. "Just glanced through it."

"What's the last place to request a transcript?"

"Nowhere. She didn't finish her master's."

"What?"

"Dropped out. Never showed up for the fall semester. I guess Andre really hurt her that second time around."

"So tell me what's on your mind," Frank said as we began the drive home.

I tried to go over all I had learned that day. It had been a long day, and when the story was starting to take longer than the ride home, he took an unexpected detour.

"Keep talking," he said. "We can drive around for a while. This way you won't get distracted or attacked by twenty-pound tomcats or hear phones or pagers. Besides, we've got a sitter."

"Good old Jack. Hope he doesn't feel like we're taking advantage of him."

"Are you kidding? He gets all of the benefits of having pets, with none of the vet bills, food bills, or shovel duty. Quit worrying about him. Go back to your story."

"I can't help but believe that what happened in town this past week—Ben's suicide, Allan's resignation, Lucas's death—this attack on Roberta—all have something to do with what went on in the summer of 1977."

"When Selman's first redevelopment study had been accepted and was being acted upon in city hall."

"Right. In seventy-seven, Andre completed a study for the city, one that probably ensured that certain folks made a lot of money. Lucas, who knew the statistics in the study were phony in some way, was discredited, thrown out of school. The person who helped discredit him was Nadine Preston."

"The only woman Selman ever went back to," Frank said.

I nodded. "And who conveniently left town after a fishing trip with Andre. I don't know if it will do much good to locate her. She seems completely untrustworthy. She destroyed Lucas's academic career and was apparently in cahoots with Andre. She probably knew she had Andre and his friends over a barrel, so she used Lucas to make her threat clear."

"You think she never intended to go into that hearing?"

"Exactly. I think Andre got the message and bought her off somehow. And Andre made other people buy him off, too—Ben Watterson was involved in it in some way, and Andre blackmailed Ben into giving him the Bertram for a song."

"How can Selman afford the slip fees and maintenance on something that size?" Frank asked.

"That was my question. I'll bet you'll discover that consulting fees and all kinds of other income find their way to him."

"Hmm. So you want to try to find Nadine Preston. You'll have her Social Security number tomorrow?"

"Yes, Ivy's faxing it to me. I know you can't look her up for me," I said, coaxing all the same.

"Oh, that would be illegal, wouldn't it?" he said, barely suppressing a grin.

"Yes."

"Don't worry. I think I can convince Reed that he ought to pursue her as someone who may have information on a possible homicide. That is, if you don't piss him off again tomorrow."

"Listen, Frank—I'm looking into all of this because I owe this much to Lucas, and for my own peace of mind. But it's also a story—one that John has been waiting for with more patience than I thought he possessed. Can Reed be trusted to keep this to himself?"

"He's trustworthy, so is Vince. But this gets tricky."

"If this gets into the hands of a competitor—I don't even like to think about it. I won't be working for a newspaper. My former coworkers would drive through my new workplace just to hear me say, 'May I have your order, please?' "

"Can't have that," he agreed. "Those places are bad for the

complexion, too. Wait a minute—would you give me extra fries?"

"You'd be looking for your beef."

"Okay, okay. I'll try to work something out with Reed. He owes me a couple of favors."

"I need for you to look up something else."

He shook his head in disbelief. "May I have your order, please?" he mimicked.

"This is serious. Could you look up Jeff McCutchen's suicide?"

He looked out at the darkened road. "August of 1977?"

"Right."

"Selman loses a lot of friends to suicide, wouldn't you say?"

"The thought did occur to me. They happened fairly far apart, and there are reasons to believe they were both suicides," I said. "I guess I still want to know where Andre was on the night Ben died."

"Carlos is pretty certain on that one, you know. Lots of people wanted to implicate your friend Claire—rich young widows don't get a lot of genuine sympathy. The note, the powder residue on Ben Watterson's hand, the angle of bullet wound—lots of other things make that one hard to question."

I shrugged. "Claire just admitted to me today that he was subject to depression—although she immediately minimized it. You think about Ben, how he usually did business, the reputation he had built. A leading citizen in every sense of the word. But if Lucas could prove that Ben knew Andre's studies were phony, Ben's reputation would go into the toilet."

"And the confidence of the bank's board of directors would probably go right with it."

"Yes."

" 'There is no cure.' Isn't that what the note said?"

"Yes. And he added something about avoiding days of pain."

"What about McCutchen?" Frank asked.

"Ivy said he used drugs and alcohol, left notes, looked like a very depressed individual when he visited her—a loner whose closest friend had run off with his girlfriend—and he made her say something that he referred to in his note. I guess it's hard to question. But just to make sure . . ."

"Yeah, I'll look into it."

"Thanks. One other thing."

He raised a brow. "Just one?"

"For now. Seeing Becky reminded me of it. If Andre Selman didn't have his heart medication with him, maybe it's because he gave it to someone else."

"Hmm. You think he slipped heart medication to Lucas?"

"Admit it's possible."

"Andre climbed all those flights of stairs with a heart condition?"

"No. He didn't have to. He just had to give the thermos to Lucas."

"Lucas wouldn't be very trusting of Andre, would he?"

"Probably not. Still, I think Lucas was seeing all of those guys who were hanging out with Moffett. I'm not sure what he said to them. Maybe he was trying to work his twelve-step program this way—you know, forgiving people. Maybe he was blackmailing them. So what if, on a cold night, someone makes a peace offering. A thermos full of nice hot coffee?"

"I'll talk to Carlos. He's undoubtedly asked them to look for those kinds of drugs in the toxicology screen."

I sighed and leaned my head back. "Thanks, Frank."

"Don't thank me. Theories are one thing, proof another. Conviction . . . well, don't get me started."

I thought he would head home then, but he took another detour and headed up the highest hill in Las Piernas, a hill that leads to a place called Auburn's Stand.

Auburn's Stand is what locals call the hill itself, but it's actually the name of a house that a rich guy owns. Halfway up the road to the house, there's a turnout that faces the ocean. Las Piernas becomes a sea of lights from this vantage point, which was the really hot makeout spot when I was in high school. Not that I was ever taken there, but I drove up there once during my junior year and had some pretty great daydreams about this guy who was a couple of years ahead of me in school. That was before the road was closed, and before the kid got drafted.

These days, the road is private, and to get to the turnout, you have to pass a security guard at a gate. So making out on Auburn's Stand has gone downhill, you might say.

We drove right up to the gate, though, and when the security guard stuck his gray head out of his booth, Frank rolled down the window and said, "Hi, Mackie. How have you been?"

Mackie smiled and said, "Not bad for an old coot. Long time no see, Harriman. Never expected to see you here this time of night. How's it hang—ooops, didn't see your lady friend there. Come back and talk to me some other time, Harriman."

The gate arm lifted and we drove through. Frank waved and rolled the window back up.

"You know I'm going to ask," I said.

He smiled. "Mackie's a retired cop. You know the guy who owns this place?"

I nodded. "Garth Williams. I like him."

"Me, too. He's good to Mackie."

"So are we going to find a bunch of squad cars parked at the old turnout?"

"How do you know about the turnout?" he asked.

"I grew up here, remember?"

The turnout was empty. We had the best seats in the house.

"Tell me you aren't a regular," I said, and he laughed.

"Not a regular. This is the first time I've been here to do something other than roust teenagers."

"Ah. Must have been patrolman days."

"That's what I wanted to talk to you about."

This sounded serious all of a sudden, so I waited.

"Let's get into the backseat," he said.

I want it said in my eulogy that I was a good sport.

From the backseat, the view was still spectacular, and we got to sit closer. He had an arm around me, I had my head on his shoulder, and he felt big and warm and almost perfect. But just when I thought he might lean down and kiss me, he said in a dreamy voice, "Remember Bakersfield?"

"Who could forget it?"

He looked at me as if he was trying to figure out if I was being sarcastic. "I meant, when we first met."

"So did I."

"We were attracted to each other, right?"

"Yes." The windows were starting to fog up, and I wanted to undo his buttons. But I didn't. He's being serious, I reminded myself.

"Well, tonight—listening to your friends? For the first time, I understood why I could never get to first base with you back then."

"Forgive me, Frank, but I don't remember an attempt to step up to the plate. After a while, I figured you thought of me as your sister."

That got a laugh. "No way. But give me credit for knowing that any move on you then would have been the wrong move. I always figured someone must have mistreated you. Someone had hurt you. You never talked about it, though."

"After Andre, I felt ashamed of myself." I shifted closer to him. "I got over it. But you're right—I was really attracted to you, but I didn't trust myself then. The last time I had been attracted to someone, it hadn't worked out so well."

"So, like I said, no first base. I might have taken you up to a place like this."

"Really?"

"No," he said after a moment. "I was too shy around you in those days."

I took his face in my hands and said, "It's the top of the first, Frank Harriman. Play ball!"

30

The house was dark when we got home. Jack was asleep on our couch, surrounded by animals. The dogs wagged their tails, waking him. He smiled sleepily, said he was going home, and walked back next door without another word.

We went straight to bed, tired and happy.

Edison Burrows called way too early in the morning—about five o'clock—but I managed to roust myself out of bed and arranged to meet him in an hour at the beach parking lot where I had last seen his son.

I was putting a piece of bread in the toaster when I noticed the glass bowl covering the note, the pager next to it. Through the bottom of the bowl, I saw these typewritten words:

```
Mr. Watterson,
   This is a copy of a note Jeffrey Mc-
Cutchen left for me just before he killed
himself. I didn't know what it meant then,
but I think I understand it now. It might
take me some time to convince others. Why
don't you save me the trouble? There is
no point in fighting this; I won't give
up.
   You were very generous to me once be-
fore. This photo proves I have not for-
gotten that.
```

"Frank!"

He came bounding out of the bedroom, half-asleep. "What?"

"Didn't mean to alarm you."

He rubbed a hand over his face. "What's wrong?"

"This note—it fell out of Ben's calendar. I think it's the one Lucas sent him with the picture!"

"What makes you think so?"

I showed him Lucas's distinctive typing trademarks.

"It was a 1977 calendar," he said, yawning. "Maybe it's an old note."

"You aren't awake yet, are you?"

"No," he answered truthfully.

"Claire said Ben had been getting nostalgic, remember? I think Lucas sent Ben a copy of Jeff McCutchen's suicide note."

"Hmm." His eyes were drifting shut.

"Frank, wouldn't the detectives investigating Jeff's suicide make copies of the suicide note?"

"No."

"No?"

"They'd keep the original."

"Can you get a copy from McCutchen's file?"

His eyes came open. "Huh? Oh. Maybe. Probably in storage by now." He yawned again. "I'm going back to bed."

I watched him pad back toward the bedroom, and wondered if he'd remember any part of our conversation. I recorded a memo for him on the answering machine before I left, and also included all the other items I had asked him to check on the previous night—asked before he hit a grand slam in the bottom of the ninth.

Before I left the house, I took three months out of Ben's calendar for 1977: July, August, and September. They made a thick stack of paper, which Cody eyed covetously. Before he could do more than that, I put them into a big manila envelope, along with my notes on Moffett's secret meetings. I'd

have to write the story on Moffett when I first got into work—
that was a bone that would hold the editorial wolves at bay
for a while, give me more leeway to pursue the stories that
interested me more avidly: stories of misrepresentation in redevelopment studies, suicidal bankers, and murdered friends.

It was chilly and gray out, the beginning of spring weather
on the southern California coast: cloudy in the early morning
clearing to hazy sunshine in the afternoon. Sometimes better,
sometimes worse, mostly little changed. It made the drive to
Blue's section of the beach a cold one; I spent most of the trip
trying to figure out when I was going to find time to have the
window repaired.

Edison Burrows was waiting in the parking lot, leaning
against the hood of a white Taurus station wagon. He was staring toward the ocean until he heard my car.

"Haven't seen any sign of him," he said, pulling his jacket
up against the brisk breeze.

"It's pretty early."

"Yes, I suppose so."

There was very little activity around us—a few joggers, a
walker or two. It was prime surfing time, but the surfers were
all down at the other major section of the beach, nearer the
house. Here, though, there were no real waves. My father once
told me that before the breakwater had been built, this section
of beach was a surfer's paradise. That was in the pre–*Beach
Blanket Bingo* days, not long after World War II. Annette was
still in mouse ears. Surfers weren't so numerous or organized
here then, and they lost this beach to harbors and marinas.

I heard someone coughing, a deep, barking cough, and
some loud swearing in response. I looked up and down the
beach, but couldn't tell where the voices came from.

A Parks and Recreation Department tractor started up, and
we watched it move out to clean up the sand. I glanced at one
of the closed-up lifeguard towers and saw four tousled heads
rise above the railings around it, then four faces scowling at
the tractor in annoyance. Looked like Blue and a few of his

best friends had tried to get out of the wind the night before.

"Is that your son?" I asked Edison, nodding toward the man I had been thinking of as Corky.

He gave a nervous smile. "Yes, that's Joshua."

Joshua saw us in the same moment. He lifted a hand in a stiff wave, then slowly made his way down the tower ladder. A fit of coughing stopped him partway down. Didn't seem to be doing too well. I figured that in addition to whatever was making him cough, he probably had a hangover.

I glanced at Edison and saw his mouth tighten.

Joshua Burrows carefully eased himself from the ladder to the sand. He rested his head against one of the rungs for a moment before turning toward us and beginning a slow trek across the beach. He was walking with a limp, holding his ribs on one side. Coughing. As he came closer, I could see that his face was bruised. His eyes were clear. Not hungover. Hurt.

"Hello, Dad," he said in a raspy voice when he reached us, and then nodded toward me. Anticipating his father's question, he said, "I got rolled a couple of nights ago."

Edison looked down at his shoes, but his voice was calm, undemanding, when he asked, "Have you been to a doctor?"

"No, no. Not yet." It seemed like he was worn out, out of breath. "Thinking of going, though. Maybe I'll go later today." He turned away as he started coughing again. When he stopped, he winced and shifted over to lean on the car.

"Ms. Kelly tells me you've met before?" Edison asked.

I felt like I had suddenly landed in a strange country where people have nothing left to live for but their manners, or think so. Sort of like the old movies where the aristocrats on safari stop in the middle of the jungle and have tea and crumpets, not realizing the local lions are planning a picnic, too.

Joshua nodded. "I've had the pleasure." He seemed out of breath, and took a moment to add, "So what brings you here?"

"Something Lucas said in a note." Edison started to reach inside his jacket, but paused and said, "Want to sit down? Out of the wind? We could sit in the car."

"No, thanks," he said, then looked at his father's face. "Well, sure. Why not?"

"You two take the front," I said.

"You take the front. I'll get in back," Joshua said.

Keep that distance, I thought.

When we were inside, the rank smell of Burrows the Younger's clothes and body were nearly enough to make me want to go outside and try to read their lips through the windshield. He leaned back in the seat, glanced over at me, and smirked. "Better crack a window for Ms. Kelly, Dad. Her sense of smell is more acute than yours."

Edison turned red.

"Forget it," I said. "I'm fine."

Joshua laughed and set off another coughing fit, this one doubling him over. "Hot," he said, breathing in odd, quick and shallow breaths, holding his ribs. "Damn, it's hot in here." It was quite cool, but a sheen of perspiration was covering his face. With clumsy fingers, he began unbuttoning his fatigue jacket. Beneath it, his clothes were stained with sweat.

Edison exchanged a glance with me. There was no confidence anywhere on his face.

Joshua leaned his head back again and closed his eyes. "So, you got a note from the Prof?" Back to talking like his street pals.

Edison pulled out the letter Lucas had typed at his home and handed it over the seat to his son.

Joshua read it, stared at it a long time. "Stupid damn thing for him to say. He should have known better."

"Never mind the part about coming home," Edison said, reminding me of what Lucas had written. "Just help Ms. Kelly understand what her part means."

His eyes didn't look as clear as they had a few moments ago. He closed them and murmured, "Too late. He could never get that through that thick skull of his." He had another coughing fit, then said wearily, "Too late for him. Too late for Las Piernas, and sure as hell too late for me."

I'm not noted for having a long fuse, so maybe it was my temper that made me say, "Edison, I can't take this. Either you drive him to the hospital, or you sit on this side and let me drive him there."

Edison looked startled for a moment, then locked the car doors and put his key in the ignition. Hearing them lock, I had a moment of panic as my claustrophobia kicked in. I looked for and found a release on my side. I moved my fingers over it, but didn't press it.

Joshua saw the gesture and smiled. "You sure you want to be locked in here with me and my B.O., Ms. Kelly?"

"No, but I'll live. You, I'm not so sure about. Start the car, Edison," I said. "Take him to the hospital."

"I don't need a fucking hospital."

"Joshua Burrows!" Edison said, just like a father. It was about time, though I would have picked a different issue.

"Sorry, Ms. Kelly, Dad. But I still don't need a hospital." There was no fight in it.

Edison drove off. We were closer to St. Anne's, but he was heading toward Las Piernas General. It only took me a minute to figure out why. Las Piernas General was closer to his house.

Joshua was staring at the letter. "I won't tell you, you know."

He was talking so low, I barely heard him.

"I don't need you to tell me, you spoiled brat."

That brought his head up. I glanced at Edison. He was smiling in spite of himself.

"Sure you do," Joshua said. He was wearing down, still having difficulty breathing, and he started to speak in short sentences, halting to breathe between them. "It says right here . . . 'PS23' . . . You don't know what it means."

"Yeah, well even though you look more like something out of the valley of death than my shepherd, I shall not want. I was supposed to go to Lucas's Bible, open to Psalm 23, and find the note. I hope he told you what that scrawl on the note meant, because I never would have figured out that it said 'cherubs' without help."

He closed his eyes.

"The bar in the Angelus, right?"

He swallowed hard, nodded.

"Look, Joshua—"

"Forget it. Lucas said . . . you were a quick study." He kept his eyes closed, but a slow smile crept up on his face, making him suddenly seem about fifteen years younger. "Ironic hiding place . . . for a guy in AA."

I smiled back, even though he didn't see it. "Yes," I said. "It fits his sense of humor, doesn't it?"

He nodded, opened his eyes, watched me.

"Is there more to the message?" I asked.

He started coughing again. Each time, it seemed to take him longer to stop. Edison kept looking in the rearview mirror.

"Secret panel in the bar . . . Lucas figured it out . . . said it was from . . . Prohibition days." He smiled again. "Couldn't fool him."

"Do you know what he hid there?"

"Papers."

"What kind of papers?"

He shook his head. "Wouldn't tell me. He said it might not be safe to know . . . always watching out for me."

He dozed most of the rest of the way.

"I think he has pneumonia!" Edison whispered to me. "I'm a terrible father."

"This does some good?"

"No," he said. "No."

Joshua woke up when we were just a few minutes away from the hospital. When he stopped coughing long enough to speak, he said, "Don't take me there. You can't force me—"

"Don't be ridiculous," Edison said. "You're going to the hospital and that's that! Just because you won't be able to drink for a few days—"

They started arguing loudly, saying pretty much the same thing over and over, with Joshua not sounding any better as it went on.

"You can keep tabs on a mutual friend," I said quietly.

They both shut up.

"I'm assuming you know Roberta Benson?"

Joshua nodded. "We all do . . . runs the shelter."

"She's in Las Piernas General."

"Why? She's not sick, is she?"

I was expecting cynicism, some remark about her being a

shrink—not this unabashed concern. "She's in a coma. Someone bashed the back of her skull in."

What little color he had beneath the bruises faded. He leaned his forehead against the window. "Why?"

"Walked in on someone robbing her office—that's the official theory. But she knew Lucas, and saw him as a client. I think someone was looking for a file on him. Or just trying to make sure her mouth stayed shut."

"Doesn't keep files on people. Just shelter business. Her policy." More coughing.

"She knew Lucas. You knew Lucas, too, and it's no secret. You want to tell me who hurt you?"

"Doesn't have anything to do with this."

"Tell me anyway."

He brooded for a moment, then said, "You don't tell the cops?"

"No. That's your business."

He looked toward his dad and shook his head. "He'd tell." But while Edison vehemently denied the accusation, Joshua held my attention, and very clearly held up two fingers, then pointed to the tip of one of his dirty running shoes.

Two Toes. My jaw dropped. Joshua was watching me. Watching me with bruises all over his face, maybe a few broken ribs, and God knows what else. Attacked in his sleep by the man who considered himself my guardian angel. "I thought Blue was going to protect you—"

"Blue wasn't around," Joshua said.

"I don't know who attacked Roberta," I said. "I don't think it was—the one who attacked you, but I don't know. I'm just trying to say that you and your dad need to watch each other's backs—that's too hard to do if you're on the streets, Joshua. You'll be safer here."

He didn't say anything.

"Maybe they can even help you get rid of that cough," I said.

"Why should you care?"

"I owe somebody."

"Lucas?"

"Yes."

"You knew what the note meant . . . why'd you come looking for me?"

"Two reasons. I didn't really know all of it, did I? And I've already told you the other reason."

"You owe Lucas."

"Right. So do you."

"I'm so tired," he said, but was completely docile after that.

31

Nina Howell, my pal in the Zoning Department, was delighted to be of help when I called her. Ray Aiken was acting city manager now, and her own boss was learning that administrative support personnel—which included secretaries—would be treated differently as long as Ray had anything to say about it. Nina's work life wasn't completely transformed, but it had improved.

"How can I get in touch with Charlotte Brady?" I asked her.

"Allan Moffett's former secretary?"

"Yes."

"Mr. Aiken asked her to come back. She's one of his assistants now. Want me to transfer you to her?"

I said I did, and spent the next five minutes listening to Charlotte rave about her new boss. I was feeling a little impatient; I needed to get a story in on Moffett's secret meetings, but I was also anxious to get back to following up on other matters.

"Ray Aiken always did all the real work around here anyway," Charlotte said in what I hoped was conclusion.

"Workhorses don't always make the best administrators," I said. "I'm glad Ray is doing so well."

"He's great. Now what can I do for you?"

"I wondered if you might verify a few items for me." I read off some of the information I had gathered from Ben's calendars.

"So what you want to know is, did Allan Moffett call these meetings in defiance of the Brown Act?"

Can't put anything over on Charlotte Brady. "That's what I want to independently verify," I said. "I already know it."

"Until I talk to Mr. Aiken about this—hmmm. You know nothing will come of it, right? I mean, even under the terms of the Brown Act, there won't be much you can do?"

"Of course not. In the first place, the law only concerns legislative bodies and their committees, not the city manager himself. But those meetings were held illegally, and Allan was the one who put them together. The public has a right to know that the man they entrusted over all those years abused that trust."

"He'd never make a comeback, would he?"

"It would be doubtful at best."

"Oh, I am so tempted! Tell you what. Off the record? You are right on target. That little bastard had more secret meetings than J. Edgar Hoover and his dressmaker."

"Now Charlotte . . ."

"But I can give you the name and number of someone who would probably love to verify it on the record."

"Who might that be?"

"Why, Allan's ex-wife."

"I don't know—"

"Are you kidding? Double check with whoever gave you those names in the first place. Nancy went to half of those meetings. She was a looker, and Allan liked to show her off."

I called Claire first.

"Irene! I just read about Roberta in this morning's paper!"

I talked to her about the events of the prior evening, then said, "I talked to Becky this morning. She told me Roberta's color is better today, but otherwise there's no change."

"I should call Becky. Maybe I can help her somehow, make it easier for her to spend time with Roberta when she's off duty."

"She'd probably appreciate that. I have a favor to ask, too. Do you know who 'N.M.' is in Ben's calendars?"

"Sure. Nancy Moffett. Allan's ex-wife. He used to bring her everywhere. Boy, was he ever nasty to her in the divorce. Nancy and I are friends. Do you need her number?"

I called Nancy Moffett, and got an earful.

When I called a few of the other attendees at these secret meetings, I was able to truthfully say, "I've verified this from three different sources . . ." and ask if they had anything to add, or say in their own defense.

People will talk, especially if they think others are talking about them. I had everything in place on one side of the story. Moffett's turn.

He surprised me by answering his phone. Every other time I had called in the past week, I got a machine, and though I had left messages, my calls were not returned.

"Mr. Moffett, this is Irene Kelly. I've talked to several people today who will go on record as saying that while you were city manager, you asked them to attend meetings which—as you were fully aware—were in violation of the Brown Act. I wanted to give you an opportunity to respond to these allegations."

He let me list a few of the meetings before he said, "Well, Ms. Kelly—off the record, which is the only way I'll talk to you—if you know your Brown Act so goddamn well, you know that the worst you could do would be to demand the reversal of some of the decisions made in those meetings, which is not likely, since they almost all fall under protected categories. And you also know that I can't be held personally responsible for those violations. You know that my position was not subject to the Brown Act, but that even if I had been a council member, you'd have to sue the city, not me. So screw you."

"Now Allan, that's a little hostile. I don't even know how I find it within me to do this, but I'll ask again, and for your own sake, this should be *on* the record, Allan. Do you have a response to the allegations?"

"No comment."

"Okay, well, that takes care of that. I suppose I should mention that I completely understand that you probably can't be jailed or sued for being underhanded, and no one I know wants to bother suing the city over the acts of a—well, over someone like you—and it is too late to undo most of the damage you've done. Still, the public will not be pleased to learn you spent the last twenty years sneaking around in clandestine meetings, privately deciding how to spend their tax dollars. They may have suspected something like this all along, but once it hits print, it's sort of a declaration that you've made them out to be fools. It's a mistake, Allan, to underestimate just how cranky the local citizenry may feel when that happens."

"You miss the point, Kelly. I don't plan to return to public life, and one of the best things about being a private citizen will be to tell you—you and your friends at the *Express*—to fuck off."

Thank goodness he told me to fuck off. It conveyed more than how he wished to say good-bye. Hearing that phrase, I knew he was nervous, maybe even scared. Moffett never uses ye old f-word unless he's afraid. He's fairly foul-mouthed as public servants go, and he'll say all kinds of other nasty things, but Allan never uses that one unless he's feeling rabbity. Sort of a "best defense is offensiveness" philosophy.

Well, as far as I'm concerned, Allan can say "fuck" every fifteen seconds if he wants to. What mattered to me was knowing he doesn't say it so often; he says it only when he's close to freaking out. I make it my business to know things like this about Moffett and other officials. In his case, I learned these habits of speech because I've listened to him for a dozen years—in meetings and interviews—and during that time had so little cooperation from him, I had to learn to read whatever clues his habits gave me.

"So you have no plans to return?" I asked.

"None."

"Then why insist on being off the record, Allan?"

No reply.

"I think you do plan to come back. Resignation is sort of like marriage—resign in haste, repent at leisure, right?"

Silence, but I could hear him breathing, and he was breathing almost as hard as Joshua Burrows.

"You probably had a moment of panic the other day," I went on. "You resigned, lived to regret it, and now you figure once you've tied up some loose ends, you'll be back. But you should get used to it, Allan. This time, the mess is too big. And someone's screwing up the cleanup, don't you think?"

"What the fuck are you talking about?"

"I'm talking about Lucas Monroe," I replied.

"I don't know any Lucas Monroe!"

"You used to go fishing with him."

"I've been fishing with lots of people."

"He even took your picture on a fishing boat."

"Lots of people have taken my picture."

"He was in your office last Wednesday—a week ago today. I'll bet the cops have already talked to you about it."

"A black guy insisted on seeing me on Wednesday. I didn't know his fucking name. Wanted help with the homeless shelter. I explained to him that I was planning to retire and couldn't help him."

"Some nameless, homeless, African American man was the first person to get the announcement of your retirement?"

"Funny world, isn't it?"

"No. I don't think it's so funny right now. He's dead."

"I don't know a thing about that."

"I suppose you don't know anything about what happened to Roberta Benson?"

"Roberta Benson . . . the shelter lady?"

"Don't play dumb with me, Allan. It's in today's *Express.*"

"Never read the rag."

"Even if you haven't read it, you know exactly who she is. Someone attacked her in her office last night. She's in a coma."

"What in the fucking hell is going on?" he said vehemently, then catching himself, added lamely, "I mean, it's sad, but what does it have to do with me?"

If I had been sitting across from him, I would have been able to pick up other cues from his posture, his eyes, what he did with his hands. As it was, I couldn't be certain, but it seemed to me that Allan didn't know who hurt Roberta, but was scared all the same. Why would he be? Because he was afraid it was someone who could be connected to him?

"No idea who might be taking care of your potential enemies, Allan?"

"What the fuck are you talking about? No fucking way is the fucking shelter director my fucking enemy! I'm not going to sit here and listen to this kind of fucking nonsense!"

He hung up. Didn't matter. I'd hit the mother-effing lode.

I scrolled through the story on my screen, typed "Contacted by the *Express,* Moffett declined to comment on the allegations," and hit the keys that file a story on the computer. I called Murray, having made a promise, and told him he might be interested in the story I had just filed.

John had asked me to let him know when I filed it, so I went into his office and watched as he pulled it up. He read it, keeping his face expressionless, which is something you get used to when you work with John.

His comments to me were strictly along the lines of follow-up, and I told him that I had already talked to Murray. "Moffett thinks he's out of reach," I said, and repeated a few of Moffett's off-the-record ratings on the subject of the Brown Act.

John grunted in disbelief. "Moffett might be beyond the reach of the law," he said, "but he's not beyond the reach of public opinion. No politician in this town is going to want to be tarred with the same brush—they'll all steer clear of him. And even if he tried to get hired somewhere else, a scandal here would make him too risky to touch. Scandal's worse than a lawsuit to a guy like Moffett."

"At least Moffett deserves his damaged reputation," I said, thinking of Lucas. "And I'm not done with him. This isn't why he resigned."

We talked about my progress on that part of the story. John seemed less irritated with me now, probably because I had handed something in. Not just any something—we both knew that Wrigley would quickly calculate how many papers a "Secret Meetings" headline would sell.

As if Winston Wrigley III—"Duck and cover, here comes WW III," the staff would say—had crossed his mind, too, John said, "Kelly, would you happen to know anything about Mr. Wrigley's pager number being widely distributed?"

"Why, now that you mention it, he did ask me to give it to a good-looking rich widow. Is he being pestered by gangs of them now?"

"No, but he's been paged by several funeral homes, pet hospitals, psychiatric facilities, and other establishments in the last twenty-four hours. And surprisingly, they always seem rather annoyed at him, and don't seem to understand why he's called, even though their numbers are on his pager. He said it was going off all night. He couldn't figure out how to set it to the vibrating mode, so he finally put it in the glove compartment of his car. Then he worried all night that someone important might be trying to reach him."

"A pager would hardly seem worth it, would it?" I said.

"He just might be seeing it that way himself, Kelly."

I went back to my desk and checked my voice mail. There was a message from Lisa Selman, sounding forlorn, asking me to call. I did and got her father's machine, and left a return message with my pager number. In spite of my glee over Wrigley's torture, I had to admit the pager had been handy. Still, I bridled at the thought of being forced to carry one at all times.

I called Keene Dage and left a message on his answering machine. "Keene, you'd be surprised at what I've learned lately. I know you can tell me more. Let's get together and talk."

He'd probably ignore it, but you never know when being a pest will pay off. I called Jerry Selman's number again, this time leaving a message for him to call me. I was hoping he could shed some light on his father's ex-girlfriend. I thought of calling Corbin Tyler and leaning on him, too. Because I chicken out sometimes, I convinced myself I had better things to do.

I took a few pages of Ben's calendar out of the envelope I had stuffed them in—end of July and early August. The pages were filled until August 8. That day was blank. So was the one after it. And the one after that.

When looking through the pages of the earlier months of 1977, I had found other blanks, but only one here or there. August 9, August 10, August 11. On and on, nothing. Claire had said Ben wouldn't write if he felt depressed. This must have been a major blue funk. I went as far as August 16, the last of the pages I had pulled out, without seeing another entry. I was going to try to pull out the next set, but Ivy called to say she was about to send Nadine Preston's records by fax.

I hastily put the calendar pages back into the envelope and carried it with me to the fax machine. The fax chirped, and the transmission began.

It was a long one, about fifteen pages, which caused complaints from a couple of people who wanted to use the fax machine. But bigger problems came from those who were curious about my hovering over it, shielding the pages of the fax so they couldn't be read as they were received. I eventually grabbed a copy of yesterday's late edition and propped a tent of classified ads over the receiving tray. The fax wasn't important to any of them, but some of my coworkers seem to think that if we aren't pesky with each other, we'll get out of practice for the job.

As the last page was coming through, the fax machine made a high-pitched squealing sound and stopped working.

"What's wrong with it?" I called to Lydia. Among the people who happened to be in the newsroom at that moment, she was the only one I trusted.

She came over, pressed a button that shut off the squealing sound—much to everyone's relief—and said, "It needs a new cartridge."

"A toner cartridge?"

"No," she said, opening the lid of the machine. "This is a plain paper fax. Doesn't work like the old ones." She looked over to see Dorothy Bliss edging closer. "Buzz off, Dorothy. Irene gets it."

Dorothy left sputtering, while I wondered what on earth Lydia was talking about. As I held my faxes close, Lydia pulled a gray object out of the machine.

"Hold this," she said. "Don't give it to anyone. It's the printing cartridge."

It looked like a square, gray, plastic frame; two long, enclosed spools were braced together at each end by thinner side pieces. Stretched between the spools was a thin film, shiny black on one side, dull black on the other.

Lydia glanced over, saw me examining it. "That's the ribbon," she said.

On the ribbon, there was a perfect negative image of the page I had just received. I suddenly understood why Lydia was giving it to me. I held it while she found a replacement cartridge and inserted the new one in the machine.

I went to my desk and sat on the fax pages. Now that I had both hands free, I examined the cartridge more closely. Somewhat like a film cartridge, one of its spools was made to hold unused ribbon, while the other acted as a take-up spool after exposure. I started to pull on the take-up spool. Out came a length of images, black and white reversed. The thin ribbon crackled, but was stronger than it looked. It reminded me of the carbon ribbon in an electric typewriter, but it was much wider. When I had all my pages, I took out a pair of scissors and cut them from the film. I got an envelope from my desk, and put the ribbon clipping in it, then placed the actual pages in a second envelope. Keeping hold of both envelopes, I took the cartridge back to Lydia.

"Thanks," I said. "I never knew that the machine held a second copy of everything that was faxed here. Kind of dangerous, when you think about it."

"People fax things all the time without knowing about that. Think about what happens at businesses," Lydia said. "Someone does what you just did; stands by the fax and picks up a confidential memo, not knowing that anyone else in the office could open up the fax and read the image in negative. Or obtain signatures and credit card numbers and all the other sorts of things that people fax in 'confidence.' "

She stopped talking, then said, "You're pulling on your lower lip."

"Thanks, Lydia," I said numbly and went back to my desk. I wanted to read the faxes, but what Lydia had said about the machine stirred a memory.

I called Charlotte Brady.

"Charlotte, it's Irene. Couple of things. First of all, I don't think you need to worry about Allan coming back."

I waited for her to stop cheering, then asked, "Was his fax machine a plain paper fax?"

"Yes," she said. "With the volume of material we receive in this office, that saves a lot of time. Why?"

With my fingers crossed, I asked, "Has the printing cartridge been replaced since Allan left?"

"No . . . oh. Uh-oh."

It took me about fifteen minutes to cajole her into even handing the phone over to Ray, since she wasn't going to consider just giving me the cartridge. Ray was a hard sell, but eventually I got him to agree to let Charlotte unravel the spool and clip out any pages Allan Moffett had received from Ben Watterson on the day Ben killed himself. I told him I had at least one page of it, and was bound to get any others from other sources, but time was of the essence, and I'd appreciate his help. Maybe not entirely true, but good enough to get Ray to bend a little.

He decided I could see the fax ribbon under three conditions. First, I would see it only if it was not confidential accounting information—Allan's or the city's. Second, Ray would get to look at it first, and could withhold it, if it was something that might make the city look bad. Third, I swore not to reveal my sources.

Although I could live with the third one, I didn't like the first one much and the second one not at all. But he wasn't going to budge, so I took the best I could get. Charlotte asked me to stop by in an hour.

I went back to the faxes Ivy had sent to me.

It was totally illegal for a college employee to give me access to Nadine's transcripts, of course, and I was very protective of any sources (in this case, Ivy and her friend) who took this kind of risk. I was sparing in my requests of such sources, having once—in younger days—cost someone their job over information that didn't seem so important after all. There were other reporters in that newsroom who would have loved to learn who my source at the college was, how I got my hands on protected records. Most understood I'd never let them know, and that was that. They might be envious, but they'd live with it. In a few of my more aggressive, competitive colleagues, it inspired a near-rabid desire to turn their investigative talents on me. It gets tiresome. I've learned a few tricks for avoiding them when they are in that sort of mood.

That's why, when Lydia came to tell me I had a call, I was sitting—fully clothed—on a toilet in a closed stall of the women's room, going over Nadine's transcripts and registration records.

"Keene Dage is on the phone," she said.

32

I folded the faxes and stuffed them into the same big manila envelope that held Ben's calendar pages before unlatching the stall door. When I got to my desk, I kept my elbows on top of the envelope while I talked to Keene.

The connection was noisy, with the sound of a motor in the background.

"I just picked up your message from my machine," he said. "I'm here in Las Piernas. I had to come up here today."

"So you want to get together and talk?" I asked.

Silence.

"I'm learning more about this every day, Keene. I now know enough to have a pretty good idea about what has been going on."

"So you say."

"You think I'm bluffing? Okay, fine. I'm picturing a boat with a group of men on it. You're one of them. There's a young woman named Nadine Preston."

"Shit." Afraid, not angry.

I pressed my advantage. "Oddly enough, this isn't about fishing. It's about buildings. And about a man being cheated out of his future. And other things. It hasn't been easy on you to be a part of it, has it Keene?"

"No! It hasn't!" He paused. "I'm surprised you still think enough of me to figure that out."

"I do have faith in you, Keene, or I wouldn't be trying to get you to tell me your side of the story. Sooner or later, someone is going to talk to me. It can be you, or it can be someone else. But the first one to get this off his chest has the best chance to tell it his way. You want one of the others to give me his version instead?"

"No."

"You want to talk to me, Keene?"

Even over the noisy connection, I could hear his sigh. "Believe it or not, yes, I do. This has gone far enough. Moffett just called me a few minutes ago. Madder than a wet hen. Bastard thinks I've already talked to you."

I thought of how quickly word seemed to pass between the members of this group. "Are you on a cellular phone?" I asked, wondering if I was acting a little paranoid.

"Yes, I'm in the car. Are you having trouble hearing me?"

"No, and I'm afraid someone else might not be having any trouble hearing us. Cellular phones aren't very secure."

"Oh, I see what you mean. But the odds—"

"Too many people around here have been unlucky lately."

"I'll call back from a pay phone."

He called back just when I was sure he had been mugged or shot or dispatched by some other means. "Goddamn, it's hard to find a public phone that works around here!" he said.

"Just glad to know you're safe. What are you doing in town?"

"Had to check up on a property I just acquired."

"The Angelus?"

He grunted. "I shouldn't be surprised that you already know that, but I am. Yes, the Angelus. I was going to talk to you about it anyway. I saw my kids today and—well, never mind, I'll explain all that later. Do you believe me?"

"Yes."

"I have to do this my own way." There was a silence, then he said, "Why don't you meet me at the little park on the corner of Twentieth and Laguna?"

I wasn't too familiar with that area, but I had seen the park and supposed I could find it easily enough. "When?"

"Two-thirty okay with you?"

I looked at my watch. It was one o'clock. I figured I could make a phone call, get over to Ray Aiken's office, and still have plenty of travel time to spare. "Sure."

"See you then."

I called Frank, told him about my morning, and gave him Nadine's Social Security number. When he'd asked the coroner about heart medications, Carlos had told him yes, they'd thought of that, and to be patient, the toxicology work would take at least another week.

"Jeff McCutchen?"

"It's really weird, I know, but sometimes these guys at the police department—my lieutenant, people like that? They like to look over at my desk and see me doing work on the cases *they've* assigned to me."

"Sorry. I know you're busy. Thanks for all you've done— I'll leave you alone for the rest of the day."

"Don't you dare. I'm just saying it might take a little time, okay?"

"Okay. And I do appreciate it. I'll try to think up some suitable reward for you."

"Extra innings?"

I laughed. "Sure. But what are we going to do for you?"

We talked for a while about household matters—what was

needed from the store, who would pick up the dry cleaning, and was the bank deposit made.

"I called a couple of repair places," he said, and quoted a range of prices, naming the two shops which were most reasonable. "Which one do you want to take your car to?"

"You didn't have to do that on top of everything else you've got on your plate," I said.

"I knew you'd put it off," he said with annoying accuracy. "They're saying there's a chance of rain tomorrow. Let's get your window fixed today."

"Don't know if I'll have time."

"Take the car in. I'll pick you up after work."

"I'll see what I can do."

That didn't make him happy, but he got another call, so we said good-bye with the understanding that I'd phone again a little later in the afternoon.

My phone rang a few minutes later. As soon as I picked it up and identified myself, I got an earful.

"Are you trying to kill him? I don't know what the hell you think you're up to, but I won't stand for it!"

"Jerry?"

"My father's relationship with that woman is none of your business. I won't have him upset. Do you understand?"

"Jerry, I called you, not your father. I'm not trying to harm him. I just want to know about Nadine Preston."

"No good will come of this," he said. "Leave us alone."

He hung up.

I was disappointed, but figured his father's illness had placed him under a strain. Maybe he'd settle down and talk to me later.

I took my pager out, saw that it still had Ivy's old message on it, along with all the others I had received. I tried to clear them. All the functions on the pager were handled by pressing two buttons, both made for someone with fingers the size of a chipmunk's. I pushed the buttons in frustration, ultimately succeeding in my task by default—I have no idea which combination of button-pressing did the trick.

Feeling that unparalleled sense of satisfaction that comes

to a conqueror of electronic devices, I dropped the pager into my purse. (The manufacturers should give out karate-type belts: yellow belt, can use memory dial on the phone; brown belt, can use all the functions on a VCR; black belt, can install peripheral devices on home computer.) I told Lydia where I'd be, grabbed the fax envelopes, and took off.

"Here you are," Charlotte said, handing me a section of black fax ribbon that was about two feet long. "Ray said that if you could make anything of this, you were welcome to it. I just think it's sad, myself."

I held the ribbon up to the light. The first page was a cover page with Ben Watterson's letterhead on it. Written in the same handwriting I had seen in his calendars was a brief note:

> *Here it is.*
> *Now what will you do, Allan?*
> *I don't believe I can bear to learn the answer.*

The next page was the note to Ben from Lucas, the one I had already seen, saying that what followed was Jeff McCutchen's note.

McCutchen's note began in a tight, careful hand and ended in a loose, erratic scrawl:

> *After all he has done, I should want revenge. I don't. I wish I did. It would be something to look forward to. Alas, I'm nothing more than a miserable son of a bitch who can no longer afford nor find pleasure in his vices. A sad state of affairs, my friend. I can't feel a thing. Starvation without appetite. Emptiness. Worse than pain.*
> *I just want out.*
> *Don't blame yourself for any of this. I've always had less courage than you, Lucas. If I had any courage, I would have told you about him a long time ago.*
> *I owe you something for that.*
> *I watched from a distance the last time you were be-*

*trayed by him. It only cost me a quarter. Jeff McCutchen,
Budget Spy.*

*What good is the truth if you don't have the power to
make anyone believe it? I don't have to tell you the answer
to that one. And I don't have the truth. I just have a guess.
My curiosity is gone, Lucas. Here's my last guess about
anything:*

33 44 30
118 9 36

*I won't make this easy for you, simply because I believe
you would be better off not knowing. But my judgment is
notoriously poor, so if you decide you must know, this hint
should be enough.*

Maybe this will never do anyone any good.

Am I Judas if he is not Jesus?

Will the dead rise again?

*You're good at math, Lucas, but how are you with
numbers?*

Charlotte was watching me. "You're right," I said. "It's sad
that anyone should have ever felt this way." I didn't say more
because I didn't want Charlotte or her boss to believe they
were giving me something important. No matter how rambling or affected by drugs Jeff McCutchen's words were,
these were his last. I've yet to read an unimportant suicide
note.

I tucked it into the envelope which held the other section
of fax ribbon, asked Charlotte to give Ray my thanks, and left.

I thought about the note as I drove to meet Keene Dage.
"How are you with numbers?" McCutchen had asked. What
could they represent? A pair of combinations for a safe? Was
the second set "118 and 9" or "11 and 89"? Perhaps these were
some kind of computer passwords. If Ben Watterson had so
quickly understood their meaning, perhaps they were terms of
a loan, or dollar figures. But what had only cost a quarter? The
more I thought about the note, the less sense it made to me.

* * *

"What happened to your window?" Keene asked when I stepped out of the Karmann Ghia. I told him and he shook his head. "Supposed to rain tomorrow. I know a guy not far from here that does good work. Reasonable. Come on, follow me over there and we'll get it fixed."

I was about to protest, but figured the time I'd save in answering questions about my broken window would make up for whatever it'd take to drop the car off. Besides, I didn't want to start out on the wrong foot with Keene.

He was right, the shop was close by, and the one he had in mind not only specialized in VWs, Porsches, and Audis, but was in a sort of minimall of repair shops, including a glass shop. One way or another, I'd get a new window. "I built this place," Keene said, with not a little pride. "Lots of special considerations in this kind of building, but the auto guys appreciate the thought that went into it. I never have vacancies here. Minute a shop opens up, someone wants to rent it."

The owner greeted Keene like a long-lost cousin, quoted me a price that was just above being suspiciously low, and said he could have it ready for me the next day. I called Frank, but he was out, so I left a message on his voice mail saying where the car was and taking him up on an offer for a ride home.

"Come on," Keene said, after I had signed the paperwork. "I want to show you my city."

"What's in the envelopes?" he asked as I settled them under my feet in the big Mercedes.

"Some stuff for work," I said.

He laughed. "Not exactly a two-way street with you reporters, is it?"

"No, so don't take it personally."

That seemed to amuse him, too.

He started talking about O'Connor, the man who had taught me most of what I know about reporting. They were drinking buddies, Keene said, which put him in a group that might not fill a stadium, but which would probably sell enough tickets to allow a home game to be shown on TV.

"That was before I quit drinking," Keene said, "almost thirteen years ago. I still spent time with O'Connor—early on he let me know he wouldn't try to tempt me. He'd call me up and say, 'Let's have lunch, you rich and sober son of a bitch. You buy the sandwich, I'll buy the water.' Good man. Everybody knew it. Had his faults, but he was a good man."

He was silent for a time, and I didn't ask him any questions. I was thinking my own thoughts of O'Connor.

He took me downtown, and until he drove past the paper, I worried that he might have changed his mind about talking to me, that he was going to take me back to the *Express* and go home to Fallbrook. But about half a block past the Wrigley Building, he started pointing out his work.

"Corbin Tyler did a great job on that restaurant design," he said, pointing to a popular eatery. "My company did all the work. Lovely building to start with—a Schilling. You don't know of him, I suppose, but he was very popular in his day. Lots of work in Las Piernas. Corbin studied all of the old prints, drew his lines to complement the original design. Owners were pleased." He pointed to the monolith that was the BLP. "We did the new bank building, of course. There was an abandoned drugstore there before. And here—this clothing store? That was a massage parlor. Not much of a building there before, so we didn't save it. The masonry was unreinforced, so it probably would have cost a fortune to bring it up to code."

Cars were passing us, drivers giving him dirty looks, but Keene paid not one bit of attention. He was so preoccupied with looking up at buildings, for a time I worried that he would rear-end somebody. But he seemed to have this style of driving down to a science, and I began to relax and enjoy the show. He pointed out building after building, some new, some remodeled; some for Roland Hill, some for other developers; a favorite here or there, a story behind each one.

"Do you remember what it was like before?" he asked, when the tour seemed to be over.

"Yes. The skyline was lower, and many of the buildings were getting run-down, but—"

"Run-down! Twenty-five years ago, downtown Las Piernas was a pukehole! It was the three Ds—dirty, dangerous, and dying."

I didn't argue. He was right, but still . . .

"You miss the old buildings," he said, reading my mind. Or maybe my obstinate look.

"Not all of them, but yes, there was a charm and beauty to them that I just don't find in the BLP building—no offense."

"None taken. I'm with you."

"What?"

"I just build them the way they tell me to build them. Unless I'm the owner, there's only so much say a construction man has over a project. Don't get me wrong—I take pride in my work—every nail and brick of it. But would I have destroyed the Gergans Building? Never."

He was referring to a beautiful old building that had been near the shore. The Gergans was one of the battles preservationists in Las Piernas had lost. I had been in it once or twice before it was torn down, seen the carved woodwork and marble, the loving detail work that had graced every corner of it. To some it was probably made in a cluttered style and hopelessly busy; to me, it seemed to say "I'm filled with visual pleasures and surprises. You could work within me day after day, and still you would find something new to see and discover." The photos, all that remained of it, never would do it justice.

"If you're trying to tell me there are no easy answers—"

"Oh," he said, "you know that already."

"Then why the tour?"

"Bear with me. Bear with me."

I hoped I could. I was fairly sure I knew where he was driving now, and I wasn't sure I was ready to see the Angelus again.

But we were about a block away from the old hotel when Keene pulled his Mercedes over to a curb and stopped the car.

He looked down the filthy street and asked, "What do you see here?"

"Nothing too lovely," I admitted, looking at the decaying, boarded-up buildings that lined the block.

"A long row of shitholes, is what you mean."

"Maybe if the people who lived here a few years ago had been allowed to stay, it wouldn't be like this. Maybe it wouldn't have become a place where only rats could survive."

"Maybe," he said, "but I don't picture them having the kind of bucks it would take to paint one of these places, let alone do the earthquake work."

"Well, if they'd had the kind of bucks the city gave to Hill and Associates, if someone could have taught them how to bamboozle limited partners out of ready cash, if Ben Watterson had loaned money to them on a handshake and at a big discount, hell, who knows what they could have done to the place?"

His mouth flattened into a tight line, but then he sighed and said, "You could be right. Who am I to say? Maybe this neighborhood wouldn't have gone into the crapper like it did—or, I should say, could have crawled out of the crapper it had already become. But you'll forgive me if I say I don't think it would have been so simple to save it, either."

"No," I admitted. "We started out saying there weren't easy answers, right?"

"Right. Well. Let me tell you what else I see here—"

"We could call your vision 'economic opportunities,' " I interrupted, "and fight over whose opportunity, or we could settle for 'convention center.' "

He looked surprised, then started laughing. "Shit. Are you the kind of person who calls up the birthday girl and says, 'I can't make it to your surprise party?' "

"No," I said, smiling, "I just enjoy pissing off rich, sober sons of bitches."

"God, you're good at it," he said, wiping tears from his eyes. He drew a deep breath and let it out slowly. When he looked over at me again his expression was grim. "Well, no use taking up more time. I just bought a building that looks like a damned church. It's as good as any place to make a confession."

He started the car again and pushed the automatic door locks.

33

"Unlock the doors," I said as we turned a corner. "Unlock them now."

"Why?" he said, glancing over at me.

I reached for the button on my side, hit it. The door unlocked. No problem. I was still staring at the button, wondering why I had expected it to remain locked, when Keene pulled the car over to a curb.

"Here we are," he said. "You're right. Probably silly for such a short trip—probably silly not to walk. But you mentioned rats and there are lots of two-legged ones around here. You wouldn't believe the character my security man kicked out of here earlier. I told the guard we'd be coming back here, and he promised to run off any other weirdos. The place should be safe enough now."

We were at the Angelus.

It looked different. The sagging fence had been replaced, as had the broken windows on the bottom floor. I glanced up and heard him say, "We started on the lower floors. The window your friend broke hasn't been replaced yet."

"I'll pay for it," I said.

"Don't be silly. I wasn't dropping hints."

"You've done a lot in two or three days," I said. "When I was here on Sunday, it looked different."

"When the police called and told me what had happened here, I had my kids do some work."

"So you knew? You knew when I called you on Monday?"

"No! They called up my kids—the police called my son—and— Wait. Let me back up a minute."

He exhaled, long and slow.

"The building is owned by my company. It's a family business in every sense of the word. I've got five boys and two girls."

"I didn't know you had so many children."

"Yep, seven. One of the girls and one of the boys didn't give a damn about the business, which is fine, and they're happy doing other things. But the others—they run the business here in town."

"While you stay in Fallbrook?"

"I'm down there most of the time. So Monday morning, the kids get a call from the police. Later, my youngest son lets me know about it, but I don't get the details."

"What did he tell you?"

" 'Dad,' " he mimicked, holding his thumb and little finger to his face like a phone, " 'the police called to say a homeless guy climbed up to the upper floors of the Sad Angels Hotel—' "

"Sad Angels?"

"That's what my kids call the hotel. Anyway, he called to say this bum climbed up and had himself a heart attack." He went back to his imaginary phone. " 'Poor guy was in there dead for days, Dad. Some women were looking for him and found him—one of 'em broke a window so she could call the police.' "

"And did the police ask any questions?"

"Yeah, they asked him if we gave permission to a transient to sleep in the Sad Angels. He told them no, which was the truth. Then he called me to ask if I wanted him to start the work on the place, get it cleaned up."

He paused, looking out at the fence. " 'Yeah,' I told him. 'Start getting that place cleaned up. New fence, new locks. Get a security company to cruise by the place. I don't want any more people dying in my old angel hotel. Those angels are sad enough.' "

"And that's all you knew when I called?"

He nodded. "That's all I knew. I didn't know it was Lucas Monroe. I didn't even know Lucas was dead. I didn't know that you and your friend were the women—I found all that out late Monday, when one of the older boys called. He had called the police to find out if it was okay to do some work around the place, and found out more than his brother."

"This has all been done in one day?"

"You teach seven kids to work as a team, they can get anything done! But to be honest, we were already making plans when this happened. The windows were already ordered. Fence wasn't a problem for a construction company. Same with the general cleanup of the grounds, and the first floor. They probably called in some favors. The kids are fond of the place, believe it or not. Talked me into buying it so Roland wouldn't level it."

"Roland Hill?"

He nodded.

"Why the attachment?"

He smiled. "See those angels on the corners? Well, we used to live not far from here when the kids were little. I was just starting to make my way. My wife was alive then, of course. We were driving past the place one day—a day when the kids had been giving my wife fits. The youngest looks up and asks his mother why those angels are so sad. 'Why, those must be your guardian angels,' she said. 'And who could blame them for being sad?'

"Well, my oldest girl pipes up and says, 'There are seven of us and eight angels.' Without missing a beat, my wife says, 'The saddest angel up there is your father's.' "

I smiled, but when I looked back at him, his face was full of regret.

"She was right," he said. "Back then, I used to drink pretty heavy. Left her with so much work, I sent her to an early grave." He opened his car door. "Come on, I'm getting tired of sitting in here."

I got out, taking my envelopes with me. I watched him take out a separate set of keys and unlock the gate in the fence. He looked back at me, and said, "We won't go upstairs, if that's what you're worried about. I know that's where he was. But how about the lobby? Have you been in the lobby?"

"No, I haven't."

"Oh, you're in for a treat. You're gonna love it."

A security company cruiser stopped by just then. Keene talked to the guard for a moment, then motioned me to follow him through the gate. He locked it behind us, and seeing my face said, "You want to hold the keys?"

"Yes."

He handed them to me, but didn't make a move toward the hotel. He was waiting for an explanation.

"I had a bad time once," I said. "Being locked in a place."

He nodded, opened his mouth as if to say something, then closed it again. He started walking toward the hotel, across grounds that were now swept clean.

I followed him to the top of the steps, where he stood looking up at the sad angels, then smiled at me. "One night," he said, "while my wife and I were out, my second-youngest son was shoved into a broom closet by his older brothers, who thought all his screaming and carrying on was funnier than hell."

I think my face went white.

"They didn't let him out for over an hour," he said, not smiling now. "Kid had nightmares for years after that. To this day, he can't sleep in a tent, won't go into a phone booth. Has to know where the doors are. Hates being in any closed place. One day, I had an idea. I let him carry my keys. As long as he had the keys in his hand, he was okay. Discovered it made life a little easier for everyone."

"I guess there's not much that raising seven kids won't let you experience."

"Not much. In some ways, we're all kids, I suppose. So, would you please unlock the front door?"

I did as he asked. The glass-and-brass doors were almost as shiny now as they must have been in the 1920s. Keene stepped inside.

"They've done good," he said with pride.

I followed him into the lobby of what must have been a

grand hotel in its day. It wasn't perfectly restored by any means, and it was empty and devoid of furniture, but it was also clean and smelled of wax and polish.

We stood on a large mosaic entry depicting Botticelli-like celestial beings. There were angels everywhere. A dry fountain in the entry was graced with carvings of embracing seraphim. Behind it, a grand staircase ascended to a wide balcony on the next level. Except for the angels and the elaborate woodwork, the Angelus seemed an entirely different hotel than the one I had been in on Sunday.

The room was open and the ceiling a full story above us. Marble columns rose to meet it. It was painted a twilight blue with gold stars, and all around its edges bemused cherubs looked down on us. Several walls were painted with murals; there was wood paneling elsewhere; the windows were tall and their casings ornate. Afternoon sunlight streamed in.

"Well?" he asked.

"You're right, I love it."

"Here, sit with me on the staircase," Keene said.

We sat there in silence for a moment, then he said, "I'm not sure what you already know about all of this. I've spent the last two days trying to figure out what I should and shouldn't tell you. At first, I was just going to try to point you in the right direction. But things have changed."

"Changed how?"

"Someone is just going crazy now. Honest to God, if I thought I knew who it was, I'd go to the police. You have to believe that."

"Tell me what you mean by 'going crazy.' "

"Hurting people! Maybe—maybe even worse. Hell, probably worse. When I heard about the woman who runs the shelter getting hurt, I guess I decided I'd tell you just about everything."

I waited.

"I've got one or two promises to ask you to make. First, promise you won't drag my kids into this. They've never known any of it, and I owe my late wife that much."

"If they haven't had anything to do with it, I won't be the

one to drag them into it, as you say. But I can't make promises about what other reporters will or won't do."

"I understand. The second promise is more selfish, but I'm not ready to give up my hide yet, and I'm afraid that's what I'd be doing if whoever is going around hurting people knew I talked to you."

"What's the promise?"

"You protect me as a source—keep my name and any description of me off the record. I'll tell you all I can. But nobody knows I'm the one that talked to you. Not the police and not the public."

I hesitated.

"I won't do it any other way," he said.

"Okay, I'll protect you as a source. But if you're investigated by the police, they may learn things on their own. I can't protect you from the law."

"Married to a cop, I suppose not."

"Does that make you mistrust me?"

"Hell no. I know how you reporters work. You ever leak this to your husband, pretty soon you've got no reputation as someone who can be trusted. No one talks to you. You go nowhere, because no one will tell you anything they wouldn't want the cops to hear."

I nodded. "I guess you do understand how it works. But the cops are working on this, Keene. They aren't stupid. Reed Collins, Jake Matsuda—the guys who are working these cases—they make connections on their own."

"Good. I want the person who's doing all of this to be caught. I just don't want to be crucified while they're looking for the guy."

"So talk to me."

He stared off toward the fountain, but I don't think he was looking at it.

"Jesus, this is gonna be tougher than I thought," he said.

"I'll give you some help. Someone saw an opportunity in Las Piernas. In redevelopment."

He cleared his throat and said, "Allan Moffett and Roland Hill. It started with them."

"Allan gave inside information to Roland, and Roland gave Allan kickbacks." It was a guess, but I wasn't out on any limb.

"Yes. And I went along with it. I don't mean they ever cut me in on their deals, but because I was willing to keep my mouth shut, a lot of business came my way."

"How much business?"

"Millions of dollars' worth. Millions. I wouldn't be sitting here calling this my hotel if it wasn't millions. Not all with redevelopment. But because Roland used my company, other developers came to me."

"And I'm sure Allan helped you to put in competitive bids for city projects."

"There was that," he admitted. "They weren't stingy with financial advice and inside info—as you know. They hand-picked all of us."

"What do you mean?"

"They knew Selman was weak: guy had two separate child-support payments, expensive habits, and was always trying to impress young broads. I had seven kids, and even though the business was growing, I was having trouble keeping ahead of my suppliers' bills. Corbin Tyler, he just had one kid, but she had some heart problem that kept him in the red. Booter Hodges is just a damned glad-hander. That joker would do anything to rub elbows with money, 'cause unless he brings the bucks into the college foundation, he's out of a job. He was the one that suggested Selman."

"And Ben Watterson?"

"Watterson came into it a little later, more reluctantly, I guess I'd say. He liked what it did for his business, liked what it did for the city. But it ate at him. I'll tell you something. It ate at me. Still does. Maybe I'm telling you this because I don't want to end up like Ben. I don't want my kids to find me in a shower with my brains blown out. How he could do that to Claire, I'll never know."

"I've tried to understand that myself. Maybe he was afraid she'd be ashamed of him if the truth came out. Maybe it was easier to die than to see all those people disappointed in him."

"Nuts to that," Keene said. "People expect too much. Ben was only human. We all are."

"Ben was in a position of trust. I can try to understand him, but I also have to be concerned about what he may have done to the city."

"The city! Christ, that's what gripes my ass. The city benefited like crazy. Jobs, retail sales-tax income—I could go on and on. Sure, a couple of projects didn't work out, but most of them pulled lousy neighborhoods out of the toilet. The people I hired—they're part of this city, too."

"I see. 'The poor you have always with you,' unless you can make them move to some other town."

"It's not so simple!"

"No. Neither is fixing a deal so that your competitors don't have a fair chance to provide those jobs."

When he finally answered, his voice was much quieter. "No," he said.

"And for that matter, neither is murder."

"No. But will anyone else see it that way? That's what scares the shit out of me."

"You know something about murder, Keene?"

The cavernous room was silent, so silent that I heard Keene Dage swallow hard before he said, "I'm not sure. I'm not sure, but I think I do."

"Then tell me what you think you know."

He looked down at his shoes and said, "Numbers. It all started with numbers."

34

"The numbers Andre Selman cooked up?"

He nodded. "Allan didn't like the original numbers Selman was coming up with on his study."

"Too many people being evicted?"

"Jesus. You do know. Yeah, Allan didn't think he could make his projects fly if there was some big protest over the number of people who'd have to move out. Allan and Roland called him in to talk things over. It was the first time they had worked with him, and Selman was smart enough to figure out just what kind of bonanza he had lucked into.

"So he starts giving his research assistant a hard time. This was Lucas. Lucas was ambitious, you know? Selman thought he could convince him that he had figured the statistics wrong, that Lucas wouldn't risk pissing off his—what do they call it?"

"His advisor for his thesis."

"Right."

"Andre was also his employer," I said. "Lucas needed the job to stay in school. But he didn't understand that he was supposed to compromise his principles, did he?"

"Oh, I think he understood, although no one spelled it out—that would have been too dangerous. He just refused to do it. Selman's not stupid. Fire this kid, and he's going to have all kinds of trouble. This kid might turn his ass in, let it be known what the professor is up to."

"So he found a replacement," I said, "and a coconspirator in Nadine Preston."

"Replacement, coconspirator, typist, bedmate—you name it. She was a piece of work."

"I've seen her transcripts," I said. "She got a D in Andre's upper-division stat class. She's got a D, and he hires her as a graduate assistant on a largely statistical study. She retook the class from him, and she got an A. Quite an improvement."

"Yeah, well, I can tell you she truly studied under him."

"So Andre's foofing Nadine, and Nadine is retyping Lucas's thesis."

"Shit, you know all of this already."

"Some of it. You're filling in a lot of gaps. I know that Andre managed to discredit Lucas. I'm not so clear on what happened after that."

"That should be plenty, right? I've just told you enough to get you a headline or two, right? Why not leave it there?"

"Because I'm not your chump, Keene. You said it yourself. I knew almost all of this. You've confirmed a few things for me, filled in some details. But you really haven't told me much at all. Where's Nadine Preston now?"

He looked away from me. "I don't know."

"Keene, this is not the time to get mule-headed. You think this will all stay a secret? Roland Hill's little gang is coming apart at the seams. You know it is."

"I don't know!"

Too vehement. He knew something, but he was scared. I decided to take a softer approach. "Something happened. Something that made Nadine decide she would offer Lucas an opportunity to prove that his thesis had been tampered with. What happened?"

"Selman's inability to keep his pud in his pants, that's what. He got bored, found another broad, and Nadine learned about it. They broke up. Selman was such a stupid ass. Here he knows not to out-and-out fire Lucas, but when it comes to women, he's not so bright. Roland blew a gasket—asks him if he's been taking drugs like his pal—I forget the kid's name. OD'ed later on."

"Jeff? Jeff McCutchen?"

"Yeah, that was it. Jeff. I'd forgotten about him. He used drugs all right. You'd never know it just to see the guy out on the street—that's this myth. People think they know who's a druggie because they've seen a few druggies who are out of control. Figure all druggies are like that. Just like they think they know who's a drunk because they figure sooner or later a drunk will put a lampshade on his head at a party or live on the streets like your friend Lucas. Hell, I was a millionaire drunk. No one ever saw me drunk in public. Same with this Jeff. Hid it."

"He hid it from me. I didn't learn that about him until recently," I said.

"The McCutchen kid was brilliant," Keene said. "Brilliant in every way but two: drugs and people. He couldn't keep away from pills and dope, and he was a social zero. Sometimes I think he was just such a smart kid, the only way he could stand to be around anyone else was to get loaded, you know, make himself as dumb as the rest of us. Sad kid. Lonely, I think. Odd."

"Let's go back to Nadine," I said.

"Oh, right. Well, Moffett tells Selman he should have at least stayed with her until the final acceptance of the redevelopment proposal. Selman says there's a problem. Turns out this Jeff is on to everything. He's caught Nadine going through Selman's papers."

Keene paused, then shook his head. "Now whatever else I could say about Selman—and don't get me started—he could charm the horns off the devil himself. He gets people to be devoted to him, although I don't think he's ever truly cared about another person in his life."

"Not even his son?"

"Not his son, and sure as hell not his daughter."

"Hmm."

"I'm telling you the truth. Anyway, this McCutchen kid thinks the world of Selman, and he starts warning him that Nadine's on to his scheme."

"Jeff knew about Moffett and Roland?"

"Figured it out very early on. Bright kid, like I said. Selman said he could be trusted, and it seemed like he was right. So Selman tells Roland that he wanted to get Nadine out of the picture before she learned too much."

"But she didn't stay out of the picture, did she?"

"No. She already knew everything she needed to know. She waited a while, probably planning her strategy, then she goes up to Lucas Monroe and promises him the world."

"What did she want out of it?"

"I don't think she ever planned to help Lucas out. She was the perfect match for Selman. She was right about that. He didn't exactly appreciate it when she told him so. Came over to his place one day, told his current lover to scram. Then she announced to Selman that she wanted to get back together. And she wanted money."

"I can imagine how well that went over with the others."

"Roland and Allan were furious, but honest to God, Selman frightened me. Not because he was losing his temper. He was coolheaded, not panicked at all. You ever see him when he's angry with his daughter? With Lisa?"

I nodded. "Different than with other people."

"Yeah, only it's the same this time. Pleasant, but icy. I can tell he's really pissed at this woman who would dare to presume to threaten him."

"So he's angry. But what could he do about it?"

"Selman tells Roland and Allan not to worry. Says he's got a plan. Get everybody together for a fishing trip. This can all be worked out. So we've got this 'drop everything' command from Roland and Allan to go fishing. I used to hate this crap. But I go."

"This was on Ben's boat?"

"Yeah, that big Bertram. Same one you saw in that photo Lucas took. Different day, though. He took that photo back when Andre was still inviting him along. Nadine's first trip out on it. Big Boat. More than big enough to live aboard.

"Anyway, on this day I'm telling you about, there sure as shit weren't any photos being taken. Allan and Roland come aboard carrying this huge canvas bag, and it's got some kind of heavy chain in it. Ben asked them 'What's that?' and Allan shoots him a dirty look, but Selman's the one that speaks up. 'It's a new anchor for you, Ben. We bought a spare. You should always have one.' Ben was just looking at Roland. Nadine—oh, Christ!—she says, 'Aren't you going to thank him?' "

He put his head in his hands, stared at his feet on the stairs.

"Who went out on the boat that day?" I asked.

"Ben, Selman, Allan, Roland, me, Corbin, and Nadine. Booter wasn't there. Booter used to get seasick. We're out fishing most of the day. Fishing and drinking. I'm thinking, 'What the hell is going on?' Nadine is there, she's all over Andre. They're so huggy and kissy, it's awkward for the rest of us. Ben tries to stow the canvas bag, Selman says leave it there on the deck, he'll take care of it. So all day, Ben keeps looking at the canvas bag like it's a snake. Ben's unhappy, Corbin's unhappy, I'm unhappy. I had this bad feeling, I'm drinking a little more than usual. Roland and Allan don't seem to be bothered in the least."

"Where did you fish?"

"All over. I'm no sailor. I can't even tell you where we were."

He fell silent.

"What happened next?"

He looked up, glanced over at me, but then kept his eyes straight ahead. When he spoke again, his voice was strained.

"We're out fishing, like I said. At one point, that sick bastard Selman takes her below. Ben Watterson looks like he's going to faint. Roland tells him to relax. Just like that. Cold. 'Relax, Ben.' "

He shook himself.

"So Andre went below with Nadine," I coaxed.

"Yeah. Then I realize they're down there getting it on. They come back up, all smiles. Then a little later, this call comes in over the radio from Booter. He calls to say, 'All clear.' "

"The meeting with Lucas? The one when Lucas waited for Nadine to show up and clear his name?"

"Yes. It's like Selman wanted to be screwing her right when he knows this meeting is going on. She doesn't even see what's coming. No, that call comes in, she figures she's sealed the deal, and she gives Andre this big face-sucking kiss. He really gets into it. I figure, this time, he's going to take her on the deck, right here in front of God and everybody. So I'm a little relieved when Allan says, 'Ben, take the boat in.' "

"And then?"

He was silent.

"There's more to this, isn't there, Keene?"

"I don't know!"

"Allan tells Ben to head back to the marina. Did he?"

"Yeah," he said. "Ben takes the boat in. I'm feeling a little relieved. I don't even know why. But then, all of a sudden, Roland says, 'Andre and Nadine and I have some business to discuss. We're going out again.' "

"Everyone?"

"No, just the three of them. Ben protests, but Roland just says, 'If anything happens to the boat, I'll buy you a new one, Ben.'" He shook his head. "Can you believe that? Ben said, 'It's not the boat I'm worried about.' Roland gave him this look—I don't know how to describe it. It just made us all shut up and get off the boat."

"Nadine stayed aboard?"

"Yeah. With Selman and Roland."

"What happened next?"

"Allan tells us to go home, but Ben wasn't as afraid of Allan. He keeps trying to watch where they're taking the boat. Allan said, 'Ben, don't you realize what Roland is trying to do for you? Go home.' Ben started looking green. He got sick, really sick, right there at the dock. Corbin and I started to worry about him. But after a minute, he said he just wanted to get out of there. We all walked to our cars and drove home."

"When was this?"

"August 8, 1977."

"You remember the date that clearly?"

"For a lot of reasons." He rubbed a hand over his face. "God knows I'd love to forget that day."

I waited.

Long minutes passed before he went on. "You asked me how I remembered that date? Everything changed that day. Everything. I stopped drinking. Ben sold the boat to Selman. I don't think you can get Corbin Tyler to step on a dock. Corbin and I stopped speaking to Selman; made Roland handle everything with the studies. Didn't matter. We all kept working together, speaking or not."

"You haven't told me why everything changed."

"I don't know! It just did."

"Bullshit, Keene."

He didn't answer.

"Okay, I'll ask the obvious question. Did you ever see Nadine Preston after that day?"

"No."

"The canvas bag and chain?"

"I never went back to the boat. Maybe it was there, maybe not."

"Nadine never went back to school after that semester."

"No."

"No parents?"

"Her parents were dead. I heard . . . I heard that a brother was looking for her, but she had been gone a long time by then."

"Where do you think she is?"

"I don't know! We didn't see what happened to her or the bag." He paused. "Roland picked us out to be his business associates because we were the kind of people who didn't have to be told things," he added bitterly. "To Roland, this was business."

"You didn't see anything, but you were there."

"It was a lesson. He taught us what happens to spoilsports."

"What happens to spoilsports?"

His voice was no more than a dry whisper. "They don't make it back to shore."

"They killed her."

"Yes, I think they did."

"You *think?*"

When he didn't answer, I reached into my purse and found the cocktail napkin he had left behind at the Terrace. "The night of Moffett's dinner, you wrote the letter *N* on a cocktail napkin. Nadine, right?"

He nodded.

"She's haunting you, Keene. Admit it. You only 'think' they killed her?"

He shook his head. "No, that's not true. I know they did."

I had figured that Nadine Preston was living in high style somewhere far from Las Piernas. What had happened to her shouldn't have been surprising. She was a schemer and a blackmailer. A foolish one, out of her league. There was nothing to admire in her, but I couldn't help but feel outraged on her behalf. And truthfully, I was no less angry that Andre had fondled her, had made a spectacle of his pretended passion for her, knowing all the while that he would take part in her death. As I thought about Keene's story, I found myself concentrating on details, trying to prevent myself from becoming as nauseated as Ben had been that day.

"You've known these men for years. Who do you think actually killed her?"

"I've thought about that a lot. You want my best guess? Selman."

"Why?"

"Roland would never let Selman have that kind of power over him. Selman benefited, but he didn't control. Roland controlled us all. After that, he never had to worry again that anyone would break ranks. He had us all by the balls and he knew it. He kept up his side of the deal. We made our profits. But it had changed."

"I don't understand how it's possible that all of you stayed silent all this time."

"What you think someone might have done, and what you know they've done—those are two different things."

"Suspicion of murder, Keene, not anything less. If one of you had stood up and said you suspected murder, maybe her brother wouldn't still be wondering where she is."

"And maybe six other people would have said she was alive and well two days after you said she was dead. Or they might have said *you* were the last one anyone saw her with. Or maybe everyone would have shrugged and said, 'We don't know what happened to her,' but you wouldn't be doing business in Las Piernas."

"How did Roland know he could count on you?"

"I've thought about that myself. I've had to. The easiest answer I can give you is that Roland knew who he was dealing with—from the beginning. You dated Selman at one time, right?"

"Yes."

"All those women—some guys look at him and say, 'He's got to have some kind of touch.' Do you think Selman had some magic power over people? I mean, actual voodoo or something?"

"No, but I think I see where you're headed with this. He picks his victims."

"Right. He doesn't get there without the woman's cooperation. He knows her better than she knows herself—that's the key. Makes a woman feel mad at herself afterward, maybe, but the truth is, you probably didn't stand a chance."

"Played with fire and got burned," I said. "That's all."

"But the first time you see fire—especially if you've been in the cold and dark up until then—it's damned inviting, isn't it? We wouldn't even have that saying if there weren't lots of people walking around with their fingers singed."

"So you're saying Roland knew that you'd all keep your mouths shut."

"Roland knew that, and we each knew Roland wouldn't have invited a man into his inner circle unless that were true. If you didn't have the makings of a good conspirator, you weren't going to be asked to the dance. You had to have a real talent for whatever it was you did, but you also had to be someone who wouldn't get too big for his britches, who'd keep his mouth shut, who was climbing, maybe needed something—and you had to be greedy. But above all? You had to be someone who wanted to feel like he was an important man around town."

He paused, then said, "Weaknesses and strengths. Roland is like Selman in that way. He knew more about us than we knew about ourselves. But he's smarter than Andre, and even Andre knows it. Andre takes all he can get; Roland knows what he can take and who he can take it from, but he doesn't take too much."

"Murder was not too much?"

"Apparently not, right? You know what I think? I think that was Selman's idea, start to finish. But it would have been Roland who said who should stay on shore. Being a party to it would be hardest on me and Corbin and Ben. Selman, Moffett, they don't give a shit about anybody."

"What about Booter?"

"Booter? What a joke—he's the monkey they make those 'See No Evil' statues from."

"I'd think you'd be the biggest risk."

"Maybe. But then, maybe not. Corbin and Ben, they were probably doing the same thing I was doing. Probably at least once a day, they'd look in the mirror and say, 'Maybe I'll have the balls to do it today. I'll tell Roland to shove it up his ass. I'll come clean.' And you know what that mirror answers back? 'Who are you trying to kid, you big phony?' "

He sighed. "The best design I ever saw Corbin Tyler come up with was right after that boat trip. He wasn't sleeping. Stayed up all night, night after night, working on it. It was magnificent. The Haimler Building—you know it?"

I nodded.

"I admired that set of plans," Keene said. "I told him so. You know what he said? 'I had to do something I'd be proud of.' I knew exactly what he meant. Exactly. So I put my heart and soul into building it."

I considered what he had said. "You're talking to me now. Maybe your reflection was wrong."

He smiled a little. "I wouldn't bet on it. I'm doing this in a pretty chickenshit fashion."

We were quiet again.

"I think Lucas was murdered," I said.

"Oh yeah?" He shifted a little.

"You do, too, don't you?"

"Yes," he said after a moment. "I don't know how they did it—I didn't even like to think it could be murder at first—but it was just too convenient, you know? And after the lady at the shelter got hurt, I said to myself, 'Keene, someone is shutting people up.' "

"It's why you're talking to me."

"Yes. Maybe whoever did this to Lucas and the shelter lady will come after me and Corbin. Ben killed himself, but Corbin and I, we aren't the type for that. Not so obliging. Still, no one's been arrested yet, so I'm not feeling so safe."

I had no argument to give him. "What is it you think I can do for you?"

"If something happens to me," he said, "I don't want them to get away with it. I don't want my kids to find out what I've done, but I'd rather have that than just go quietly, if you know what I mean. I go, this whole thing is blown wide open."

I looked at him sharply. "You're planning to use me as your triggering device."

He nodded.

"And you plan to let them know that?"

"Not unless absolutely necessary. Not unless they try something with me."

"Christ, Keene, do you think they'd have any more trouble getting rid of me than they would you?"

"None, and I'm sorry if it's put you in danger."

"Sorry!"

"Yes, sorry! But I couldn't think of any other way to work it."

"You're putting me in the line of fire!"

"You were in it anyway. All those phone calls you've been making? You've stirred up the hornets' nest all on your own. Do you believe for one moment that your car window was broken by a thief?"

I was silent.

"No, missy, you've got something that worries somebody." He slanted a sly look toward my hands. "I'll bet it's one of those envelopes."

I clutched them tighter.

"I'm not your thief," he said. "You've figured that out by now."

"Why don't you get a lawyer and go to the cops? Try to get immunity."

"Immunity means I still have to open up a can of worms. A lot of people would be hurt—and not just my kids. Corbin would be hurt. His kid would be hurt. So would investors, officials, my workers, lots of people."

"You have a big goddamned ego, you know that?"

He smiled. "I do."

I looked up at the cherubs, smiling down at us. The last of the innocents, in a twilight sky.

If I wanted to stay healthy, I had to find a way to open up that can of worms he worried over—without breaking my promise to keep what he told me off the record. The "cleanup man"—as I was beginning to think of whoever had killed

Lucas—only had something at stake if his reputation was protected. If the redevelopment scam could be exposed, then there was no reputation to protect.

I could think of only two ways of exposing it. One would be to find the original data, have a statistics expert look at it, and hope the expert could find the holes in Selman's study.

The other would be faster—which appealed to my desire to live. I could find Lucas's hidden papers and pray that they would be enough to get Selman and his buddies in trouble. Maybe the hidden papers would indicate which figures were changed. That in turn might show which numbers to question in the study on file with the Redevelopment Agency. I might still need a statistics expert, but it would take less time.

Time. I looked at the long windows across from the staircase. There were still a few hours of light left.

"I have a request," I said.

He looked over to me.

"I want to look around in the Angelus for a while."

"By yourself?"

No, not by myself. But I didn't want him with me while I looked for Lucas's papers. "I guess so," I said.

He was about to answer when my pager went off, startling both of us.

"Sorry," I said, "I thought it was set to just vibrate." Lydia's number was on the display. "Could I use your cell phone?"

"Sure, let's go out to the car."

I locked up behind us, not knowing if the phone call would mean I'd have to leave. If not, I'd ask Frank to pick me up at the Angelus. If I had to go back to the office, it was probably because Wrigley had figured out who passed out his pager number.

"Lydia? It's Irene. I need to make it quick. I'm on someone else's cellular phone."

"I'll transfer you down to Geoff then. Your friend Lisa is here."

"Lisa Selman?"

"We told her you weren't in, but she seems pretty upset, so I thought I'd call you, let you talk to her."

"Okay, transfer me."

Keene had heard me say Lisa's name. "Don't tell her I'm with you!" he said, panicked, looking around. "I need to get out of here."

Geoff came on the line, handed me over to Lisa.

"Irene?" She sounded as if she were on the verge of tears.

"What's wrong?"

"I have to talk to you. About Roberta. I was sorting through some boxes in my old attic room at my father's house. I found some papers. I—I think they have something to do with Lucas and Roberta. I thought—this is such a mess! I think Andre's— I can't even say it. I need your help. I borrowed Jerry's car. Can I meet you somewhere?"

"I can be back at the paper in a few minutes," I said.

"I don't want her to see my car!" Keene was whispering furiously. "She might tell her father!"

At the same time, Lisa was saying, "No, no. We can't talk here. Not in front of other people."

I sighed. Keene and Lisa waited.

"Do you know where the Angelus Hotel is?" I asked.

"Yes," she said.

"I need to look around there. I just got a set of keys from Keene Dage's kids." The lies started coming easier. "I told them I was doing a story about the restoration of historical buildings. Give me about twenty minutes to get there," I said, and hoped she didn't hear Keene's sigh of relief.

35

I borrowed Keene's phone to make one more call, and left a message for Frank saying I'd get a ride home from Lisa.

Keene started to get into his car, but went back to the trunk. He pulled out a big flashlight. "Take this. We don't have the power on in there yet, and once you're off the first floor, it gets dark . . . but I guess you know that."

"Thanks, Keene."

"You sure you'll be okay waiting here?"

I nodded. "I'll lock myself inside the gate."

He stood there, looking at his own keys. "Anything else you need?"

"No, I'm fine."

"Yeah. Well, thanks." He gave a little smile. "I mean, confession really is good for the soul. I don't feel like mine is spick-and-span or anything, but it's a weight off, you know? I've never told anyone about it before."

"Thanks for trusting me."

He glanced up at the hotel. "I'll ask my sad angels to watch over you, Irene."

"Hope they do a better job for me than they did for you."

"Me, too." His face became serious. "I really wouldn't want anything to happen to you."

"Don't get an attack of conscience over it or anything, Keene."

He laughed. "Piss and vinegar. That's what I like about you."

He waved and drove off.

I locked the gate and walked across the grounds to the front steps. While I waited, I went back to Ben's calendar. The depression, or whatever it was that kept him from making entries, lasted a little over three weeks. There was nothing written from August 9 until then. I looked again at the note from Jeff McCutchen. Six numbers. What did they mean?

I thought about Nadine Preston and couldn't help but wonder how those men could sleep at night. I looked back at her transcripts and registration information. She did fine as an undergrad. She was a less than spectacular graduate student. The earliest registration information listed her parents as the persons to contact in case of emergency. According to the computer file, they lived in Michigan. I looked at later forms. The emergency contact field was left blank.

Parents deceased, Keene had said. Estranged from her brother. Did he still wonder about his sister?

At the thought of brothers and sisters, I heard a car pull up. Jerry's red Porsche. Disappointingly typical, I thought. Great car, but it had to be the midlife crisis car of choice, an aging philanderer's notion of babe bait. Jerry really must have felt some affection for Lisa if he let her borrow this car. Wondered what he'd say if he knew she was parking it in this part of town.

She waved and reached in the car, pulling a knapsack from the passenger seat. She put the knapsack on her shoulders and locked the car. She was dressed casually again, wearing jeans, a sweater, and running shoes. She looked very young to me. I was about to remind myself once again not to treat her as a child, when I drew close enough to see her face. It was tense and swollen from crying. I hurriedly opened the gate and she came into my arms, holding on to me, literally crying on my shoulder. I gave her an awkward hug—keys, flashlight, and envelopes not leaving my paws free.

"Lisa, Lisa," I said softly. "What's wrong, honey?"

She raised her head and rubbed her palm against her eyes, saying, "I'm sorry, I couldn't help it. This has been such a rotten week! My whole life is falling apart. Why did my father have to be such an asshole?"

"Come on, let's go inside. We'll hunt down a clean patch of floor and sit down and talk."

"Thanks. I knew you'd see me. You're so loyal to your friends, aren't you?"

I glanced up toward the top of the hotel. "Not always," I said, "but I'm glad I can be here for you."

She followed my glance and said, "Oh, I love these old buildings! I'll bet the view from the top of this one is fantastic."

"Probably not what it once was, but it's not bad. The top floor has a lot of windows facing the ocean, and if you sit up there in the right spot, you can see the water."

"Can we go up there?"

I hesitated. I had planned to go up there anyway, but only after I had talked with her. But other than having to climb the stairs twice, I couldn't think of a reason not to take her there. Nothing was out where she'd see it.

"I'm sorry, that was inconsiderate of me," she said. "If you don't think you can handle the stairs . . ."

"I can handle them," I said quickly. But when I looked at her now, she was smiling mischievously. I sighed. "You're baiting me, Lisa."

She laughed. "Yes. But I really do want to see the view."

In the lobby, she became introspective, slowly walking past the fountain, mosaic, and murals, quietly admiring our heavenly hosts. Keene's tale too fresh in my mind, I was anxious to move on. We began the trip upstairs.

As we reached the fourth-floor landing, the jingle of keys in my purse reminded me that the front door was closed, but unlocked, and the gate was wide open. I tried to tell myself that we wouldn't be upstairs very long, but even to my own ears, it sounded like an excuse whose parents were claustrophobia and laziness. I couldn't bring myself to risk vandalism to all the hard work done by Keene's kids, and headed down to the lobby.

Lisa could have waited in the stairwell, but she came along as I secured the gate and the front door, and made no complaint as we started up the stairs again. We didn't talk much on the way up, but by the time we came to the room at the top, she seemed less tense. She looked around with curiosity, marveled at the green glass doors, the carved bar, the view. "You would never expect this to be up here, would you?" she said.

I tucked the envelopes, my purse, and the flashlight on a shelf beneath the bar. I walked over to the windows where I now believed Lucas had spent at least part of one late rainy night. Ben's suicide had made headlines that morning. Did Lucas sit here wondering if he had been in some way responsible for the banker's death? On a clear day, Catalina would have been visible from this place. But the promised rain clouds were slowly rolling in, and you could barely see the oil islands, let alone any place beyond the breakwater. I wondered if the clouds would make it darker sooner.

Behind me, I could hear her shoes on the wooden floor as she explored the room. She walked over to the crate, turned her head to one side, and said, "What are you really doing here?"

Part of the truth wouldn't hurt, I decided. "Lucas died in this hotel. I guess I wanted to see what he saw before he died."

Her face grew solemn. She nodded. "You've reminded me of why I want to see you." She sighed deeply, moved the crate a little, and sat on it. She pulled off the backpack, opened it, and pulled out a folder.

"This was in a box in the attic," she said, and handed it to me.

"What is it?"

"Take a look."

I opened the folder. Surveys. Typewritten pages—just like the ones I had been shown by Edison Burrows. I held them up to the light, looked at them more closely. Lucas's pages.

"Do you know what they are?" I asked.

"They are proof of Andre's dishonesty," she said.

"How do they prove it?" I asked, wanting to know what she knew and what she had just guessed at.

"They were in a box labeled 'Monroe.' I was trying to move some boxes, to find some old books I had stored up there. I found a box full of raw data and typewritten notes and statistical calculations. It's the type of thing I work with all the time, of course—I do almost all of Barton's demographics work. So I was curious. And then the significance of the name on the box struck me. I thought about the fact that Lucas Monroe used to work for Andre."

"You know that Andre was on Lucas's thesis committee, Lisa. And Lucas did work for him on the redevelopment study. Wouldn't it be natural for him to have Lucas's data?"

"You don't trust me, do you?"

It took me aback.

"I understand," she said. "Lucas is dead, although I thought that was from a heart attack. And Roberta—all for nothing!"

"What do you mean?"

She bit her lower lip, then said, "You keep treating me like someone who can't understand the simplest things. Becky told me when I went to the hospital. Said that someone broke into Roberta's office and clubbed her on the back of the head, but that nothing was missing from the office."

"Nothing was missing? I hadn't heard that," I said. "I would imagine that would be hard to determine without Roberta's help."

"I meant, no equipment or anything obvious. At least, that's what Becky said."

"Hmm."

"I don't know how he's managing it from a hospital bed, but I know Andre is behind this. I know it."

"What makes you say that?"

She sighed in exasperation. "Andre faked data for his first redevelopment study. I'm close to proving it. I thought you'd want the story. I thought I could come to you, and you would see the importance of this, the significance, and Andre and his circle of friends could be stopped."

"You can prove he faked the statistics?"

"A few key papers are missing. I'm still looking through the things Andre has hidden in the closet, but they don't seem to be there. But I'll find them. I'm determined to. And I can tell you this much already: Andre is an academic fraud. His career as a scholar is built on a foundation of lies that started with this study. He's a phony."

"He's your father."

"Meaning?"

"You don't care about him, do you? You really don't."

"Why should I?"

"He paid the bills, if nothing else."

"Ill-gotten gains."

"He gave you a love of sociology."

"His love of it is a fake! It's as fake as the rest of him. It's a field that studies human society, relationships, mores—what does he know about any of those things?"

"Enough to win the esteem of his colleagues. Enough to give you a big boost in your own career."

"You defend him again!"

I thought back to the conversation I'd had with Keene not an hour before. I looked out of the window, to the sky and sea. Muted gray. Not this.

"No, I do not defend him. I could use your help. I just don't want you to give it thoughtlessly. I couldn't forgive myself for taking advantage of your anger toward him, no matter how easy it would make my job. You mean too much to me, Lisa."

Tears welled up in her eyes. "I believe you. I swear to you, Irene, this isn't something I take lightly. I want you to know that. This is probably the hardest thing I've ever had to do in my life."

I took a deep breath, exhaled slowly. I still didn't feel right about allowing her to help me bring down her own father, but I was pretty sure my apprehensions went back to treating Lisa as a child. Her relationship with her father wasn't typical. I had to keep that in mind.

"Then I'll say yes, I could use your help," I told her. "Any papers you can get to me—without endangering yourself—will help. And I'll admit that I was just thinking that I need a stats expert to help me understand what I'm looking at."

"Great! I was hoping you'd trust me. I'll keep looking for those missing pages."

"They may be right here," I admitted.

"What?"

"You asked why I'm here. I'm looking for the missing pages."

She looked around the room. "Here?"

"Lucas left a message of sorts for me. This bar supposedly has some kind of secret panel in it. Something left over from Prohibition days."

Her eyes lit up. "I love it! Secret panels! Can I help you try to find it?"

"Be my guest."

We went to work on the bar. We examined it from every angle we could get to. We pushed, we prodded. It started to get dark. I wanted to leave, Lisa was determined to find the panel.

"Frank will be worried about me," I said, turning on the flashlight. "I've got to go."

"Shhh!" she said. "Did you just hear something?"

I stood stock-still.

We listened.

"I guess not," she said.

Very clearly, at that moment, came the sound of the stairwell door slamming shut.

"I know you're in there!" boomed the voice of a man sometimes known as Holler, sometimes known as John Jones.

Two Toes knew we were in there.

36

I turned off the flashlight, reached for the top of Lisa's head, and forced her to duck behind the bar with me. We were in the space behind the bar, where a bartender would stand. There was enough light for me to see Lisa's face, pale and worried. What had possessed me to tell her anything about the panel, to put her in this kind of danger?

"I know you're in heee-re," he sang, as a child does when about to win a round of hide-and-seek. "I'm going to count to ten, and then I'm going to come and get yoooo-u!"

I handed the flashlight to Lisa. I reached for my purse and opened it.

"One."

I found a piece of paper.

"Two."

A pen.

"Three."

Wrote, "I'll distract him."

"Four."

Wrote, "Get help."

"Five."

Reached for the keys to the gate, holding them together to keep them quiet.

"Six."

Put them in her hand.

"Seven."

Looked into her face, saw her nod.

"Eight."

Mouthed the word "Ready?"

"Nine."

The fucking beeper went off.

I stood up like I had been shot out of a cannon.

"It's my guardian angel!" I shouted, running from the bar, veering toward him, beeper beeping.

He covered his ears with his hands and ran from me, heading for the other side of the room. Laughing.

I heard the glass door open, but didn't turn toward it, not wanting his attention on Lisa. The beeper stopped beeping. I whooped and hollered and gave the best imitation of a Tarzan cry I could, trying to cover any other sounds she might make. He loved it. He repeated them, laughing, then turned and ran toward me.

What the hell was I going to do now?

I started running again. We were running in big circles over the buckled floor. He was enjoying the hell out of himself. I was terrified, but I didn't dare head for the door yet—I had to give her time. I dodged and weaved in the darkening room.

And tripped over Lisa's backpack, then the crate, landing flat on my face.

It knocked the wind out of me, sent the beeper skittering in front of me. He caught up to me in one stride. I felt his big hands grab my shoulders, lift me. He set me on my feet, turned me toward him—all as if I didn't weigh more than a doll.

"Are you hurt?" he asked.

I shook my head.

"Sure? You fell down."

No kidding, I thought, my knees, shins, palms, and chin smarting. "I'm okay," I said.

"I'm going to let go now," he said.

"Thanks."

"Don't fall down again."

"I won't."

He took two steps away from me and pointed at me. "That's what you get for roughhousing!"

"Yeah, I guess so."

He stared at me. I thought of Joshua Burrows, ribs kicked in, face bruised. I looked at the hulking figure in front of me. Two Toes could do that much damage to someone in about thirty seconds flat. Had he hurt Roberta, too?

I swallowed hard.

How long would it take Lisa to get out of the building?

I was near the windows. I took my gaze from him just long enough to glance down at the street. The Porsche was still parked at the curb.

"She's still here," he said.

I looked back to see him calmly picking up my beeper from the floor. Shit. He knew I wasn't alone.

"You were looking for the treasure," he said, pushing on the buttons of the beeper.

I didn't answer.

He looked up at me. "Yes, you were," he chided, as if I had denied it aloud. "You were looking in the altar for the treasure. Come here."

I didn't move. He grabbed my hand and yanked me along toward the bar. He stopped in front of it, but he kept hold of my hand.

"As your guardian angel, I will lead you in the ways of righteousness. I know all the secrets of the altar."

Right at that moment, I really didn't care about what was hidden in the bar. But he pulled me over to it, back into the bartender's working space. He saw my purse and stuffed the beeper inside it, freeing his hand. He grabbed the purse and put it on his shoulder. His now, I supposed. I glanced around, but couldn't see the manila envelope. Lisa must have taken it with her. I prayed she'd figure out who to give the papers to if I ended up with my skull bashed in or worse.

He looked up at the back of the bar, its intricate carvings and mirrored panels, and smiled. "You have to rub them," he said. "I watched him all the time."

He took my other hand, guided both hands toward a panel on our left. He placed each hand on one of the wings of two cherubs which graced the sides of one panel of the mirror. I tried not to think about the smell of his breath over my shoulder. It was one of several sharp, distinctive fragrances emanating from him. The man was a riot of olfactory stimulants.

Our darkened reflections stared back at me from a mirror. Mine, scared. His, pleased.

"Both at the same time or it won't work," he said. He gently curved his fingers over mine, moved our hands over the wings simultaneously. I felt the wings move backward. They rolled on some sort of ball-and-socket joint. I heard a creaking noise.

"Now forward, and back again," he said.

We moved the wings again, making the angels "fly."

Another creaking noise, and this time, I could see that the mirror had come forward as the wings went back.

We repeated the motion with the wings, and now the mirror was far enough forward to give me a clear view of what lay behind it: a lever.

"Pull it down! Pull it down!" Two Toes said excitedly, letting go of my hands.

I did. The entire section beside the mirror swung out, away from the back of the bar. He laughed and pulled it all the way open. There was a compartment beneath it.

"I can't see what's in there," I said, curiosity temporarily overcoming all other considerations.

Two Toes fumbled in his jacket and produced a disposable lighter. He flicked it and its flame softly illuminated the area where we stood. He held it over the compartment and I saw what was hidden there.

Nothing.

"It's empty!"

"Shhh!" he said, clamping a dirty hand over my mouth. He dragged me close to him, put a big arm around my waist, pinning my arms. He straightened and my feet lifted from the ground. He rounded to the back of the bar, pulled on another cherub as he leaned a knee against a smooth panel there. It gave, moved noiselessly, turning like a revolving door, and we were suddenly in absolute darkness.

I tried to struggle, but he tightened his grip on my waist and jaw until I stopped. There was nothing but darkness and his scent mixed with that of dust and old wood. At first I thought we were in some sort of closet compartment in the old bar, but we began moving. He was carrying me down a set of stairs, it seemed. The bar must have covered some passageway, probably a means of getting booze in and out during its speakeasy days.

He stopped, then loosened his grip on my waist long enough to open a door. The air was cooler, but it was still very dark. He set my feet on the ground.

"If I let go of you, will you be quiet?" he whispered in my ear.

I nodded.

"I don't want to hit you, but I will if you make noise."

I nodded again.

He lifted his hand a little, as if testing me, then took it away completely. I rubbed my jaw.

Where was Lisa? I told myself that even going downstairs in a panic, fourteen flights would take some time.

He still had hold of my waist. His head was cocked to one side, as if he were listening to something. I heard it, too. Footsteps above us. Distant, but crossing the large room above. The old wooden floor was creaking.

Looking for me! I thought frantically. She's found help and

they're looking for me! I opened my mouth to call out, but Two Toes' big hand came over it again. As he dragged me along, I wondered how Lisa had managed to find help so quickly. The security guard? Maybe my luck was improving.

Soon I realized that we had come out into the hallway of the floor below. The one where Lucas had died.

Two Toes knew which room that was—he had been there. He was going there again. I heard myself whimper as he pulled me into the room.

"Shhh!" he hissed, and shut the door.

37

It got worse.

If Two Toes had stopped in the room itself, maybe I would have managed not to think about where I had seen Lucas's body, about the pennies on his eyes. Maybe not.

He kept moving. He dragged me first into the bathroom, but when I used my legs to kick against the fixtures, he seemed dissatisfied with it as a hiding place. He dropped my purse into the old clawfoot bathtub, then reestablished his grip on me.

"Stop it!" he whispered fiercely, dragging me back out into the room. "I don't want to hurt you! I don't!"

He moved out of the bathroom, back into the bedroom itself, where there was a little light. Very little. He closed the bathroom door with his foot, and moved toward the windows. I felt a little relief until we seemed to be going straight to the bloodstained radiator. He moved away from it, though, and into the small closet. He shut the door, and we were in absolute darkness.

If being unable to escape from a small, dark, confined space was not my worst nightmare come to life, it was only because I had failed to add the prospect of being there not alone, but with a hulking maniac. He turned me so that I faced him, pressed himself full-length against me. He had an erection.

I stopped struggling. I don't think I've ever held so still in my life.

"Oops," he whispered. "I'm not being a very good angel."

He shifted his pelvis slightly. His weight still held me against the wall, but at least I wasn't being prodded through our clothes.

It was that small act of consideration that finally made me reconsider what was happening to me. He wasn't hurting me. He was hiding me.

Then I realized how quiet the building was.

If, by some miracle, Lisa had found help quickly and the police had arrived, there would have been lights and sound. They would have treated this as a hostage situation—it wouldn't be quiet, like this.

Maybe it was just Lisa and the security guard. Maybe the security guard was trying to be John Wayne. Maybe he was silently looking for me while the police tried to find the place. After all, the Angelus probably hadn't been operating as a hotel for over a decade . . .

But Lisa knew right where it was. Lisa, who wouldn't have been out of high school when it closed. When I had spoken to her on the phone, I had asked, "Do you know where the Angelus Hotel is?" and she had answered "Yes." Without hesitation.

But the implications of that made me argue against myself. Maybe she had seen the hotel mentioned in one of the papers in the attic. Or overheard Andre talk about it. Maybe Roberta told her that Lucas died in this hotel, and Lisa came by to see it. That didn't seem likely. I tried to think of other explanations. I was sure there had to be one.

Sure, until I heard the stairwell door close at the end of the hallway. Whoever was coming onto this floor made no attempt to hide his or her presence.

She might have known where the hotel was by some other

means, but Lisa wouldn't have known which room he had died in, what floor it was on. Not unless she had been here on the night he died.

Had he been alive when she saw him?

I remembered what Two Toes, my "guardian angel," had said when he last appeared before me, in the alley near my car. He spoke of Lucas being turned away from the shelter, coming to the hotel. He had said that Lucas had a guardian angel of his own:

The one that watched over him wherever he would go. He talked to the angel, and the angel went away . . . It scared me to watch that angel.

Lucas had been alive.

Alive on a cold wet night, visited by an angel carrying a thermos full of coffee. The thermos in the room was not Lucas's thermos. Did Lisa have one? Maybe it was Jerry's, filled with hot coffee from his kitchen, with the pills taken from the spare supply of heart medication from his cabinet—heart medication Jerry kept on hand to save his father's life. This had been a different kind of emergency.

If Lucas had made it into the shelter, would she have gone in like a Good Samaritan? The director's young friend Lisa, sharing coffee and visiting with an old friend? Or did she delay him in some way, make certain that he was too late to find a bed there?

Heart medication. It wouldn't be such a difficult way to kill someone. In the coffee, it would have been tasteless. Heart medications are powerful drugs. What will save one person could kill another; enough of it will kill anyone. What had she said to him? The same thing she said to me? My father hid some papers in an attic? He's never loved me, I want to help you?

I pictured Lucas beguiled by her. Compassionate, trusting her. Drinking the coffee until he had enough in his system to do the damage. In that moment of dizziness before he fell against the radiator, did he know? Clutching his ring against his chest, did he know his trust had been betrayed again?

I shuddered. Two Toes leaned his cheek against the top of my head, moved the arm around my waist to pat my back. Childlike.

Childlike. The thought that Andre's daughter might be just as manipulative and ruthless as her father was one I didn't like to face. The apple never falls too far from the tree, Jerry Selman had quoted to me. I had been looking at the wrong apple.

Lisa. Why? *Why?*

Was she so angry with Andre for ignoring her that she'd try to frame him for murder? Was that why she had come to me? To make me a party to the accusations? Get the newspaper reporter to say it, so that she didn't have to? No wonder she was upset when I defended him in any way.

And now she had Ben's calendar pages, Ivy's faxes, the copy of Jeff McCutchen's suicide note. How ironic that she didn't need to frame Andre—he had probably already committed a murder.

The footsteps in the hallway were cautious, but steadily approaching. Two Toes seemed to notice that I wasn't trying to struggle. He relaxed his grip. I wanted to communicate my trust to him somehow, but didn't dare to even whisper. I couldn't see his face, he couldn't see the change in mine. I moved my arm a little, patted him as he had patted me. He eased away slightly. I reached for his hand, gently squeezed it. He squeezed mine back, just as gently. He stood back a little more, dropped his arms, no longer covering my mouth or holding me to him.

A moment later, any remaining doubts I may have held on to, the slim, denying hope that said no one I had cared for so much could have killed Lucas, vanished when I heard a sharp bang against the door to the hallway. It quickly banged again as it hit against a wall, sounding as if it had been kicked open.

"I've got a gun," Lisa's voice said from a slight distance. "Bring Irene out now."

Two Toes reached for my face, found my mouth, and patted his fingers on my lips. I nodded as he held them there lightly. He then turned around silently, his back to me.

I wondered if she really had a gun. We had heard her footsteps overhead, in the bar. Her knapsack. Had she gone back to retrieve a weapon?

"Do you hear me? I said to bring her out now!"

The air inside the closet seemed to be gone.

When we didn't emerge, she called out, "I have magic, Mr. Jones. I'll trade you my magic for Irene."

Mr. Jones. She had learned Two Toes' name, but not his street name. From Roberta, perhaps? Two Toes had been to the shelter. Was she hunting him, too?

Two Toes wasn't quite as gullible as she hoped, it seems. He didn't move.

"Irene?" Her voice was less cocky now. "Irene, try to make some sound. It's the only way I can save you."

Listening to her lie brought a bitter taste to my mouth.

I heard her walk cautiously into the room, her shoes making the same sound I had heard upstairs, as if she had something sticky on the soles of her running shoes.

The light of the flashlight played near the closet door. The footsteps were hesitant, unsure.

Suddenly there was a piercing noise—I barely registered what it was before gunfire rang out. The echo of the shot had hardly faded before I realized what the first noise was: my beeper, going off in the old iron, claw-foot bathtub.

The acrid smell of gunpowder filled the small room.

The beeper stopped.

"Now," she said shakily, "you know I wasn't lying about the gun."

The beeper went off again.

"Shut that thing off!" she shouted.

It continued.

She fired again; I heard the sound of something shattering, probably the bathroom mirror. The gun seemed to be fired near us. She had to be standing to one side of the bathroom door, firing through it, into the bathroom.

The beeper stopped for a moment, started up again.

"Come out of that bathroom, or I'm coming in!" she shouted, her voice not far from the closet.

The beeper stopped.

It occurred to me that with the flashlight in one hand and the gun in the other, she didn't have a hand free. Her steps moved nearer the bathroom door.

"Do it!" she shouted. "Do it now!"

As if obeying her order, Two Toes burst out of the closet like a berserker, screaming as he launched himself into the room. I followed, staying low.

Lisa had turned at the sound, the flashlight beam spinning our way. The surprise kept her from taking aim, but she fired the gun as Two Toes leapt at her.

He grunted as he tackled her to the floor, grabbing her right wrist, tearing the gun from her hand and sending it across the room. I grabbed the left hand, prying the flashlight from her fingers as she tried to hit Two Toes with it. She struggled against him, but he overpowered her. I used the flashlight to find the gun, turned to see her flailing her fists against Two Toes in impotent fury.

He backhanded her hard against the face. She lay stunned from that blow. He smacked her across the face again. He was pinning her wrists above her head in one hand now, sitting astride her. He was about three times her size. He raised his hand for another blow.

"No," I said. "Two Toes, no!"

He paused, looked up at me.

"Get off me, you filthy cocksucker!" Lisa shouted.

He smacked her again.

She started crying.

He was raising his hand.

"Please don't," I said.

"She needs to be punished," he said simply.

"Not by you," I said, trying to think of a way through to him. "You're my guardian angel."

She laughed. "What? Did he tell you he used to be a body-guard? I thought Roberta made that up."

He smacked her another time. "I'm guarding her. You hurt people. You hurt me."

For all the anger and disappointment I felt in her, I couldn't stand idle, letting Two Toes beat her senseless right before my eyes. "Guardian angels don't hurt anyone," I said. "They take care of people. You take care of me."

He paused, but seemed undecided.

One of the first prayers I ever learned, one I probably knew by heart before I was five, came back to me. I said it to him in the same singsong way I had said it as a child:

> *Angel of God,*
> *My guardian dear,*
> *To whom God's love,*
> *Entrusts me here,*
> *Ever this day,*
> *Be at my side,*
> *To light, to guard,*
> *To rule and guide.*

He smiled. "Say it again."

I repeated it.

"My side hurts," he said, and reached a hand down to the ribs on his righthand side, opposite of where I sat with the flashlight. When he brought the hand up again, it was covered with blood. "See?"

"Oh, Christ," I said, and moved so that I could see his other side. A dark stain was slowly spreading on his jacket.

"No, just an angel," he said seriously.

"We'd better tie her up," I said. "Then I'll try to help you. Do you have a knife?"

He nodded, reached into his jacket, and tossed a pocket knife to me. I used it to cut the straps off Lisa's knapsack. I tied her hands tightly.

"I don't understand you," I said to her.

She didn't say a word.

As I tied her ankles, I saw that the bottoms of her running shoes had mud encrusted in them—and little pieces of date palm debris. I was willing to bet her footprints would match the cast taken of the ones leading into the hotel. She would have picked up the mud and debris on the way into the hotel on a rainy night. She hadn't picked that up when she walked across the grounds with me this afternoon—Keene's crew had cleaned up just before then. The debris in the shoes would probably match the pulp left on Roberta's office carpet.

I untied her shoes and pulled them off.

"Hurry," Two Toes said.

I convinced him to prop himself up against a wall. I set the gun down. He eyed it.

"Forget it," I said.

He let me open his jacket, allowed me to unbutton his shirt.

He had a sly smile on his face.

"Forget that, too. Keep an eye on Lisa."

I pulled the shirt away and found another. Three layers down, I found the wound.

"Ow!" he said as I pulled his undershirt away from it.

"Sorry."

The wound was just above his hip. It looked as if the bullet had grazed him. Painful, but not too deep, and if I could staunch the bleeding, probably not fatal.

"Press on it," I told him, placing his hands near it. "Like this. Don't let up on it. I'll try to make a bandage."

"Socks," he said. "Get the socks."

"What socks?"

"In the treasure room, where we hid."

"Upstairs?"

"In here," he said impatiently, as if I really did not know a thing.

I stood up and went to the closet.

I shined the flashlight in it. There was a shelf in the closet. On the shelf was a big cardboard box.

I brought it out into the room.

"That's it!" he said. "In there, with the magic spells from the Holy Bible."

"Magic spells?" I said, and lifted the lid.

On top of papers full of facts and figures I doubted he would ever understand, Two Toes had stored two other items taken from Lucas. Dress socks and a leather belt. I pulled them out of the box and Two Toes smiled.

"Those are clean!" he said.

Clean socks. No wonder he called it the treasure room.

I used them as a bandage, the belt to hold them and put pressure on the wound.

"Why do you call them magic spells?" I asked, trying to distract him as I picked up the gun again. But he had little interest in the weapon now.

"The Prof kept them in the altar. He hid them there."

"He wasn't a professor!" Lisa said angrily.

"I don't like you!" he said, just as angrily.

"You know what, Lisa? I don't like you much, either," I said, moving to the window. Sooner or later that security guard would have to cruise by again. I didn't want to leave Two Toes with Lisa, so I would need to signal the guard from here. Taking Two Toes down the stairs with me was out of the question; it would be asking too much of a bandage made of socks and a belt.

"He was a professor!" Two Toes insisted, still glowering at her.

"Oh, what do you know!" she said.

"The Selmans know all kinds of things, don't they? Three post-graduate degrees in the family, and at least two murderers."

"Just two," she said. "Leave Jerry out of this."

"So you do know," I said.

"About Nadine? Let's say I've had a strong suspicion for years. It doesn't matter, really. I was cleaning up after Andre's other transgressions—cheating the public. I wish Lucas had just left things as they were. I didn't want to have to silence him. I really didn't. But I guess it was going to come to that, anyway. Until I took a look at that fax ribbon, I didn't even know he suspected the truth about Nadine."

I was stunned. This was too much to take in. "I've learned

some horrible things about your father today, but the idea of him using you to help—"

"Using me? Using me to help?" she laughed hysterically.

"She's crazy," Two Toes said.

"Andre doesn't even suspect that I know about his bogus statistics! Oh God! All those years I spent in that attic, that furnace vent like an intercom—and the brilliant Dr. Selman still has no idea what I know about him. That's how smart he is!"

Two Toes acted like he wanted to smack her one again.

"You'd better rest," I said to him. "You're hurt."

"I'm hurt, too," she said. "He hit me hard. And my wrists hurt. Could you loosen these straps a little?"

"You really don't have much respect for my intelligence, do you?"

"That's not true."

We were silent. Two Toes started humming a melody I couldn't place at first, then I realized I had heard it outside St. Anthony's. The "Our Father."

I watched for the security guard.

My pager went off again.

"I'll get it!" Two Toes said, stumbling to his feet.

"Be careful!" I said, but he was already on his way into the bathroom.

"You made a mess in there!" he said to Lisa, as he came back out wearing my purse. He plopped down against the wall, still clutching the purse. He busied himself looking through it.

"Gimme the light," he said.

"I need it." At his sullen look, I added, "There's a little light on my keychain. Use that."

Good enough.

"You wouldn't understand," I heard Lisa say.

"As I said before, you don't have much respect for my intelligence. I'll admit I don't understand this. I thought you were trying to pin Lucas's murder on your father. But this isn't about Andre, is it? Not about loving or hating him."

"I don't love him." She stated it as fact. "He never gave

me any love, I never gave him any. He doesn't love anyone. And hate? I don't feel enough for him to do that, either. This isn't about what Andre is, or how I feel about him. It's about what people—certain people—believe him to be."

"Especially Barton Sawyer."

She was quiet, then said, "Yes, especially Barton. Don't you understand? Who was I when Barton first met me?"

"A young campaigner."

"No, that's not all. I was the daughter of a great social science statistician. A man who was making a big splash as an expert in the field of urban populations in transition. That's the Andre the public policymakers know. There's quite a bit of truth to that. Just not enough truth."

"Lucas Monroe was about to prove Andre to be an academic fraud, and perhaps a murderer," I said. "Neither of which makes good press for a future assemblywoman."

"Do you think anyone would trust someone whose father bilked the public the way Andre has?"

"You keep talking as if that's his big sin, not the murder of a woman who was younger than you are now. I'll tell you the truth, Lisa. If Nadine's murder didn't come to light, I'm not sure the studies would matter much. I don't think very many people would understand how they had been cheated. Most don't care enough about the poor to worry about whether they've lost their housing."

"Barton Sawyer would understand it. It would matter to him."

"Oh, and there goes your money."

"More than money!" she said fiercely.

"Oh?"

"Barton would never have anything to do with me. I couldn't stand that. He thinks I'm like he is. I've tried to be, but it's not enough. He prides himself on trying to clean up politics. Do you think he'd be associated with the daughter of a murderer? Even if I withdrew my candidacy, he wouldn't keep me on staff. The daughter of a man who falsified redevelopment studies for his own gain? Don't you understand? If Andre's reputation was ruined, mine would be ruined, too.

I couldn't let those papers be made public. I had to make sure you never had a chance to study them. Now—oh God, don't you see how disappointed Barton will be?"

"Yes," I said. "I think I know exactly how disappointed he'll be."

She didn't answer.

"You know what, Lisa?" I said after a moment. "To some extent, reputations are like statistics. They stand for something larger. They aren't necessarily the facts, they're just a way to represent the facts. Poor samples, faulty methods of correlation—they all apply, don't they? Sometimes, you think you know someone, but you've based your judgments on small, carefully displayed samples of their behavior. The whole person may be different. You, for example. I've never really known who you are."

"What I said upstairs," she said, "was true. This wasn't about you and me. I didn't like hurting Roberta or Lucas. And you—you did so much for me. Try to believe that much of me, that I regret what I've done."

For once, I kept control of my temper. I actually thought before I opened my mouth.

"Prove it," I said.

"What?"

"Tell what you know to the police."

"About what?"

"Everything. Nadine, Lucas's degree, the studies. Everything."

"I don't know all of it," she said slowly.

"Your political reputation is shot. You're going to go to prison for what you did to Lucas and Roberta. If you don't want the entire focus of the publicity to be on what a little shit you are, then turn in that father you claim not to love. Turn in Andre. Maybe Barton will come to forgive you."

"He'll never forgive me."

"All right, then, suppose he doesn't. He's not God, Lisa. There are other people who've cared about you, too. Maybe later you might feel as if you did something for someone other than yourself. Maybe your mother might come to believe she had some influence on you, that you didn't turn out to be just like Andre."

"I'm not like him!"

"God help Marcy when she hears what you've done."

She started crying. "Leave my mother out of this."

"That's what you've done. You should have gone to her a long time ago. Maybe Lucas wouldn't have ended up on the streets if you had told her what you suspected. Maybe none of this would have been necessary."

She cried louder now. I thought of June Monroe and didn't care how hard Lisa cried.

"Are these your dogs?" Two Toes asked, apparently equally unmoved. He was going through my wallet.

"Yes," I said, wondering if I'd ever get it back. "Do you like dogs?"

"Do they bite?"

"No."

"I like them. What are their names?" he asked.

"Deke and Dunk."

This was apparently very funny to a guardian angel.

"Be careful, you don't want that wound to bleed too much," I warned.

I looked out at Las Piernas. I angled myself for the slim view of the water. The Pacific usually soothes my soul, but it was too dark to see much of it now. I could see the lights at the end of the pier and even the colored reflection of the lights of an oil island. I thought back to days when, on a student budget, I took Lisa to the beach or to parks or any place that offered student discounts—the zoo or the local skating rink. The beach was always a favorite with both of us, though. We both loved the ocean. Did she still love it, or had that changed, too? We talked of sailing away from Las Piernas. I remembered going out on the pier and feeding a quarter to the telescopes to look out at Catalina Island and the ships leaving the breakwater.

Ships and islands. Two sets of three numbers. Longitude and latitude.

"Say that prayer again," Two Toes said. When I finished, he said, "Amen." We were quiet for a time.

"Roland Hill was there," Lisa said into the silence.

I glanced back at her. "Who else?"

"Just Roland and my father. But Allan knew about it. He took the others away. Booter Hodges gave some sort of signal to them, but he didn't know what was going on. Not really. They wrapped a chain around her and threw her overboard. I don't know much more. Allan bought the chain. Roland was angry with him, because he paid by credit card. That's how I know. I heard my dad laughing about it when Roland told him."

"Andre, Allan, and Roland knew for a certainty that she was killed."

"Yes."

"You'll tell the police?"

"Yes, I promise," she said, then added quickly, "That probably doesn't mean anything to you."

"You might be surprised," I said.

A few minutes later, I saw the security guard cruiser coming up the far side of the street.

I didn't have a chance to get his attention before another car sped from the other direction. Keene Dage's Mercedes. He wasn't at the curb before Frank got out of the passenger side, frantic. He was looking up at the building. I flashed the flashlight. He spotted it, pointed. The security guard was fumbling with the gate. I could hear sirens. I had to let Frank know that we were okay.

"Can I have this?" Two Toes was saying behind me.

"Have what?" I asked, trying to get the window open.

"This thing that beeps."

"It's all yours," I said, using the butt end of the flashlight to strike the pane.

I was going to owe Keene for another window. If I got my wallet back, I'd pay him for it.

38

Two Toes kept my pager. The policy at the paper changed by the next afternoon, so I didn't order a new one. It had gone off because Frank had tried to get in touch with me again and again, finally contacting one of Keene Dage's kids. Keene had just left, heading back to Fallbrook after a family dinner, but his son had reached him on the car phone. When Keene heard that I hadn't come home yet, he doubled back and picked up Frank. They called in reinforcements on the way.

Lisa left with the police. I used Keene's cell phone to call Marcy and told her that Lisa had just been arrested, and that she might want to be at the police station when they brought her in. I told her that I thought it best that someone else give her the details. She wasn't happy with me about it, but I told her I had to go, I needed to take someone to the hospital.

Two Toes was afraid of the ambulance, so Keene took him to St. Anne's in the Mercedes. Frank and I rode with them. On the way, I got all of my belongings back, with the exception of the pager and the picture of the dogs. Once there, I introduced him to a favorite nun of mine, and she convinced him that St. Anne's would never mistreat a guardian angel. When we left, he was trying to trade my pager for her rosary.

Roberta came out of her coma. She was having trouble speaking and couldn't walk. But no one was giving up yet, least of all Roberta. Time would tell. I was only one of many friends who were determined to help her out in any way we could.

Some of those women, Marcy included, would probably never speak to me again. They blamed me for Lisa's being in jail, and there wasn't any point in trying to get them to see it any other way. Alicia Penderson-Duggin, of all people, was my biggest defender.

Lucas had a big funeral. A dead hero of the common man has a lot of political appeal, I found. There was lots of media coverage, and politicians and college administrators were anxious to be associated with his memory. The *Express* had taken my story and turned it into something that I probably should have been happy with, but wasn't—a big front-page tribute to him. Maybe it bothered me because they couldn't spare two lines for him a week before, and now he was selling their papers.

During the funeral, I stayed off in a corner of the cemetery, sitting on a fence with Blue, Rooster, Decker, and Beans. I don't know what was said at his graveside, and I don't really care. Like just about everybody else at that funeral—except Lucas's mother and his brother—the preacher didn't know him. Maybe I just wasn't ready to say good-bye to him. I'm not sure, even now.

Charles Monroe stayed at the grave long after everyone else had gone. He saw me sitting on the fence and nodded. I nodded back. I left after that.

I didn't see his mother until the next day. She was in Joshua Burrows' room at Las Piernas General. They must have been talking about Lucas, because she was smiling. When she saw me, the smile got bigger.

"Hello, June," I said.

"Good to see you," she said. "Corky—I'm sorry, I should call you by your right name."

"Corky's fine," he said. He looked very different from the last time I had seen him. He was clean, the bruises were fading, and although he wasn't the picture of health, the antibiotics were obviously doing some good.

"How are you doing?" I asked.

"Just taking it a day at a time," he said.

"Good for you," June said. "That's the way to recover from *anything.*"

He smiled. "She's subtle, isn't she?"

"Oh, I didn't come in here to lecture you, and you know it," she said. She looked over to me. "I've about worn him out talking about Lucas."

"I wish I could have been at the funeral," Joshua said.

"Your father was there for you," June said. "Lucas would understand. Besides, it doesn't matter so much what you do for a person after they're dead. You were his friend when he was alive."

It hit me like a slap, although I know she wasn't aiming the remark at me. "She's right," I said. "Excuse me. I'll be back later."

I hurried out of the room.

She *was* right, of course. I walked around the corner, found an elevator, and took it to the top floor. There's a little solarium there, and I needed someplace to sit, someplace where there was light.

I realized that whatever little good I had done by telling Lucas's story, his name would be forgotten. Once those of us who knew him were gone, who would remember him? The poor who had been forced to move because of Andre's crooked study wouldn't have their homes back. Redevelopment, with all its mixed results, would continue apace. New studies had been demanded, and Ray Aiken would undoubtedly allow better oversight of future projects.

The elevator opened and I stepped out into the sunlight.

I tried to look at things differently. Nadine's brother was sad but relieved. I learned he had filed a missing person's report on her, but in the six months that had passed since her death, Hill made certain loose ends had been tidied up, and she was thought to have left the area. The coordinates Jeff McCutchen guessed at from his quarter's worth of viewing turned out to be in the water near an oil island. Lots of diving and some underwater metal detectors finally turned up the chain. It was still around the canvas bag. The bag, which had been firmly anchored by the chain and sheltered to some degree by the island, was carefully raised and opened. A largely intact adult female skeleton was found within. The teeth, a bracelet, and an old fracture on the crooked left little finger were enough to identify the remains as those of Nadine Preston. No one had expected to find so much of her, the coroner had confided.

Stop it, I told myself.

Keene Dage, who probably would have been able to completely avoid the risk of criminal prosecution, instead had come forward. He was being offered immunity from prosecution in exchange for his testimony in several investigations, as was Corbin Tyler. The last time I had seen him, he was tired but happy. "My kids are behind me one hundred percent," he said. "That's all that matters to me."

"You'll have to recarve the faces of the angels on the Angelus," I told him, and he laughed.

Roland Hill and Allan Moffett were probably going to prison. Booter Hodges was looking for another job. And although I didn't know it that day when I stood in the solarium, Andre Selman would cheat the hangman. He never left the hospital. Heart failure. Perhaps there was some justice in that after all.

Some of Roland Hill's investors wanted to lynch him. Some wanted to lynch me.

Claire had thanked me. If I hadn't come to know her, to see how courageous she was, I might have been surprised at her gratitude. She was more at peace for understanding what had been on Ben's mind in those last days, she said. She thought no less of Ben. She had loved him. That's all there was to it as far as she was concerned. A pity his demons hadn't let him see that.

Word was, the college was awarding a posthumous master's degree to Lucas. Too little, too late.

Barton Sawyer had earned my respect by not distancing himself from Lisa or joining the hoopla around the newly popular memory of Lucas Monroe. Instead, he privately sent letters of sympathy to June and Charles Monroe, to Marcy and

Jerry. The only time he spoke of Lisa publicly was to say that he felt the same sadness he would feel if his own daughter was imprisoned, regardless of her guilt.

I had visited Lisa before her arraignment. Her face was black and blue and there were marks on her wrists from where I had tied the straps too tight. She saw me looking at them and said, "Remember the time you were teaching me how to ice skate? I fell and knocked you down with me, and you got a fat lip. I was crying, both because I had hurt you and because I was afraid you'd never take me skating again. You said, 'Lisa, ice is slippery. People fall down on it. Get used to it.' Remember that?"

"Yes," I said, "I remember."

She started talking of other things we had done together. They were good memories. Maybe we wanted to convince ourselves that things had been different then. I've come to believe they were, though I doubted it for a time. Before I left, I thanked her for keeping her promise to talk to the police. She asked me to come back. I told her I would.

I looked out across the view from the solarium. In the distance, I could just make out the tallest buildings downtown. Keene Dage's Las Piernas. Corbin Tyler's. The sun glinted off the glass crown of the Haimler Building.

We all have to do something we can be proud of.

I heard the elevator doors open. My husband stepped out.

"Ready to go get your car?"

"How did you know I was here?"

"I know you. There wasn't an ocean in the hospital, so I had to look for sunlight."

"They call him *Detective* Harriman."

He had reached me by then, lifted the hair on the back of my neck, put his mouth on it and blew, sort of a contact raspberry.

"Hey, that tickles," I said, laughing and feeling shivers down my spine.

"It's a neck fizz. It's supposed to tickle. You're supposed to laugh once in a while."

"Sorry. I've been a sort of morose creature, haven't I?"

He shook his head. "That's okay, too. But once you've talked to June Monroe, we're going to get your car, put down the top, and enjoy a beautiful spring day. Got it?"

"June Monroe's looking for me?"

He fizzed my neck again. "You're supposed to answer, 'Yes, I've got it.' As for June, you know she is. I told her I'd find you. And no Detective Harriman jokes, Ms. Kelly. You want to talk to her here?"

"Yes. We might have some privacy here, anyway."

He gave me a quick kiss and went over to the elevator. Every few seconds he'd look over at me and make a completely clownish face. I couldn't keep my own straight.

"Yes, doctor, her condition is improving," he said when the bell for the elevator rang. I was gratified by the clown act, knowing only his closest friends—including his wife—ever saw this side of him.

When he left, I felt his absence so strongly I almost slipped back down into my funk. Almost.

He must have told June to wait on the next floor down, because she arrived just a moment later. I smiled at the thought of how sure of himself he had been.

"I said something you took the wrong way down there," she said without preamble.

"No, you were right. I've been thinking about it a lot."

"Too much, you ask me. Let's sit down over here—just for a minute. You got that man waiting for you, and I don't need a lot of time to say what I am going to say."

Well, just try to argue against a will like that. We sat down.

"Do you know what Edmund Burke said about evil?" she asked.

This I was not expecting. But fortunately, my old friend O'Connor had been a walking quotation book, so I knew the answer. " 'The only thing necessary for the triumph of evil is for good men to do nothing.' "

"Exactly right," she said. "Not 'everything.' Nothing. You

did something. You should feel good. But no, you're too busy wishing that you were better than the rest of us."

"What?"

"Oh yes. You're up here wishing that you could be perfect. That your courage never failed you. That when some old drunk came up off a bench shouting crazy stuff at you, that you had been a perfectly charitable Christian soul and said, 'How may I help you, brother?' "

"Well—"

"Well, nothing! Do you think no one forgives you for that? Do you think Lucas himself held that against you?"

"No."

"So, then, quit wasting time with all this feeling bad about what you could have done, and just get out there and keep doing something. You don't have to do everything. Just what you can."

For some damned reason, I started crying. She put an arm around me.

"Oh, now Frank is really going to be after me," she said. "Listen to me, Irene. I know my son lives. I don't mean with Jesus, though I believe that with all my heart. I mean here. He lives, because he changed something. He made things a little better before he passed. And you helped him do that. You have done him a great kindness."

"I would have preferred to have been kinder to him for five more minutes while he was alive," I said.

"Of course you would have. But then, my son was a teacher, and you've learned something from him, haven't you? We all only have five minutes to be kind to each other. So go on down there and be good to that husband of yours."

She squeezed my shoulder.

"Go on," she said. "Five minutes. Think of some little something. It all adds up."

I could figure that much out.

I'm good at math.

ACKNOWLEDGMENTS

I owe thanks to many individuals for their help with this book. They deserve applause; if I've erred, save the boos and hisses for me.

I'm especially grateful to Laurence Whipple, a man with courage and heart, who is the Director of the Seattle Food Bank; my friend K. C. Pilon, who has worked extensively with the homeless; Steven Kingston, the original Rockford, who helped Rachel to be a better private investigator and shared many insights into his work; Susie Gibbs, for answering endless questions about alcoholism recovery programs. Emergency department physician James Gruber, M.D., and orthopedic surgeon Ed Dohring, M.D., each took time from exhausting schedules to help me with medical research. Jacquie Prebich, R.N., and Mark Prebich, Administrator of Ancillary Departments at South El Monte Hospital, helped with coronary care information. Michael Burke helped with banking and finance information, as did Thomas Burke.

Debbie Arrington, who has contributed so much to this series, did yeoman's work with this book, especially on the topic of redevelopment investments. Andy Rose and other members of the staff of the *Long Beach Press-Telegram* were also generous with their help.

Safe Navigation, West Marine in Long Beach, Charles Link of Performance Tackle, and Ron and Darlene Jack assisted with nautical matters. Professor Emeritus Rodger Heglar, who taught anthropology at San Francisco State University, Joan Parker of the Moss Landing Marine Laboratory, and forensic anthropologist Dr. Judy Suchey of California State University, Fullerton, contributed to my understanding of what happens to bones left in the ocean.

Fictional Las Piernas has fictional oil islands; Long Beach, California's THUMS islands are, in fact, found nowhere else in the world. I am indebted to Ed Fischer, Steve Marsh of THUMS, and Don Clarke, City Geologist for Long Beach, who spent lots of time talking to me about the real oil islands.

Ruthann Lehrer of the Neighborhood and Historic Preservation Office for the City of Long Beach helped me to see what the Angelus might look like. Jenny Oropeza, Cathy Keig, and Jim Hayes helped me through the political maze. Heather Cvar helped with the special expertise on pranks that only a thirteen-year-old can provide. Joe and Elaine Livermore of Footprints of a Gigantic Hound in Tucson, Arizona, are owned by the original model for Finn, a wonderful Irish wolfhound named Mr. Calder, who was gracious enough to allow his feet to be measured. That was probably one of the weirder calls the Livermores received this year, but I doubt they are surprised that I'm the one who made it.

I'm also grateful to Detective Bill Valles, Corporal Joseph Levy, and Officer Don Smith of the Long Beach Police Department, as well as Dennis Payne of the Robbery-Homicide Division of the Los Angeles Police Department.

Sharon Weissman and Tonya Pearsley provided extraordinary support, research, contacts with experts, and personal insights. Sharon even let me take her fax machine apart. Both read drafts and kept me from despairing during those days when I thought I'd never find time to get this one written. Sandra Cvar helped me find the time.

Special thanks to Michael Connelly, who helped me to keep my perspective and answered a number of pesky questions as well. (Lex and Nex are yours again, Mike.)

My family and friends are due many thanks, especially Tim, who had to read the manuscript two zillion times. Nancy Yost, superagent and *Cosmo* model, and Laurie Bernstein, the world's most patient editor, provided insightful comments and unfailing support. Jim Timmie, Charles Roberts, Annie Hughes, Rochelle Garris, Holly Zappala, Michele Pipia, Virginia Clark, and Dominique D'Anna, and so many others at Simon & Schuster—thank you, thank you, thank you.

The Trouble with Thin Ice
by Camilla T. Crespi

A bride-to-be, is arrested for a very cold-blooded murder—the week of her wedding. Simona Griffo, a friend who likes to meddle in such matters, starts asking questions. As she puts the pieces together, however, she unwittingly pushes herself onto thin ice.

Hearing Faces by Dotty Sohl

Janet Campbell's neighbor has been brutally killed, and there's no apparent motive in sight. Yet Janet refuses to live in fear. When a second murder strikes the apartment complex , Janet's life turns upside-down. Seeking answers she discovers greedy alliances, deadly secrets, and a vicious killer much too close to home.